CAN'T LOSE YOU

VOL. 1

WANN

NETCOMICS

Can't Lose You Vol. 1

Story and Art by Wann

English translation rights in USA, Canada, UK, NZ,
Australia arranged by Ecomix Media Company
395-21 Seogyo-dong, Mapo-gu, Seoul, Korea 121-840
info@ecomixmedia.com

- Produced by Ecomix Media Company

- Translator Jeanne

- Pre-Press Manager Yesook Ahn

- Cover Design Carol King

- Editor Zhanna Veyts

- Managing Editor Soyoung Jung

- President & Publisher Heewoon Chung

P.O.Box 16484, Jersey City, NJ 07306
info@netcomics.com
www.NETCOMICS.com

ISBN: 1-60009-039-7

First printing: February 2006
10 9 8 7 6 5 4 3 2 1
Printed in Korea

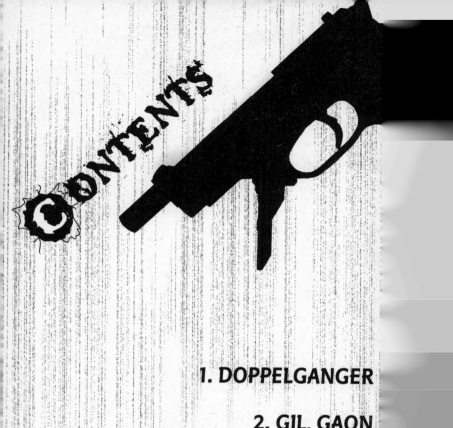

CONTENTS

1. DOPPELGANGER

2. GIL, GAON

3. THE DOUBLE

4. A CRISIS

5. IMMERSION

6. A BAIT

From the author

I am thrilled to meet a new world of readers,
yet I feel a little shy, too... Haha.
I hope you enjoy as much as possible the brief trip
you will be taking to the novel world of Can't Lose You.
I thought I had done quite a bit of traveling,
but I actually have not been to America.
To have the book land in the U.S. before its author,
I suppose that is one of the fun things of being an author.
Anyhow, I will be deeply moved to see this book
at bookstores when I visit America
in the near future.
Well, I welcome you
to my world.
On with your trip~

February 2006
WANN

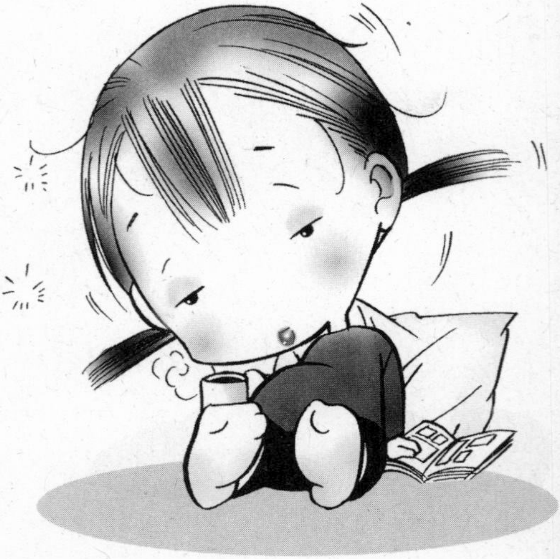

1. DOPPELGANGER

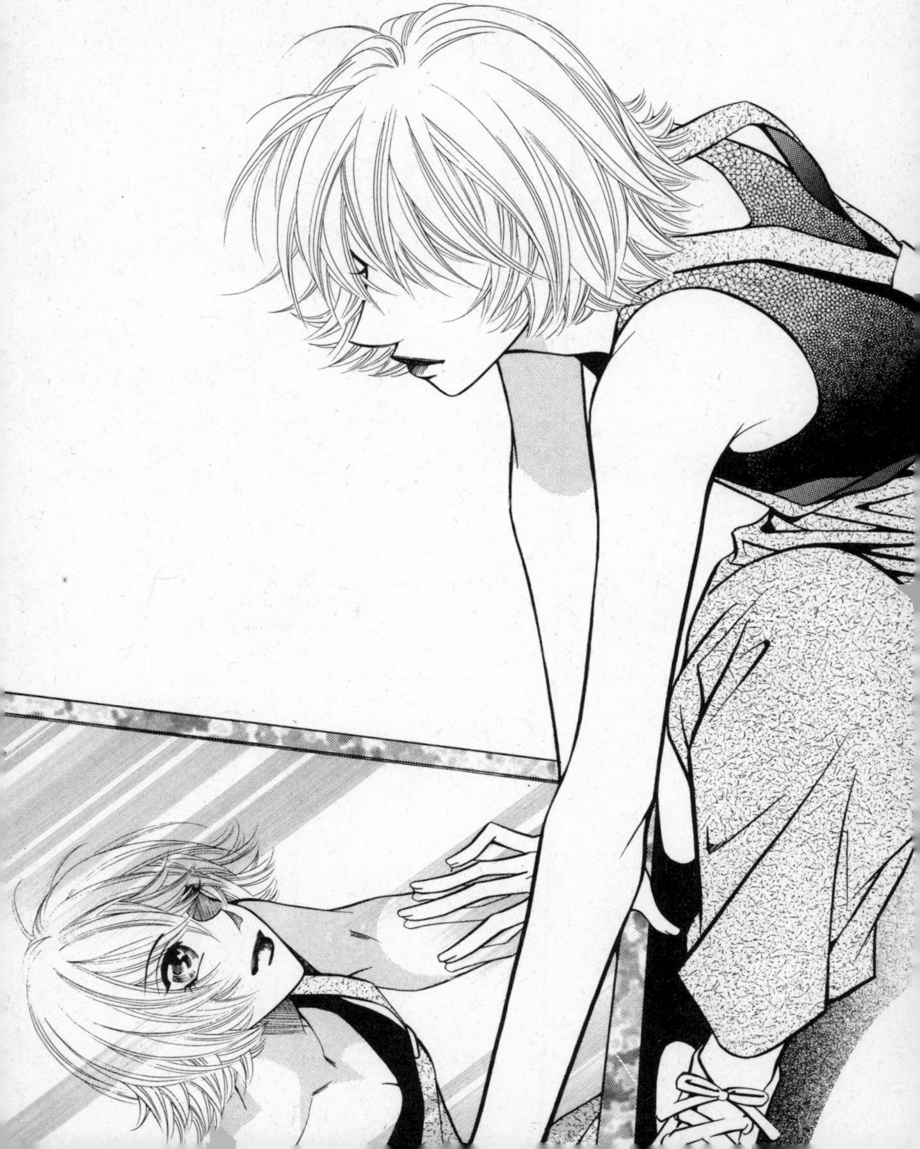

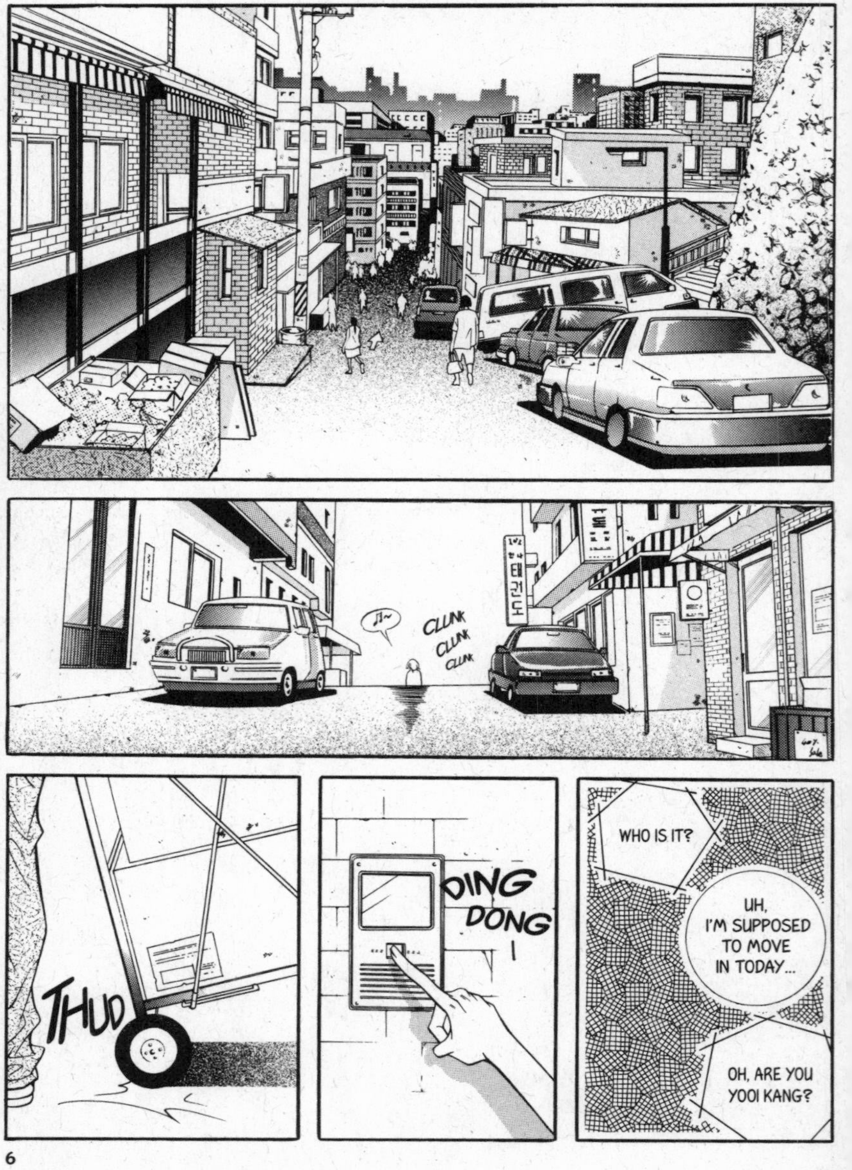

CLUNK
CLUNK
CLUNK
태권도
THUD
DING DONG
WHO IS IT?
UH, I'M SUPPOSED TO MOVE IN TODAY...
OH, ARE YOU YOOI KANG?

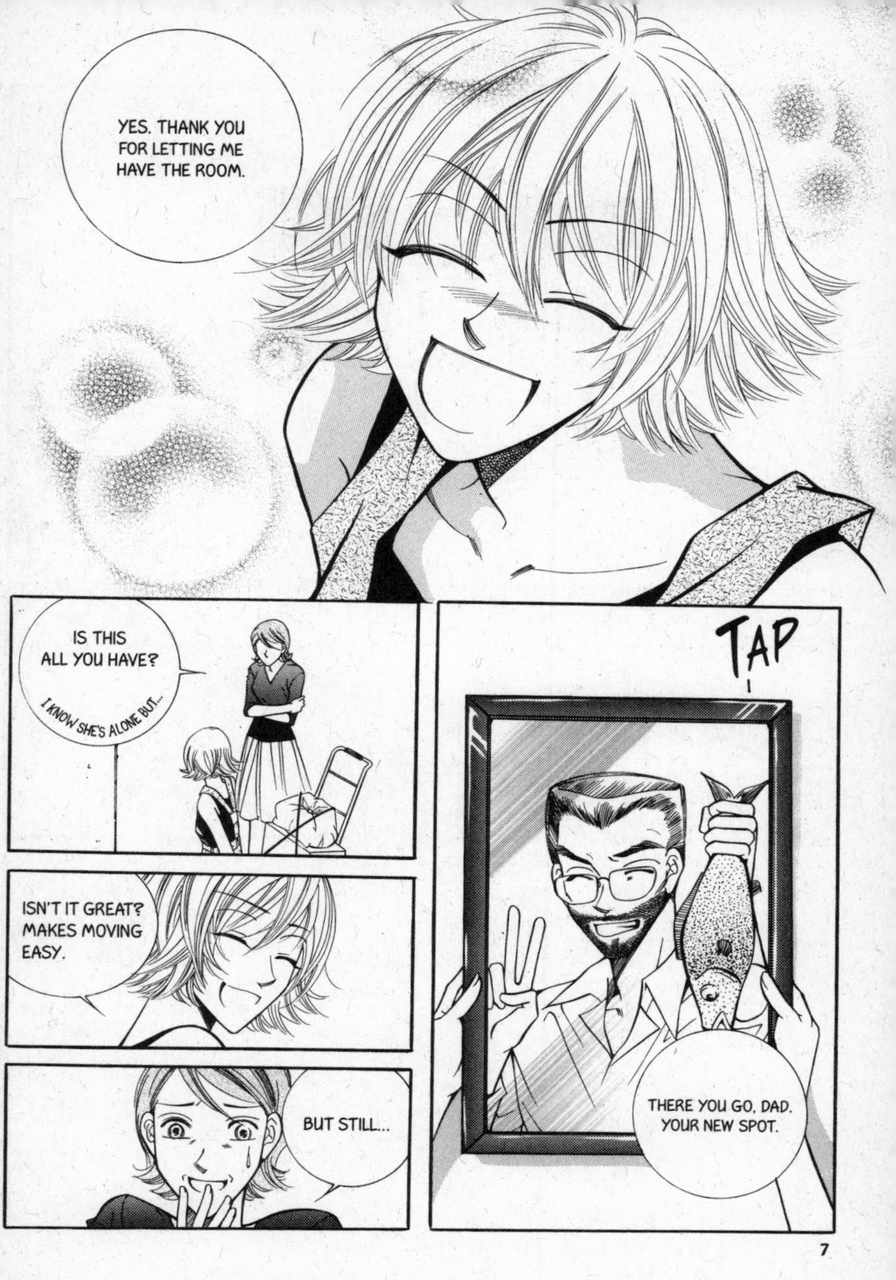
YES. THANK YOU FOR LETTING ME HAVE THE ROOM.
IS THIS ALL YOU HAVE?
I KNOW SHE'S ALONE BUT...
ISN'T IT GREAT? MAKES MOVING EASY.
BUT STILL...
TAP
THERE YOU GO, DAD. YOUR NEW SPOT.

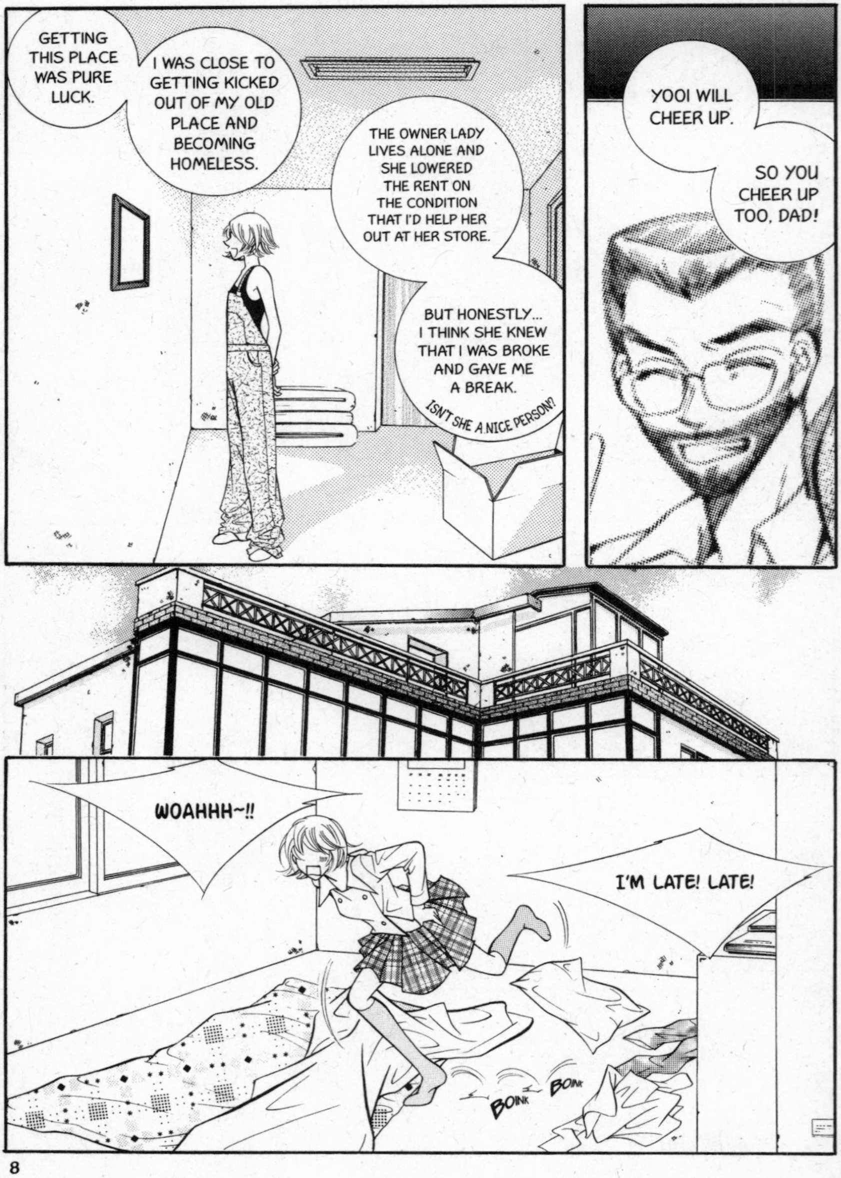

GETTING THIS PLACE WAS PURE LUCK.
I WAS CLOSE TO GETTING KICKED OUT OF MY OLD PLACE AND BECOMING HOMELESS.
THE OWNER LADY LIVES ALONE AND SHE LOWERED THE RENT ON THE CONDITION THAT I'D HELP HER OUT AT HER STORE.
BUT HONESTLY... I THINK SHE KNEW THAT I WAS BROKE AND GAVE ME A BREAK.
ISN'T SHE A NICE PERSON?
YOOI WILL CHEER UP.
SO YOU CHEER UP TOO, DAD!
WOAHHH~!!
I'M LATE! LATE!
BOINK BOINK

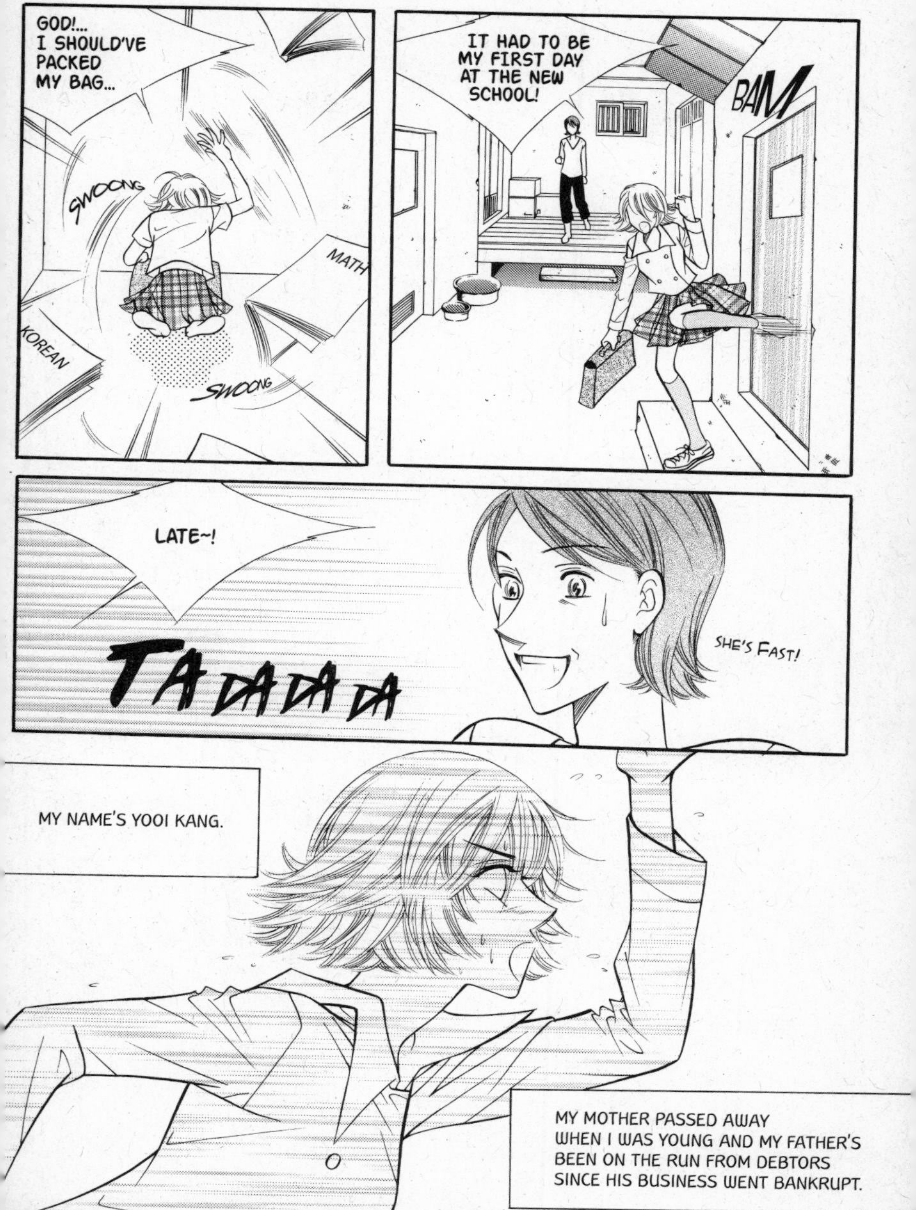
GOD!... I SHOULD'VE PACKED MY BAG...
SWOONG
MATH
KOREAN
SWOONG
IT HAD TO BE MY FIRST DAY AT THE NEW SCHOOL!
BAM
LATE~!
TA DA DA DA
SHE'S FAST!
MY NAME'S YOOI KANG.
MY MOTHER PASSED AWAY WHEN I WAS YOUNG AND MY FATHER'S BEEN ON THE RUN FROM DEBTORS SINCE HIS BUSINESS WENT BANKRUPT.

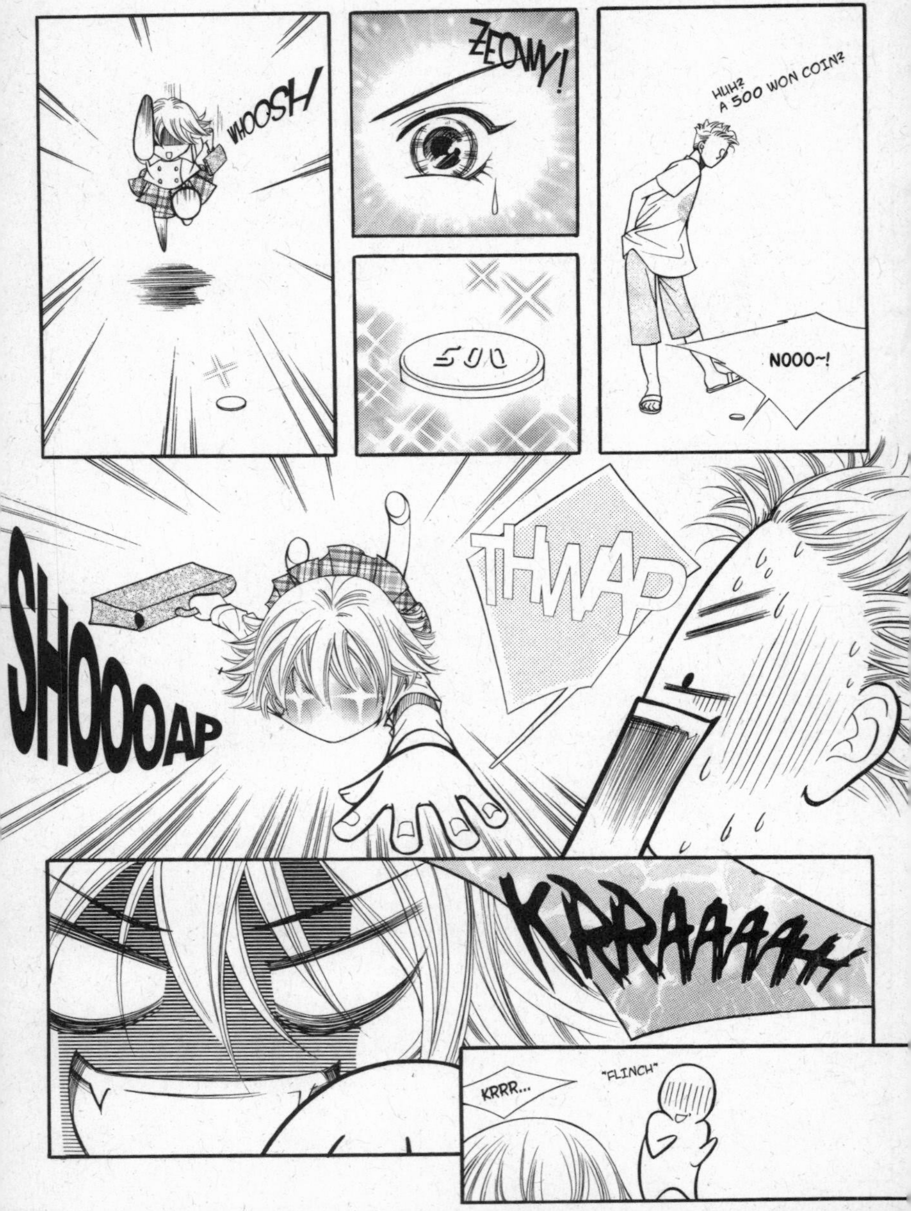

WHOOSH
ZEONNY!
HUH? A 500 WON COIN?
500
NOOO~!
SHOOOAP
THWAP
KRRAAAAH
KRRR...
"FLINCH"

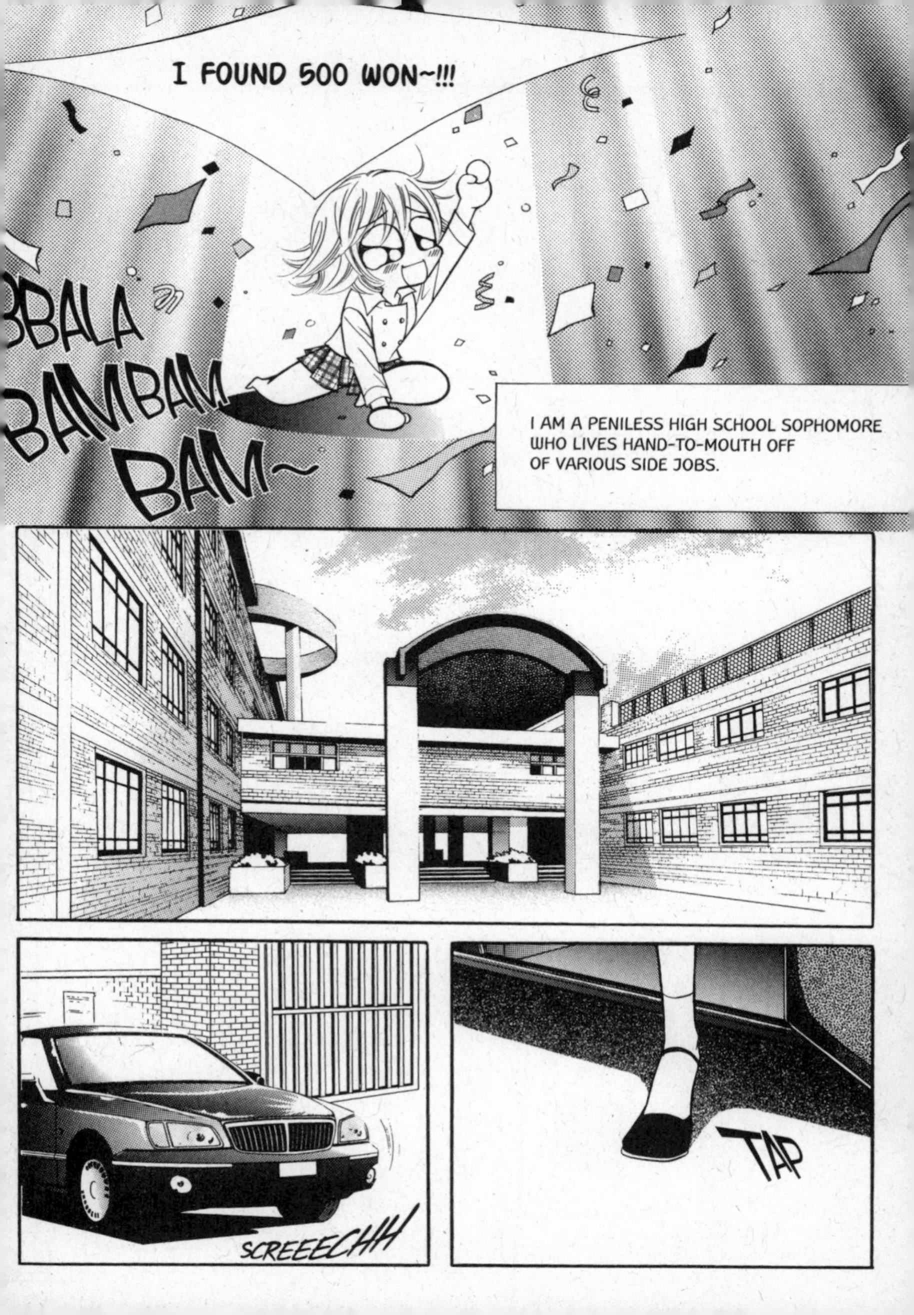
I FOUND 500 WON~!!!
BBALA BAMBAM BAM~
I AM A PENILESS HIGH SCHOOL SOPHOMORE WHO LIVES HAND-TO-MOUTH OFF OF VARIOUS SIDE JOBS.
SCREEECHH
TAP

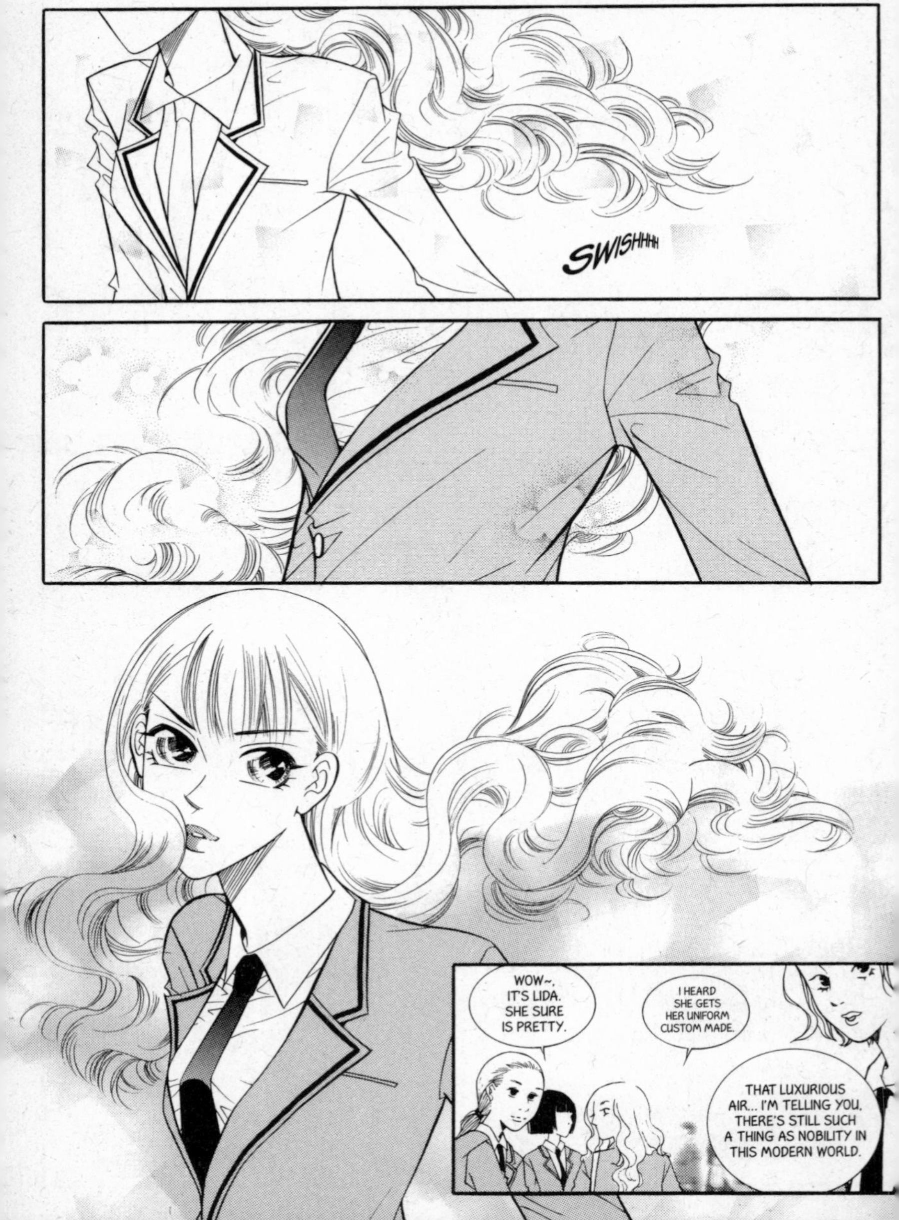
SWISHHHH
WOW~. IT'S LIDA. SHE SURE IS PRETTY.
I HEARD SHE GETS HER UNIFORM CUSTOM MADE.
THAT LUXURIOUS AIR... I'M TELLING YOU, THERE'S STILL SUCH A THING AS NOBILITY IN THIS MODERN WORLD.

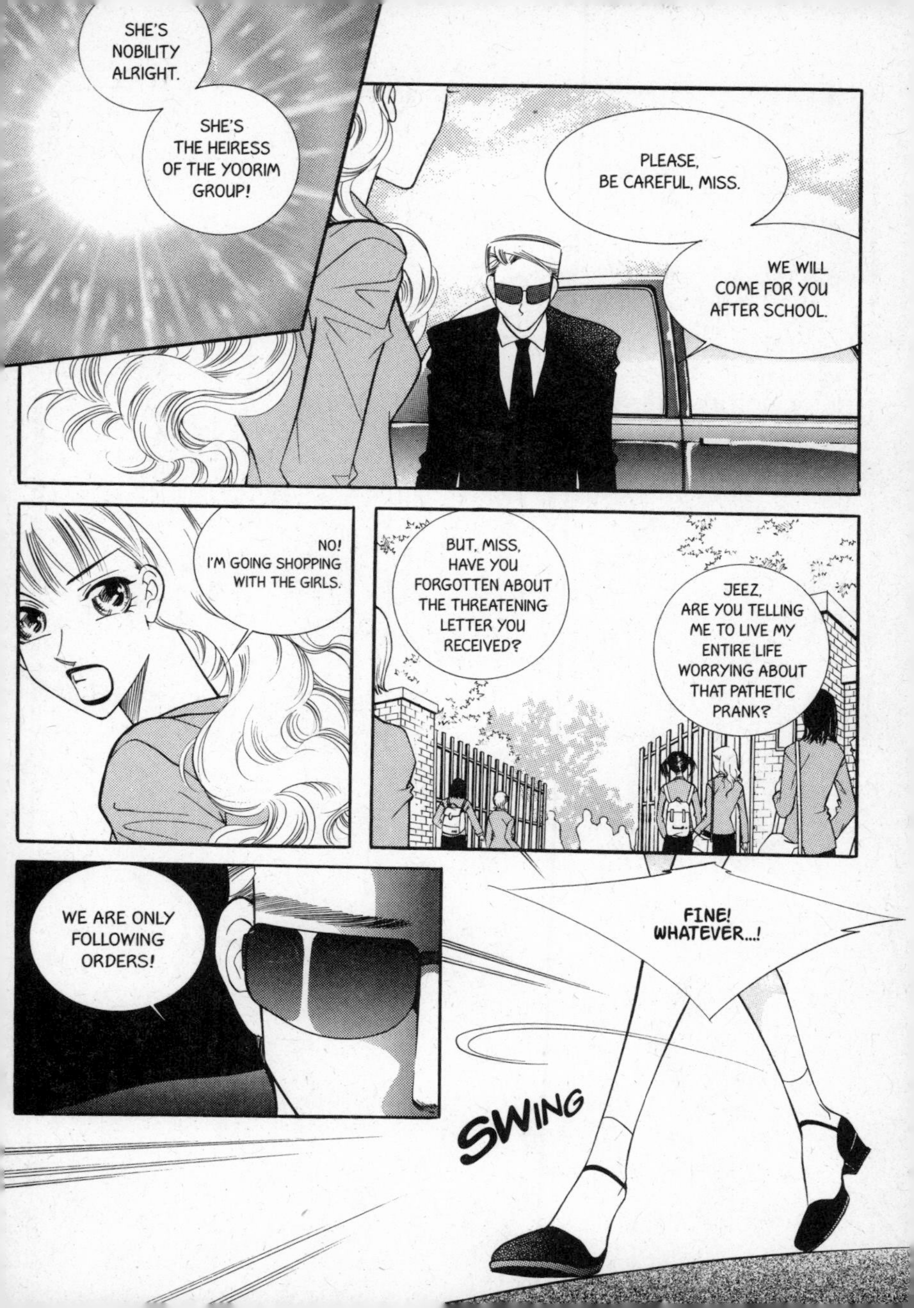
SHE'S NOBILITY ALRIGHT.
SHE'S THE HEIRESS OF THE YOORIM GROUP!
PLEASE, BE CAREFUL, MISS.
WE WILL COME FOR YOU AFTER SCHOOL.
NO! I'M GOING SHOPPING WITH THE GIRLS.
BUT, MISS, HAVE YOU FORGOTTEN ABOUT THE THREATENING LETTER YOU RECEIVED?
JEEZ, ARE YOU TELLING ME TO LIVE MY ENTIRE LIFE WORRYING ABOUT THAT PATHETIC PRANK?
WE ARE ONLY FOLLOWING ORDERS!
FINE! WHATEVER...!
SWING

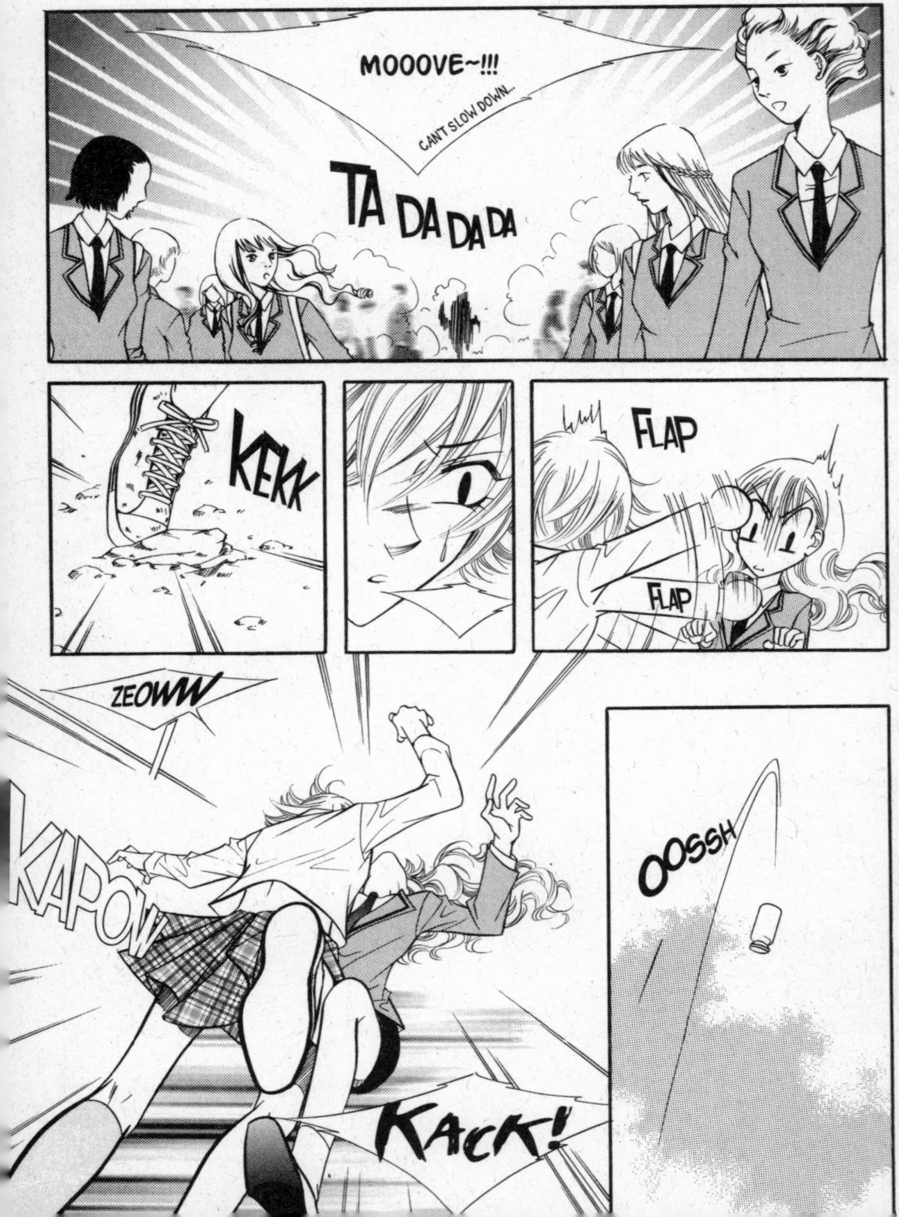

MOOOVE~!!!
CAN'T SLOW DOWN...
TA DA DA DA
KEKK
FLAP
FLAP
ZEOWW
KAPOW
OOSSH
KACK!

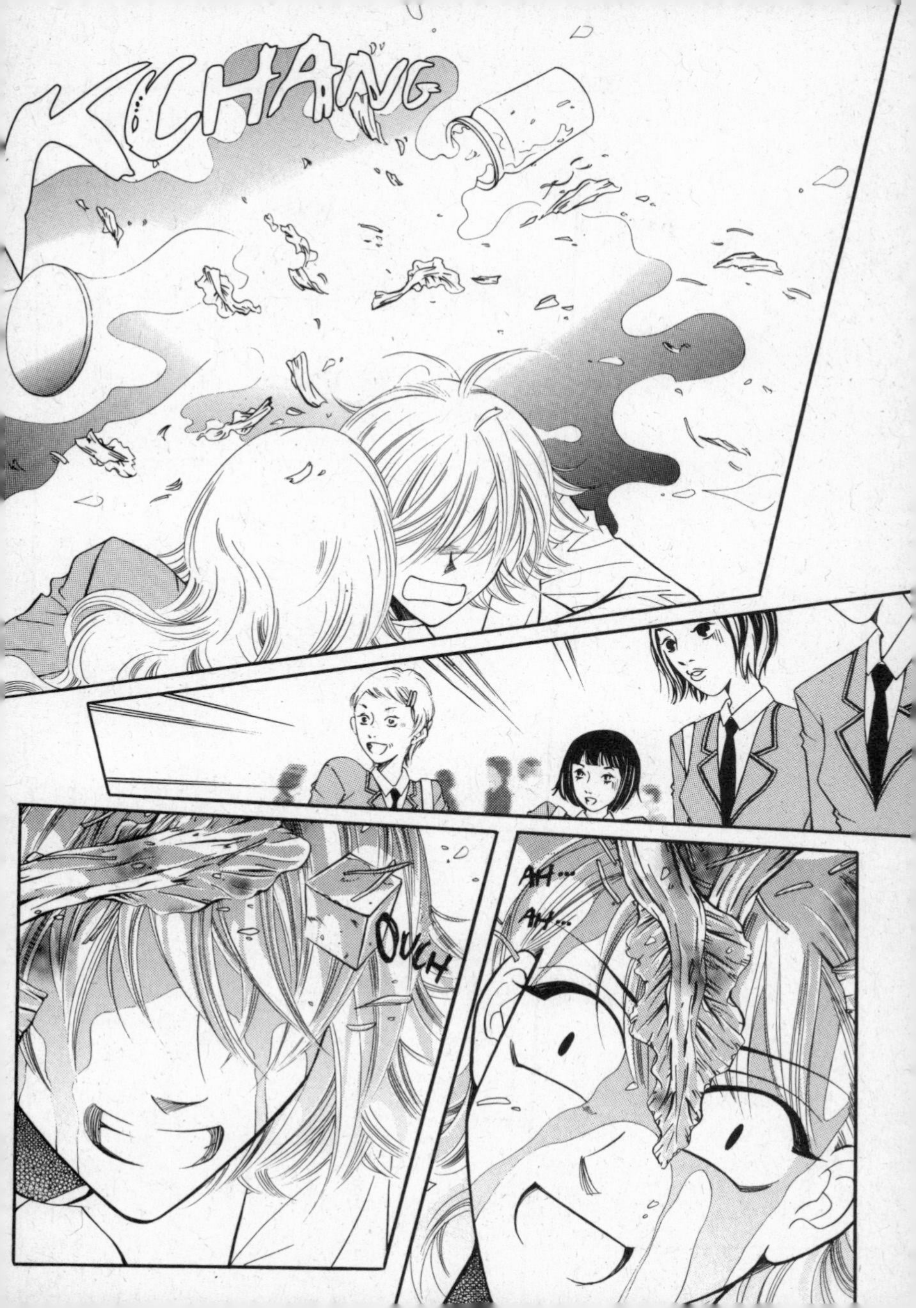
KCHANG
OUCH
AH...
AH...

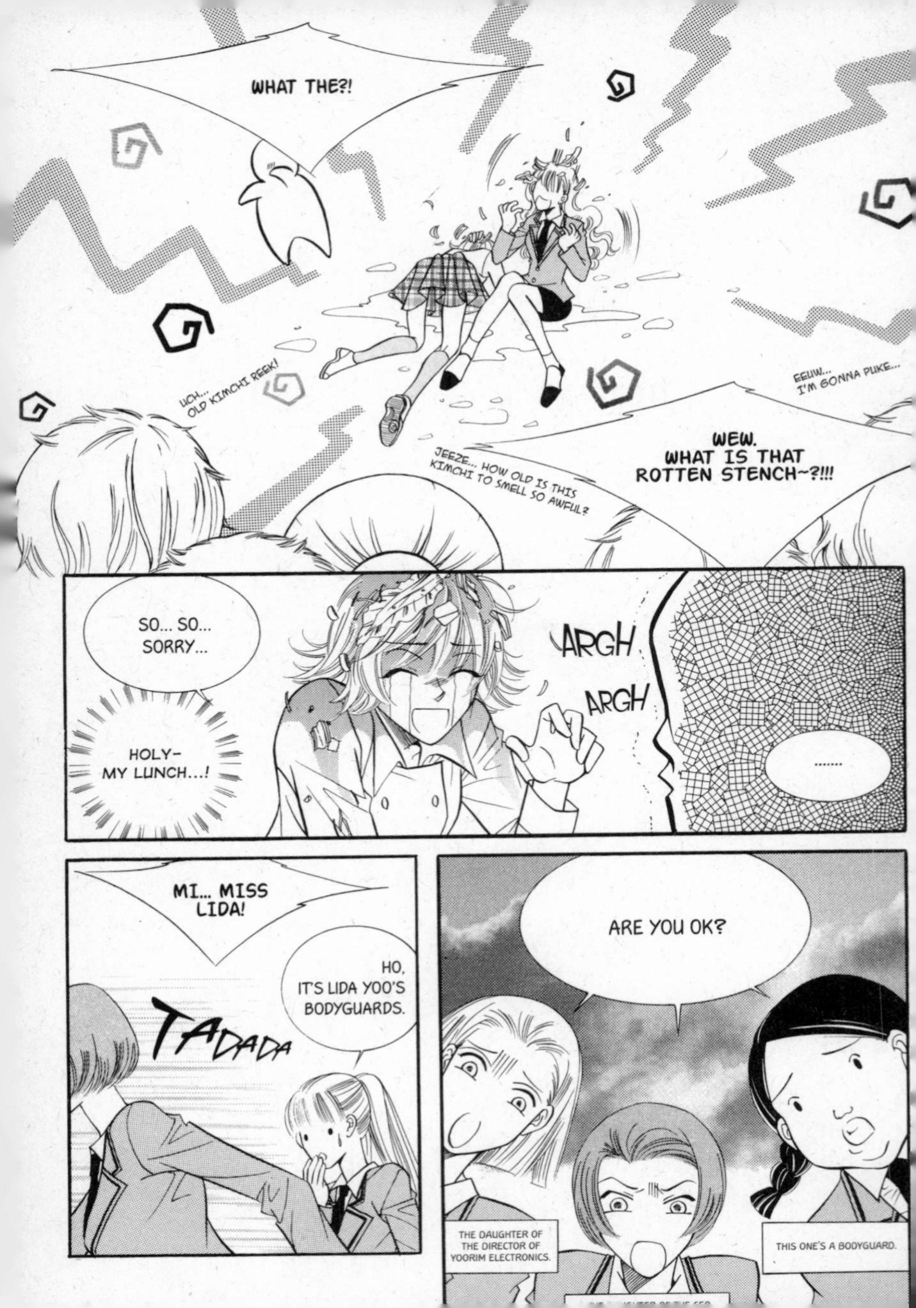
WHAT THE?!
UCH... OLD KIMCHI REEK!
EEUW... I'M GONNA PUKE...
JEEZE... HOW OLD IS THIS KIMCHI TO SMELL SO AWFUL?
WEW. WHAT IS THAT ROTTEN STENCH~?!!!
SO... SO... SORRY...
HOLY- MY LUNCH...!
ARGH
ARGH
....
MI... MISS LIDA!
TADADA
HO, IT'S LIDA YOO'S BODYGUARDS.
ARE YOU OK?
THE DAUGHTER OF THE DIRECTOR OF YOORIM ELECTRONICS.
THIS ONE'S A BODYGUARD.

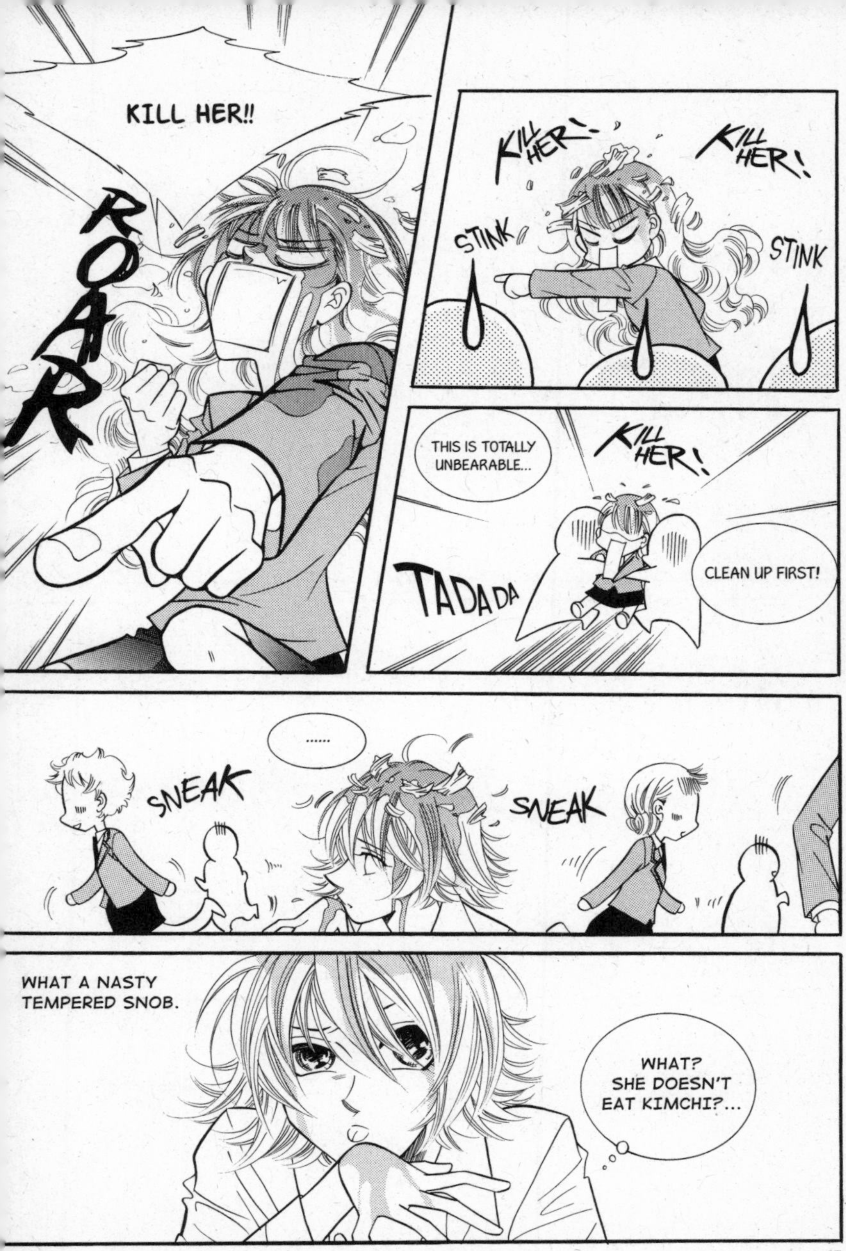
KILL HER!!
ROAR
KILL HER!
KILL HER!
STINK
STINK
THIS IS TOTALLY UNBEARABLE...
KILL HER!
TADADA
CLEAN UP FIRST!
......
SNEAK
SNEAK
WHAT A NASTY TEMPERED SNOB.
WHAT? SHE DOESN'T EAT KIMCHI?...

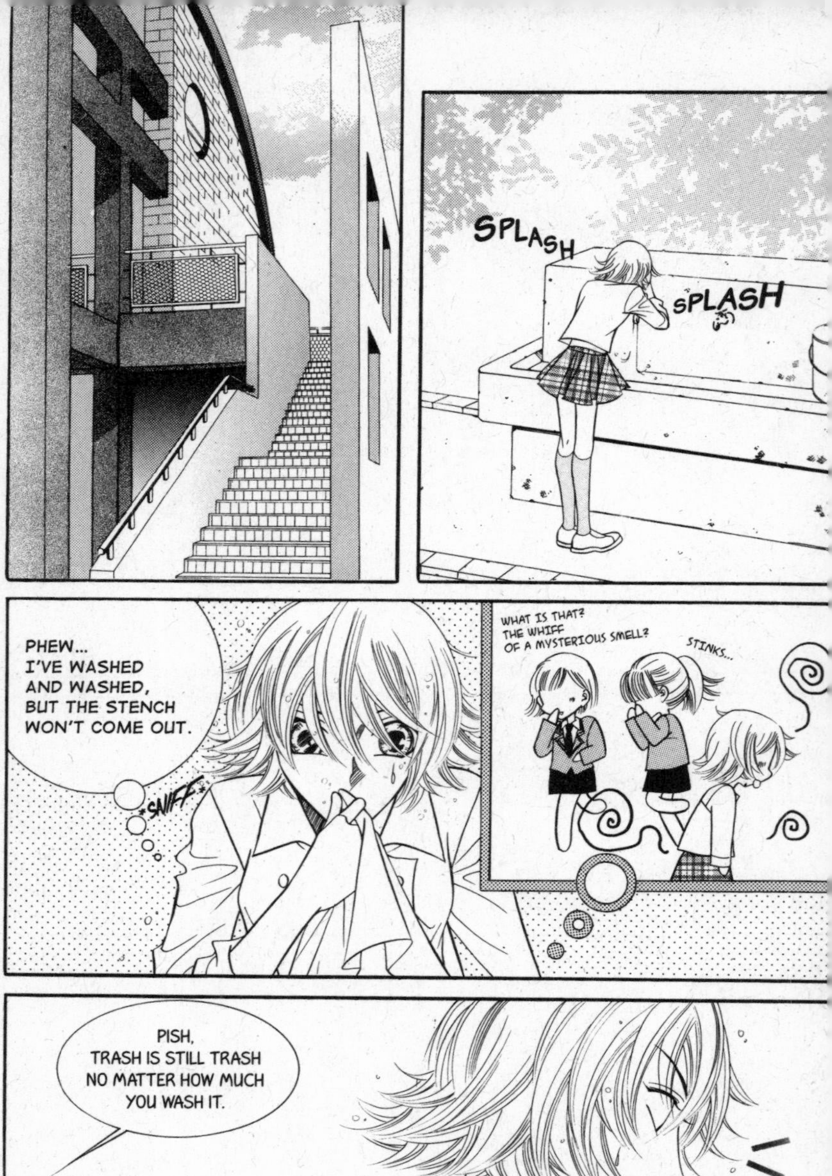
SPLASH
SPLASH
PHEW... I'VE WASHED AND WASHED, BUT THE STENCH WON'T COME OUT.
SNIFF
WHAT IS THAT? THE WHIFF OF A MYSTERIOUS SMELL?
STINKS...
PISH, TRASH IS STILL TRASH NO MATTER HOW MUCH YOU WASH IT.

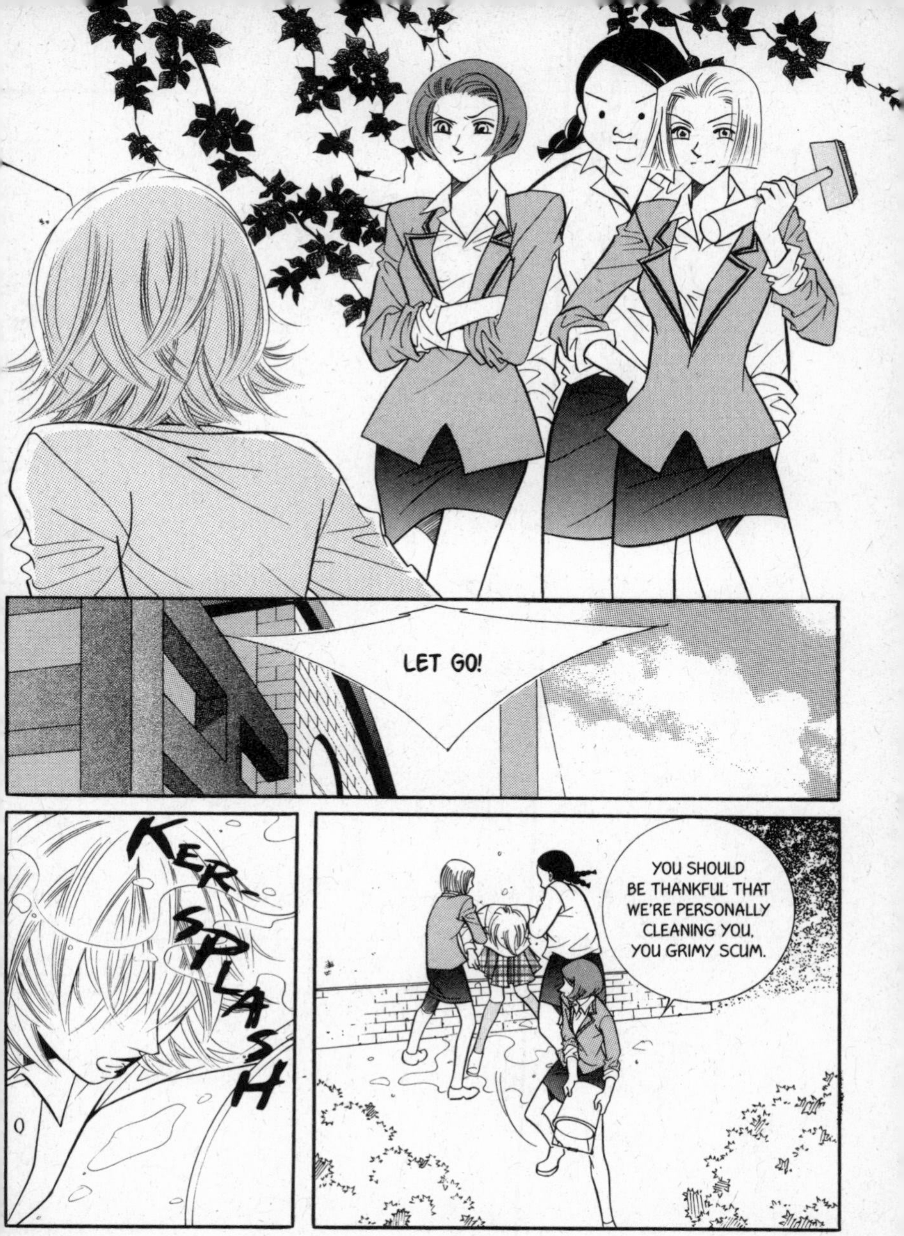

LET GO!
KER-SPLASH
YOU SHOULD BE THANKFUL THAT WE'RE PERSONALLY CLEANING YOU, YOU GRIMY SCUM.

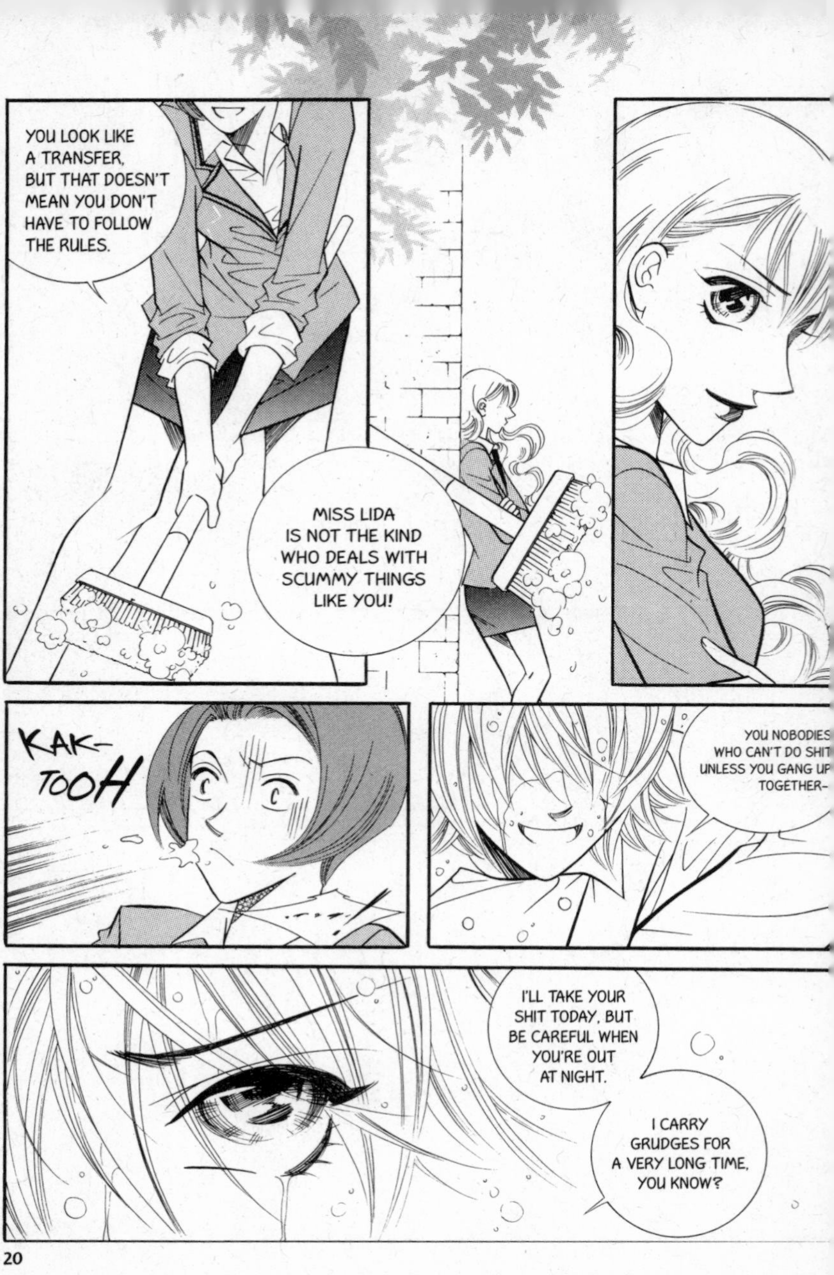
YOU LOOK LIKE A TRANSFER, BUT THAT DOESN'T MEAN YOU DON'T HAVE TO FOLLOW THE RULES.
MISS LIDA IS NOT THE KIND WHO DEALS WITH SCUMMY THINGS LIKE YOU!
KAK-TOOH
YOU NOBODIES WHO CAN'T DO SHIT UNLESS YOU GANG UP TOGETHER–
I'LL TAKE YOUR SHIT TODAY, BUT BE CAREFUL WHEN YOU'RE OUT AT NIGHT.
I CARRY GRUDGES FOR A VERY LONG TIME, YOU KNOW?

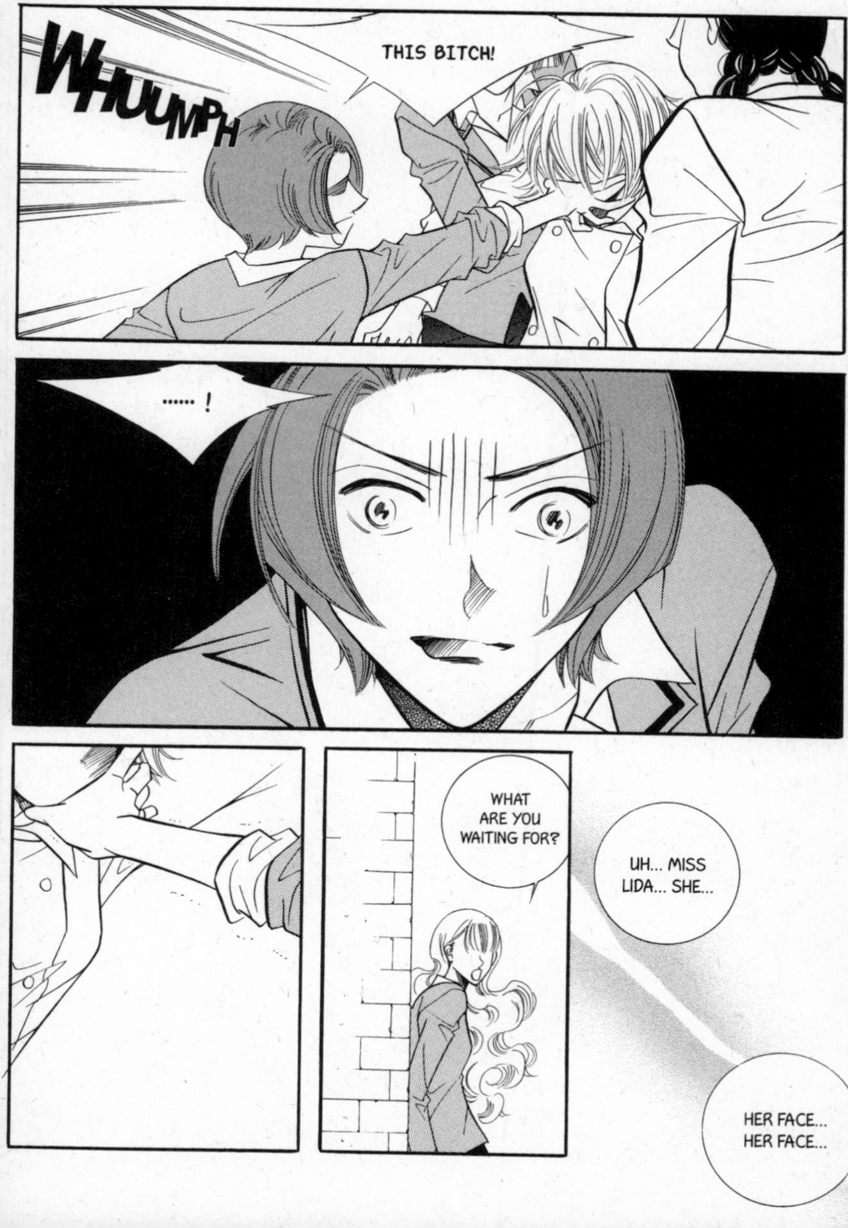
WHUUMPH
THIS BITCH!
...... !
WHAT ARE YOU WAITING FOR?
UH... MISS LIDA... SHE...
HER FACE... HER FACE...

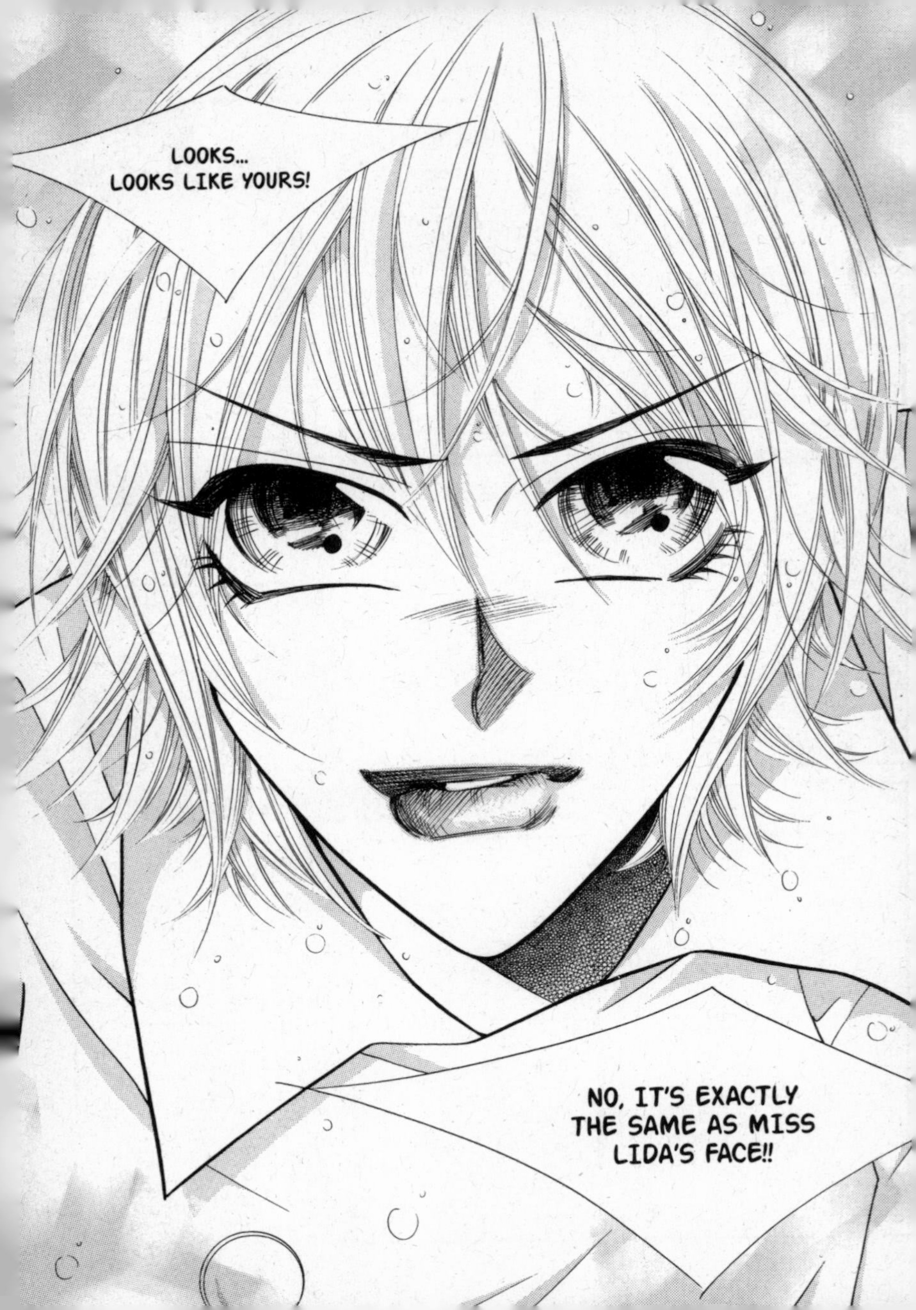
LOOKS...
LOOKS LIKE YOURS!
NO, IT'S EXACTLY
THE SAME AS MISS
LIDA'S FACE!!

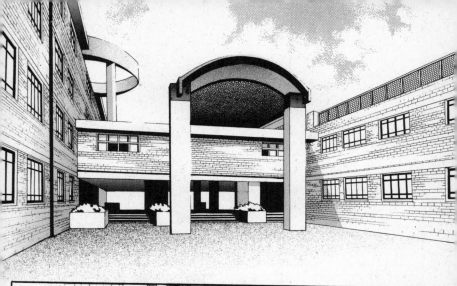

DOPPELGANGER.

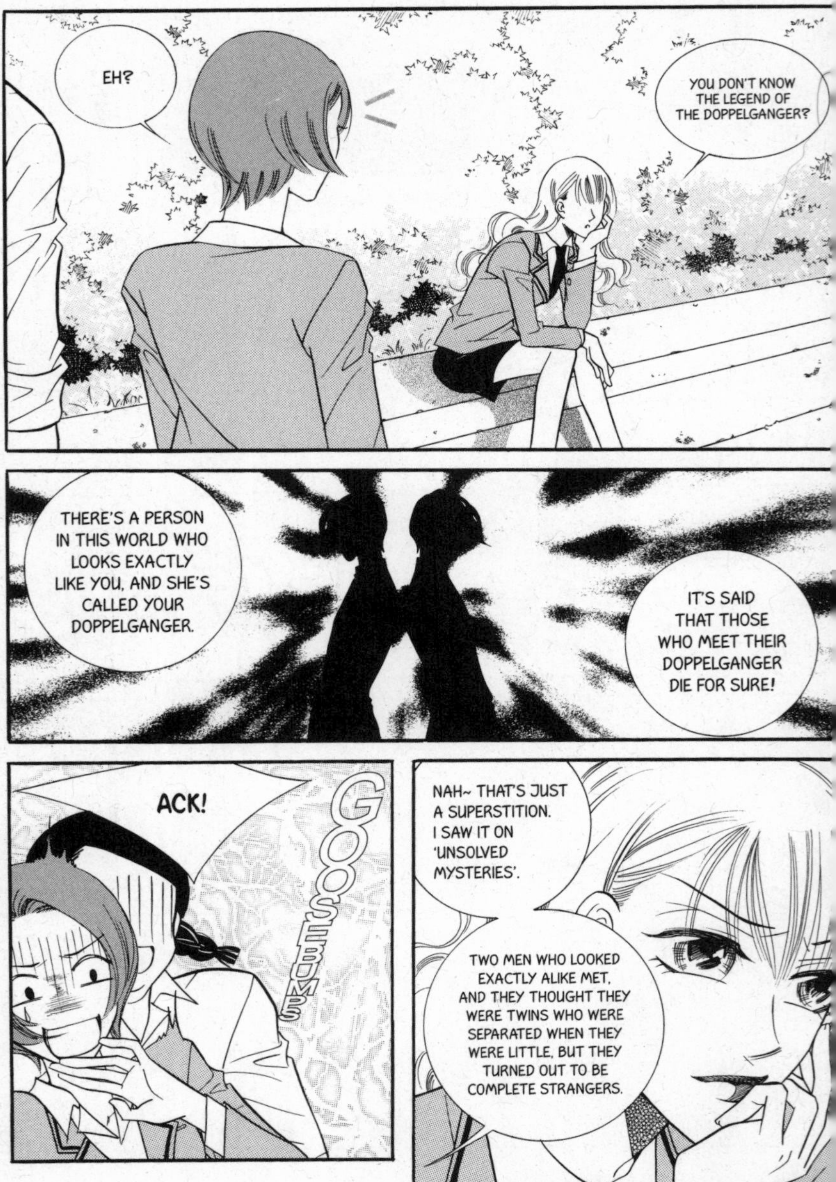
EH?
YOU DON'T KNOW THE LEGEND OF THE DOPPELGANGER?
THERE'S A PERSON IN THIS WORLD WHO LOOKS EXACTLY LIKE YOU, AND SHE'S CALLED YOUR DOPPELGANGER.
IT'S SAID THAT THOSE WHO MEET THEIR DOPPELGANGER DIE FOR SURE!
ACK!
GOOSEBUMPS
NAH~ THAT'S JUST A SUPERSTITION. I SAW IT ON 'UNSOLVED MYSTERIES'.
TWO MEN WHO LOOKED EXACTLY ALIKE MET, AND THEY THOUGHT THEY WERE TWINS WHO WERE SEPARATED WHEN THEY WERE LITTLE, BUT THEY TURNED OUT TO BE COMPLETE STRANGERS.

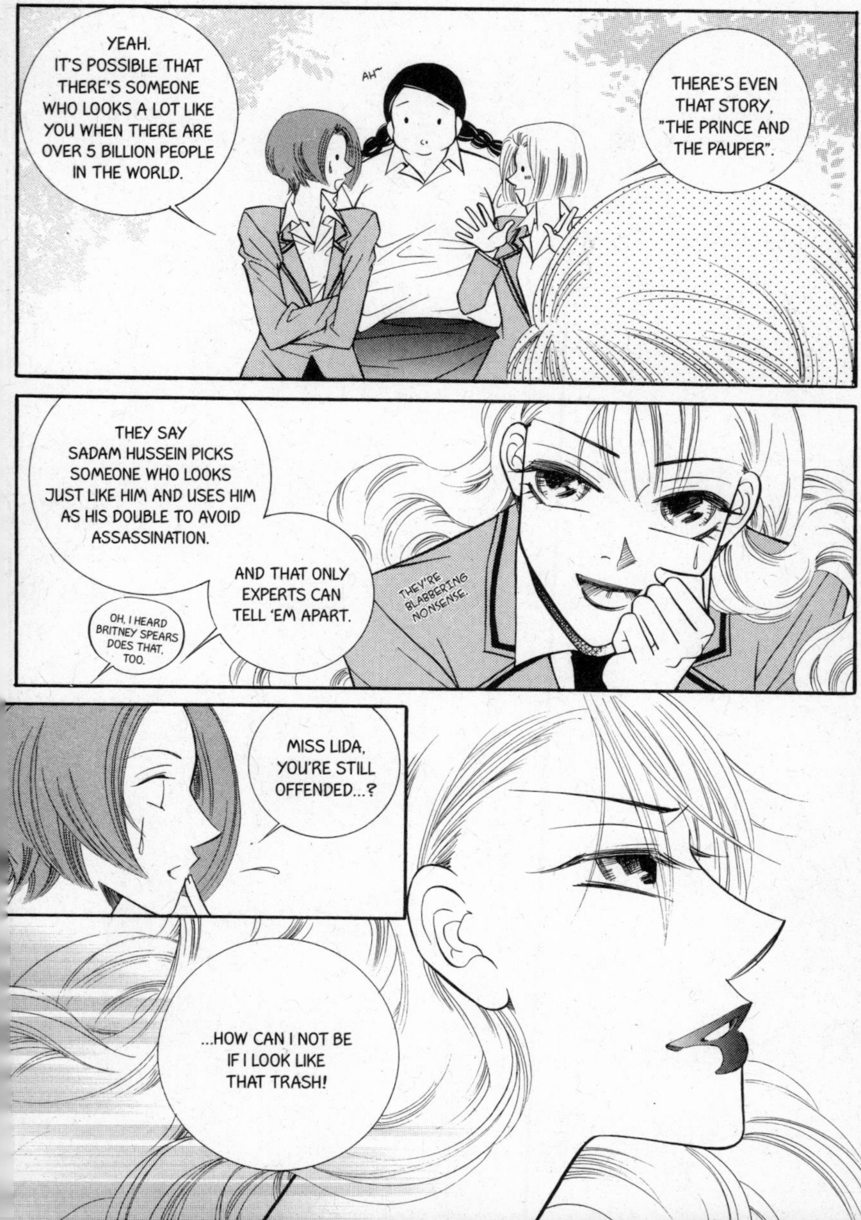
YEAH. IT'S POSSIBLE THAT THERE'S SOMEONE WHO LOOKS A LOT LIKE YOU WHEN THERE ARE OVER 5 BILLION PEOPLE IN THE WORLD.
AH~
THERE'S EVEN THAT STORY, "THE PRINCE AND THE PAUPER".
THEY SAY SADAM HUSSEIN PICKS SOMEONE WHO LOOKS JUST LIKE HIM AND USES HIM AS HIS DOUBLE TO AVOID ASSASSINATION.
AND THAT ONLY EXPERTS CAN TELL 'EM APART.
OH, I HEARD BRITNEY SPEARS DOES THAT, TOO.
THEY'RE BLABBERING NONSENSE.
MISS LIDA, YOU'RE STILL OFFENDED...?
...HOW CAN I NOT BE IF I LOOK LIKE THAT TRASH!

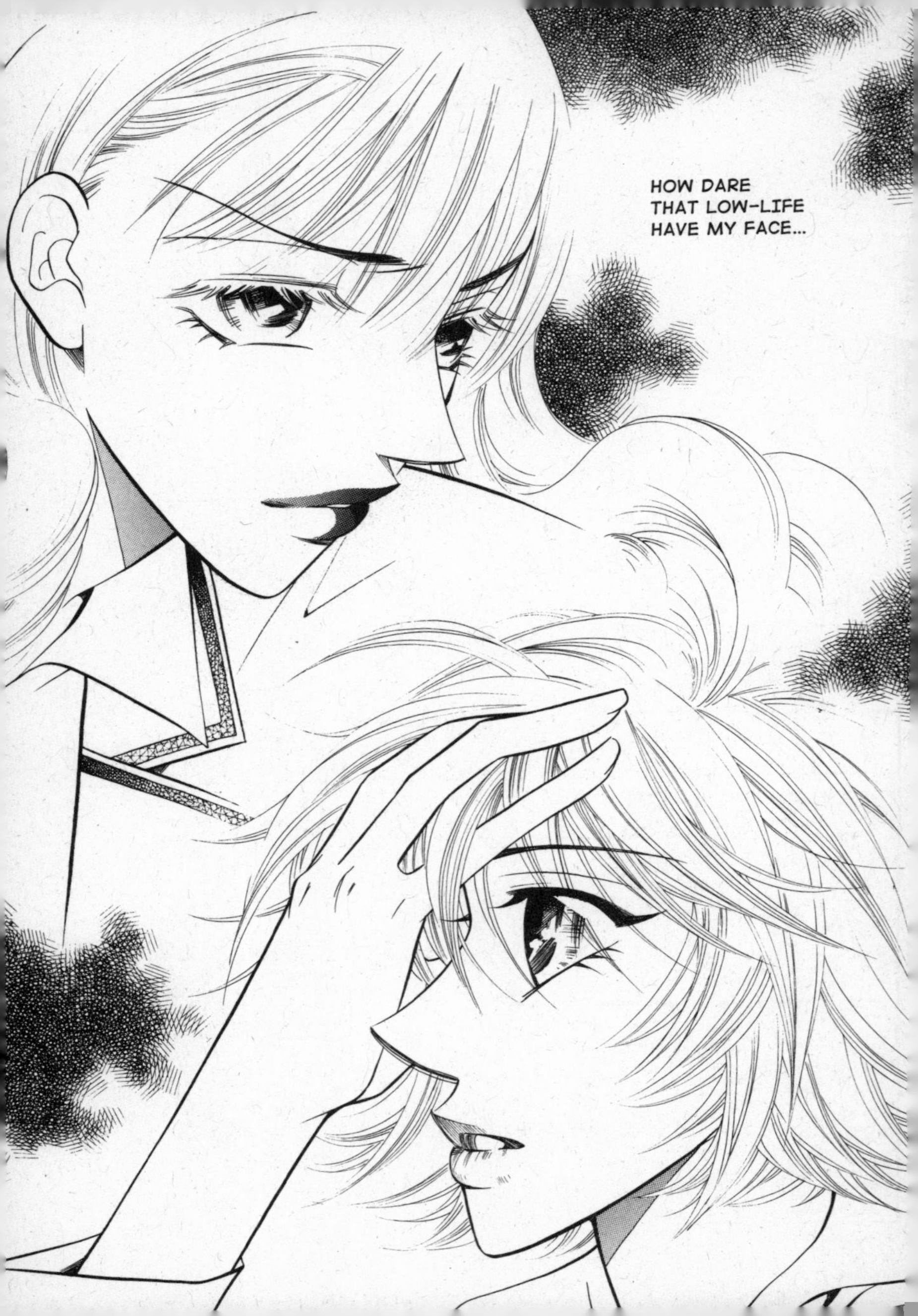
HOW DARE
THAT LOW-LIFE
HAVE MY FACE...

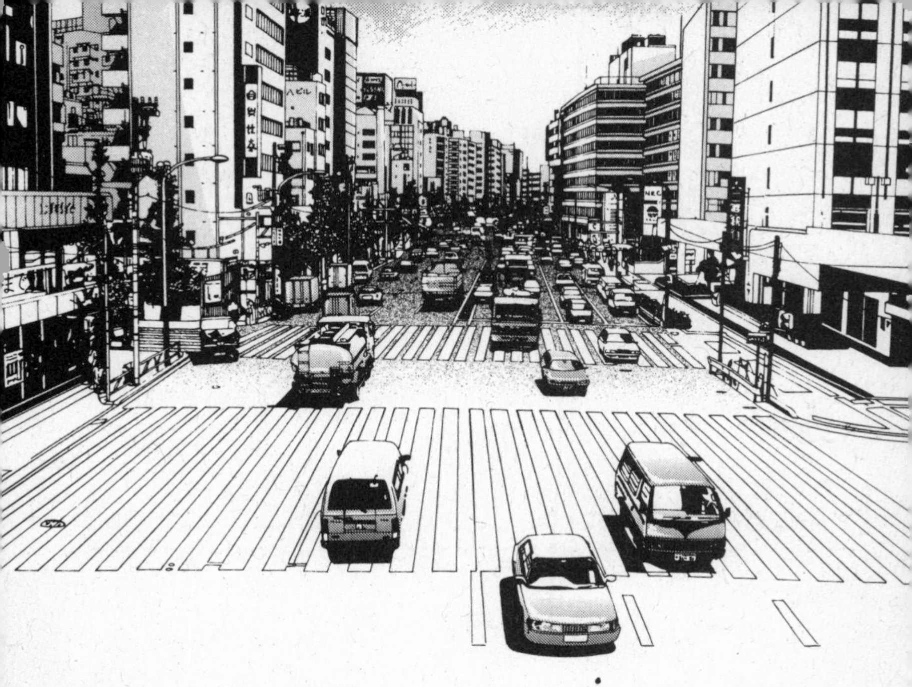

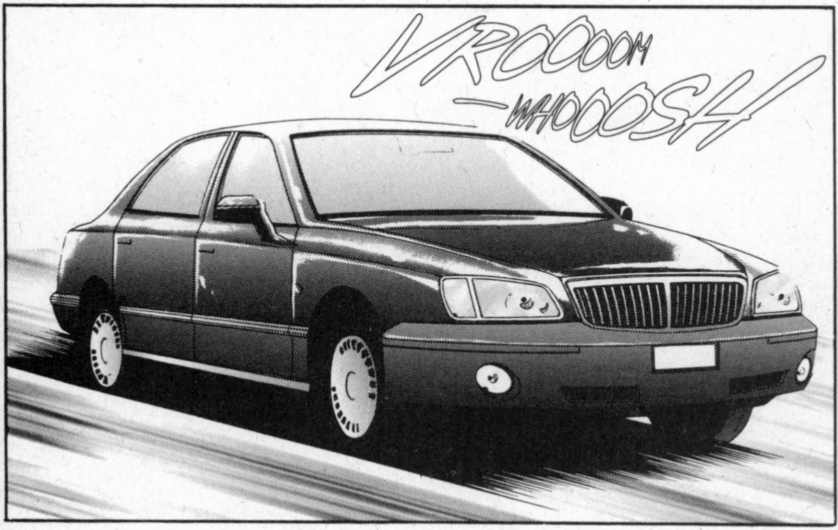
VROOOOOM
—WHOOOOSH

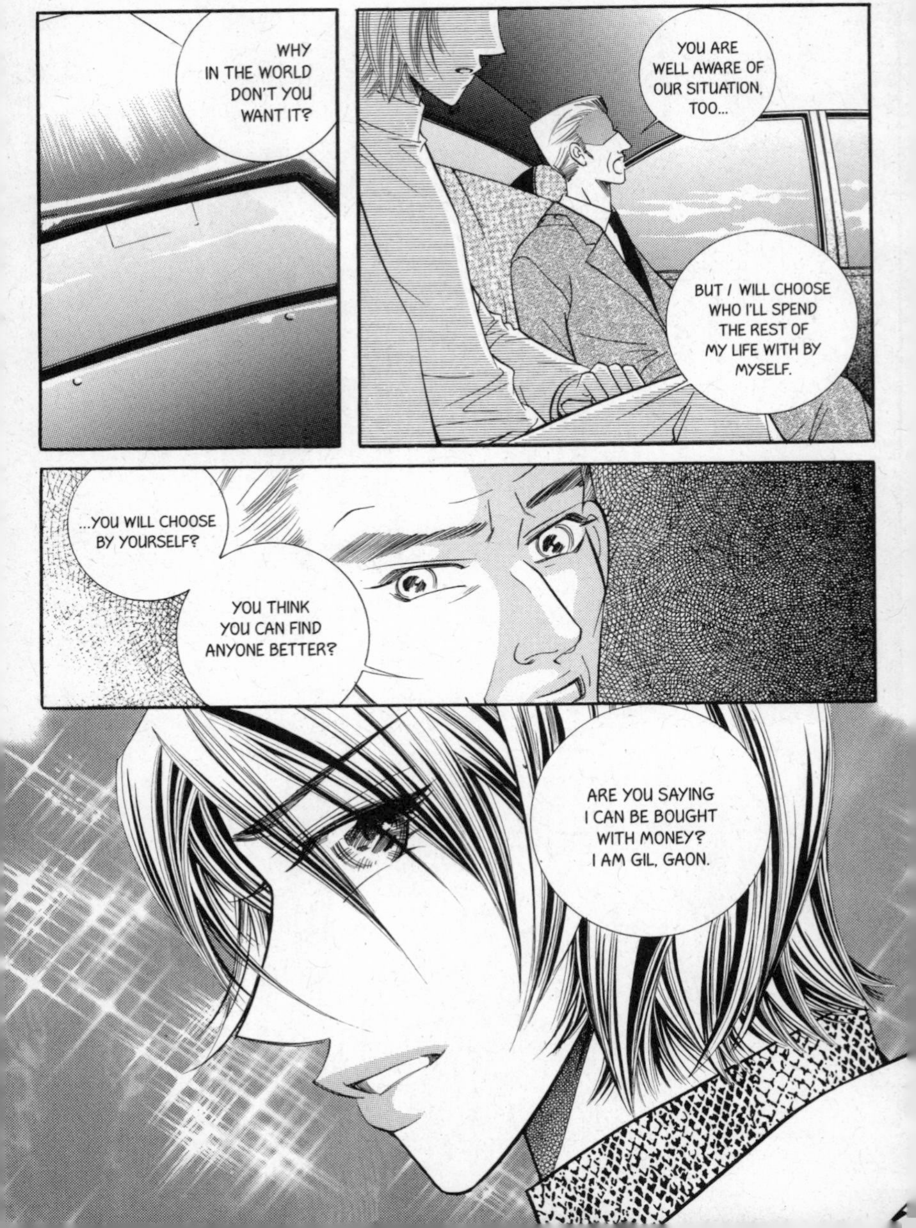
WHY IN THE WORLD DON'T YOU WANT IT?
YOU ARE WELL AWARE OF OUR SITUATION, TOO...
BUT I WILL CHOOSE WHO I'LL SPEND THE REST OF MY LIFE WITH BY MYSELF.
...YOU WILL CHOOSE BY YOURSELF?
YOU THINK YOU CAN FIND ANYONE BETTER?
ARE YOU SAYING I CAN BE BOUGHT WITH MONEY? I AM GIL, GAON.

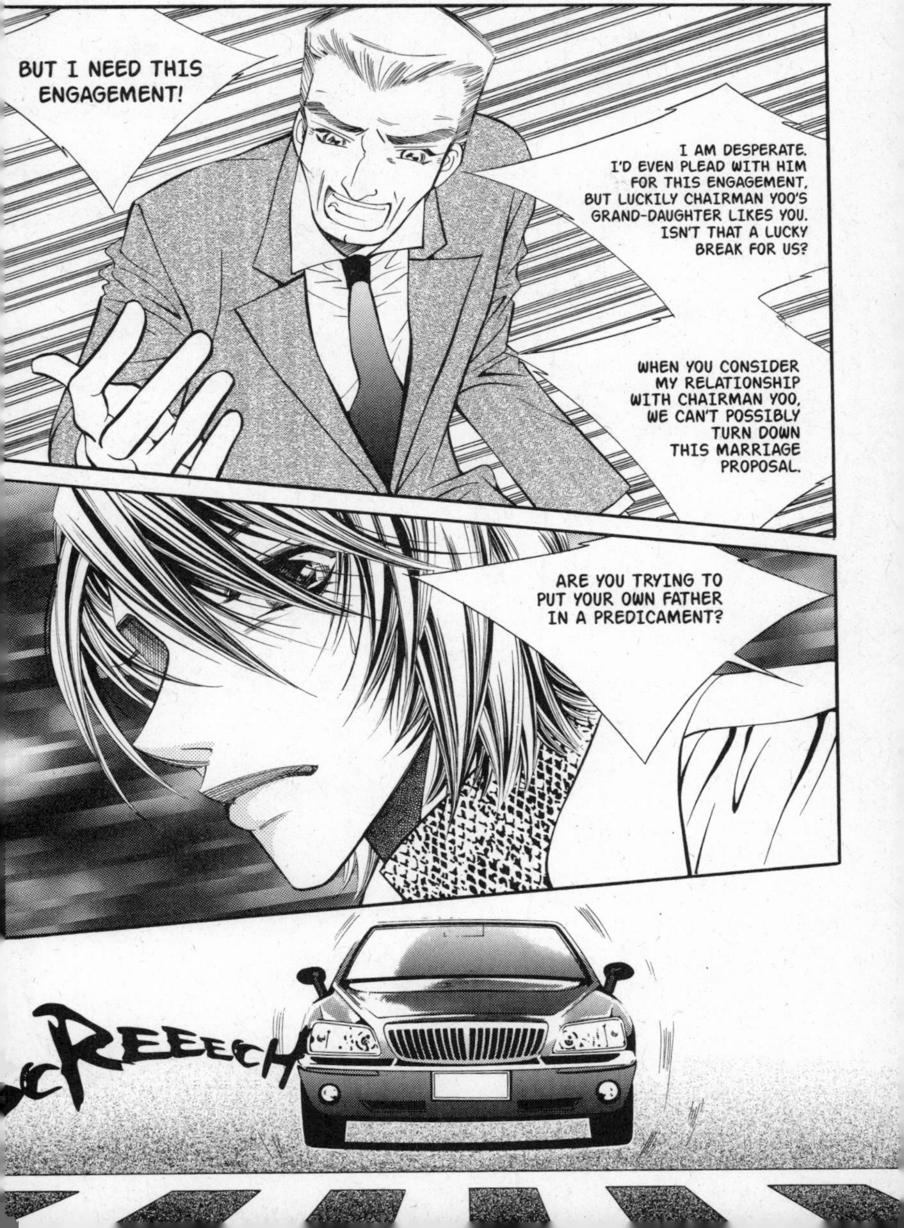
BUT I NEED THIS ENGAGEMENT!
I AM DESPERATE. I'D EVEN PLEAD WITH HIM FOR THIS ENGAGEMENT, BUT LUCKILY CHAIRMAN YOO'S GRAND-DAUGHTER LIKES YOU. ISN'T THAT A LUCKY BREAK FOR US?
WHEN YOU CONSIDER MY RELATIONSHIP WITH CHAIRMAN YOO, WE CAN'T POSSIBLY TURN DOWN THIS MARRIAGE PROPOSAL.
ARE YOU TRYING TO PUT YOUR OWN FATHER IN A PREDICAMENT?
SCREEECH

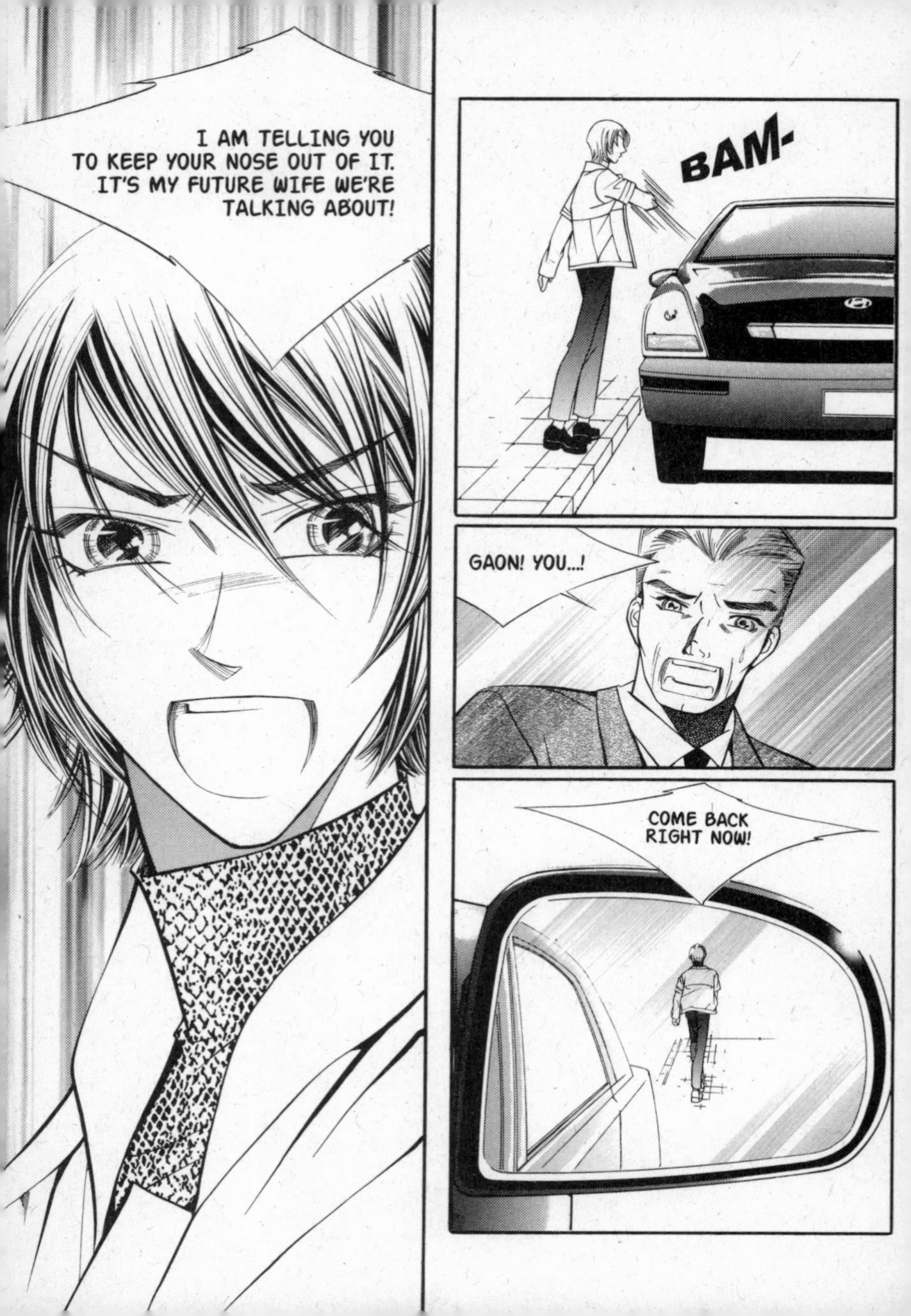
I AM TELLING YOU TO KEEP YOUR NOSE OUT OF IT. IT'S MY FUTURE WIFE WE'RE TALKING ABOUT!
BAM-
GAON! YOU...!
COME BACK RIGHT NOW!

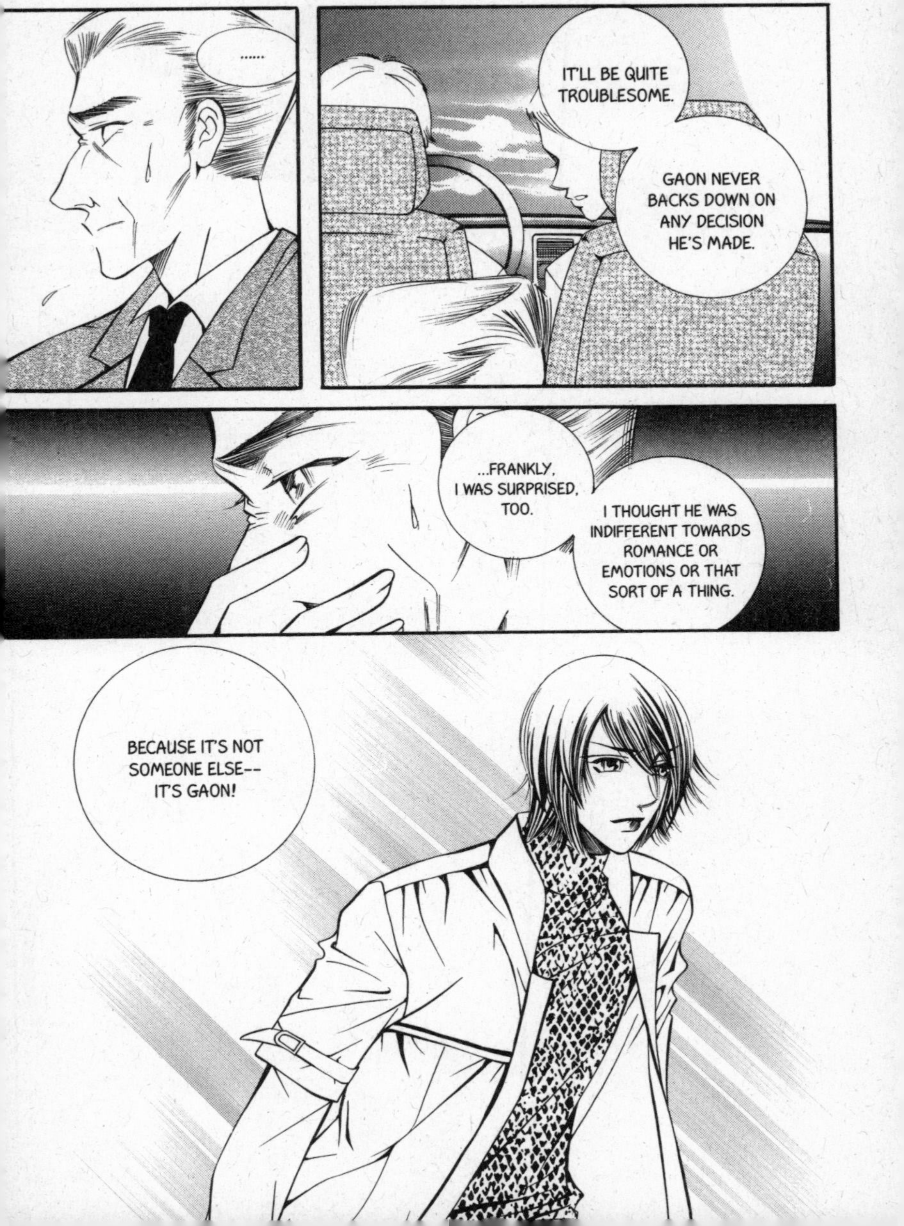

......
IT'LL BE QUITE TROUBLESOME.
GAON NEVER BACKS DOWN ON ANY DECISION HE'S MADE.
...FRANKLY, I WAS SURPRISED, TOO.
I THOUGHT HE WAS INDIFFERENT TOWARDS ROMANCE OR EMOTIONS OR THAT SORT OF A THING.
BECAUSE IT'S NOT SOMEONE ELSE-- IT'S GAON!

KANG, YOOI

2. GIL, GAON

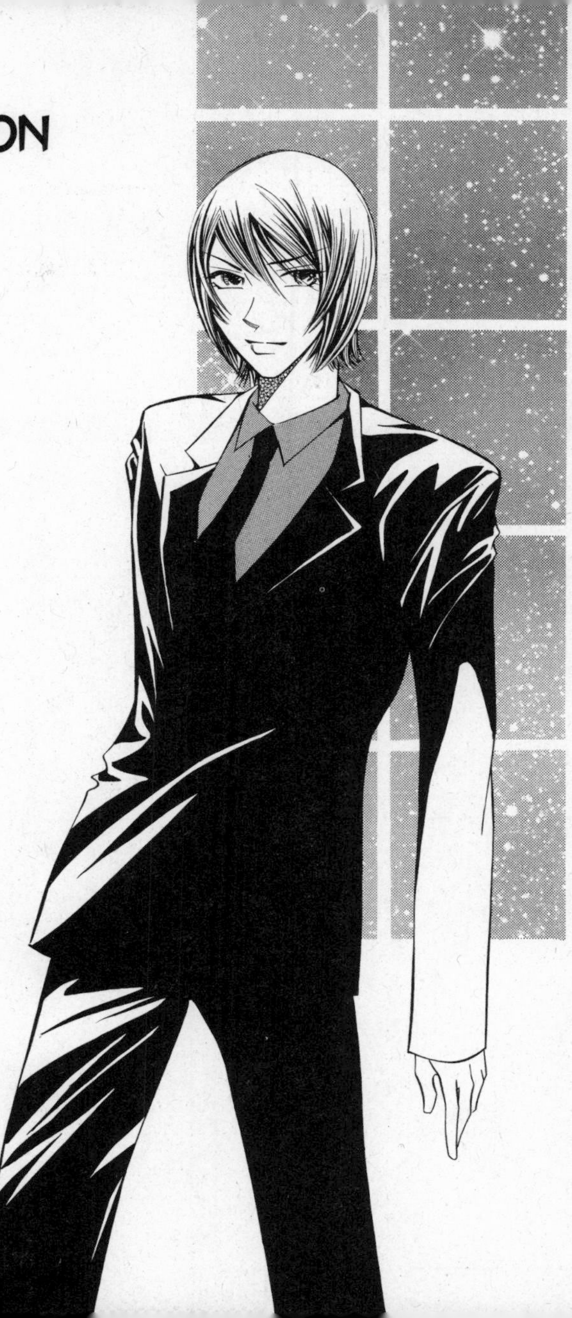

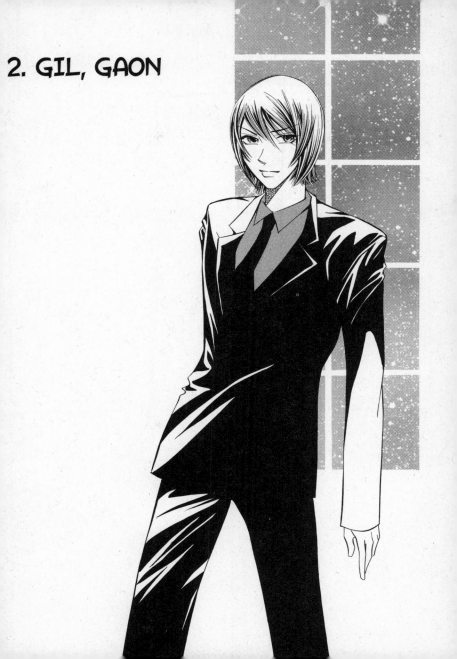

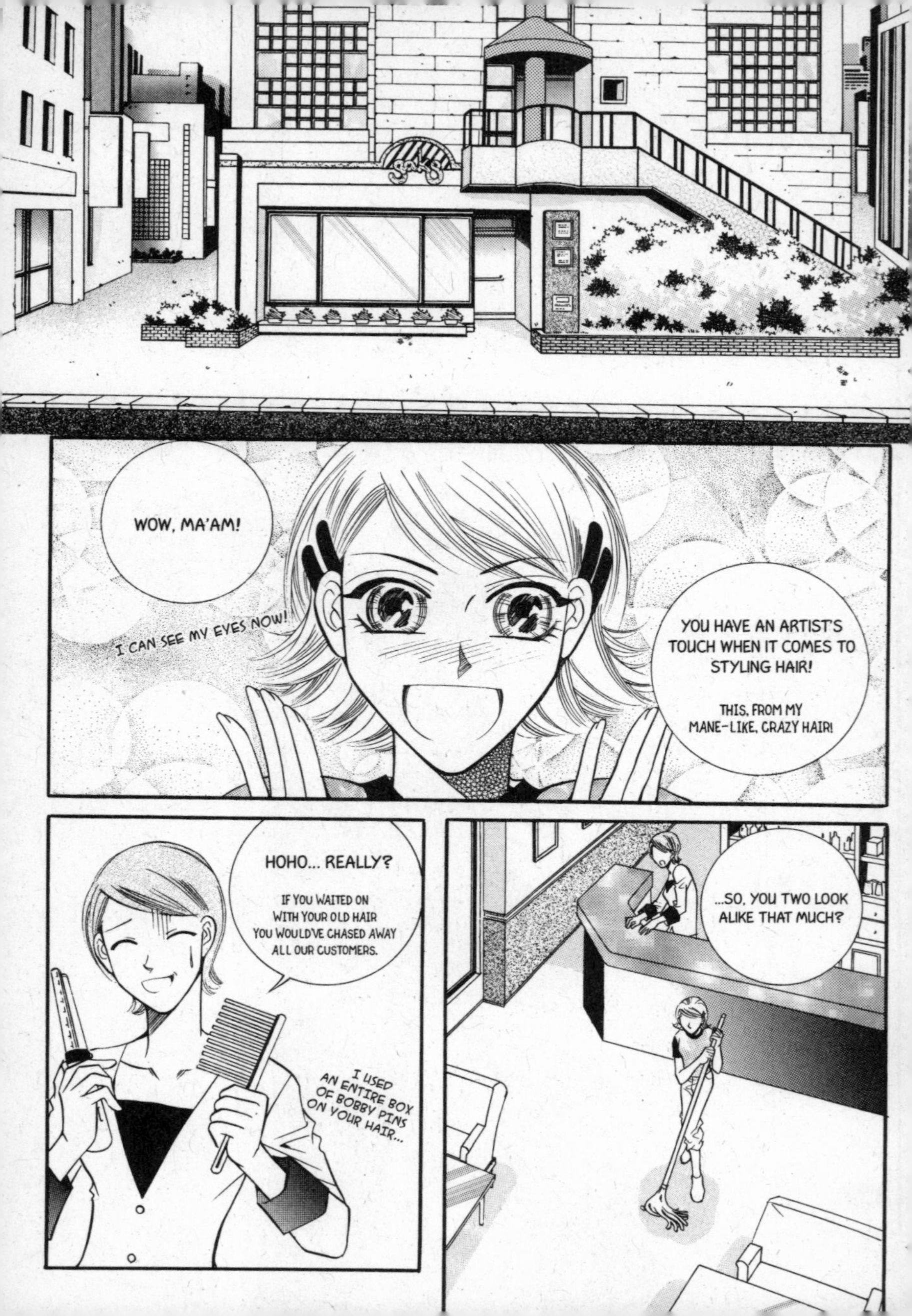
WOW, MA'AM!
I CAN SEE MY EYES NOW!
YOU HAVE AN ARTIST'S TOUCH WHEN IT COMES TO STYLING HAIR!
THIS, FROM MY MANE-LIKE, CRAZY HAIR!
HOHO... REALLY?
IF YOU WAITED ON WITH YOUR OLD HAIR YOU WOULD'VE CHASED AWAY ALL OUR CUSTOMERS.
I USED AN ENTIRE BOX OF BOBBY PINS ON YOUR HAIR...
...SO, YOU TWO LOOK ALIKE THAT MUCH?

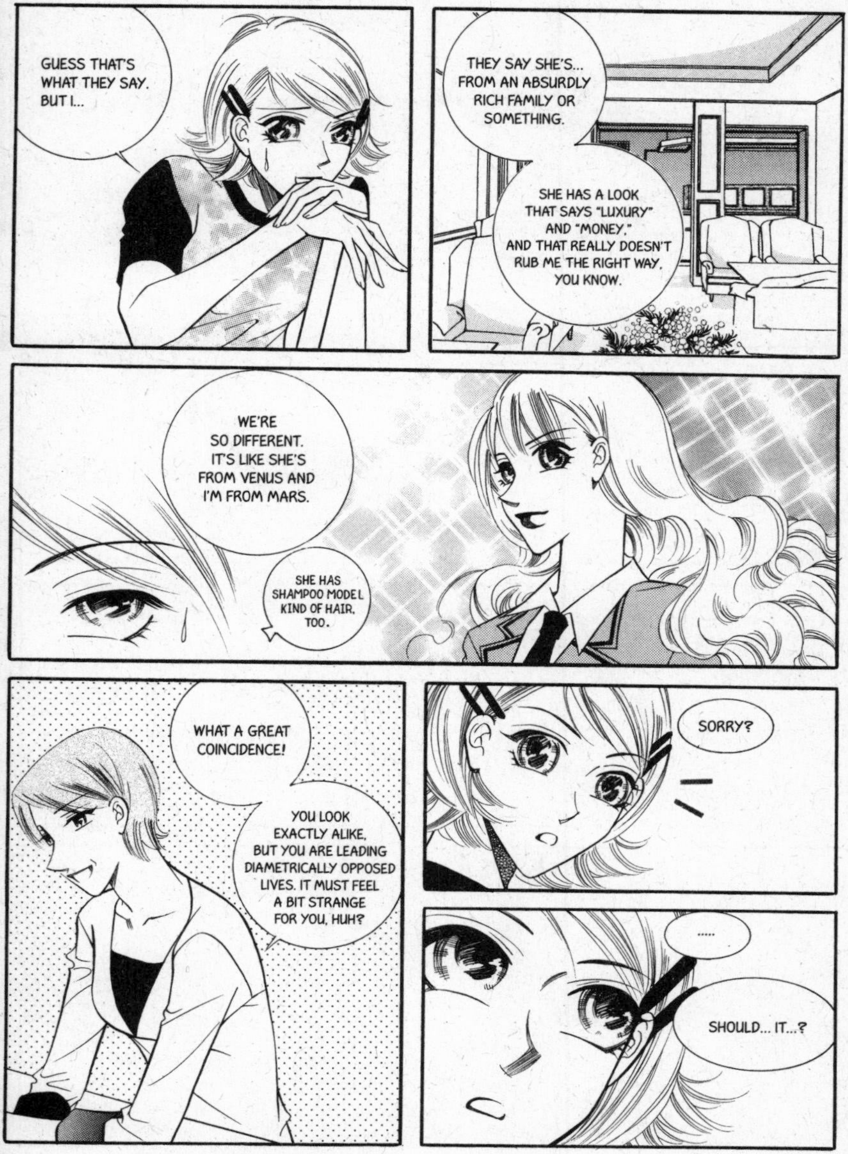
GUESS THAT'S WHAT THEY SAY. BUT I...
THEY SAY SHE'S... FROM AN ABSURDLY RICH FAMILY OR SOMETHING.
SHE HAS A LOOK THAT SAYS "LUXURY" AND "MONEY," AND THAT REALLY DOESN'T RUB ME THE RIGHT WAY, YOU KNOW.
WE'RE SO DIFFERENT. IT'S LIKE SHE'S FROM VENUS AND I'M FROM MARS.
SHE HAS SHAMPOO MODEL KIND OF HAIR, TOO.
WHAT A GREAT COINCIDENCE!
YOU LOOK EXACTLY ALIKE, BUT YOU ARE LEADING DIAMETRICALLY OPPOSED LIVES. IT MUST FEEL A BIT STRANGE FOR YOU, HUH?
SORRY?
.....
SHOULD... IT...?

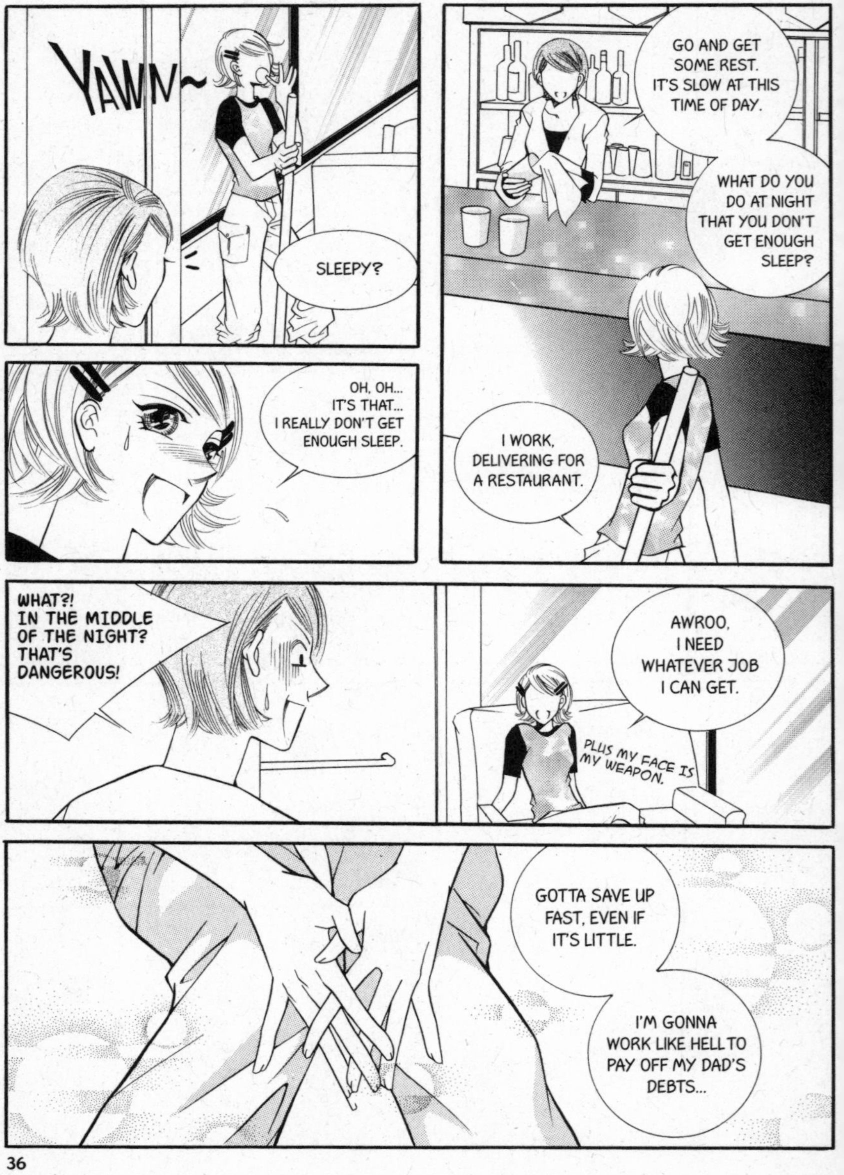
YAWN~
SLEEPY?
GO AND GET SOME REST. IT'S SLOW AT THIS TIME OF DAY.
WHAT DO YOU DO AT NIGHT THAT YOU DON'T GET ENOUGH SLEEP?
OH, OH... IT'S THAT... I REALLY DON'T GET ENOUGH SLEEP.
I WORK, DELIVERING FOR A RESTAURANT.
WHAT?! IN THE MIDDLE OF THE NIGHT? THAT'S DANGEROUS!
AWROO, I NEED WHATEVER JOB I CAN GET.
PLUS MY FACE IS MY WEAPON.
GOTTA SAVE UP FAST, EVEN IF IT'S LITTLE.
I'M GONNA WORK LIKE HELL TO PAY OFF MY DAD'S DEBTS...

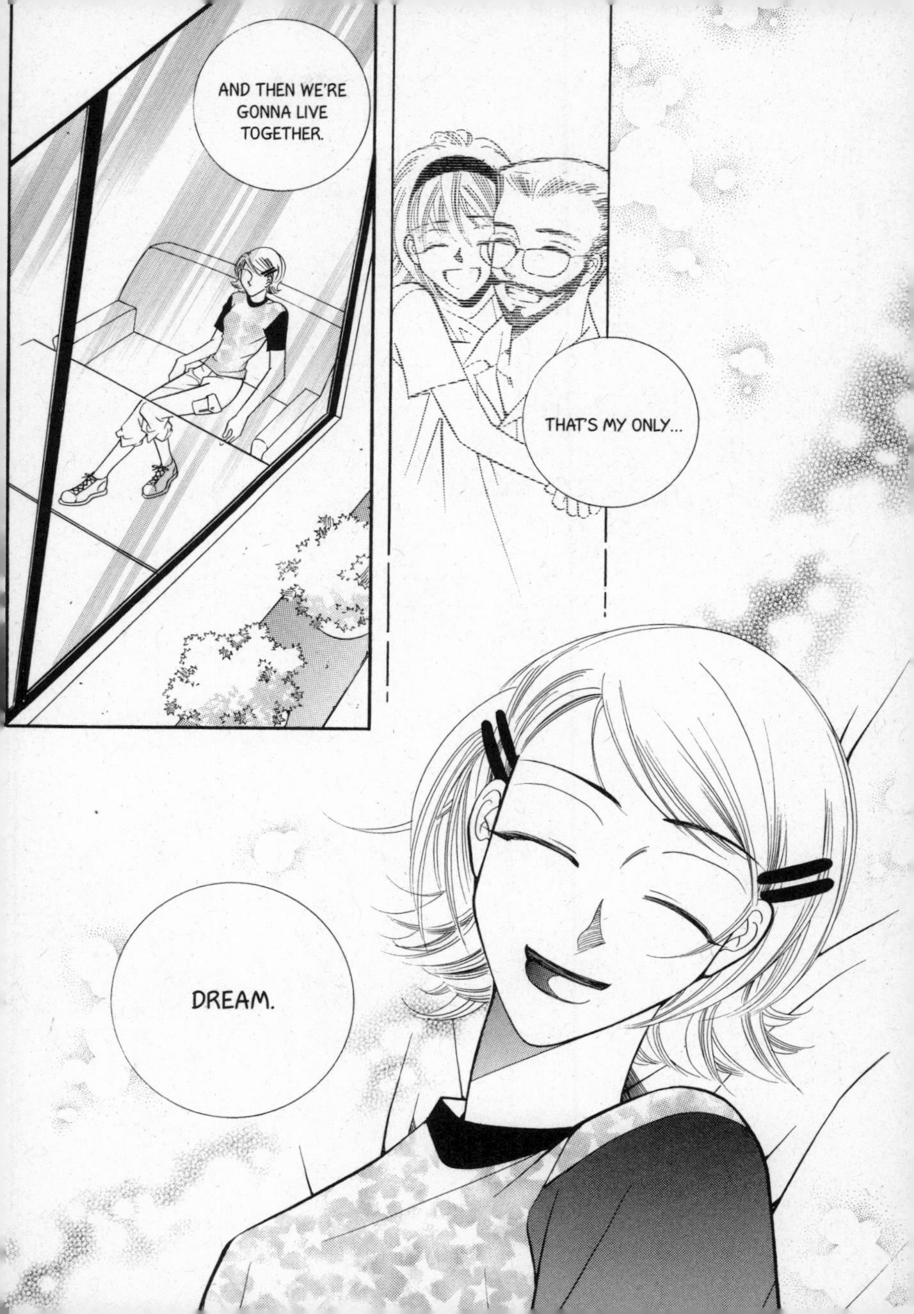
AND THEN WE'RE GONNA LIVE TOGETHER.
THAT'S MY ONLY...
DREAM.

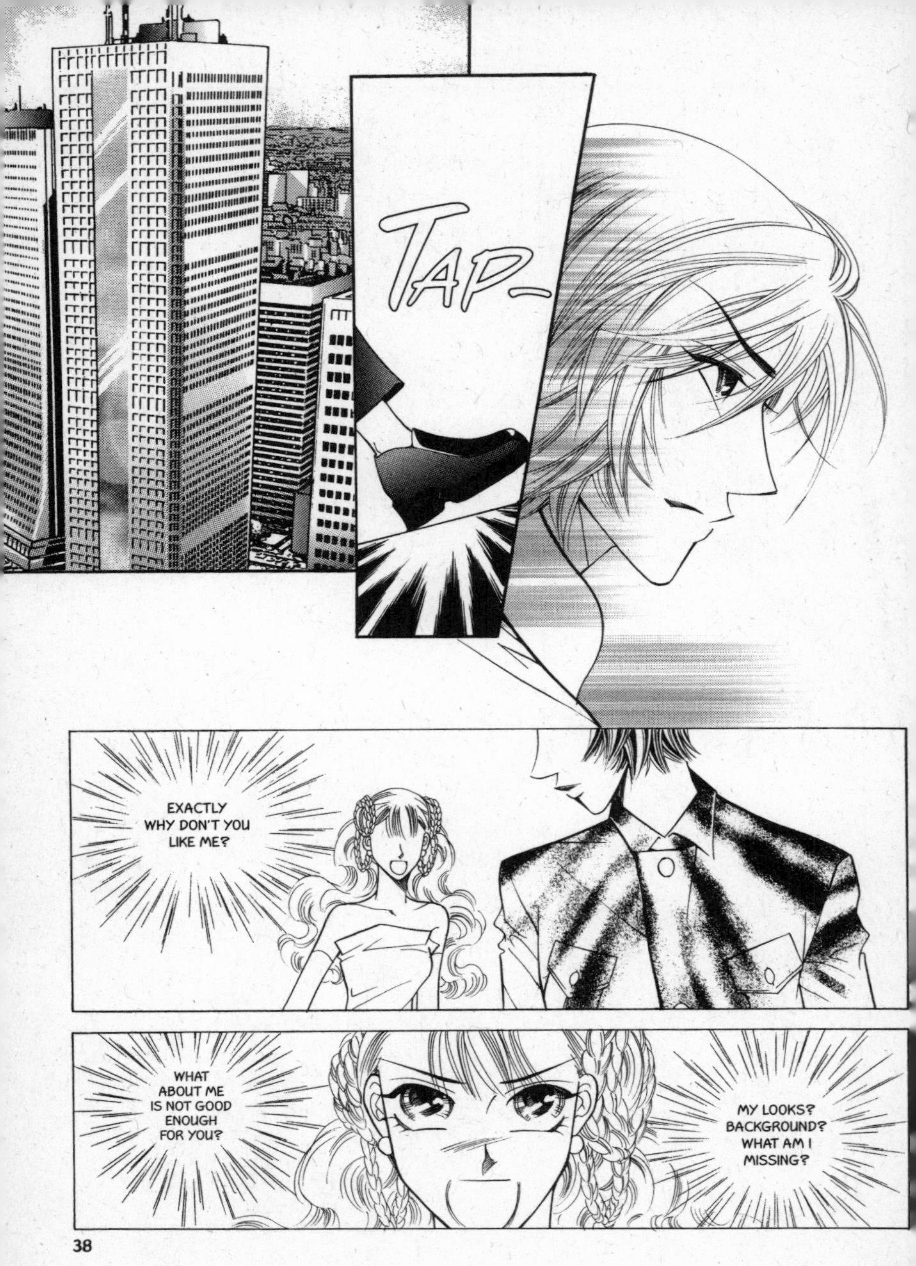
TAP_
EXACTLY WHY DON'T YOU LIKE ME?
WHAT ABOUT ME IS NOT GOOD ENOUGH FOR YOU?
MY LOOKS? BACKGROUND? WHAT AM I MISSING?

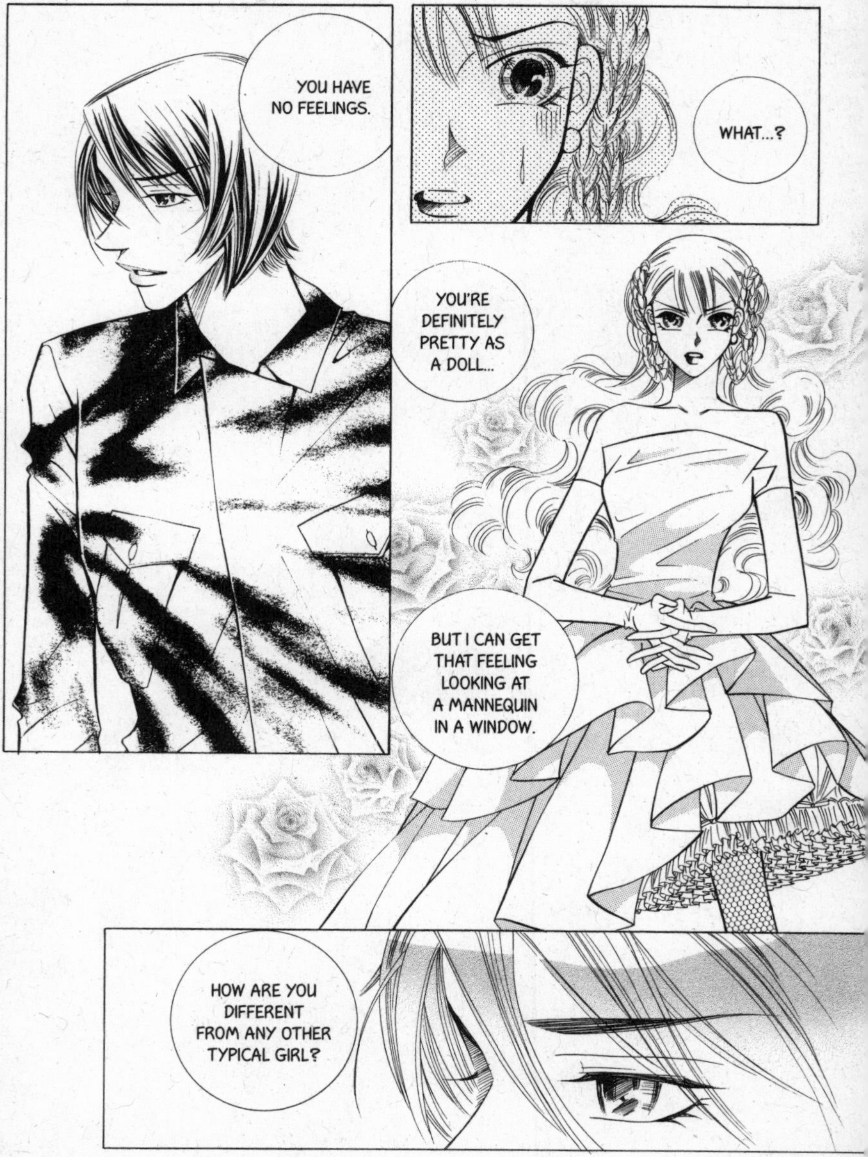
YOU HAVE NO FEELINGS.
WHAT...?
YOU'RE DEFINITELY PRETTY AS A DOLL...
BUT I CAN GET THAT FEELING LOOKING AT A MANNEQUIN IN A WINDOW.
HOW ARE YOU DIFFERENT FROM ANY OTHER TYPICAL GIRL?

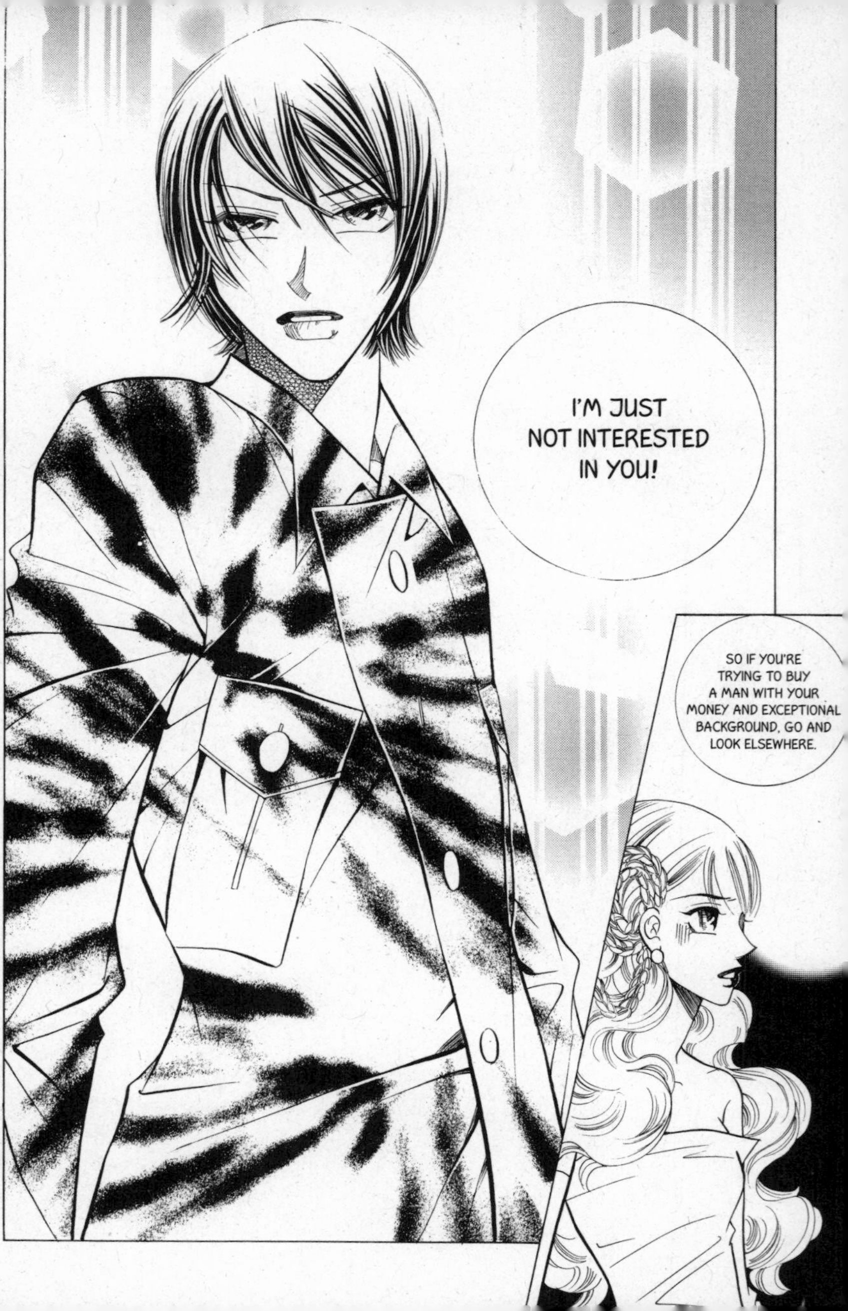
I'M JUST NOT INTERESTED IN YOU!
SO IF YOU'RE TRYING TO BUY A MAN WITH YOUR MONEY AND EXCEPTIONAL BACKGROUND, GO AND LOOK ELSEWHERE.

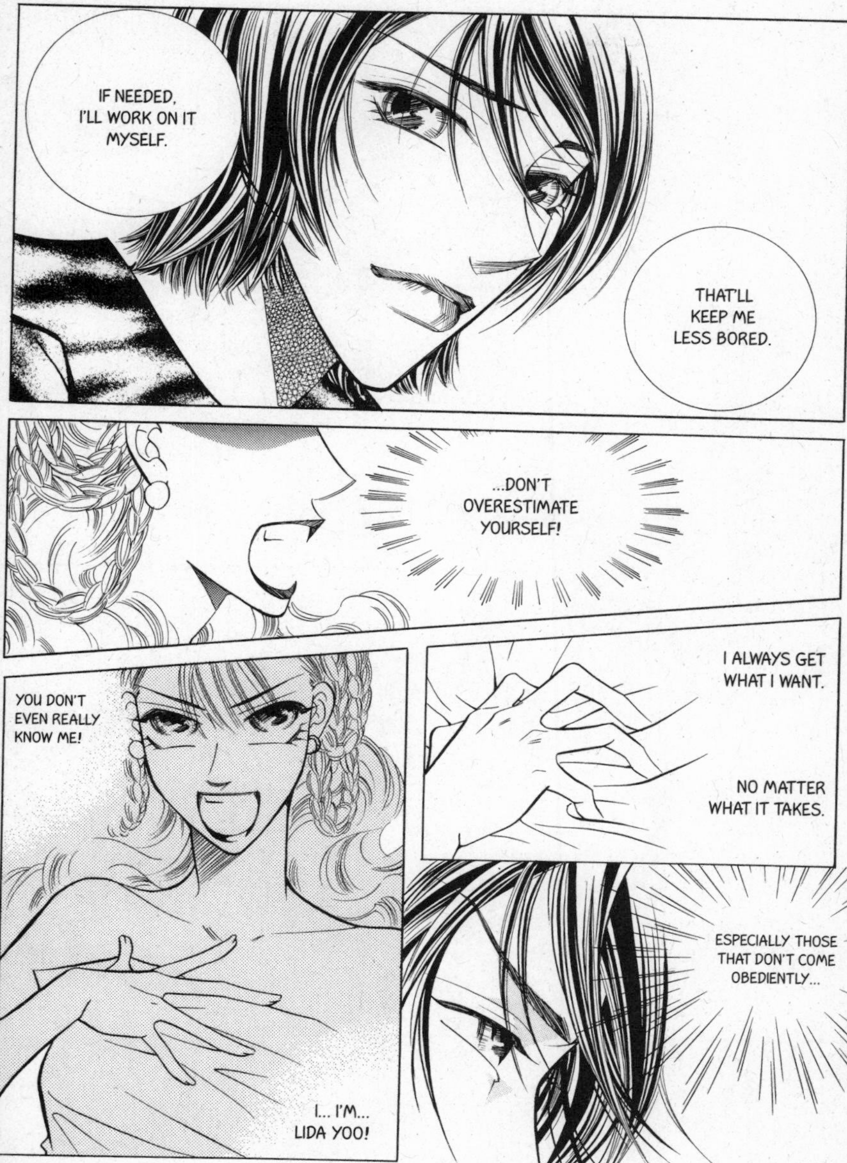
IF NEEDED, I'LL WORK ON IT MYSELF.
THAT'LL KEEP ME LESS BORED.
...DON'T OVERESTIMATE YOURSELF!
YOU DON'T EVEN REALLY KNOW ME!
I... I'M... LIDA YOO!
I ALWAYS GET WHAT I WANT.
NO MATTER WHAT IT TAKES.
ESPECIALLY THOSE THAT DON'T COME OBEDIENTLY...

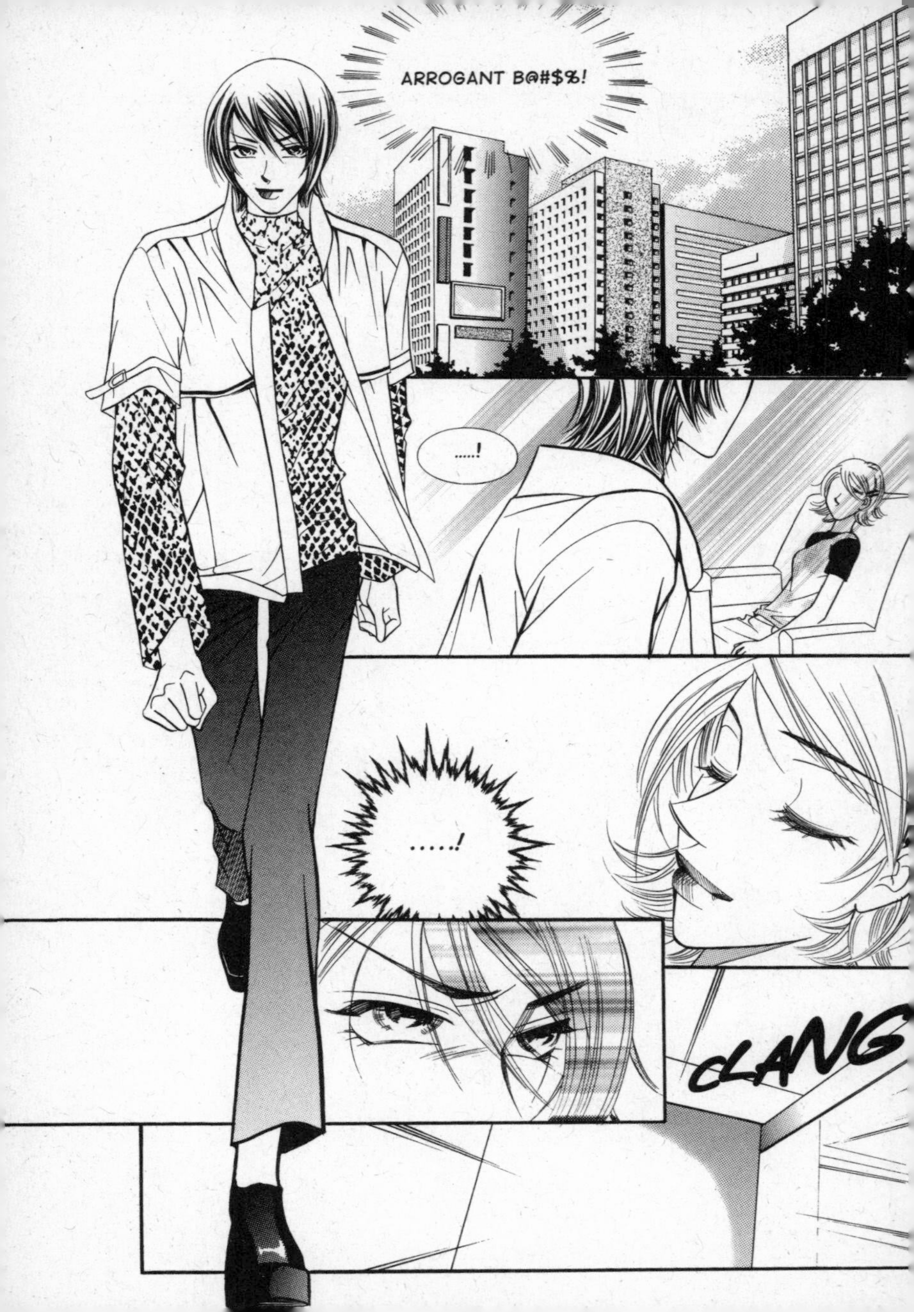
ARROGANT B@#$%!
.....!
.....!
CLANG

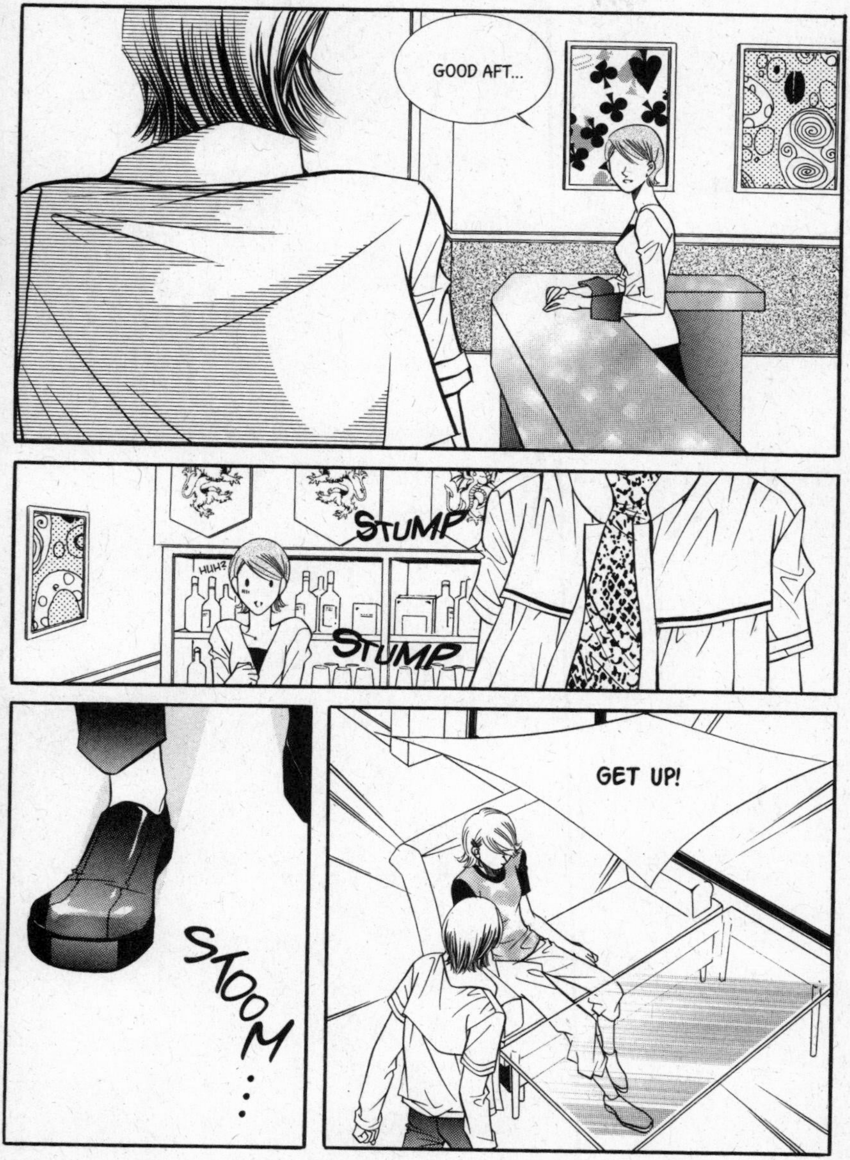
GOOD AFT...
STUMP
HUH?
STUMP
STOOM...
GET UP!

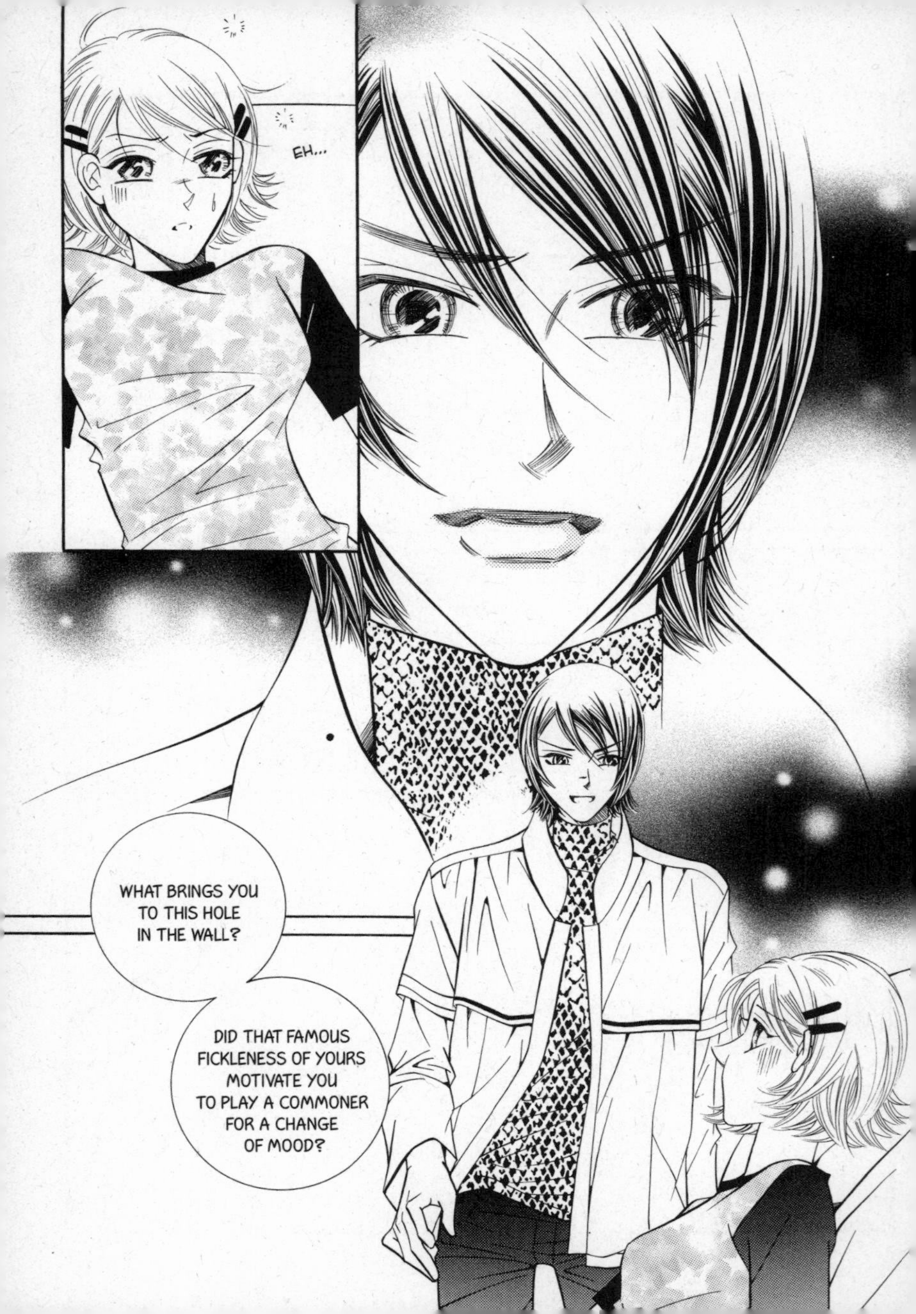
EH...
WHAT BRINGS YOU TO THIS HOLE IN THE WALL?
DID THAT FAMOUS FICKLENESS OF YOURS MOTIVATE YOU TO PLAY A COMMONER FOR A CHANGE OF MOOD?

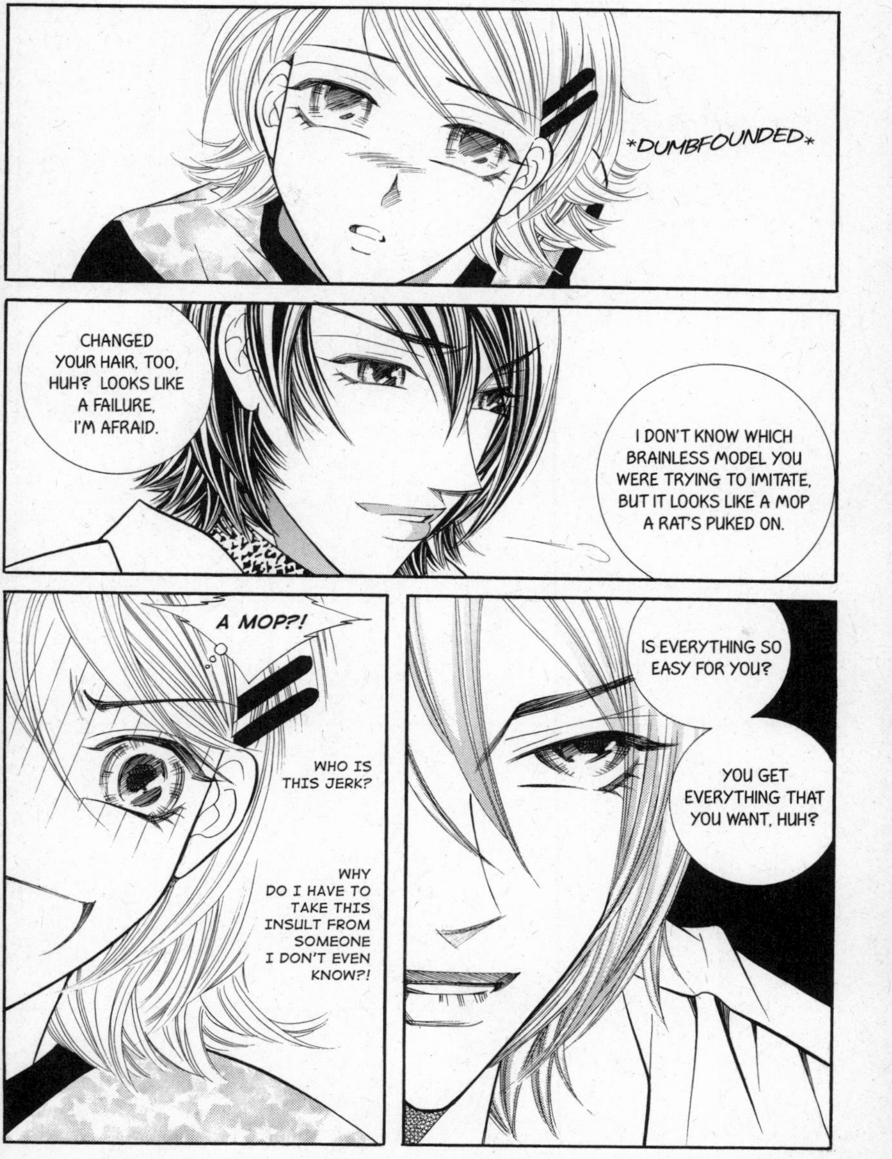
DUMBFOUNDED
CHANGED YOUR HAIR, TOO, HUH? LOOKS LIKE A FAILURE, I'M AFRAID.
I DON'T KNOW WHICH BRAINLESS MODEL YOU WERE TRYING TO IMITATE, BUT IT LOOKS LIKE A MOP A RAT'S PUKED ON.
A MOP?!
WHO IS THIS JERK?
WHY DO I HAVE TO TAKE THIS INSULT FROM SOMEONE I DON'T EVEN KNOW?!
IS EVERYTHING SO EASY FOR YOU?
YOU GET EVERYTHING THAT YOU WANT, HUH?

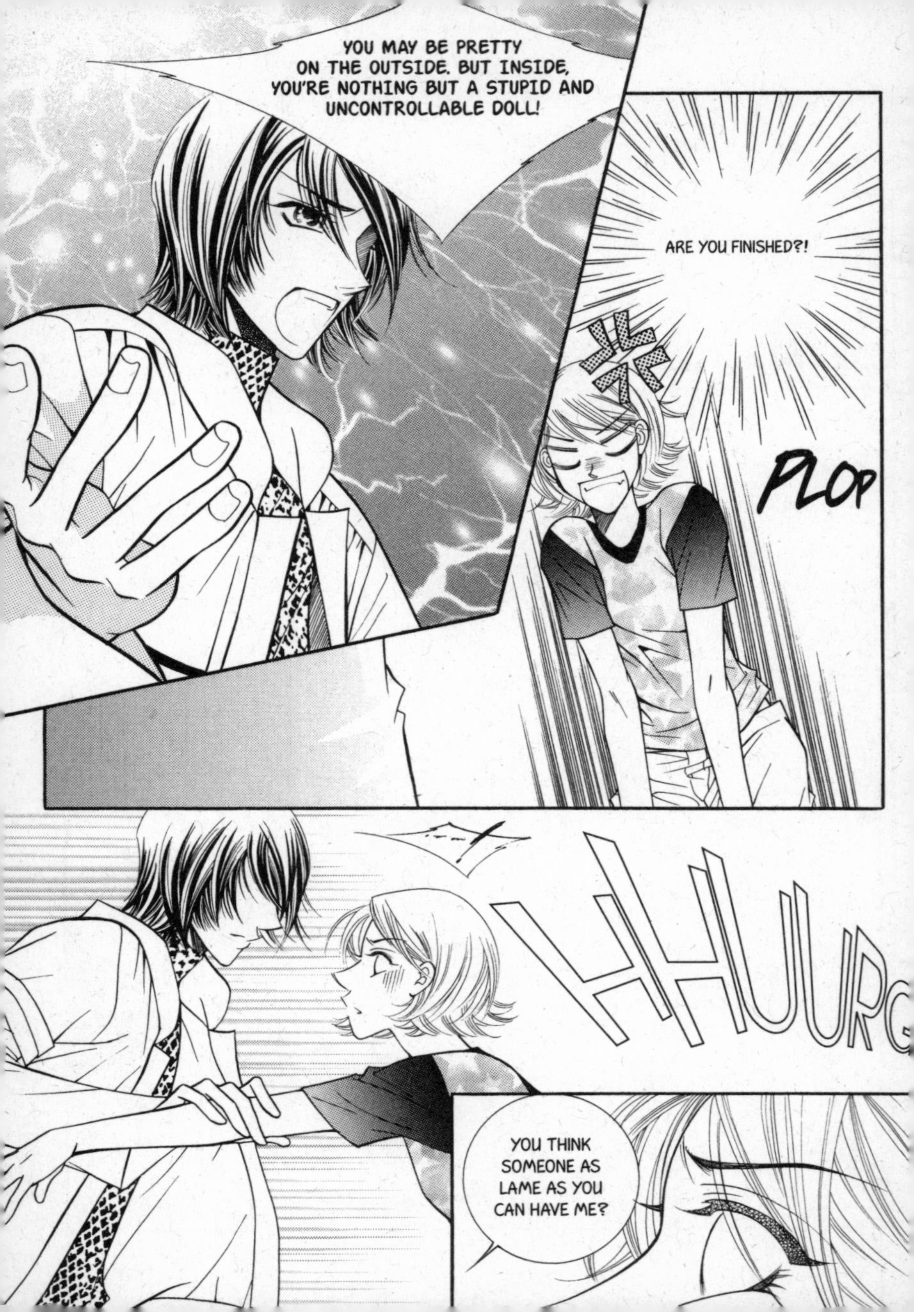
YOU MAY BE PRETTY ON THE OUTSIDE. BUT INSIDE, YOU'RE NOTHING BUT A STUPID AND UNCONTROLLABLE DOLL!
ARE YOU FINISHED?!
PLOP
HHUURG
YOU THINK SOMEONE AS LAME AS YOU CAN HAVE ME?

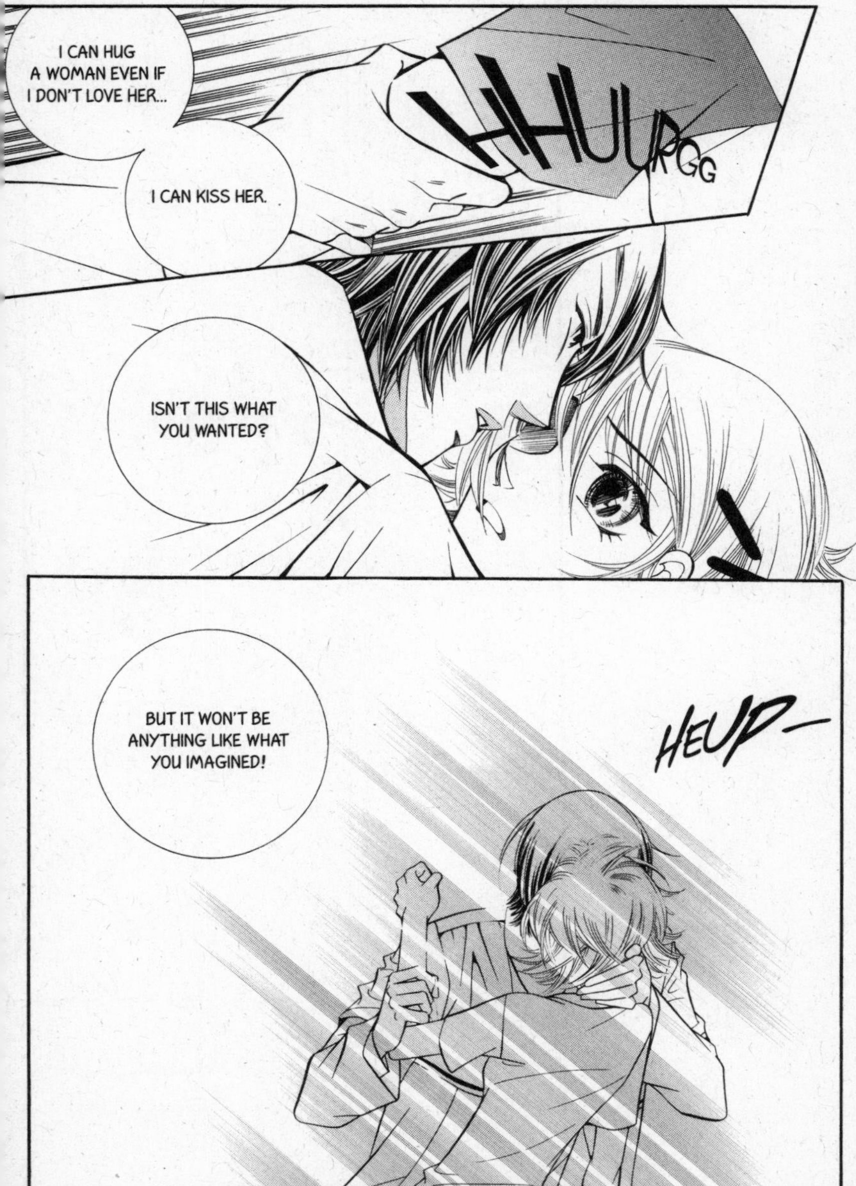
I CAN HUG A WOMAN EVEN IF I DON'T LOVE HER...
HHUURGG
I CAN KISS HER.
ISN'T THIS WHAT YOU WANTED?
BUT IT WON'T BE ANYTHING LIKE WHAT YOU IMAGINED!
HEUP—

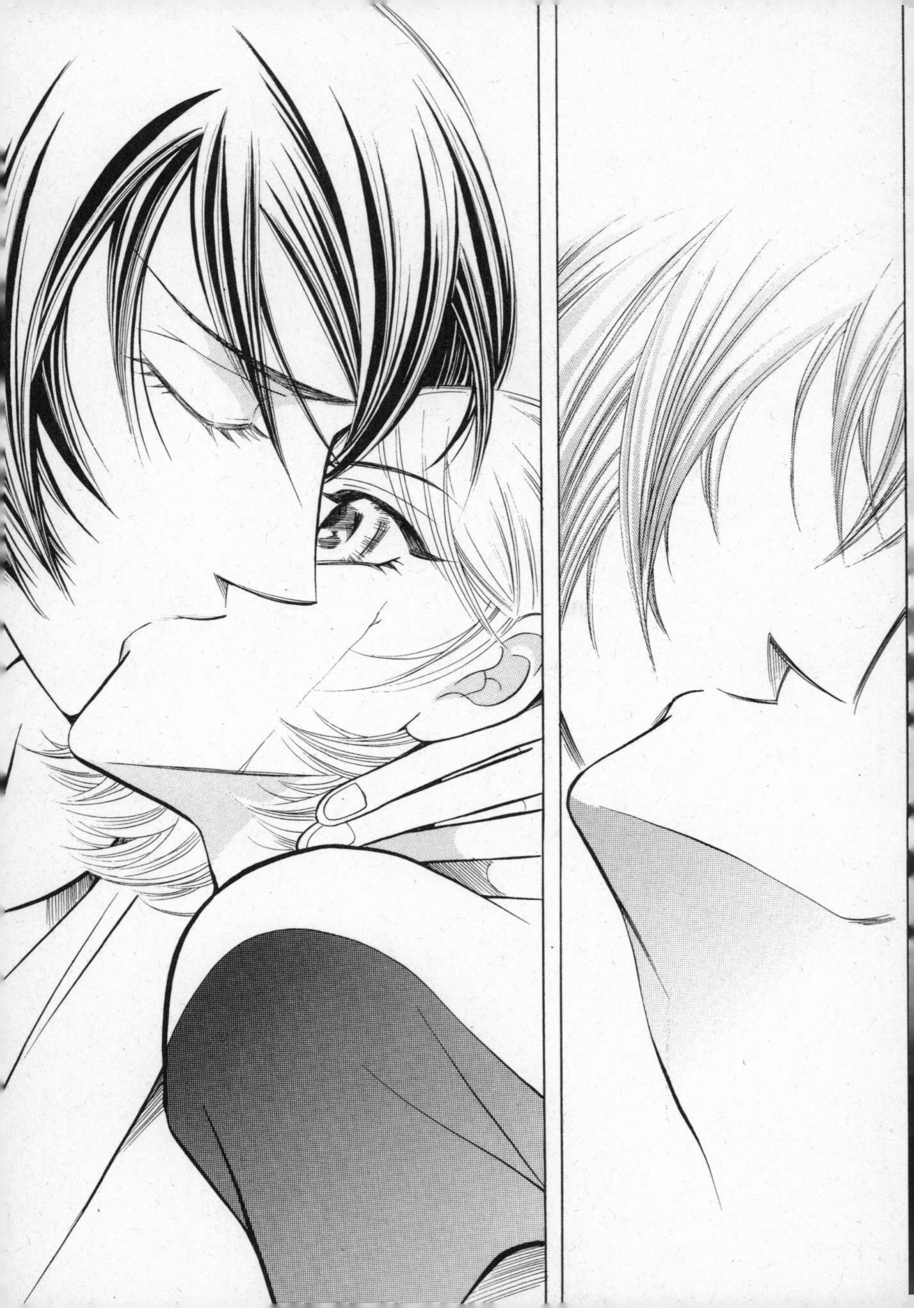

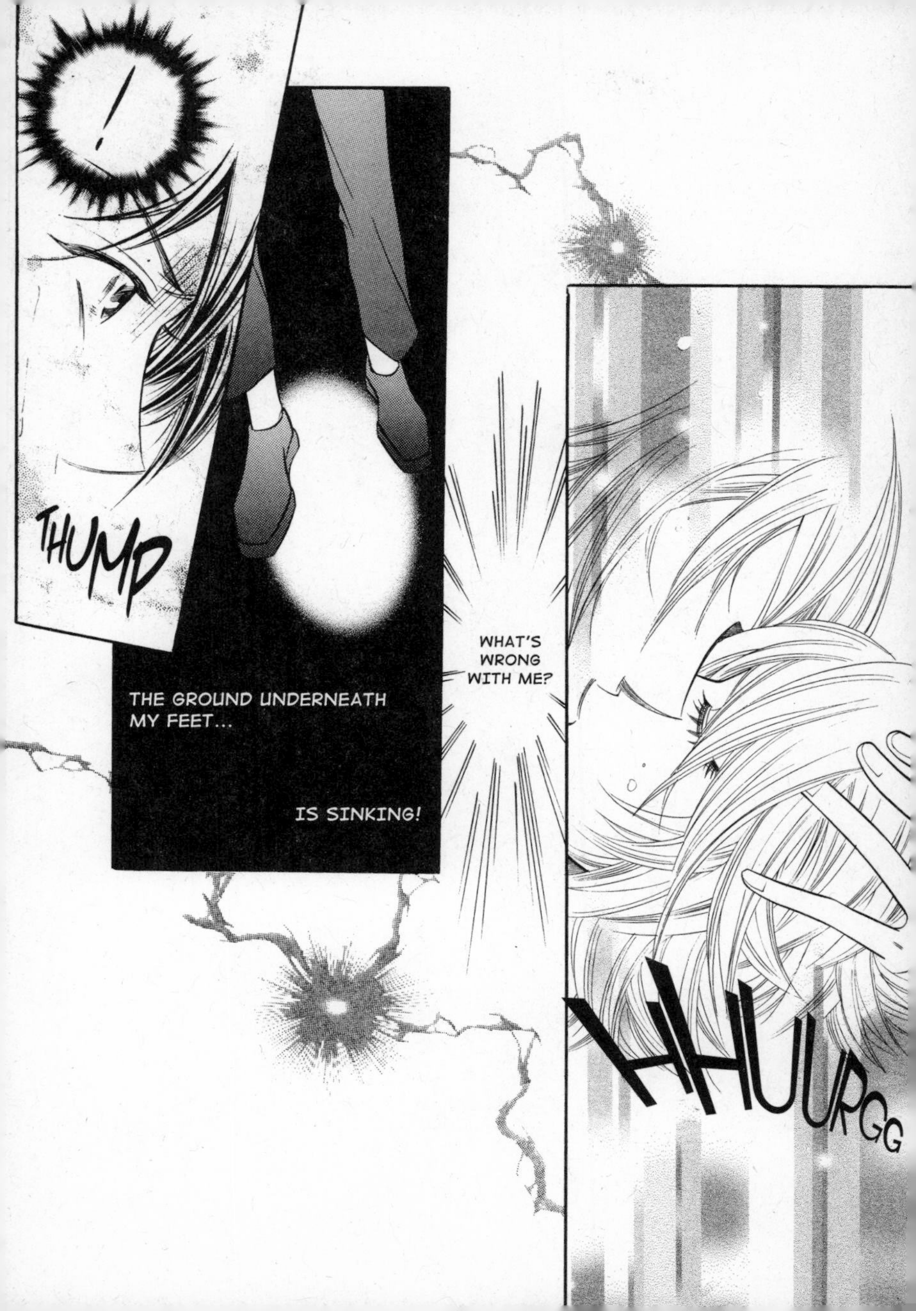
!
THUMP
WHAT'S WRONG WITH ME?
HHUURGG
THE GROUND UNDERNEATH MY FEET...
IS SINKING!

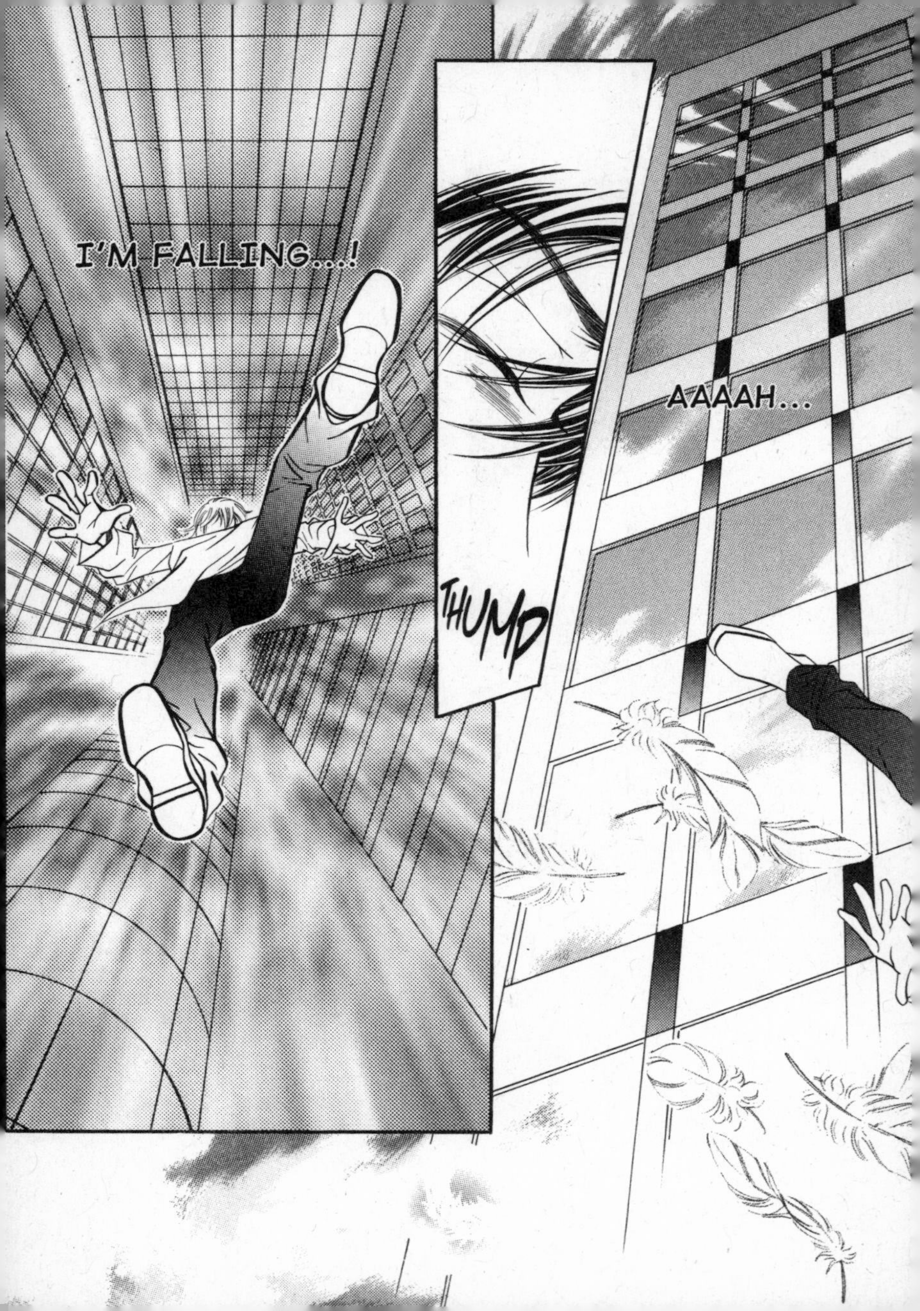
AAAAH...
THUMP
I'M FALLING...!

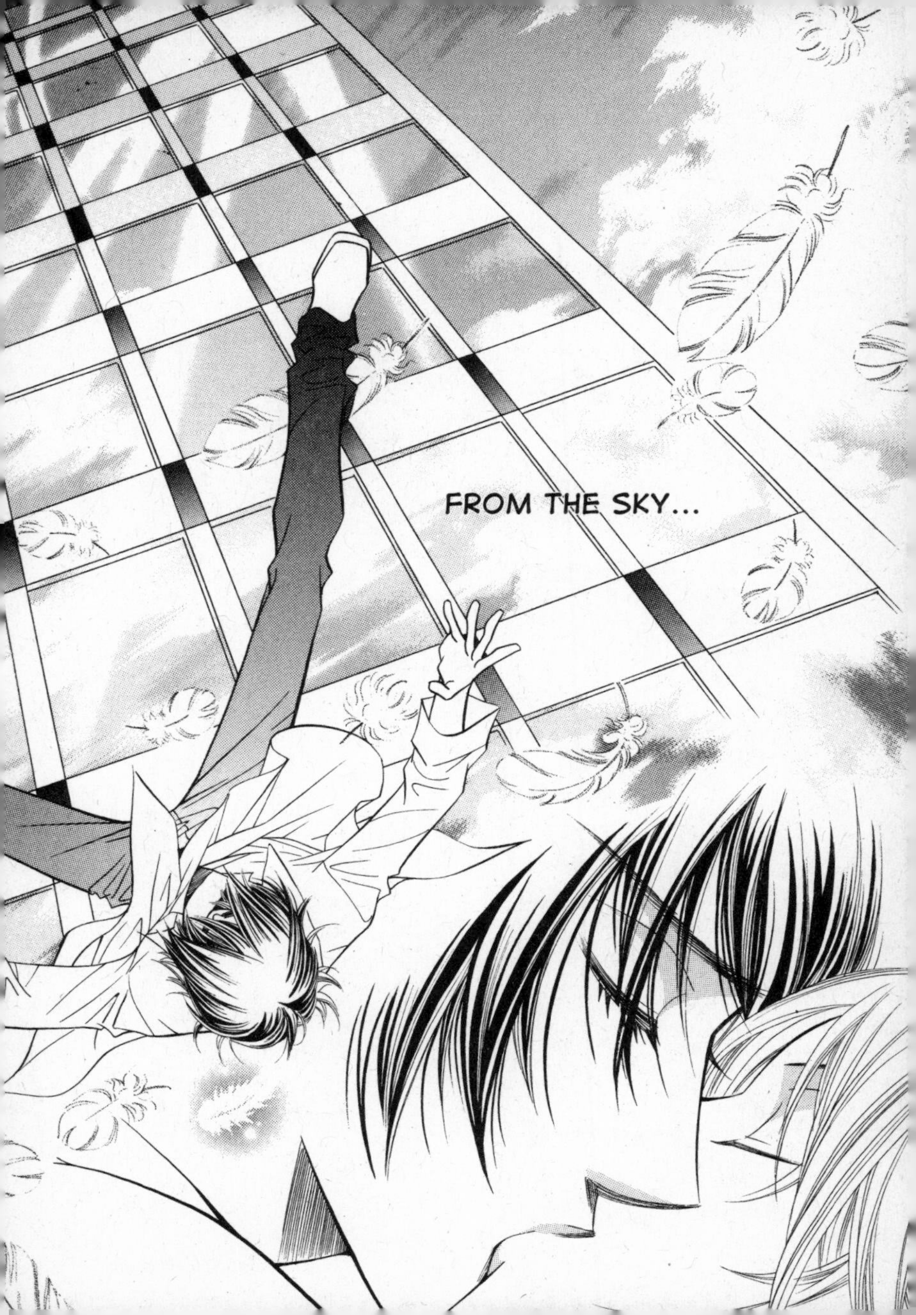
FROM THE SKY...

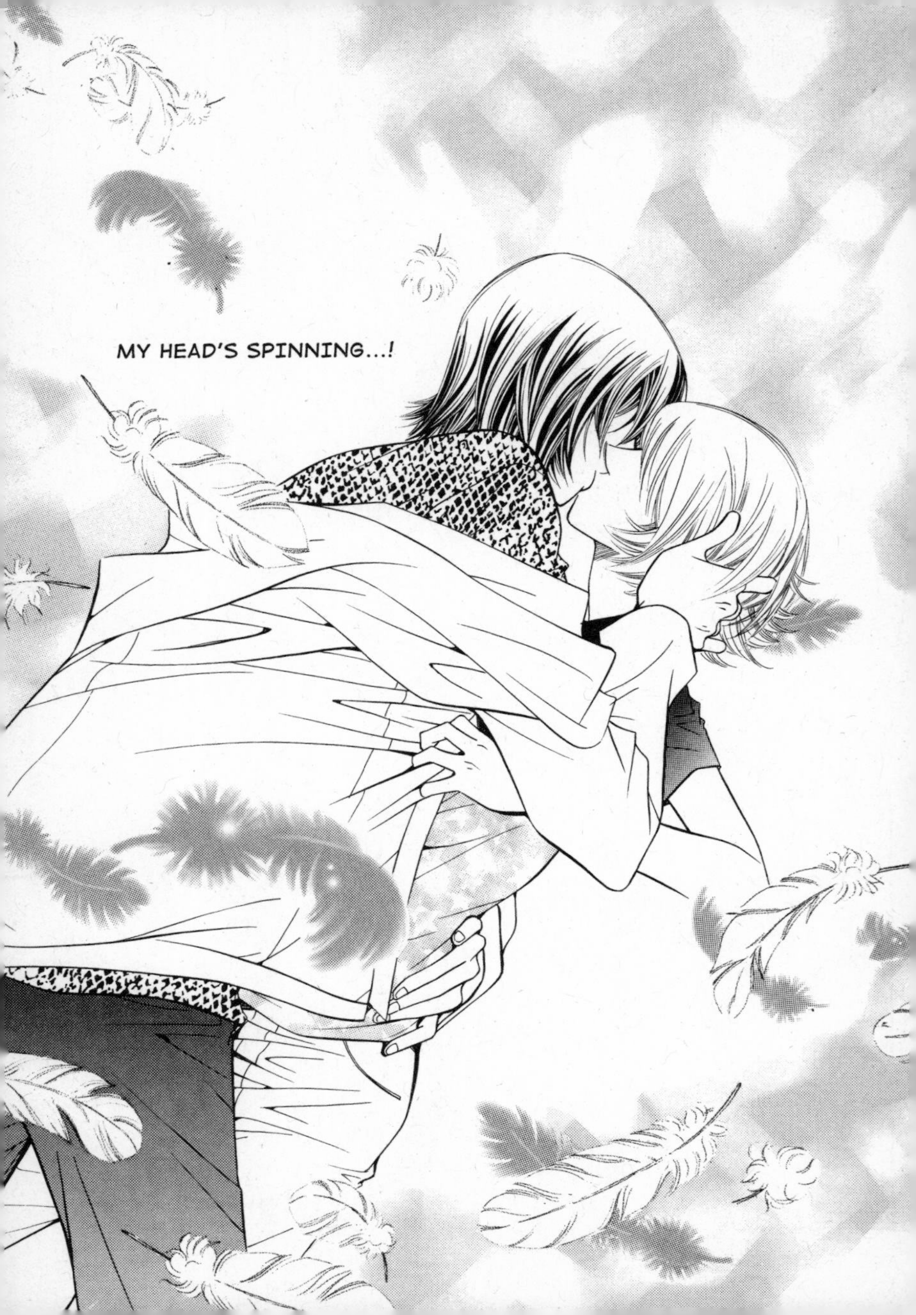
MY HEAD'S SPINNING...!

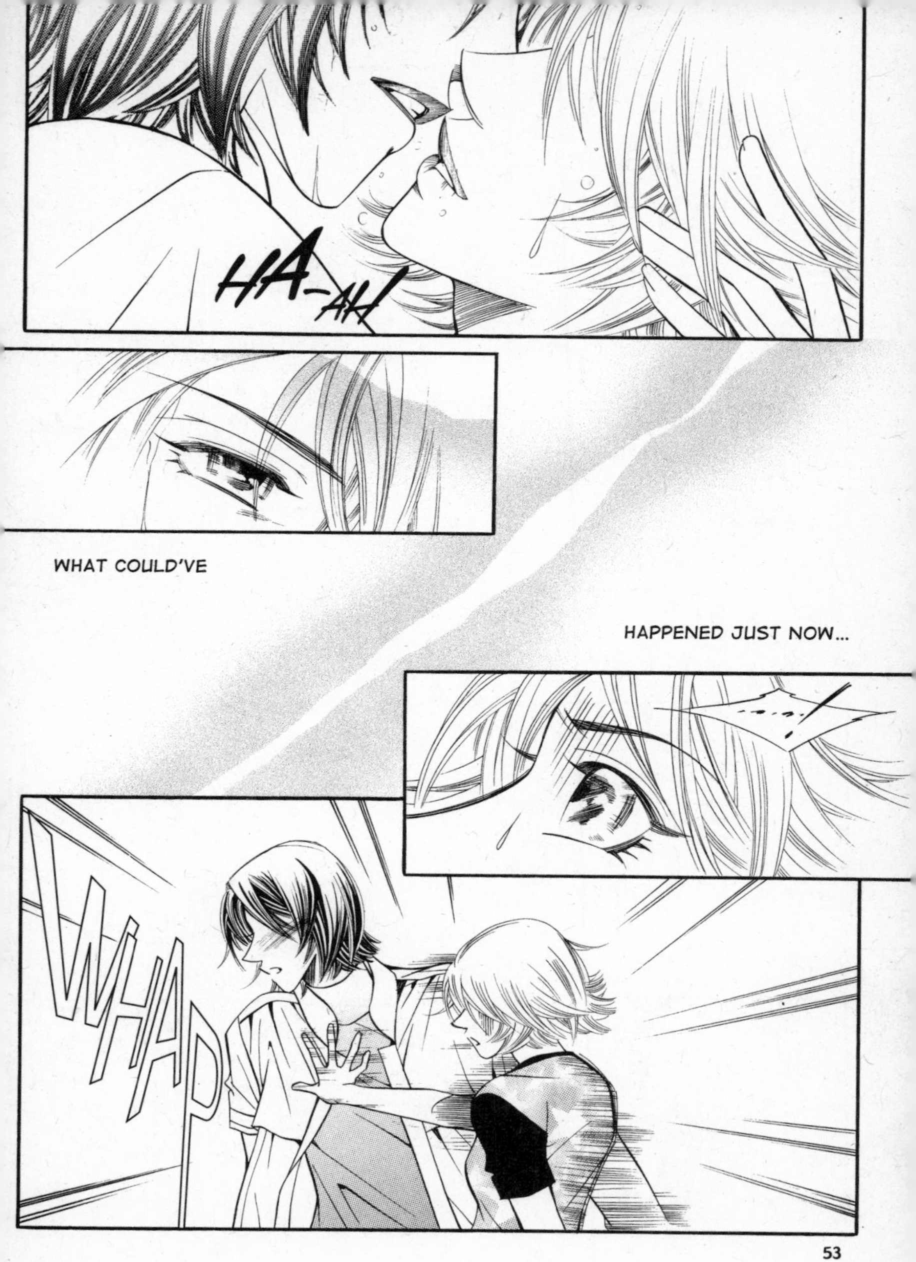
HA-AH
WHAT COULD'VE
HAPPENED JUST NOW...
WHAP

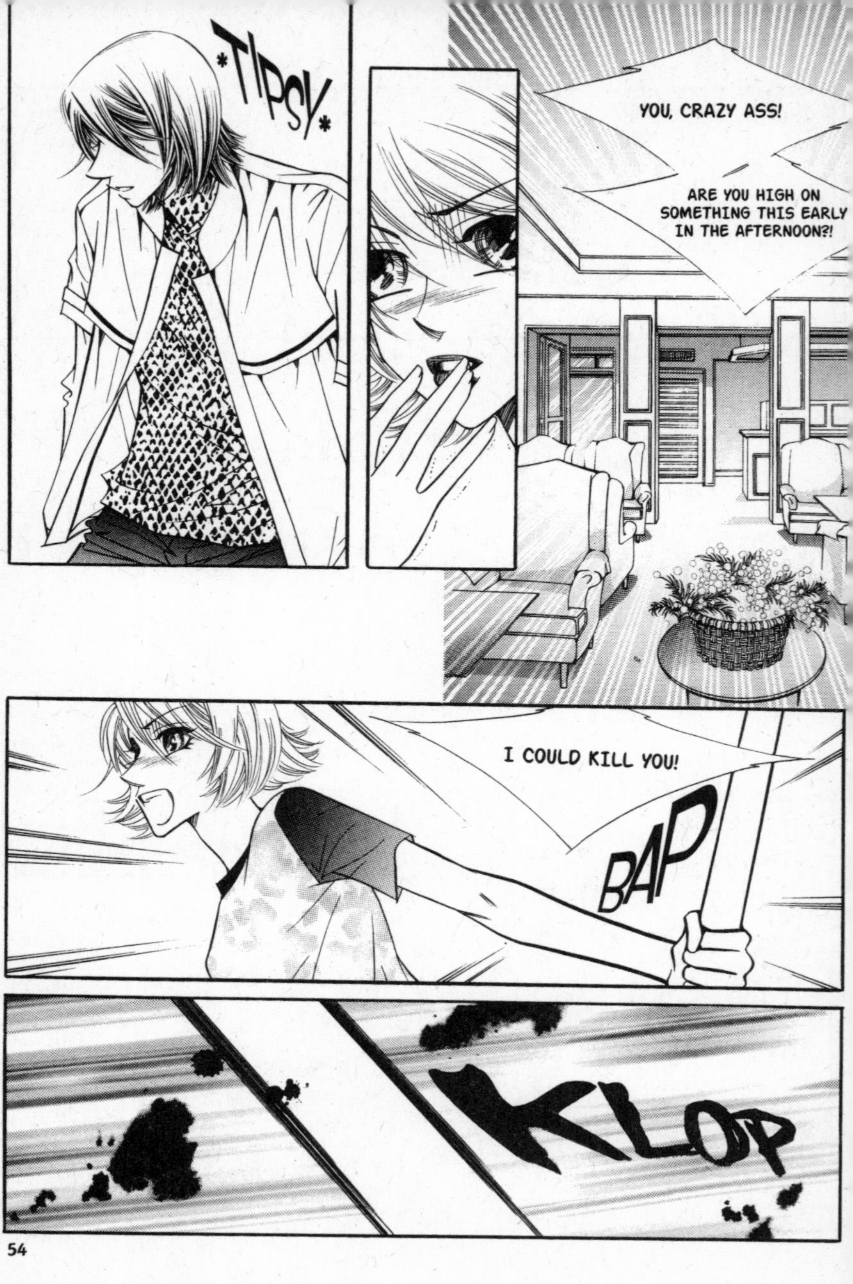
TIPSY
YOU, CRAZY ASS!
ARE YOU HIGH ON SOMETHING THIS EARLY IN THE AFTERNOON?!
I COULD KILL YOU!
BAP
KLOP

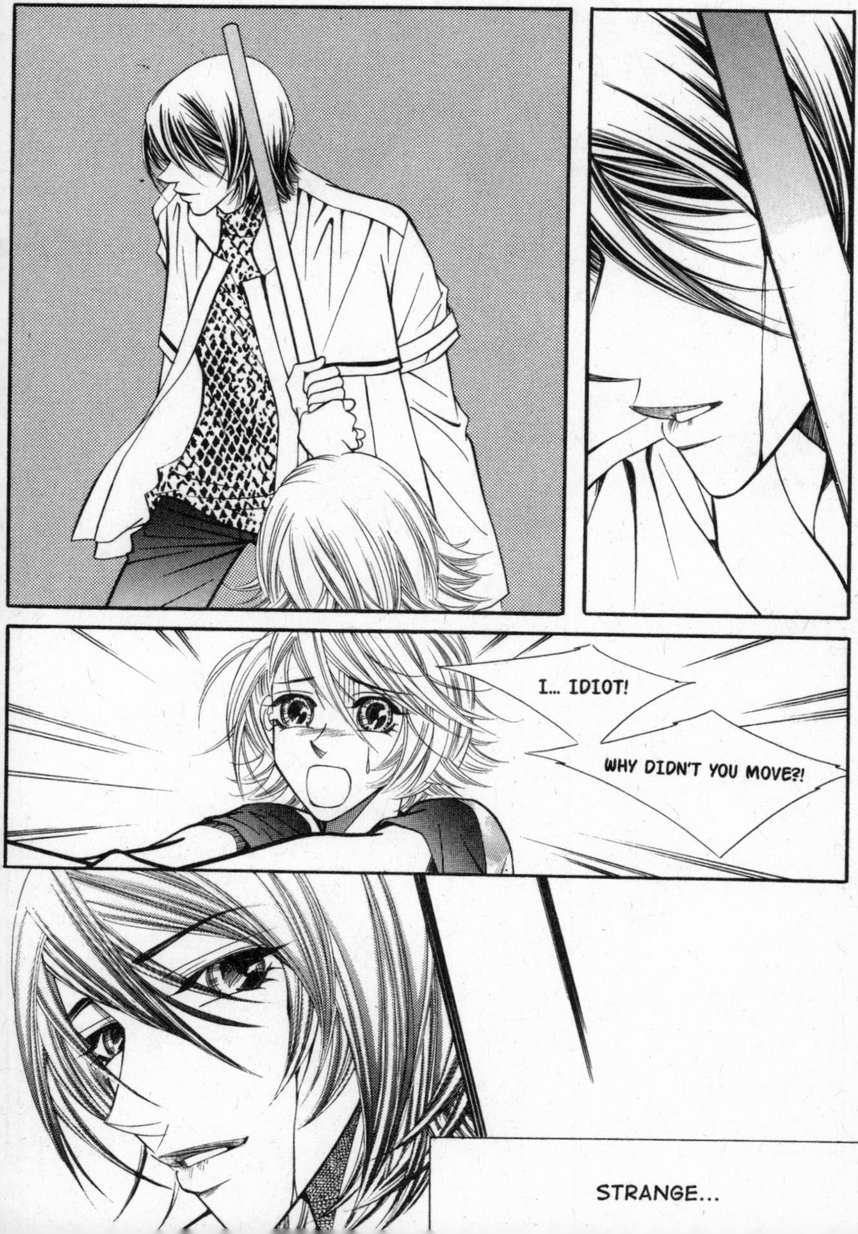
I... IDIOT!
WHY DIDN'T YOU MOVE?!
STRANGE...

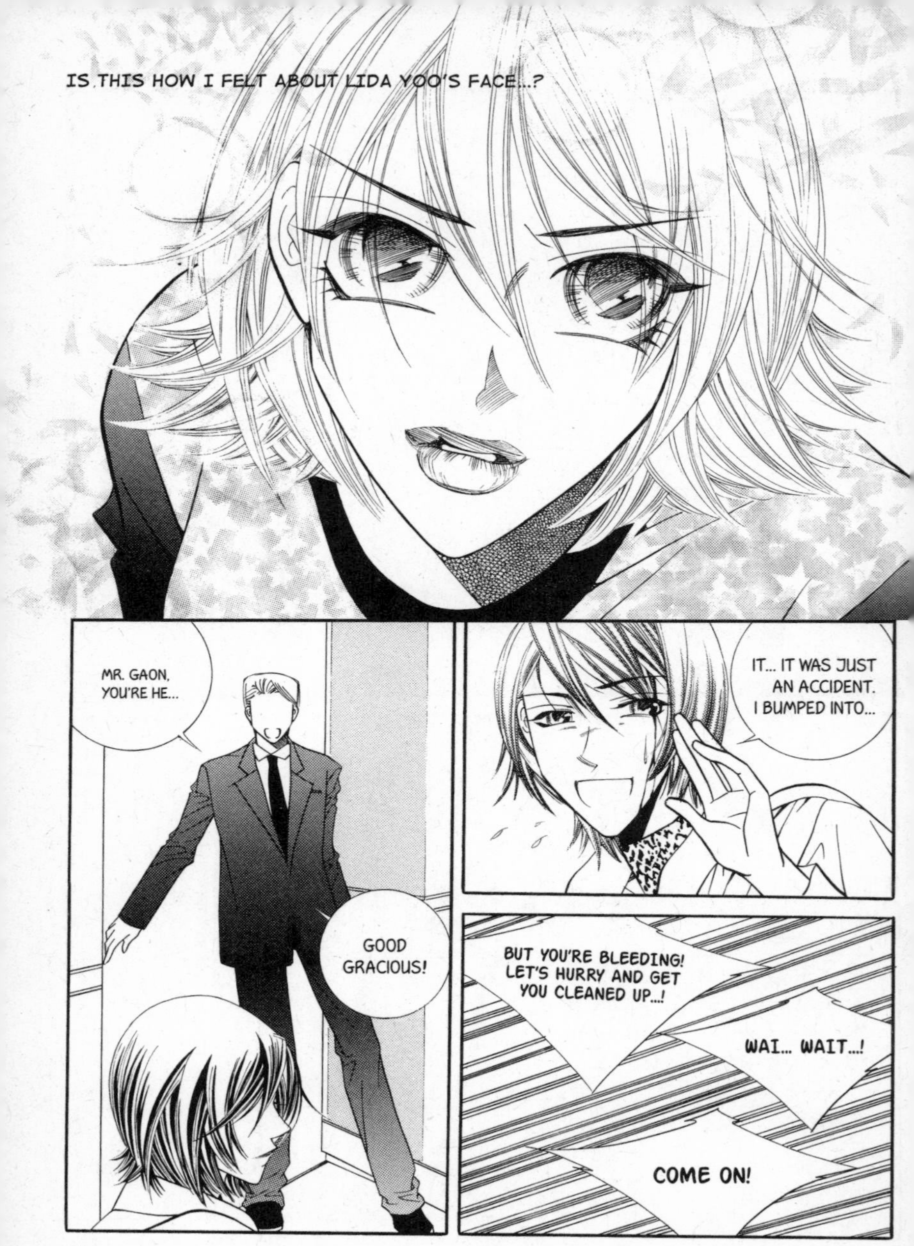

IS THIS HOW I FELT ABOUT LIDA YOO'S FACE...?
IT... IT WAS JUST AN ACCIDENT. I BUMPED INTO...
MR. GAON, YOU'RE HE...
GOOD GRACIOUS!
BUT YOU'RE BLEEDING! LET'S HURRY AND GET YOU CLEANED UP...!
WAI... WAIT...!
COME ON!

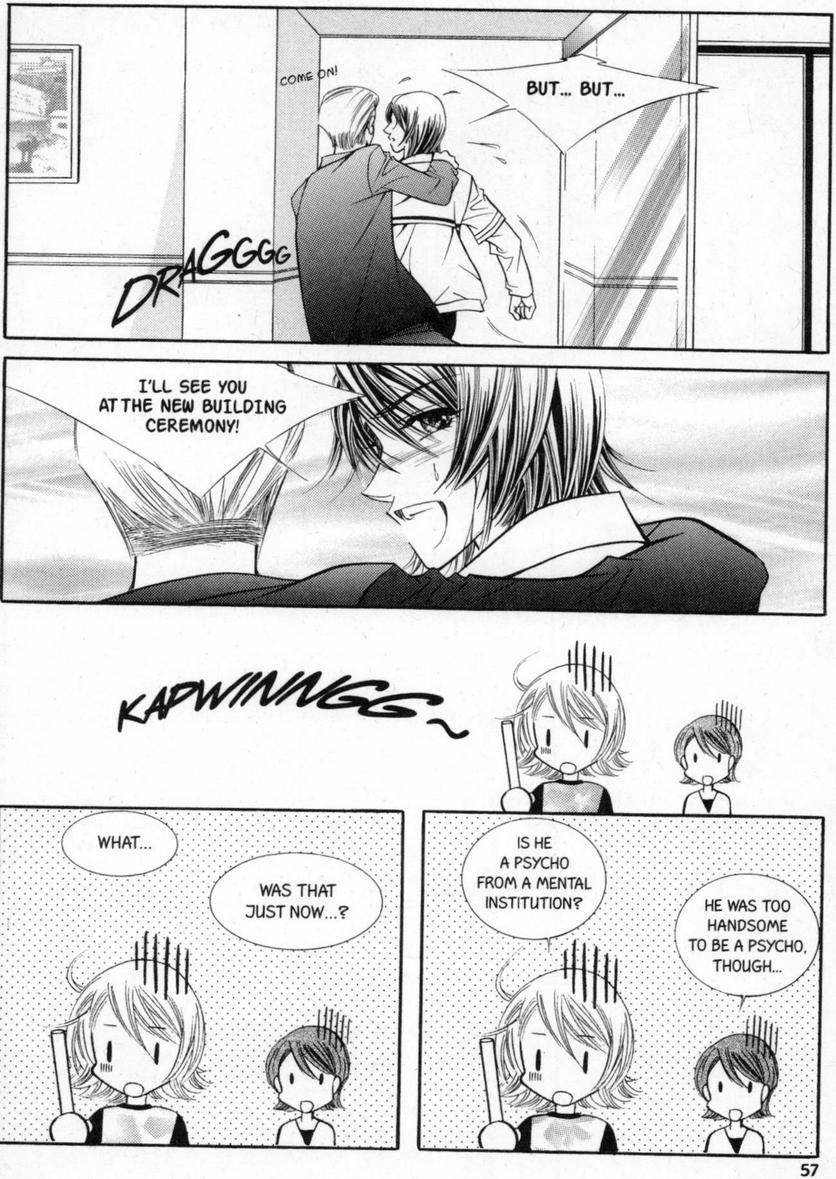
COME ON!
BUT... BUT...
DRAGGGG
I'LL SEE YOU AT THE NEW BUILDING CEREMONY!
KAPWINNGG~
WHAT...
WAS THAT JUST NOW...?
IS HE A PSYCHO FROM A MENTAL INSTITUTION?
HE WAS TOO HANDSOME TO BE A PSYCHO, THOUGH...

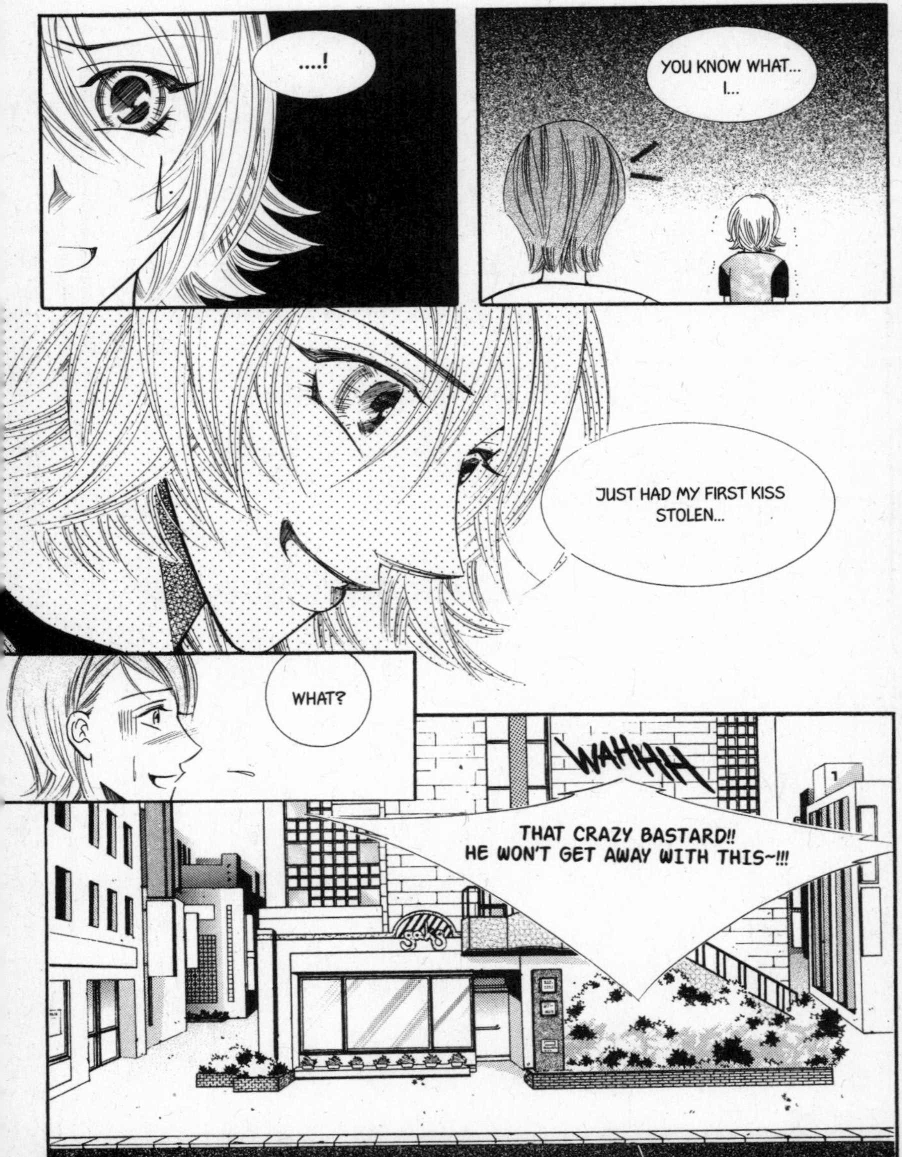

....!
YOU KNOW WHAT... I...
JUST HAD MY FIRST KISS STOLEN...
WHAT?
WAHHH
THAT CRAZY BASTARD!! HE WON'T GET AWAY WITH THIS~!!!

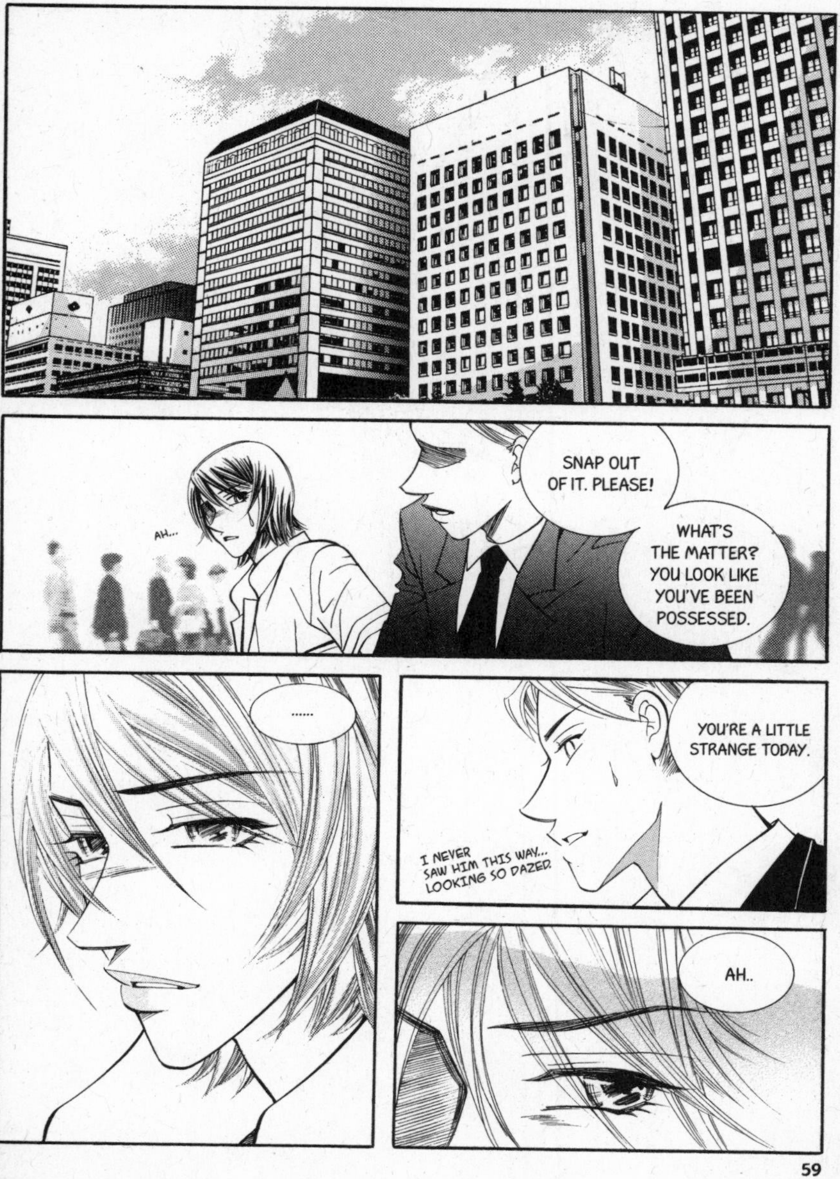
SNAP OUT OF IT. PLEASE!
WHAT'S THE MATTER? YOU LOOK LIKE YOU'VE BEEN POSSESSED.
AH...
......
YOU'RE A LITTLE STRANGE TODAY.
I NEVER SAW HIM THIS WAY... LOOKING SO DAZED.
AH..

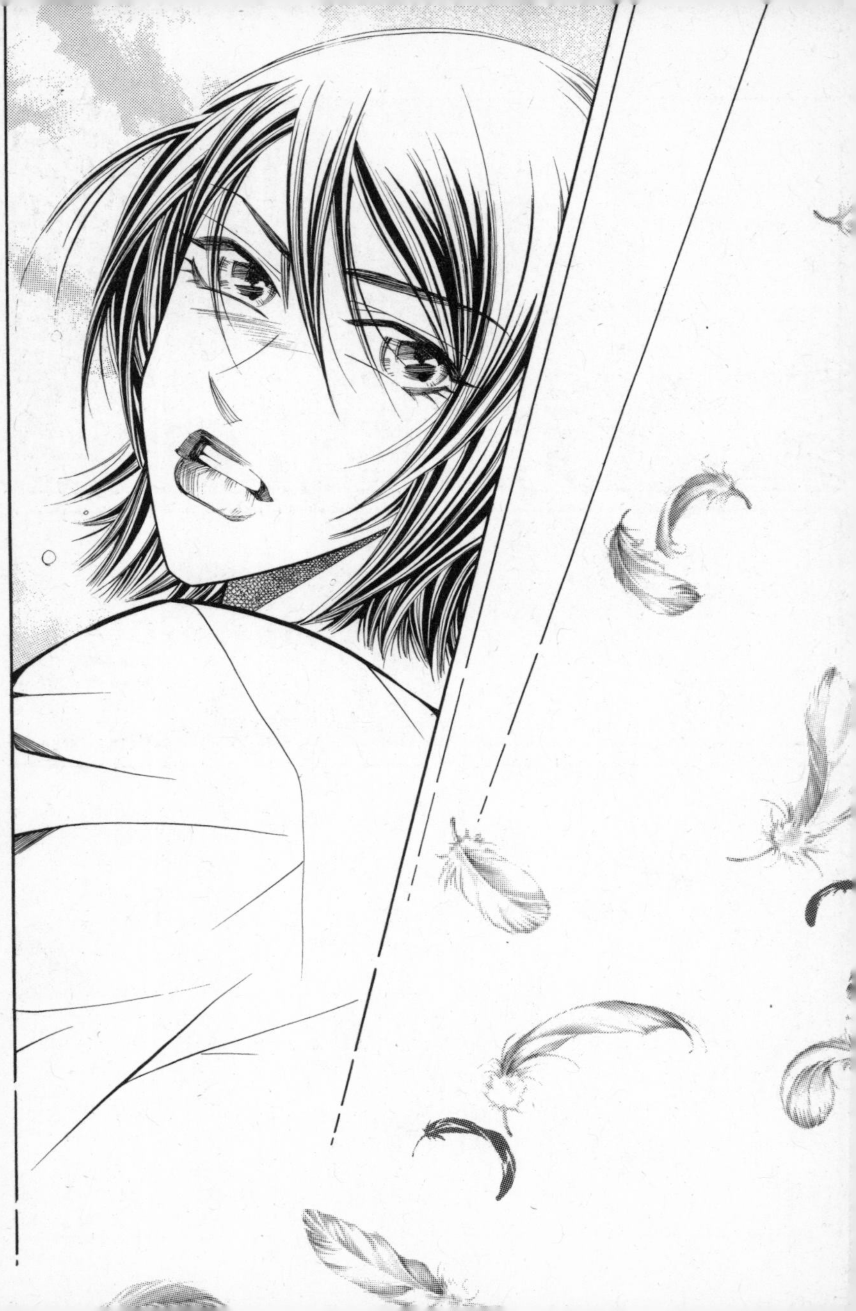

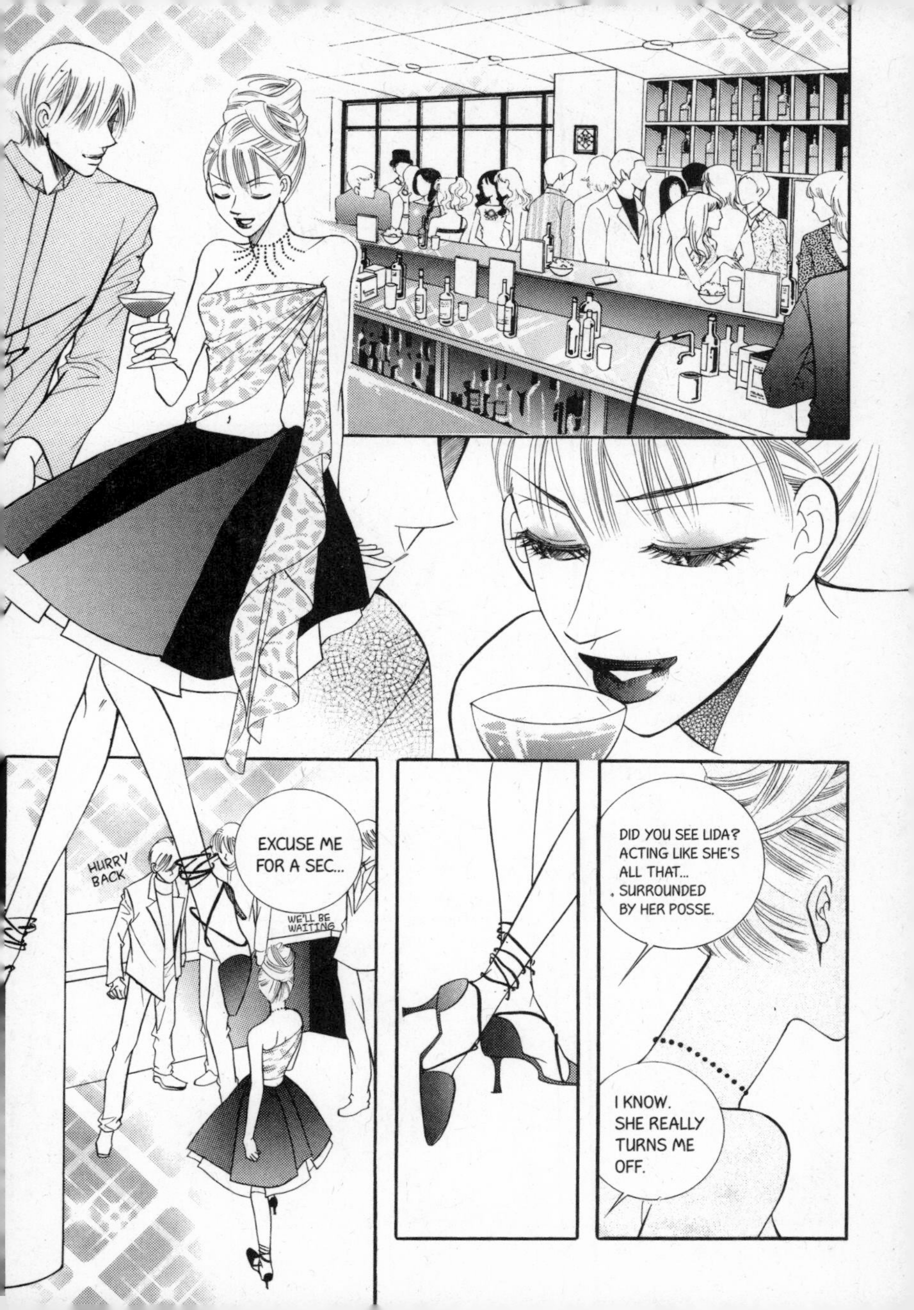

EXCUSE ME FOR A SEC...
HURRY BACK
WE'LL BE WAITING
DID YOU SEE LIDA? ACTING LIKE SHE'S ALL THAT... SURROUNDED BY HER POSSE.
I KNOW. SHE REALLY TURNS ME OFF.

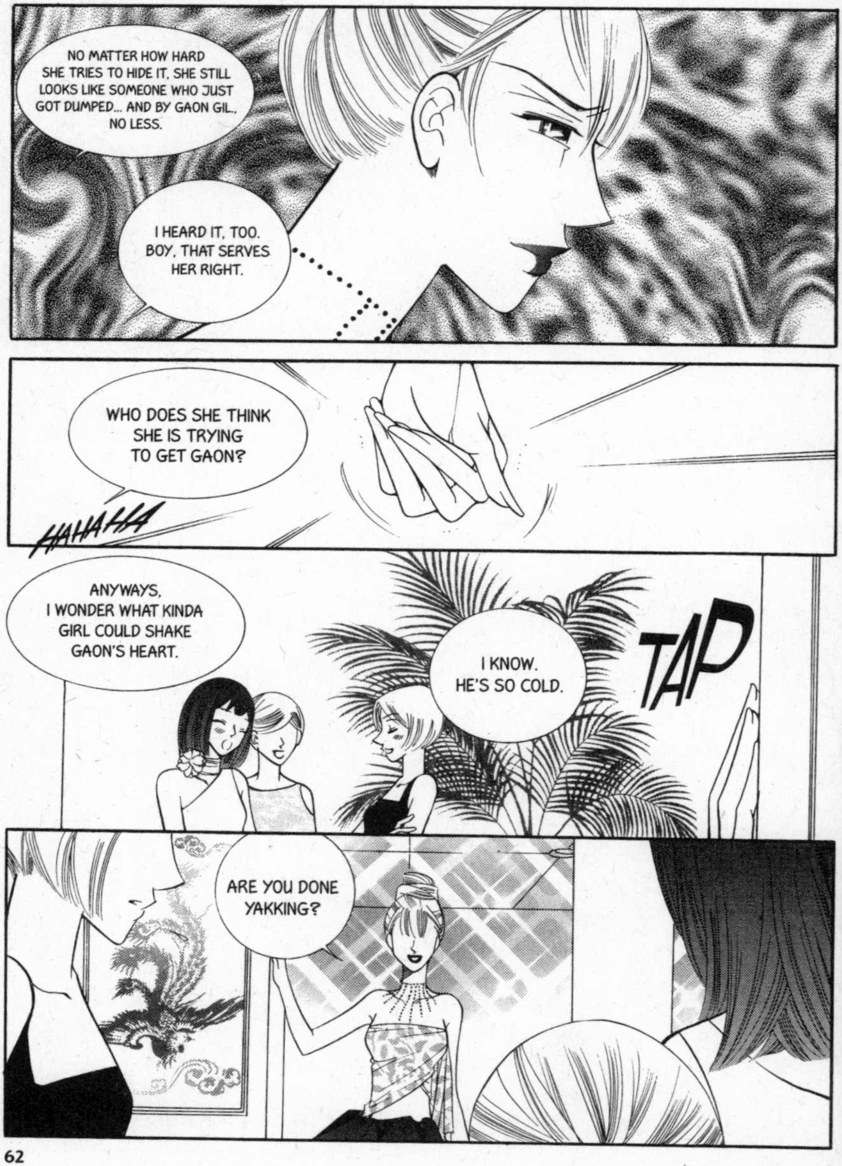
NO MATTER HOW HARD SHE TRIES TO HIDE IT, SHE STILL LOOKS LIKE SOMEONE WHO JUST GOT DUMPED... AND BY GAON GIL, NO LESS.
I HEARD IT, TOO. BOY, THAT SERVES HER RIGHT.
WHO DOES SHE THINK SHE IS TRYING TO GET GAON?
HAHAHA
ANYWAYS, I WONDER WHAT KINDA GIRL COULD SHAKE GAON'S HEART.
I KNOW. HE'S SO COLD.
TAP
ARE YOU DONE YAKKING?

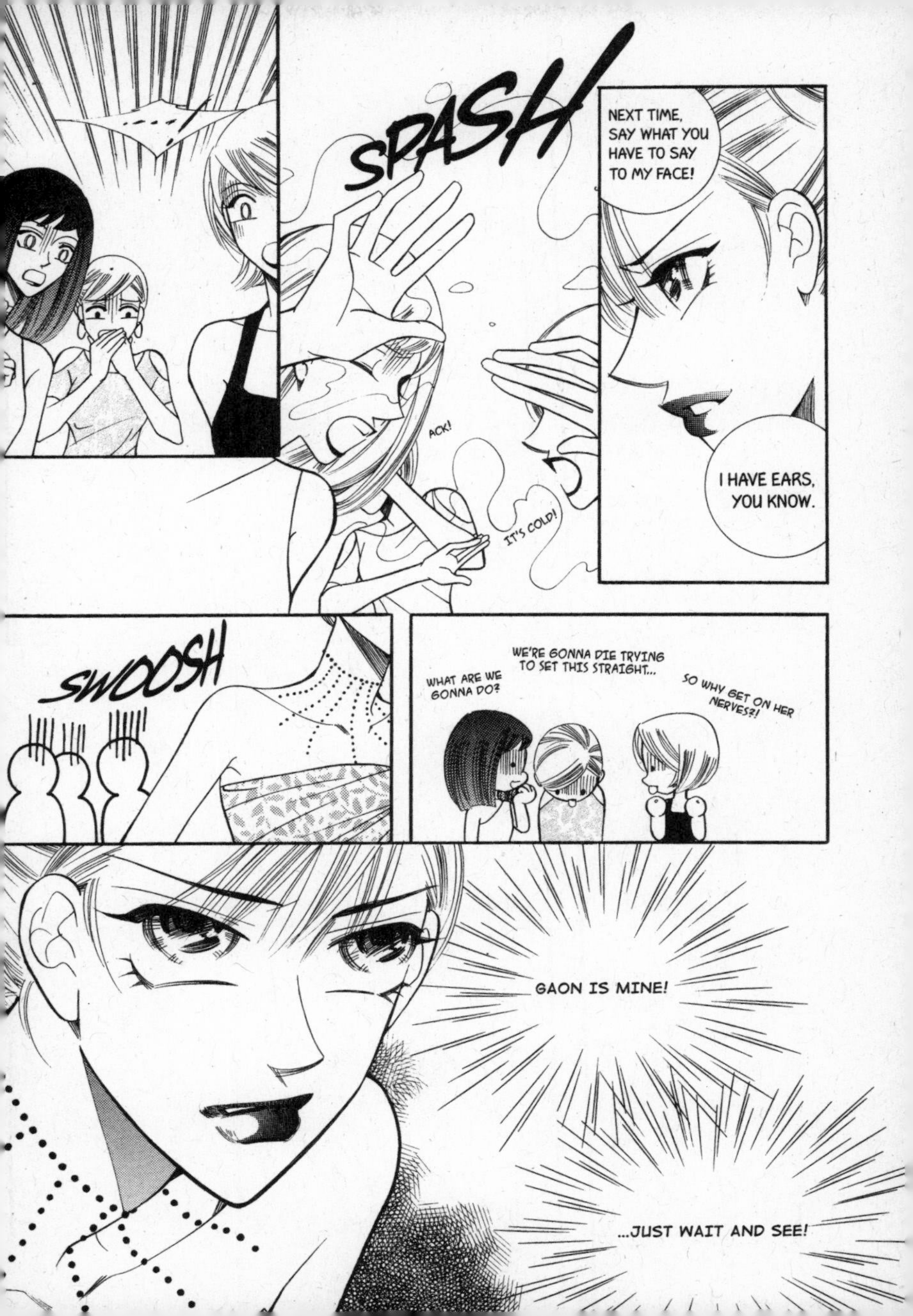

......!
SPASH
NEXT TIME, SAY WHAT YOU HAVE TO SAY TO MY FACE!
ACK!
IT'S COLD!
I HAVE EARS, YOU KNOW.
SWOOSH
WHAT ARE WE GONNA DO?
WE'RE GONNA DIE TRYING TO SET THIS STRAIGHT...
SO WHY GET ON HER NERVES?!
GAON IS MINE!
...JUST WAIT AND SEE!

GIL, GAON

3. THE DOUBLE

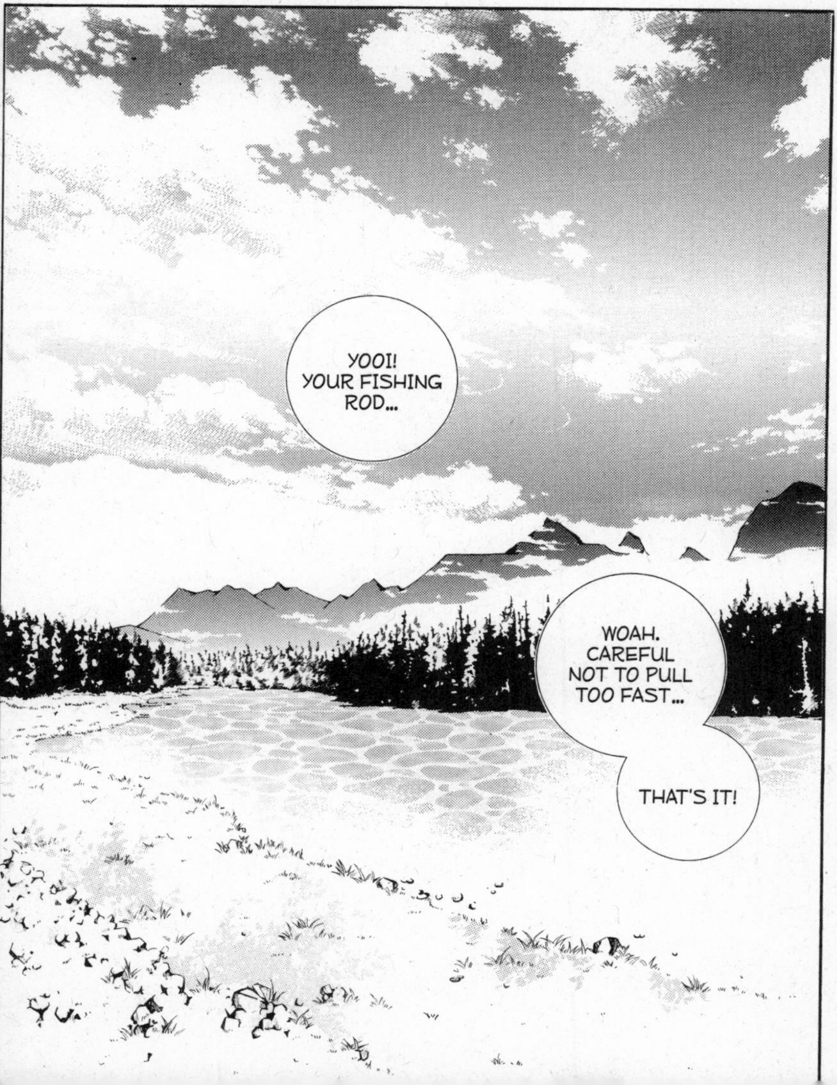
YOOI! YOUR FISHING ROD...
WOAH. CAREFUL NOT TO PULL TOO FAST...
THAT'S IT!

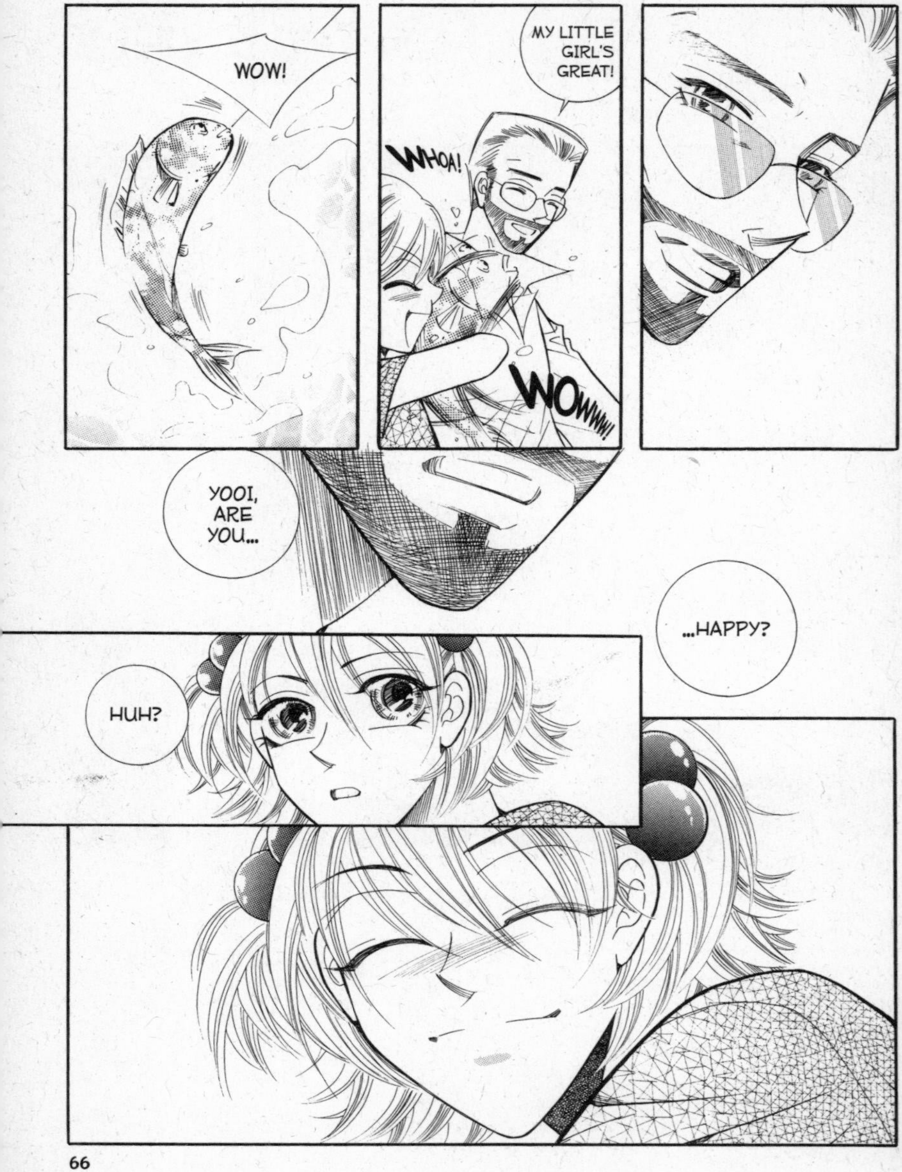
WOW!
MY LITTLE GIRL'S GREAT!
WHOA!
WOWWW!
YOOI, ARE YOU...
...HAPPY?
HUH?

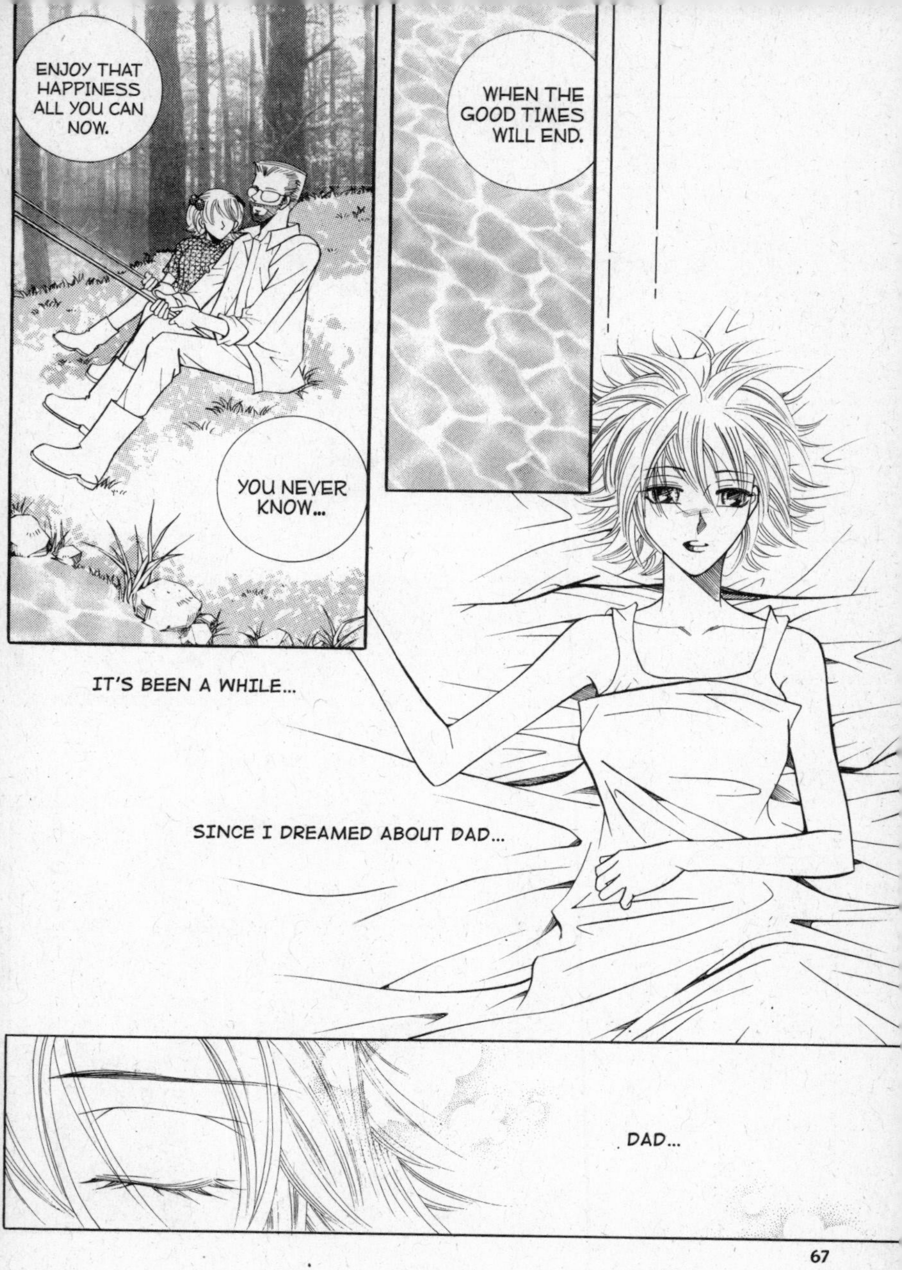
ENJOY THAT HAPPINESS ALL YOU CAN NOW.
YOU NEVER KNOW...
WHEN THE GOOD TIMES WILL END.
IT'S BEEN A WHILE...
SINCE I DREAMED ABOUT DAD...
DAD...

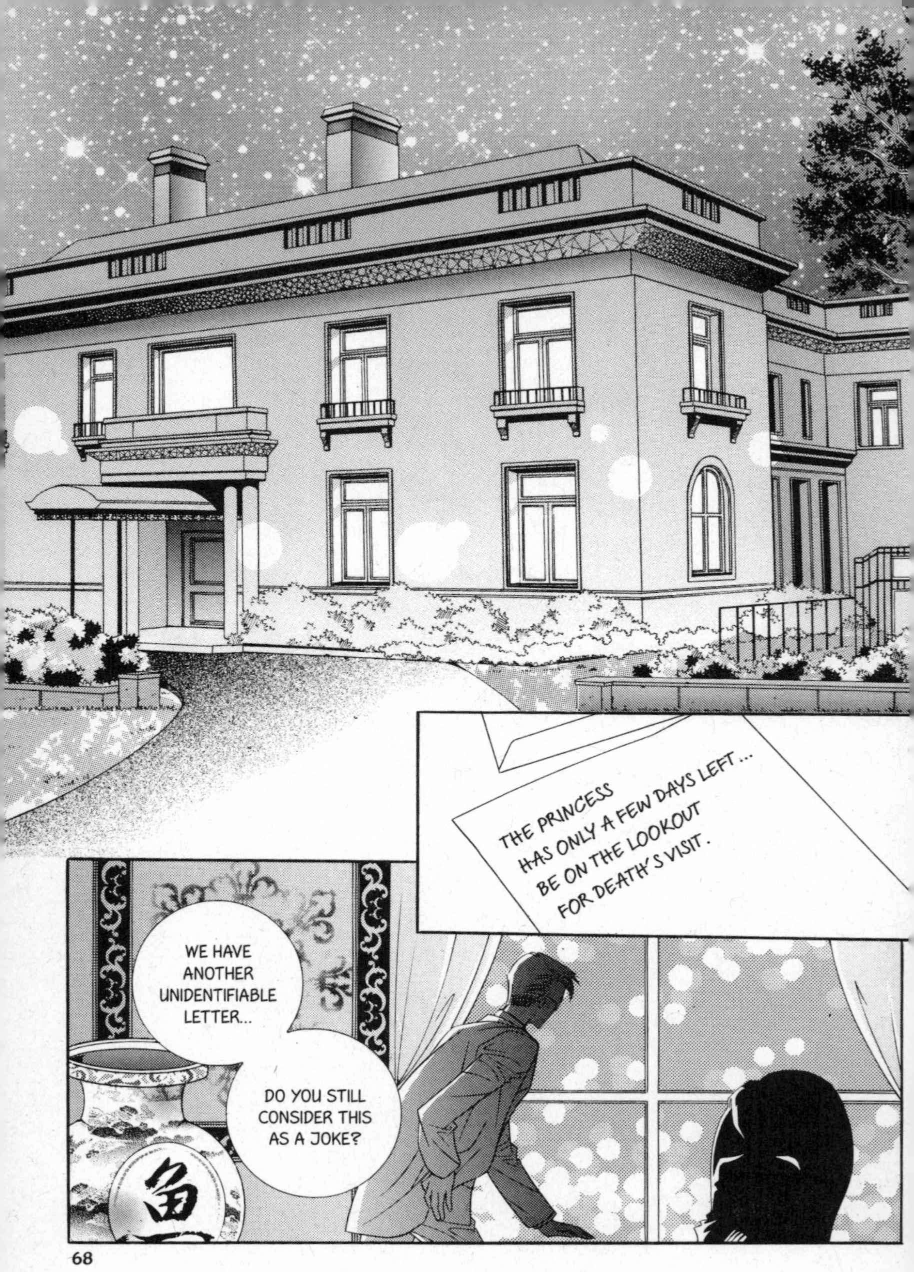
THE PRINCESS HAS ONLY A FEW DAYS LEFT... BE ON THE LOOKOUT FOR DEATH'S VISIT.
WE HAVE ANOTHER UNIDENTIFIABLE LETTER...
DO YOU STILL CONSIDER THIS AS A JOKE?

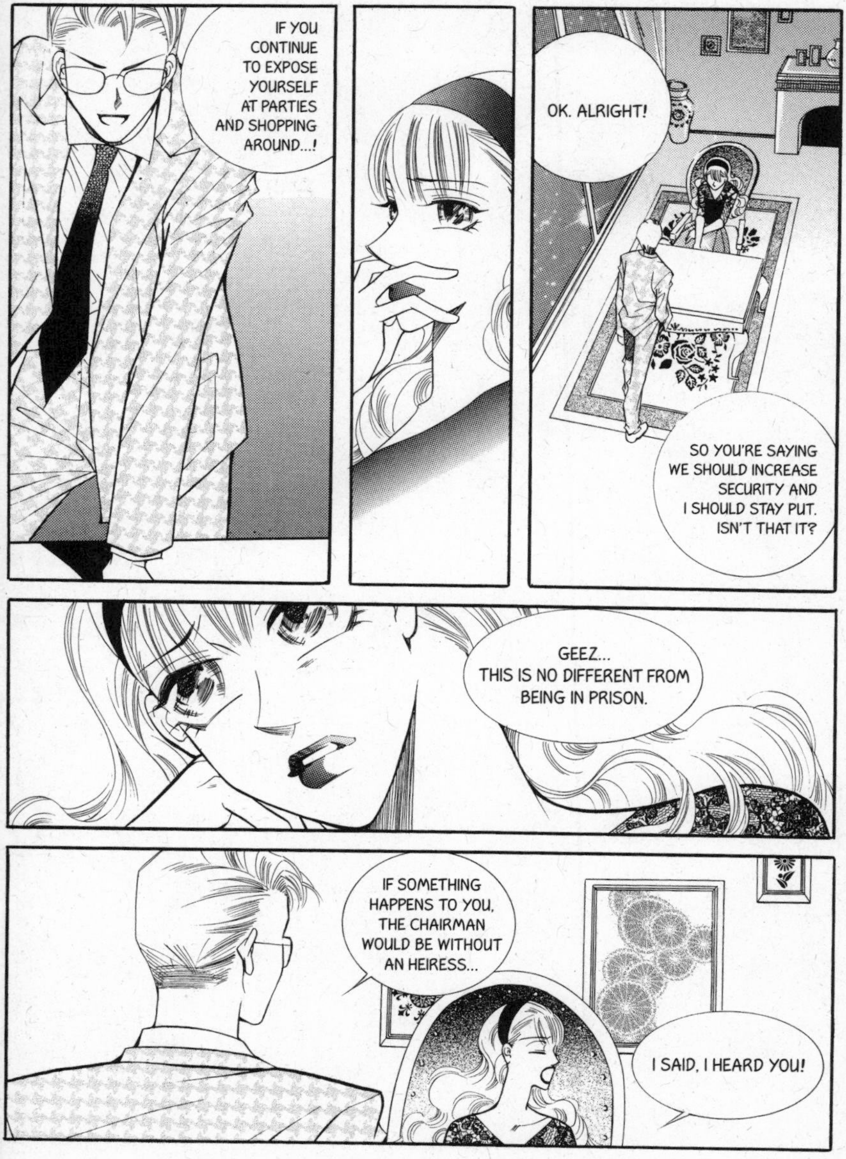
IF YOU CONTINUE TO EXPOSE YOURSELF AT PARTIES AND SHOPPING AROUND...!
OK. ALRIGHT!
SO YOU'RE SAYING WE SHOULD INCREASE SECURITY AND I SHOULD STAY PUT. ISN'T THAT IT?
GEEZ... THIS IS NO DIFFERENT FROM BEING IN PRISON.
IF SOMETHING HAPPENS TO YOU, THE CHAIRMAN WOULD BE WITHOUT AN HEIRESS...
I SAID, I HEARD YOU!

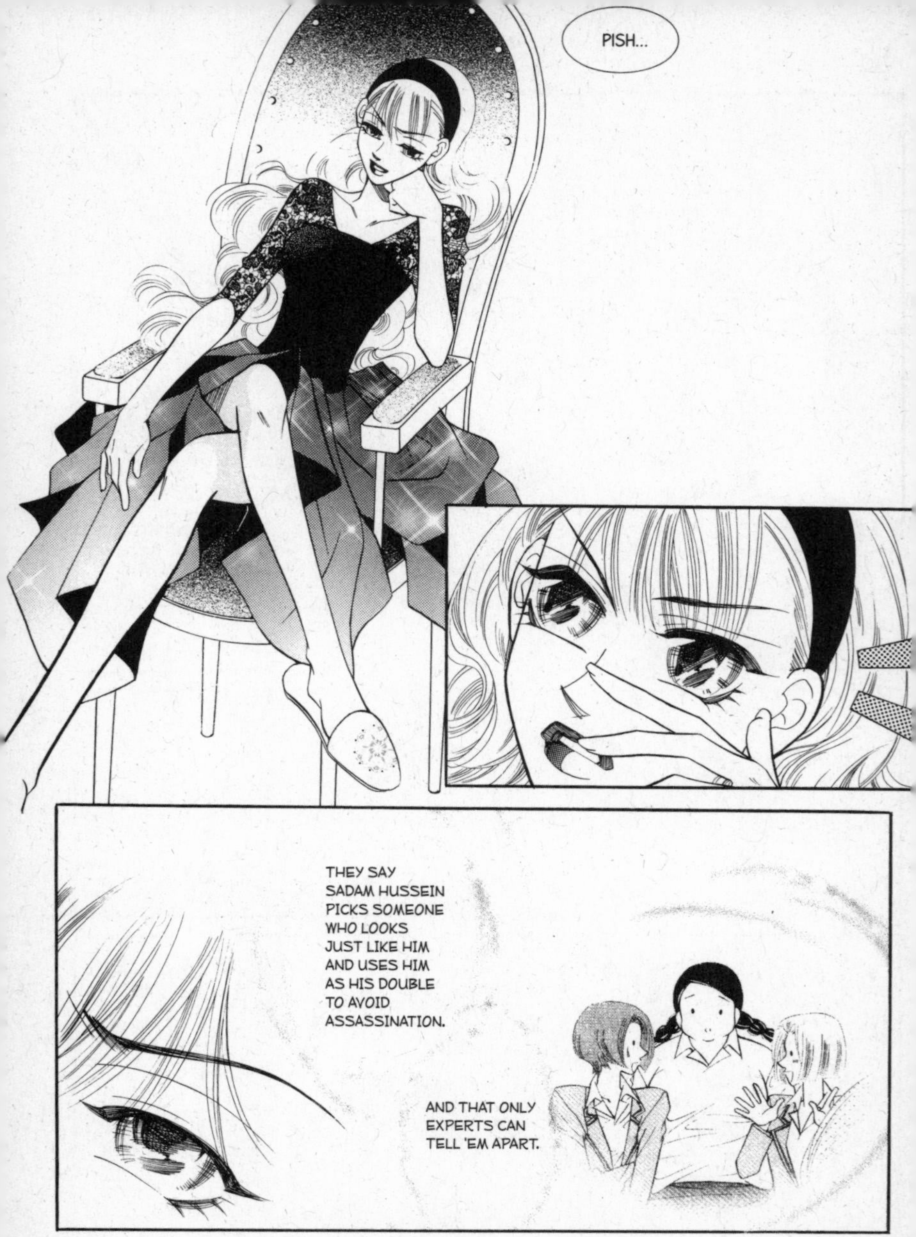
PISH...
THEY SAY SADAM HUSSEIN PICKS SOMEONE WHO LOOKS JUST LIKE HIM AND USES HIM AS HIS DOUBLE TO AVOID ASSASSINATION.
AND THAT ONLY EXPERTS CAN TELL 'EM APART.

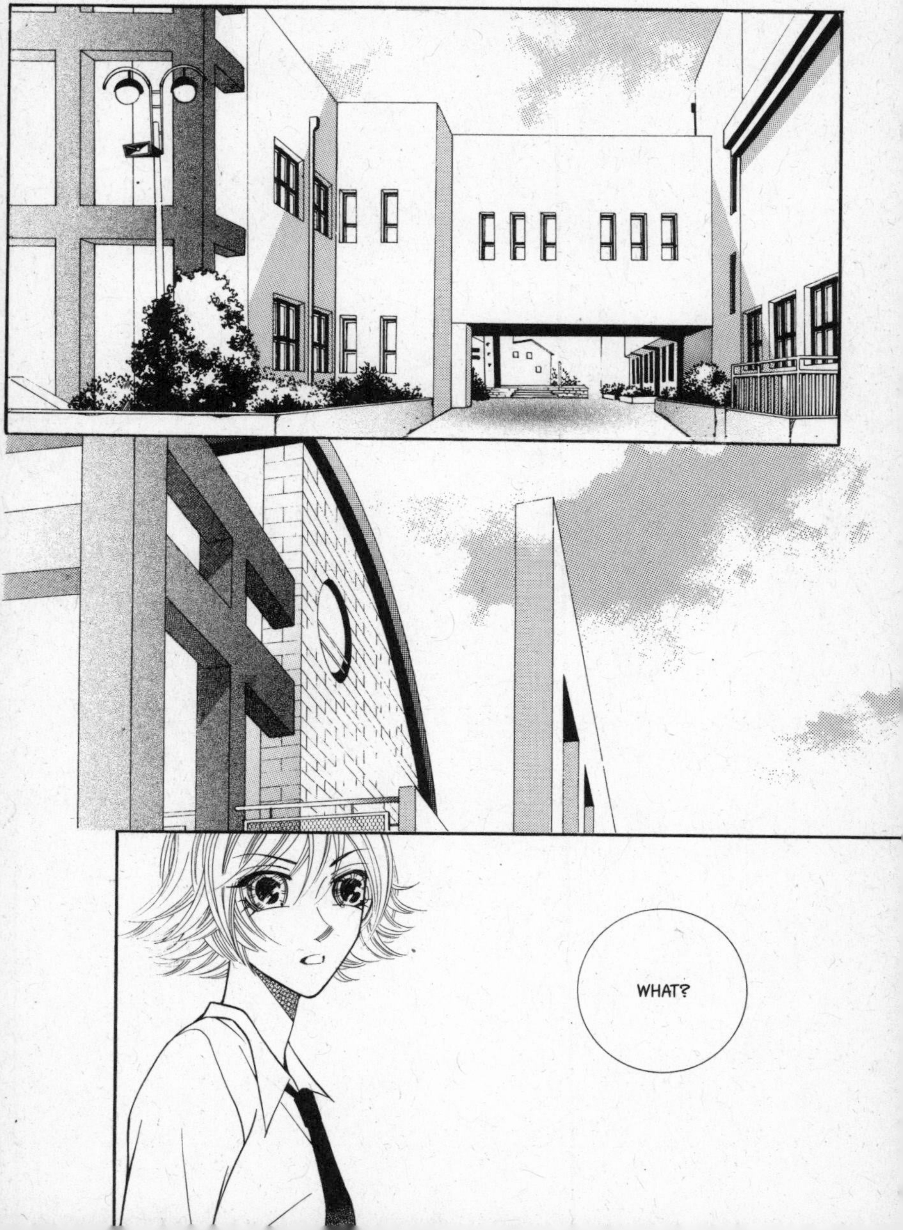
WHAT?

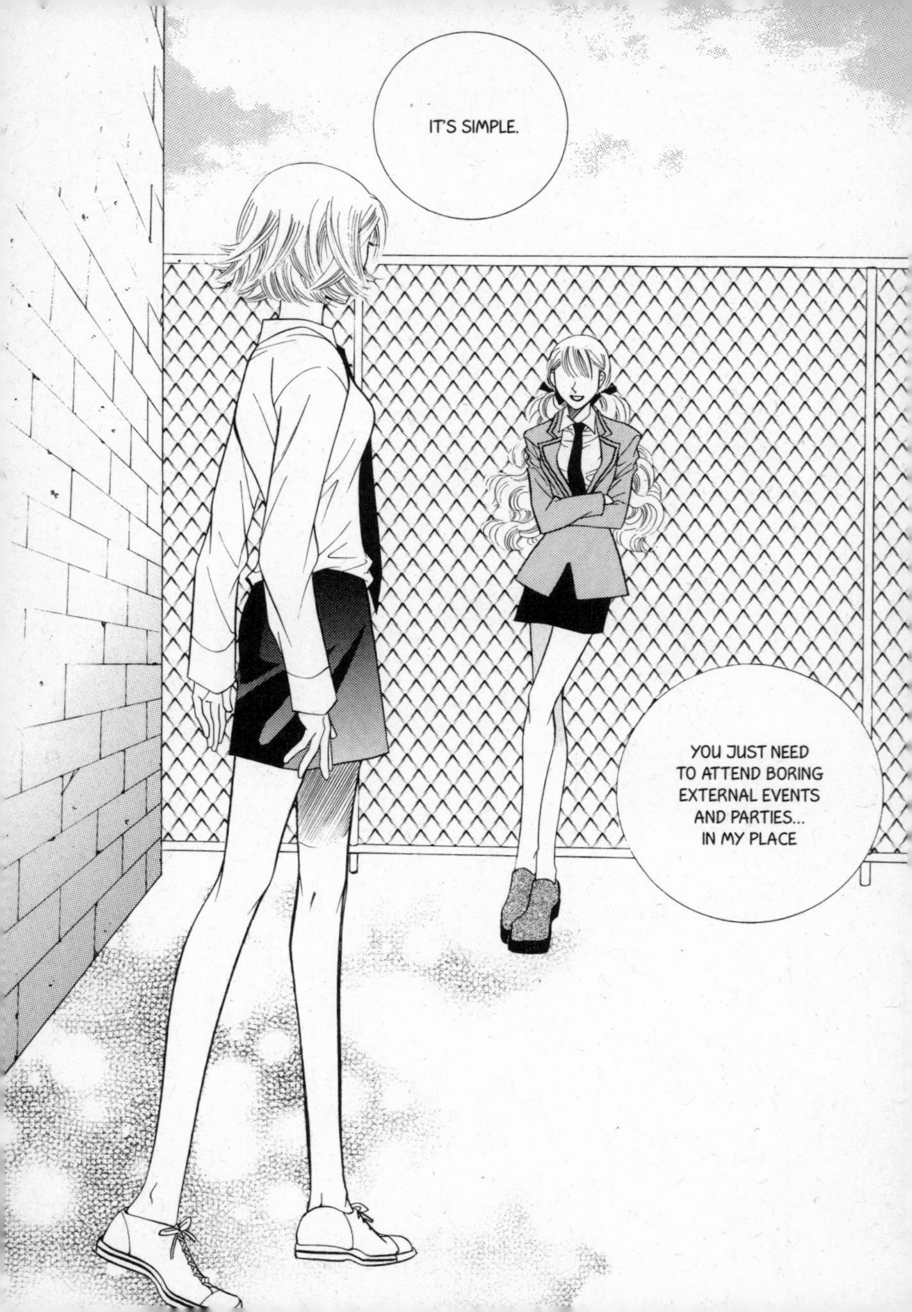
IT'S SIMPLE.
YOU JUST NEED TO ATTEND BORING EXTERNAL EVENTS AND PARTIES... IN MY PLACE

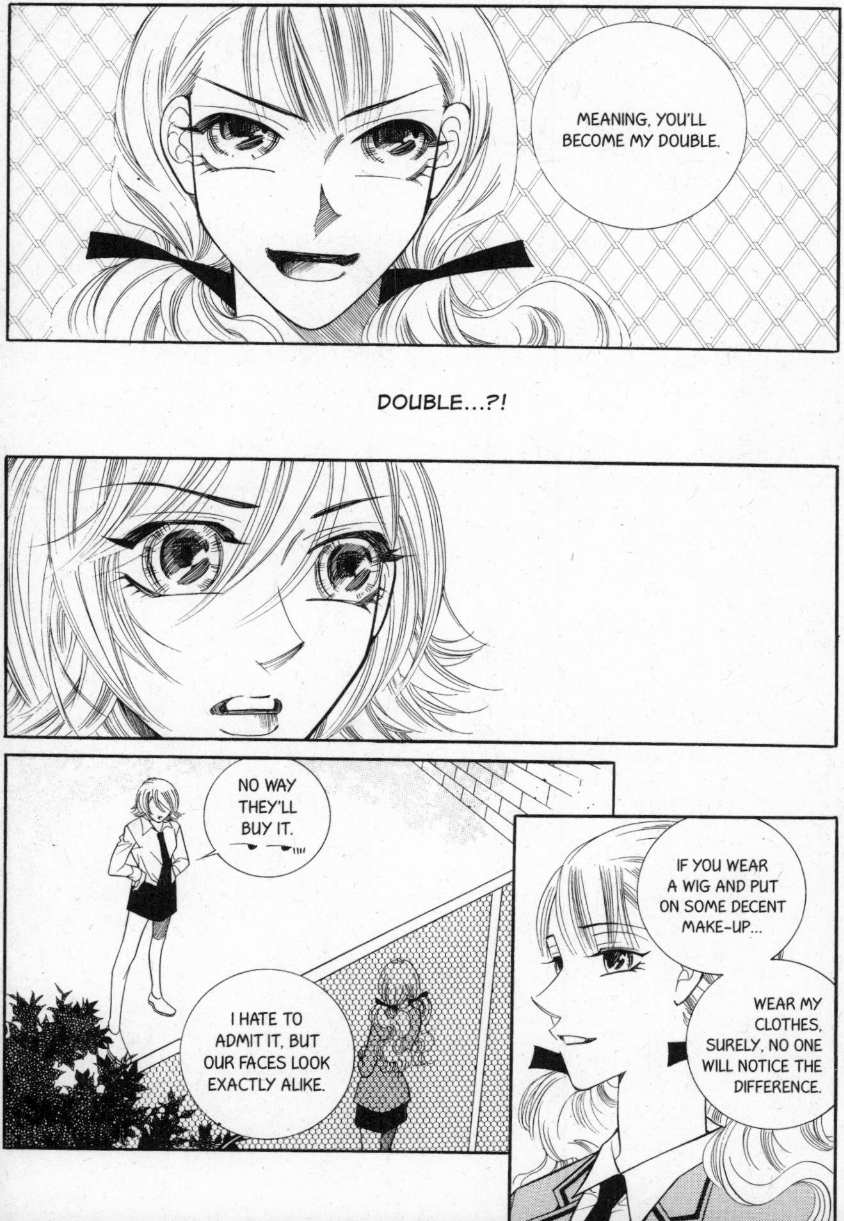

MEANING, YOU'LL BECOME MY DOUBLE.
DOUBLE...?!
NO WAY THEY'LL BUY IT.
I HATE TO ADMIT IT, BUT OUR FACES LOOK EXACTLY ALIKE.
IF YOU WEAR A WIG AND PUT ON SOME DECENT MAKE-UP...
WEAR MY CLOTHES, SURELY, NO ONE WILL NOTICE THE DIFFERENCE.

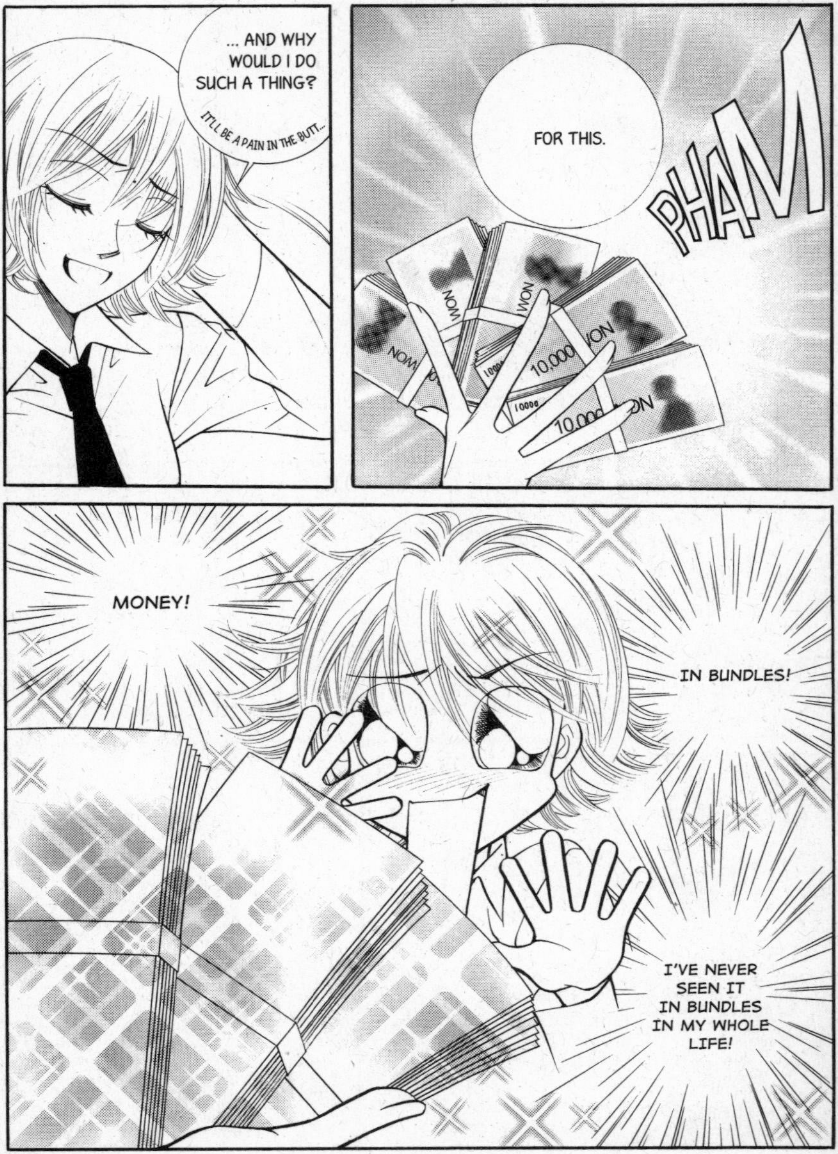

... AND WHY WOULD I DO SUCH A THING?
IT'LL BE A PAIN IN THE BUTT...
FOR THIS.
PHAM
MONEY!
IN BUNDLES!
I'VE NEVER SEEN IT IN BUNDLES IN MY WHOLE LIFE!

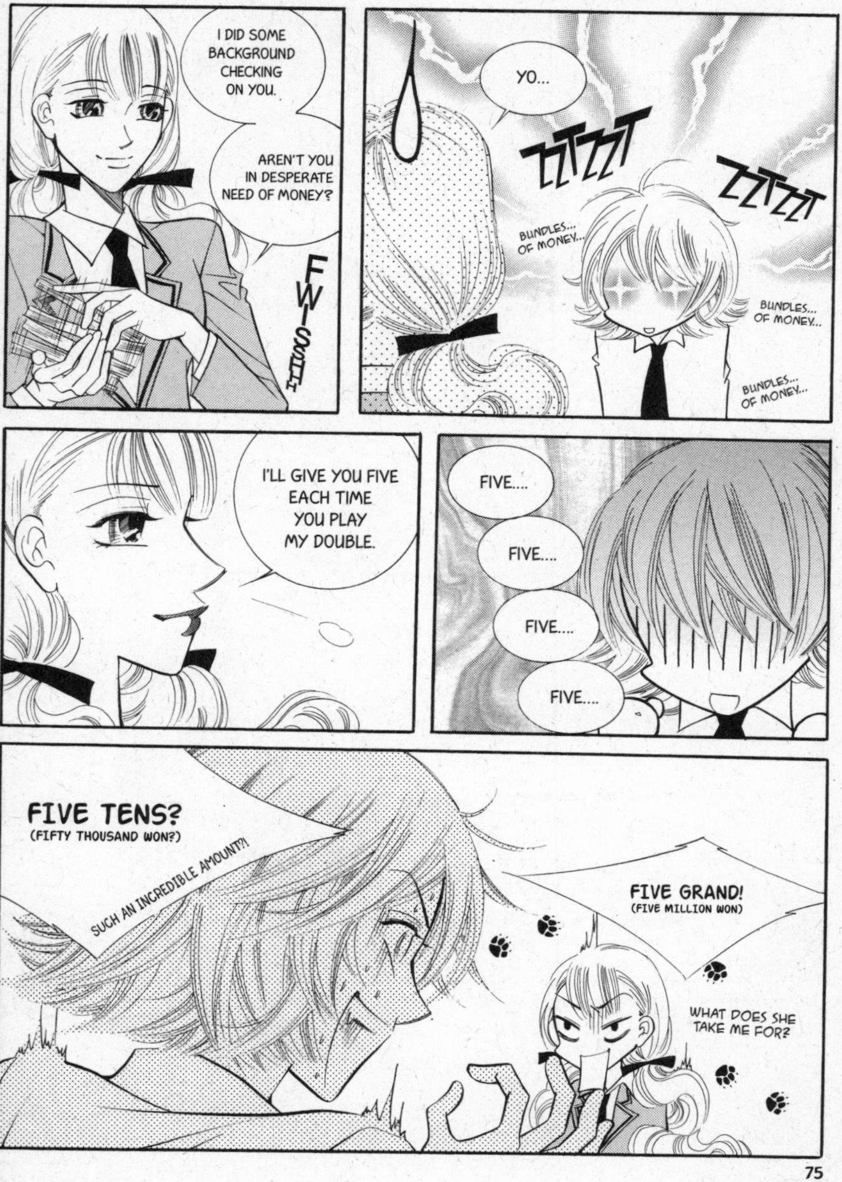
I DID SOME BACKGROUND CHECKING ON YOU.
AREN'T YOU IN DESPERATE NEED OF MONEY?
FWISSHH
YO...
ZZTZZT
ZZTZZT
BUNDLES... OF MONEY...
BUNDLES... OF MONEY...
BUNDLES... OF MONEY...
I'LL GIVE YOU FIVE EACH TIME YOU PLAY MY DOUBLE.
FIVE....
FIVE....
FIVE....
FIVE....
FIVE TENS?
(FIFTY THOUSAND WON?)
SUCH AN INCREDIBLE AMOUNT?!
FIVE GRAND!
(FIVE MILLION WON)
WHAT DOES SHE TAKE ME FOR?

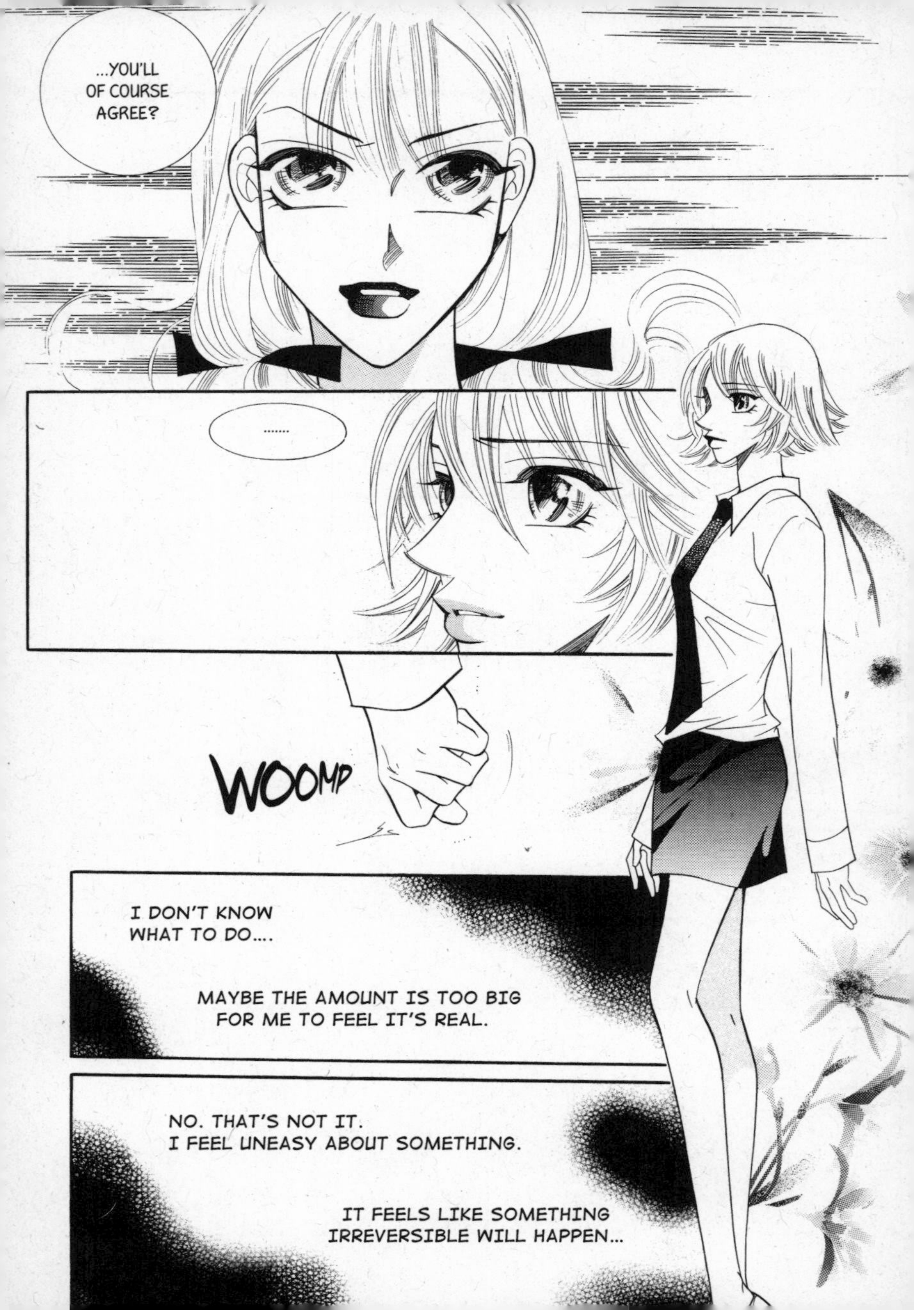
...YOU'LL OF COURSE AGREE?
....
WOOMP
I DON'T KNOW WHAT TO DO....
MAYBE THE AMOUNT IS TOO BIG FOR ME TO FEEL IT'S REAL.
NO. THAT'S NOT IT. I FEEL UNEASY ABOUT SOMETHING.
IT FEELS LIKE SOMETHING IRREVERSIBLE WILL HAPPEN...

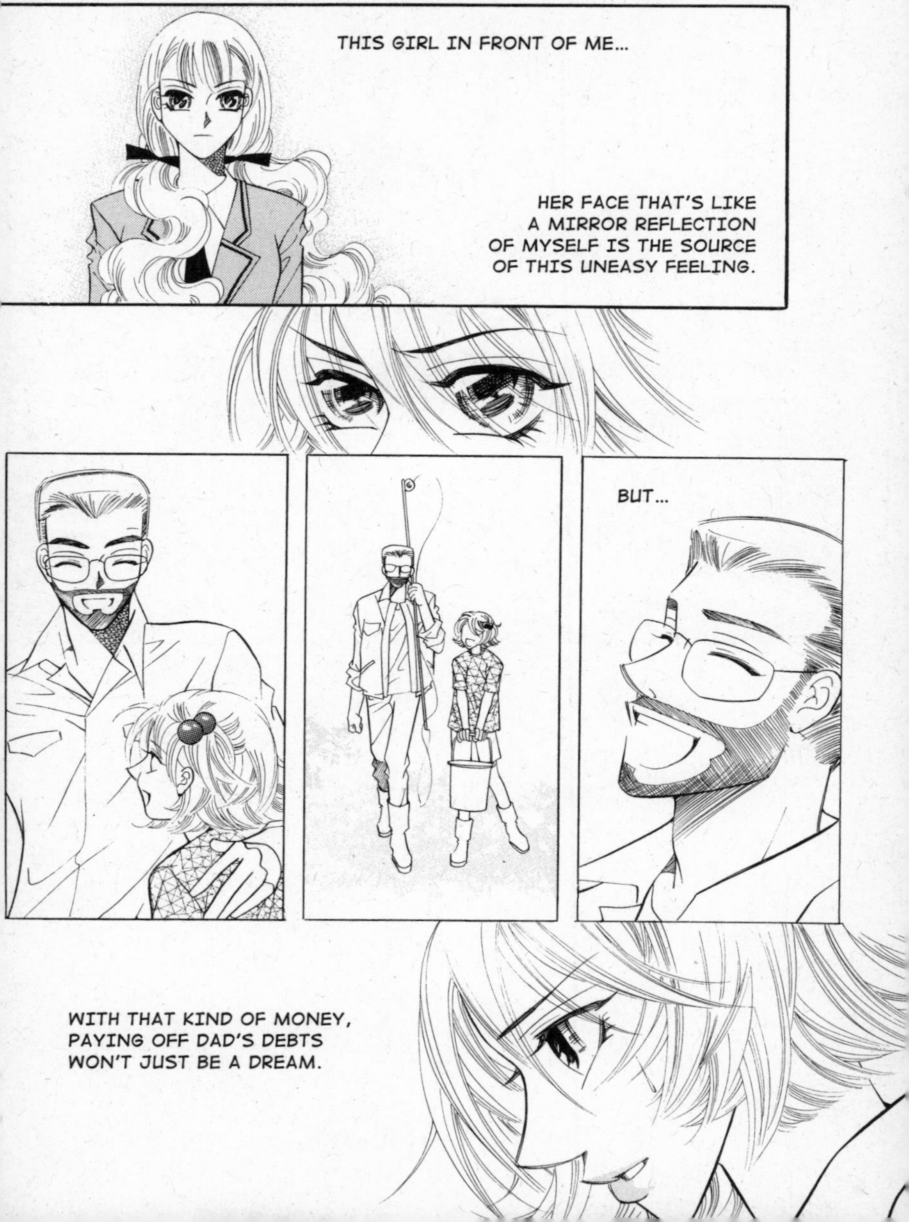
THIS GIRL IN FRONT OF ME...
HER FACE THAT'S LIKE A MIRROR REFLECTION OF MYSELF IS THE SOURCE OF THIS UNEASY FEELING.
BUT...
WITH THAT KIND OF MONEY, PAYING OFF DAD'S DEBTS WON'T JUST BE A DREAM.

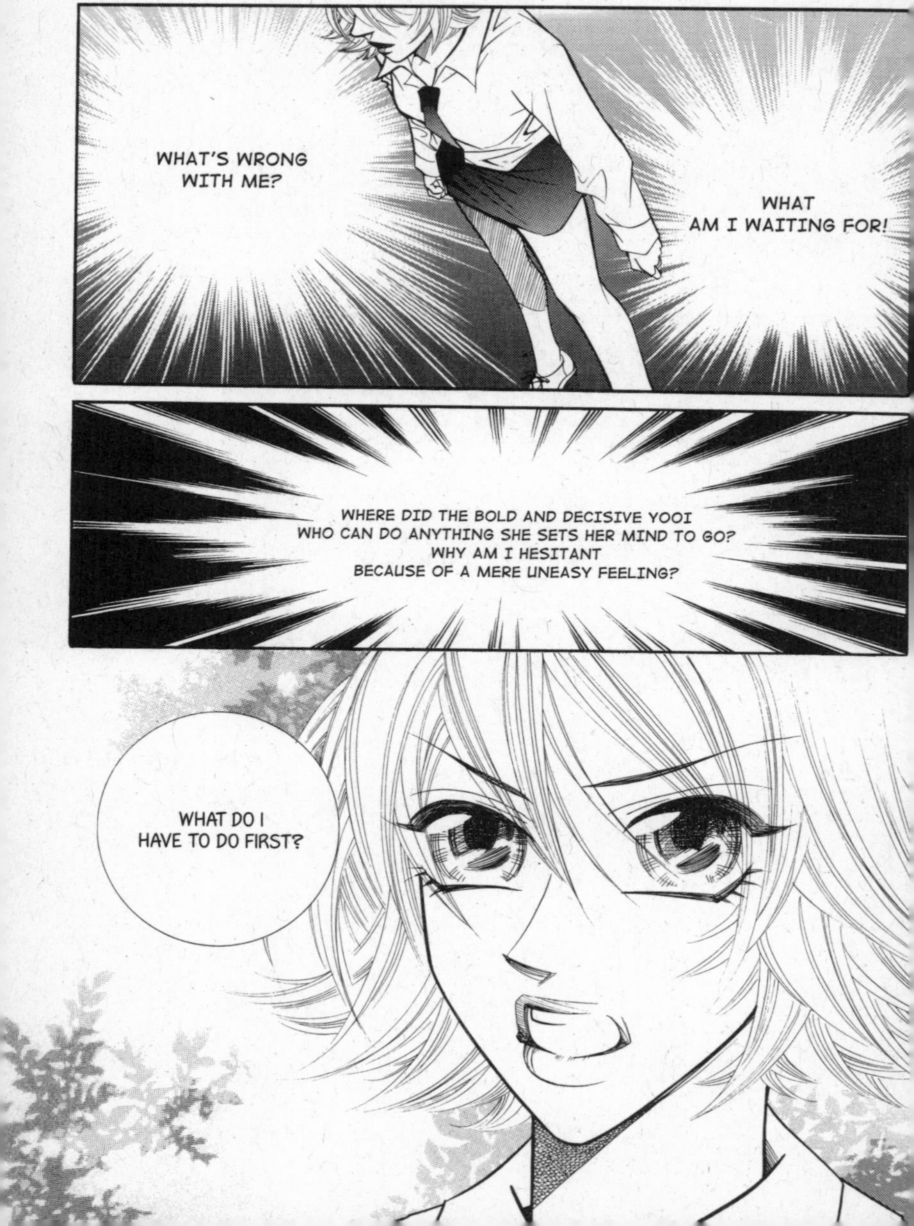
WHAT'S WRONG WITH ME?
WHAT AM I WAITING FOR!
WHERE DID THE BOLD AND DECISIVE YOOI WHO CAN DO ANYTHING SHE SETS HER MIND TO GO? WHY AM I HESITANT BECAUSE OF A MERE UNEASY FEELING?
WHAT DO I HAVE TO DO FIRST?

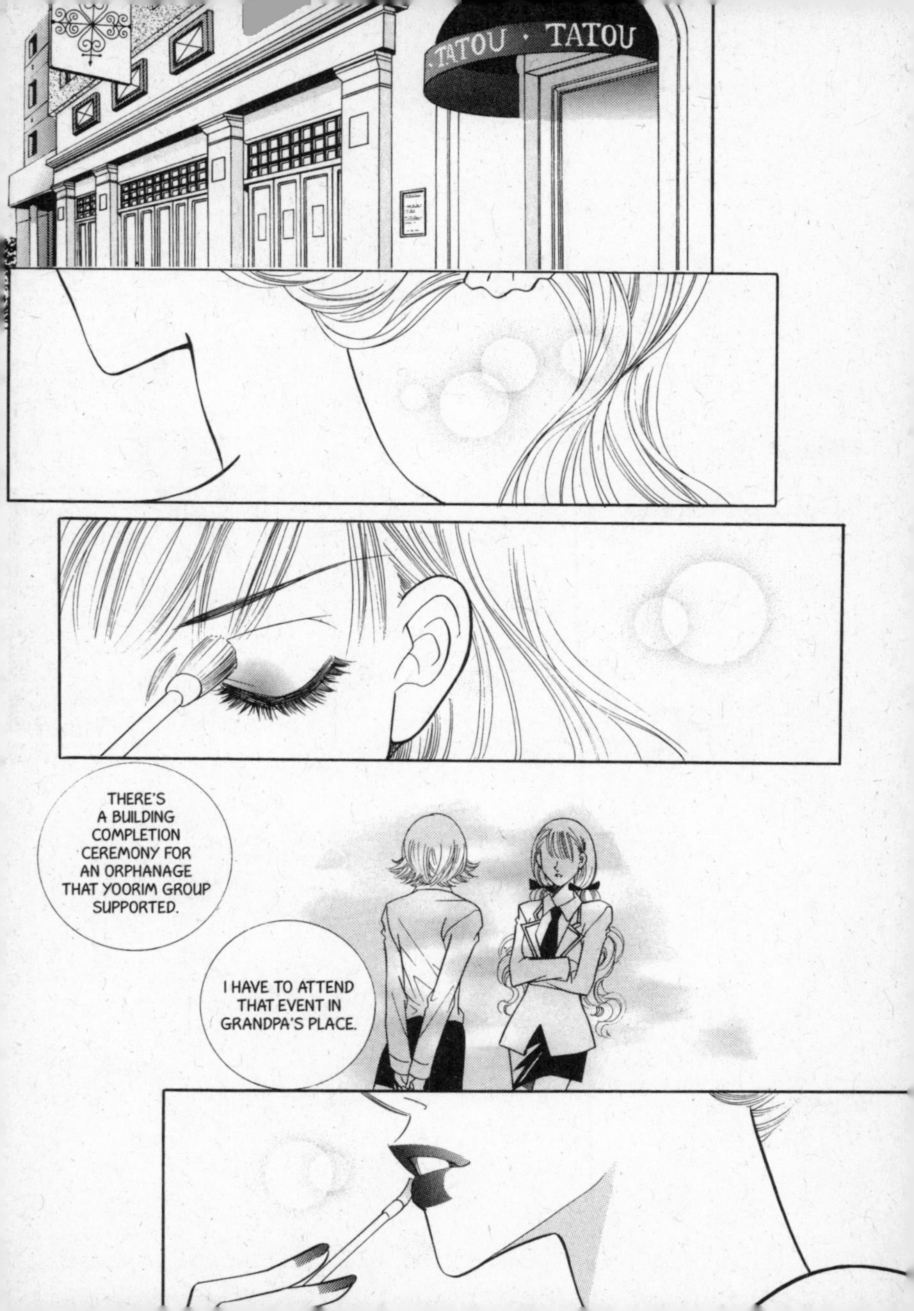
TATOU · TATOU
THERE'S A BUILDING COMPLETION CEREMONY FOR AN ORPHANAGE THAT YOORIM GROUP SUPPORTED.
I HAVE TO ATTEND THAT EVENT IN GRANDPA'S PLACE.

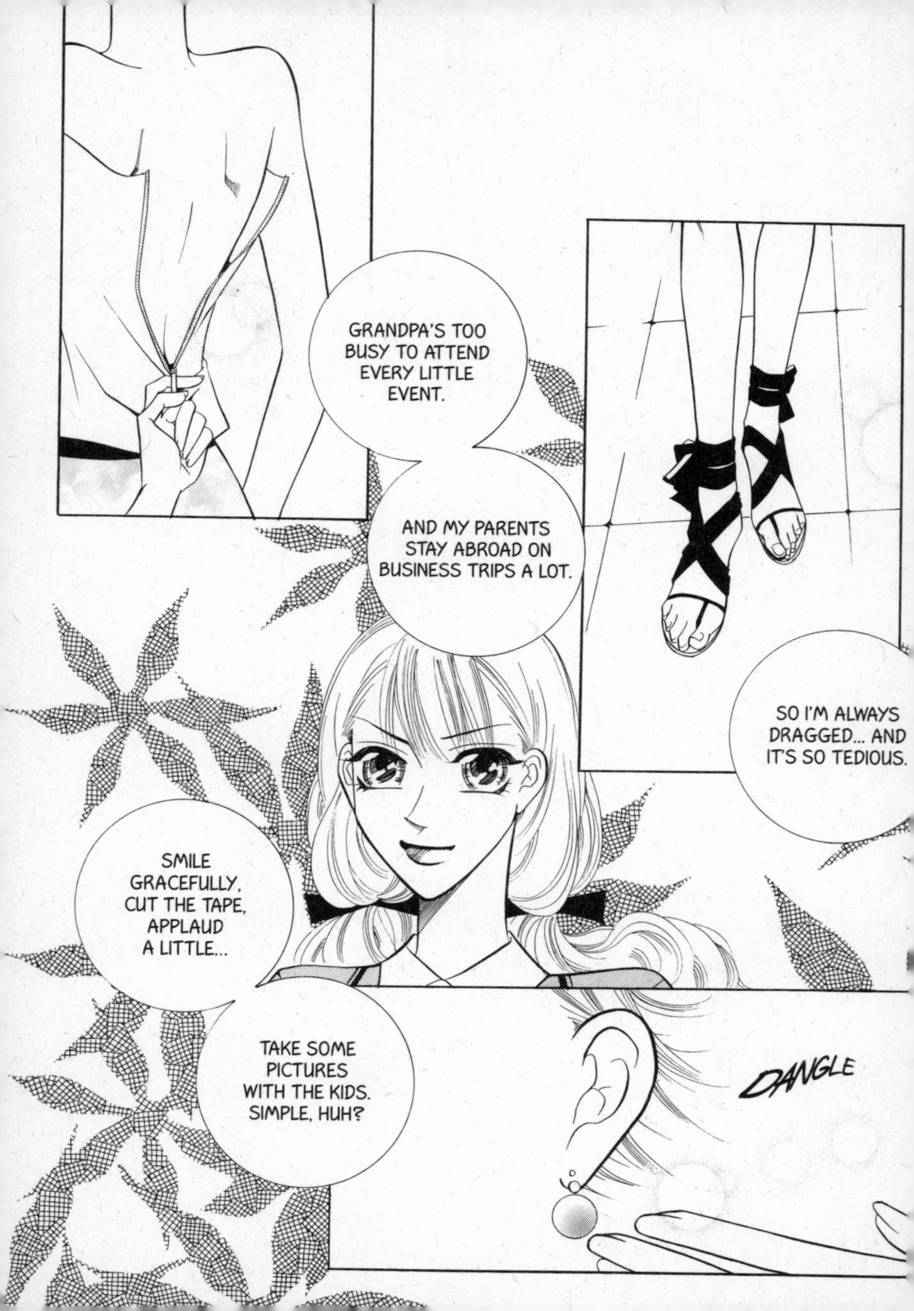
GRANDPA'S TOO BUSY TO ATTEND EVERY LITTLE EVENT.
AND MY PARENTS STAY ABROAD ON BUSINESS TRIPS A LOT.
SO I'M ALWAYS DRAGGED... AND IT'S SO TEDIOUS.
SMILE GRACEFULLY, CUT THE TAPE, APPLAUD A LITTLE...
TAKE SOME PICTURES WITH THE KIDS. SIMPLE, HUH?
DANGLE

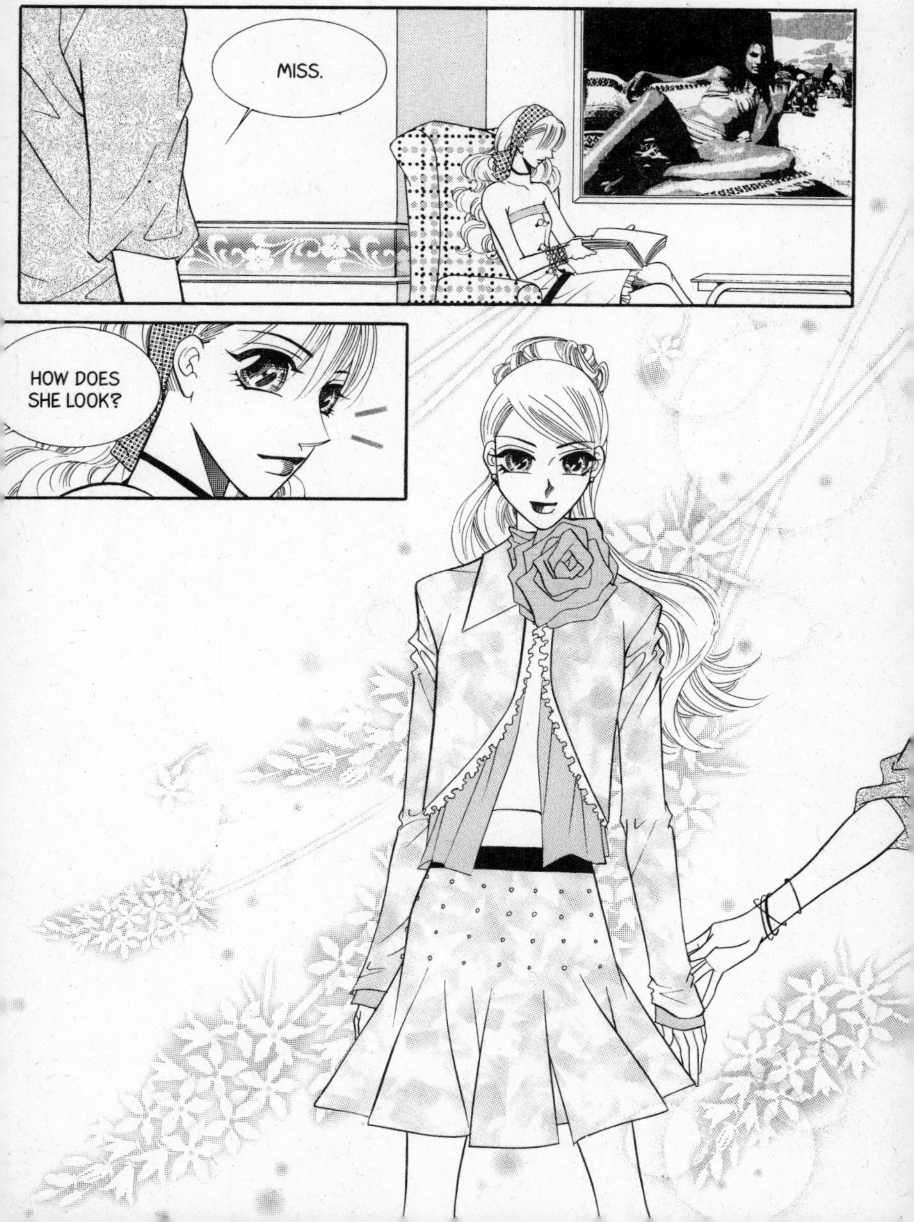
MISS.
HOW DOES SHE LOOK?

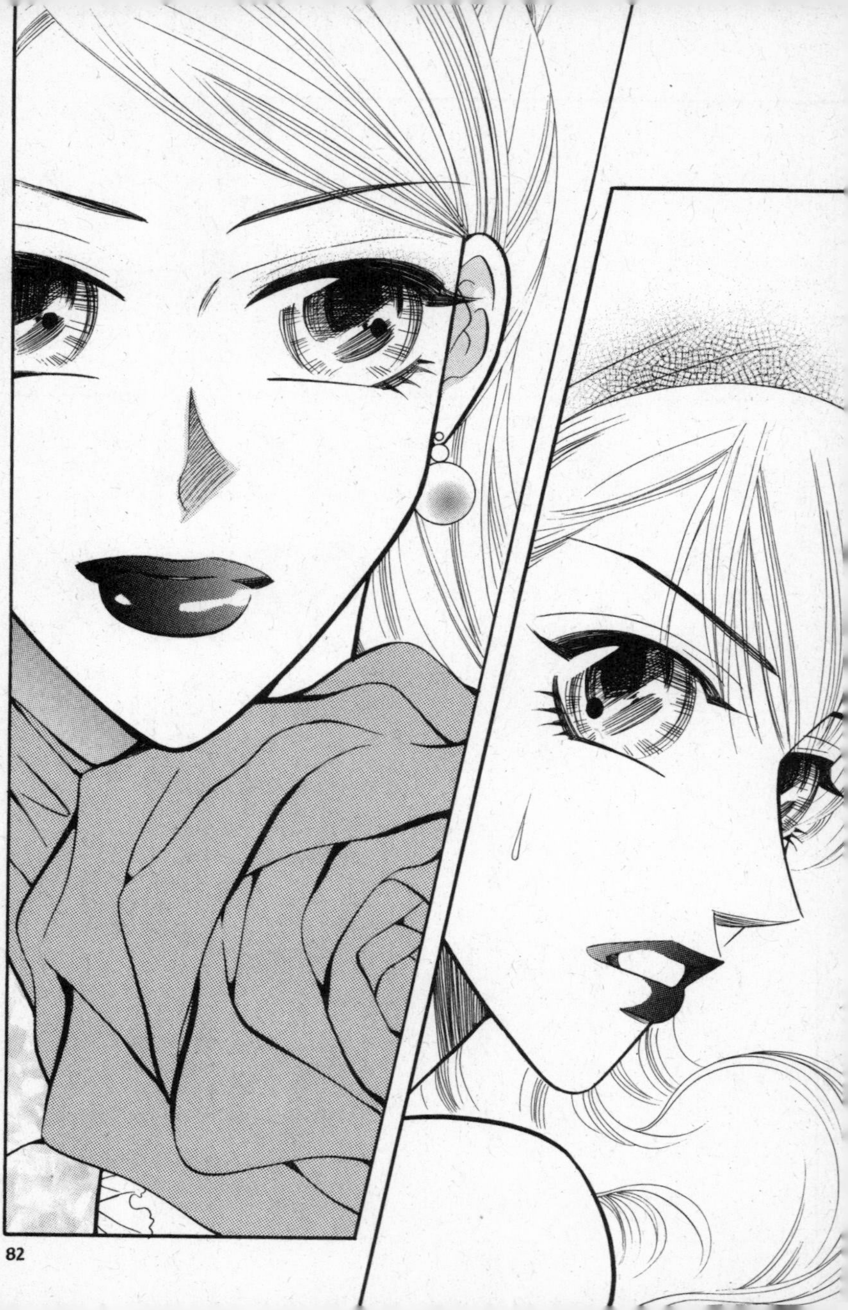

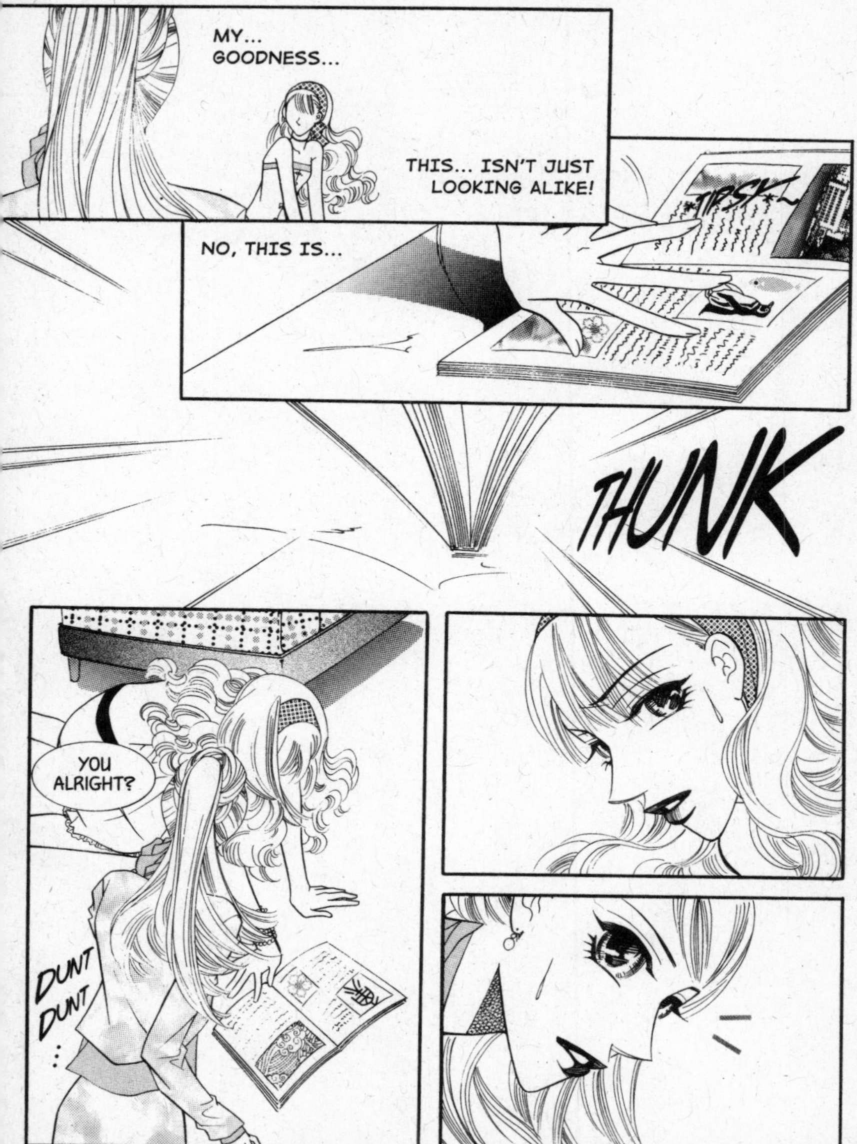
MY... GOODNESS...
THIS... ISN'T JUST LOOKING ALIKE!
NO, THIS IS...
THUNK
YOU ALRIGHT?
DUNT DUNT ...

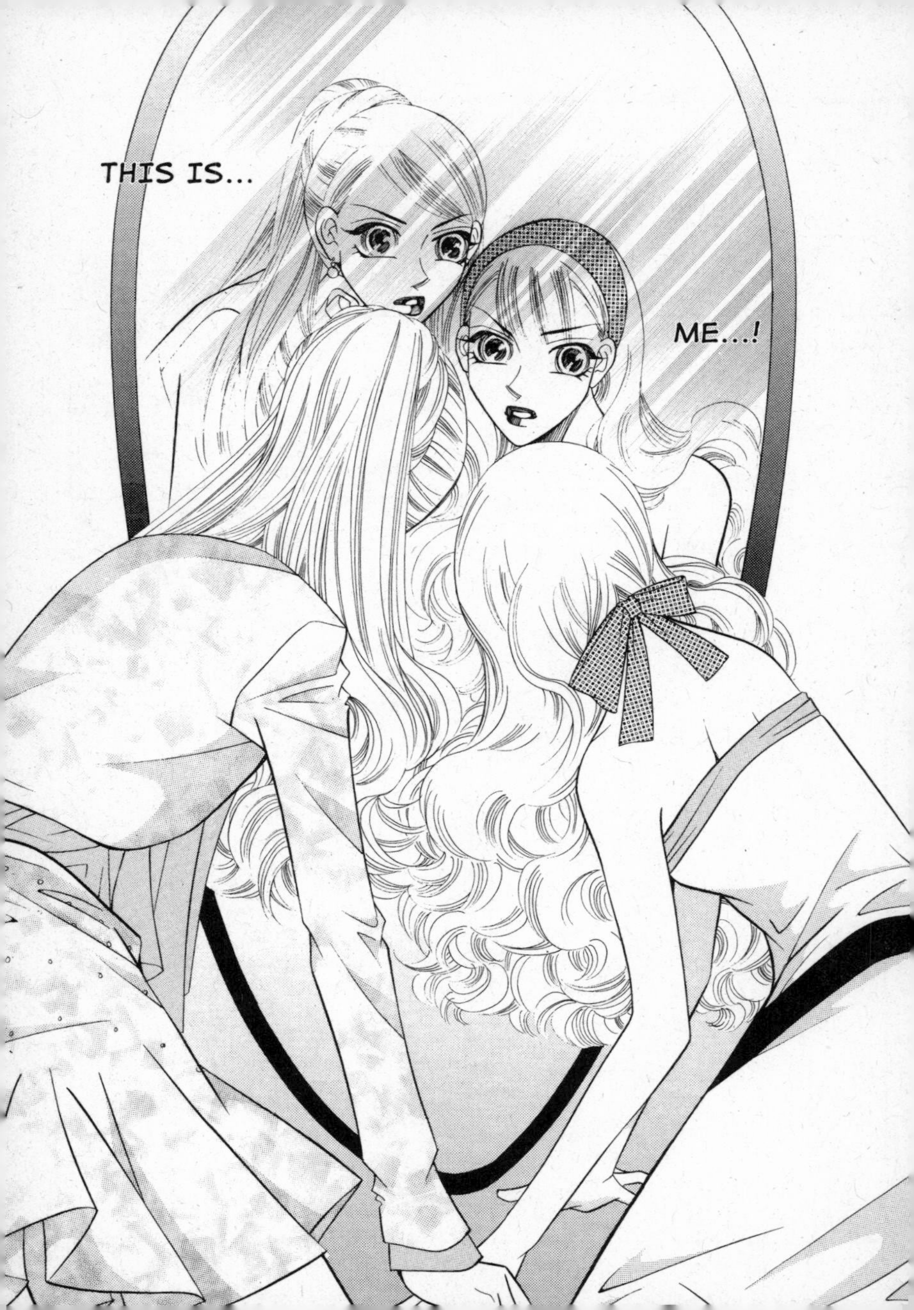
THIS IS...
ME...!

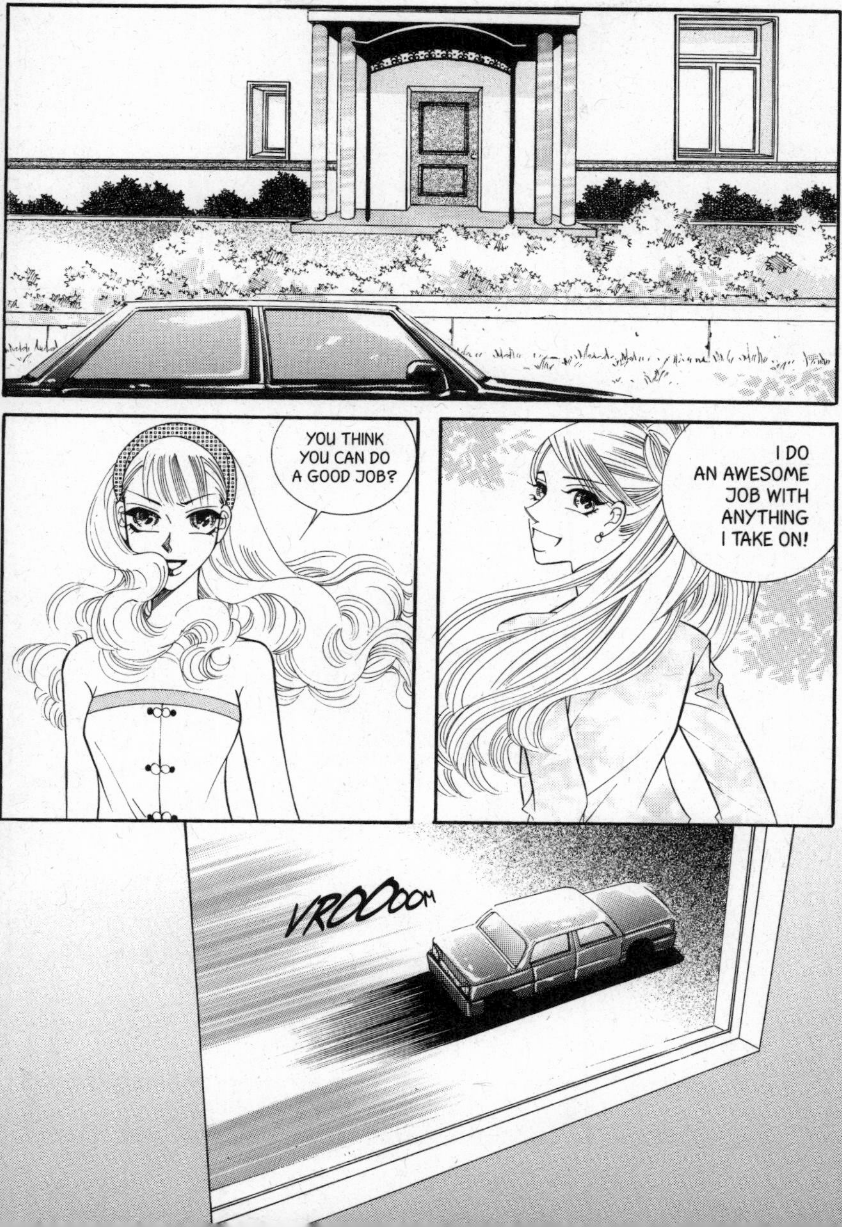
YOU THINK YOU CAN DO A GOOD JOB?
I DO AN AWESOME JOB WITH ANYTHING I TAKE ON!
VROOOoom

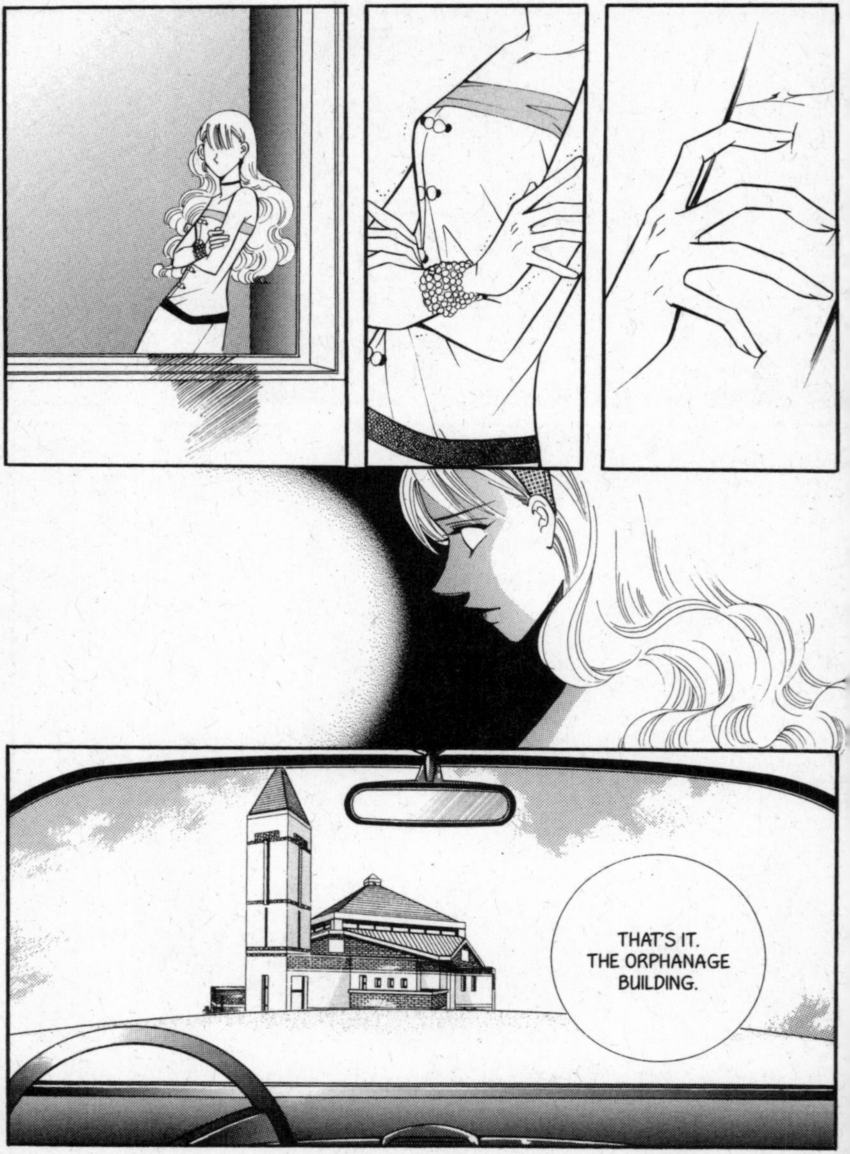
THAT'S IT.
THE ORPHANAGE
BUILDING.

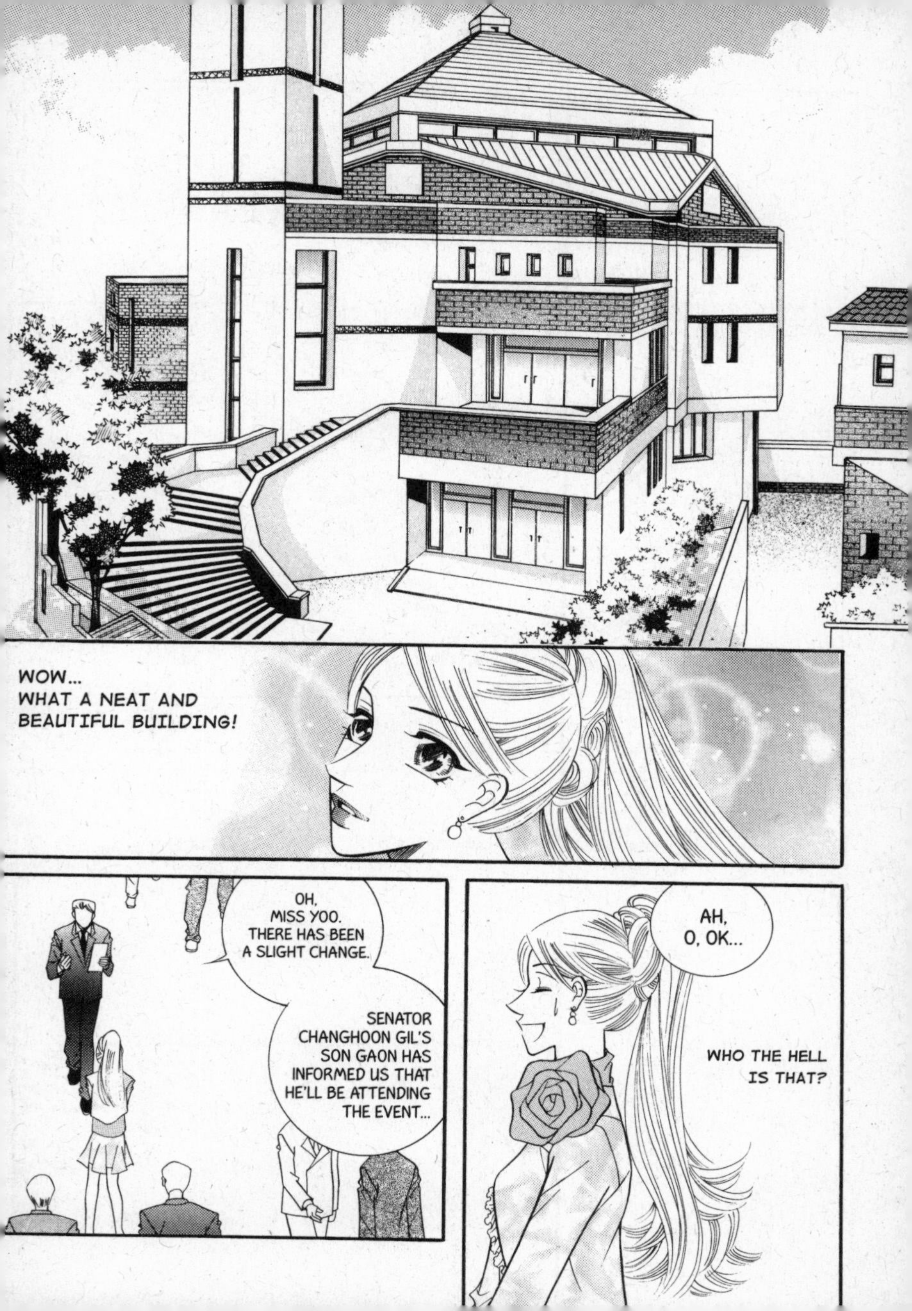
WOW...
WHAT A NEAT AND BEAUTIFUL BUILDING!
OH, MISS YOO. THERE HAS BEEN A SLIGHT CHANGE.
SENATOR CHANGHOON GIL'S SON GAON HAS INFORMED US THAT HE'LL BE ATTENDING THE EVENT...
AH, O, OK...
WHO THE HELL IS THAT?

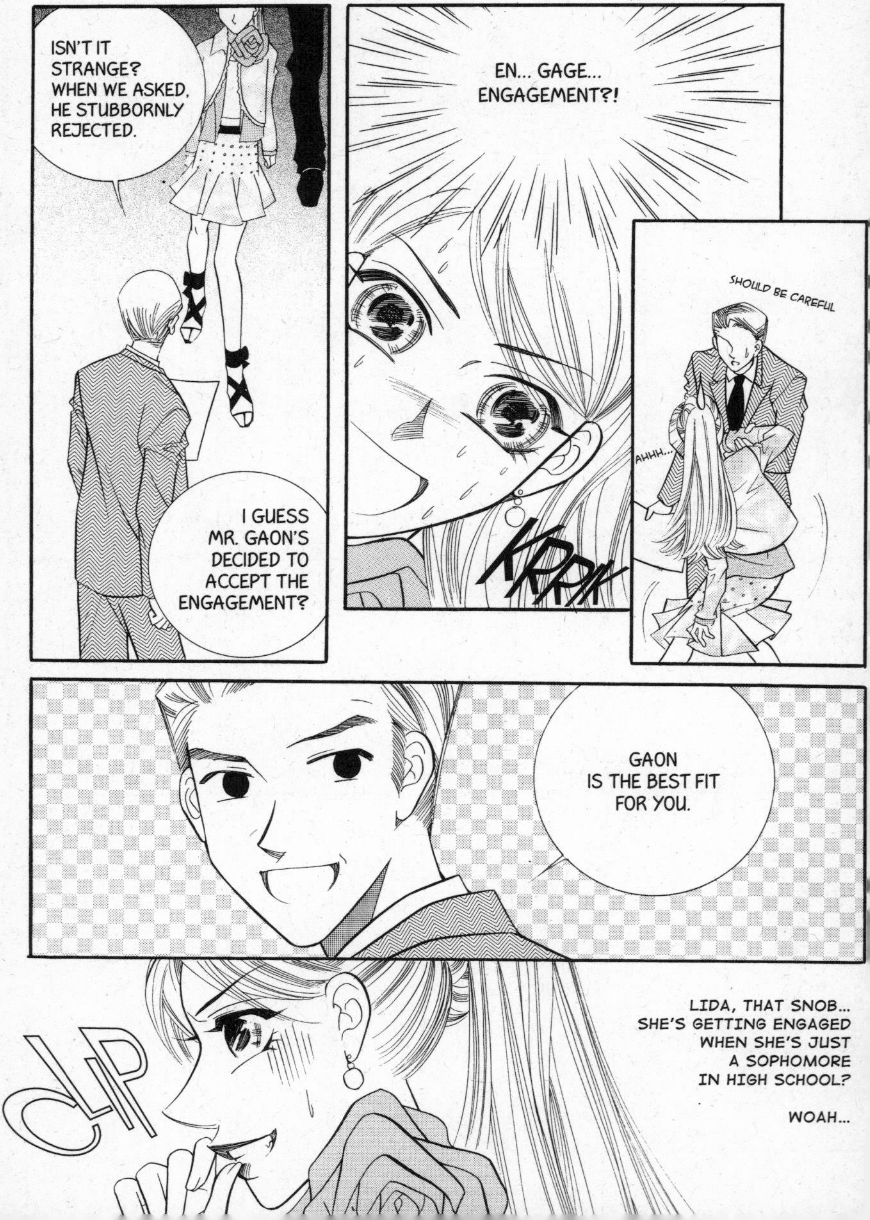

ISN'T IT STRANGE? WHEN WE ASKED, HE STUBBORNLY REJECTED.
I GUESS MR. GAON'S DECIDED TO ACCEPT THE ENGAGEMENT?
EN... GAGE... ENGAGEMENT?!
KRRIK
SHOULD BE CAREFUL
AHHH...
GAON IS THE BEST FIT FOR YOU.
CLIP
LIDA, THAT SNOB... SHE'S GETTING ENGAGED WHEN SHE'S JUST A SOPHOMORE IN HIGH SCHOOL?
WOAH...

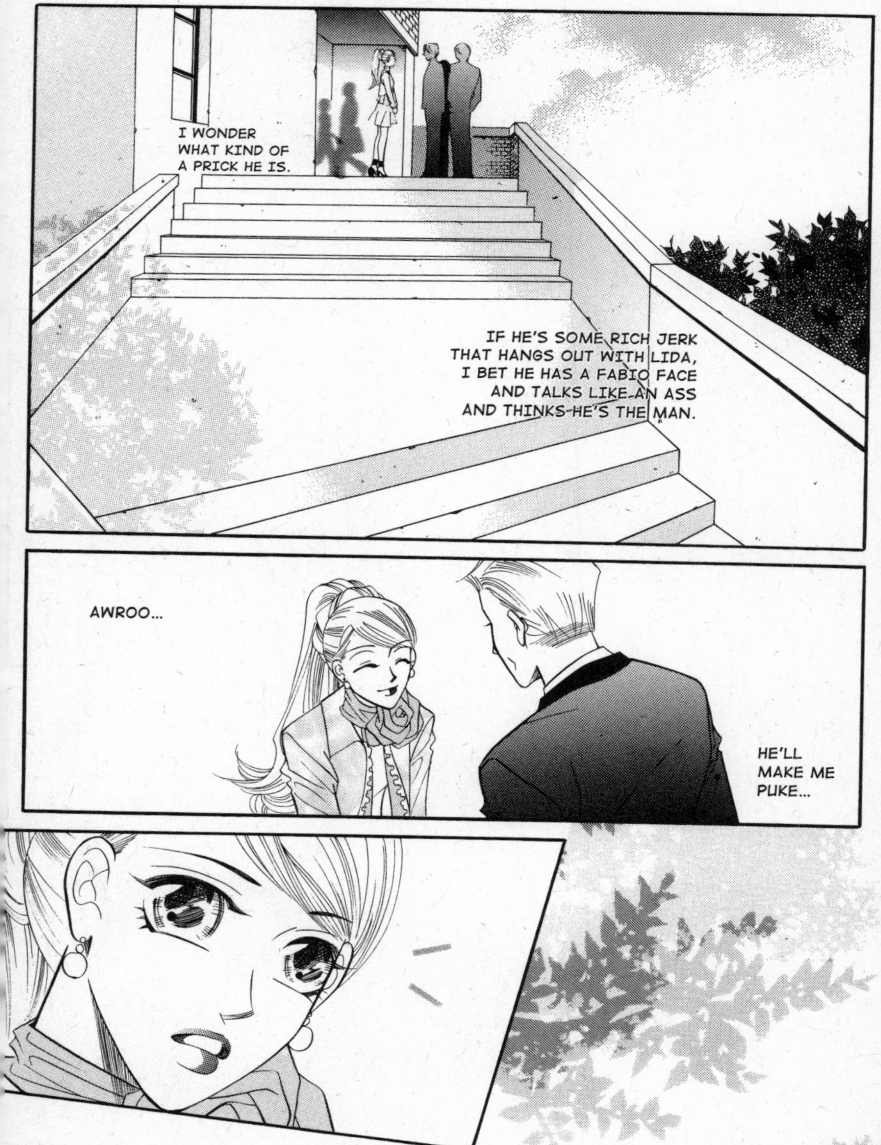
I WONDER WHAT KIND OF A PRICK HE IS.
IF HE'S SOME RICH JERK THAT HANGS OUT WITH LIDA, I BET HE HAS A FABIO FACE AND TALKS LIKE AN ASS AND THINKS HE'S THE MAN.
AWROO...
HE'LL MAKE ME PUKE...

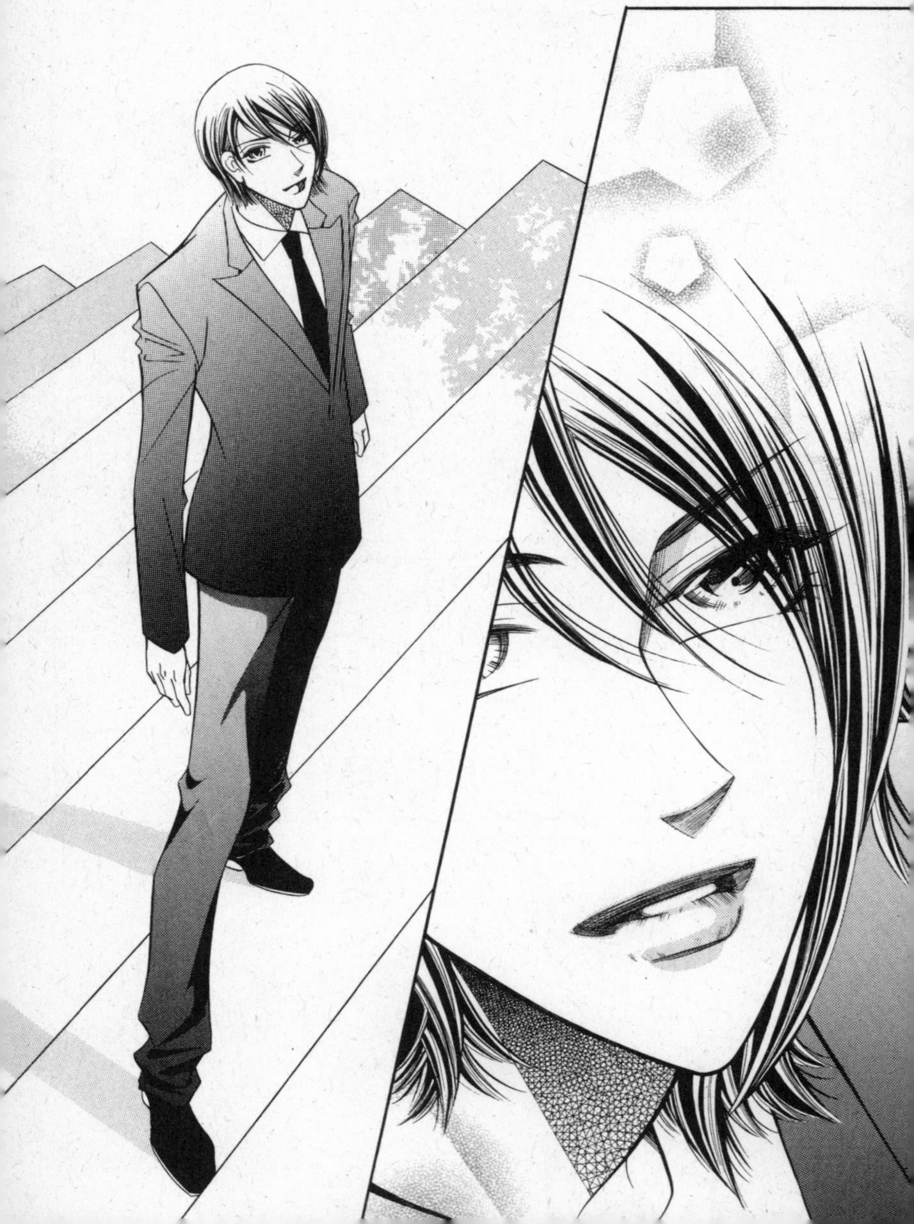

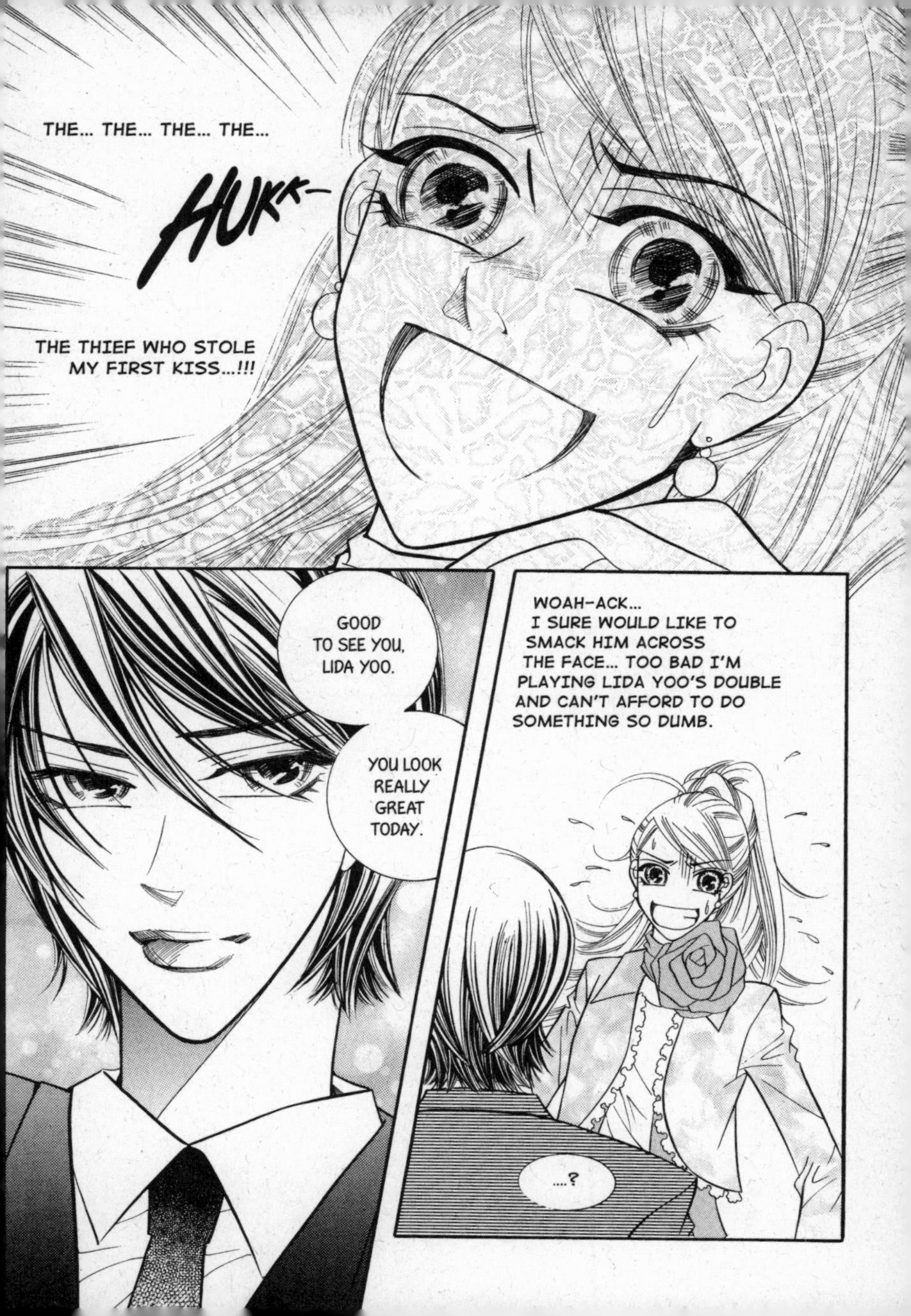
THE... THE... THE... THE...
HUKK—
THE THIEF WHO STOLE MY FIRST KISS...!!!
GOOD TO SEE YOU, LIDA YOO.
YOU LOOK REALLY GREAT TODAY.
WOAH-ACK... I SURE WOULD LIKE TO SMACK HIM ACROSS THE FACE... TOO BAD I'M PLAYING LIDA YOO'S DOUBLE AND CAN'T AFFORD TO DO SOMETHING SO DUMB.
...?

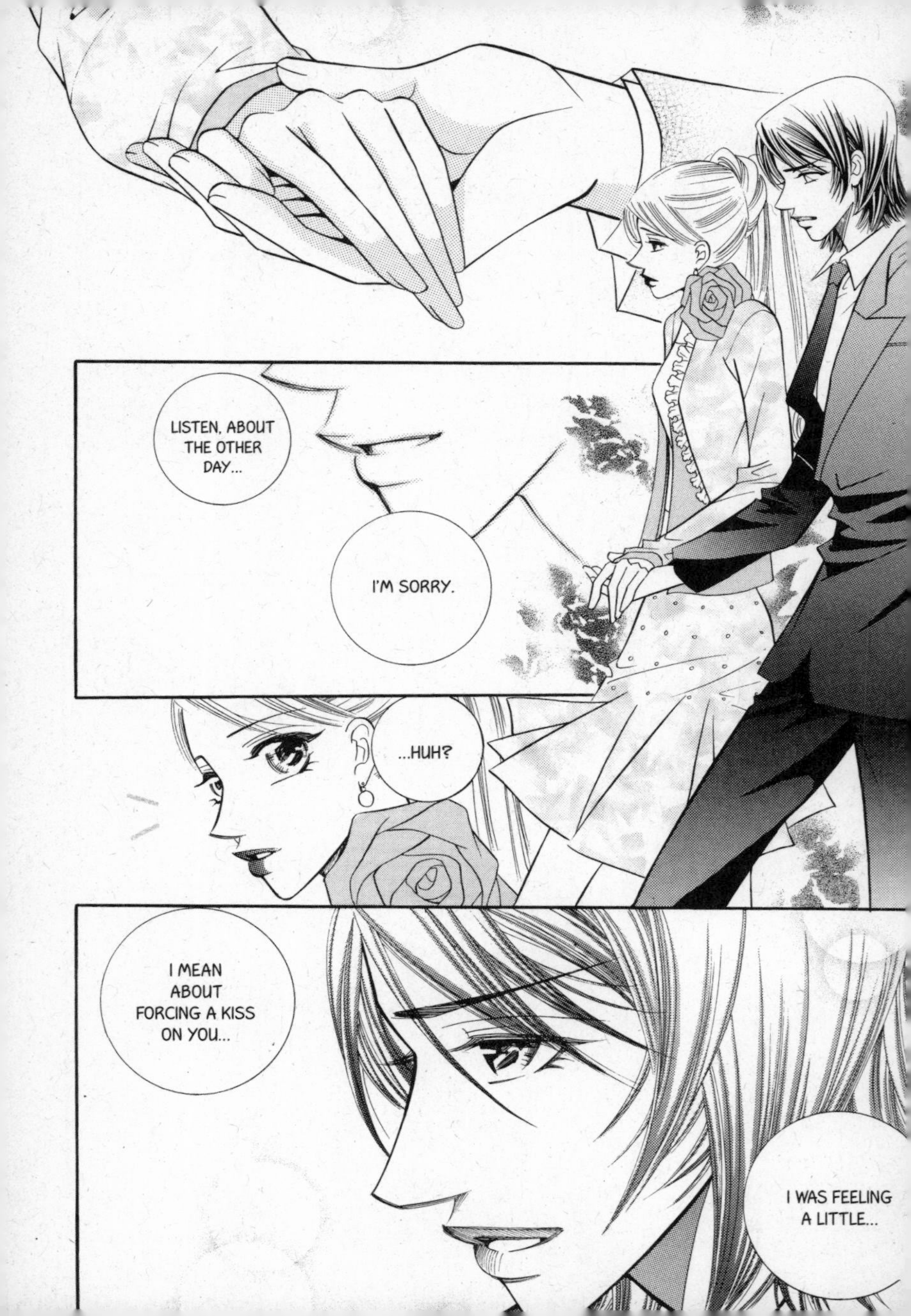
LISTEN, ABOUT THE OTHER DAY...
I'M SORRY.
...HUH?
I MEAN ABOUT FORCING A KISS ON YOU...
I WAS FEELING A LITTLE...

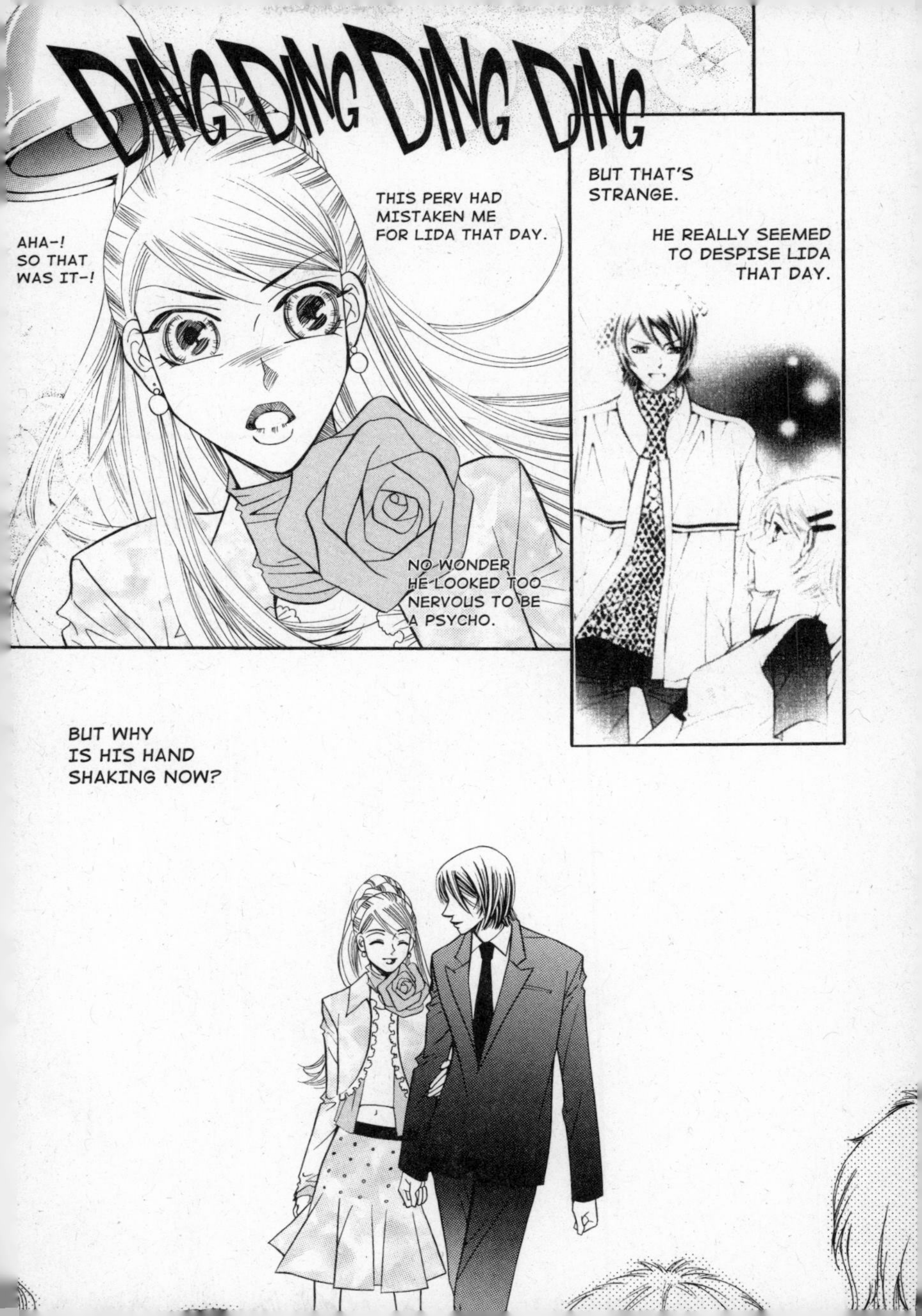
DING DING DING DING
AHA-! SO THAT WAS IT-!
THIS PERV HAD MISTAKEN ME FOR LIDA THAT DAY.
NO WONDER HE LOOKED TOO NERVOUS TO BE A PSYCHO.
BUT THAT'S STRANGE.
HE REALLY SEEMED TO DESPISE LIDA THAT DAY.
BUT WHY IS HIS HAND SHAKING NOW?

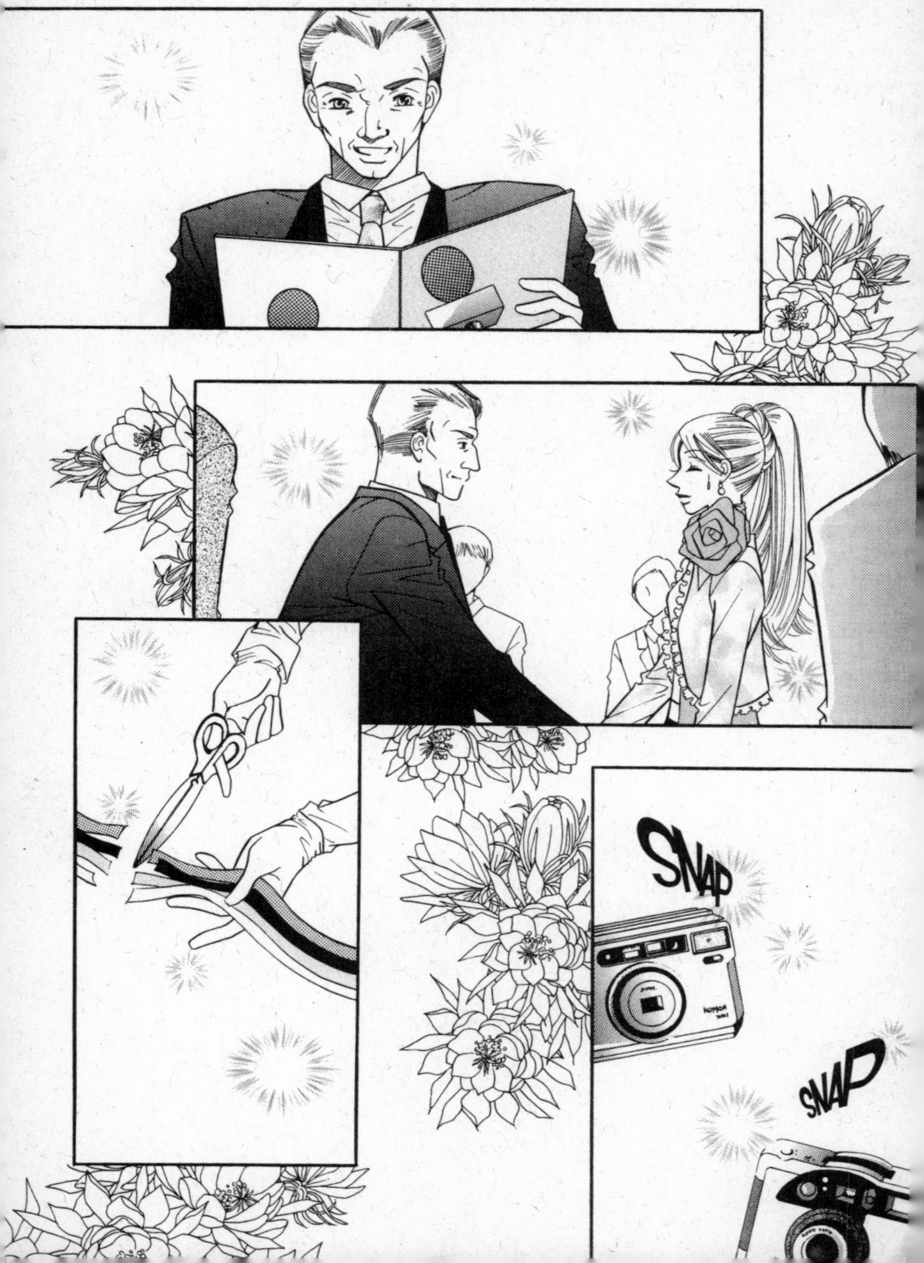
SNAP
SNAP

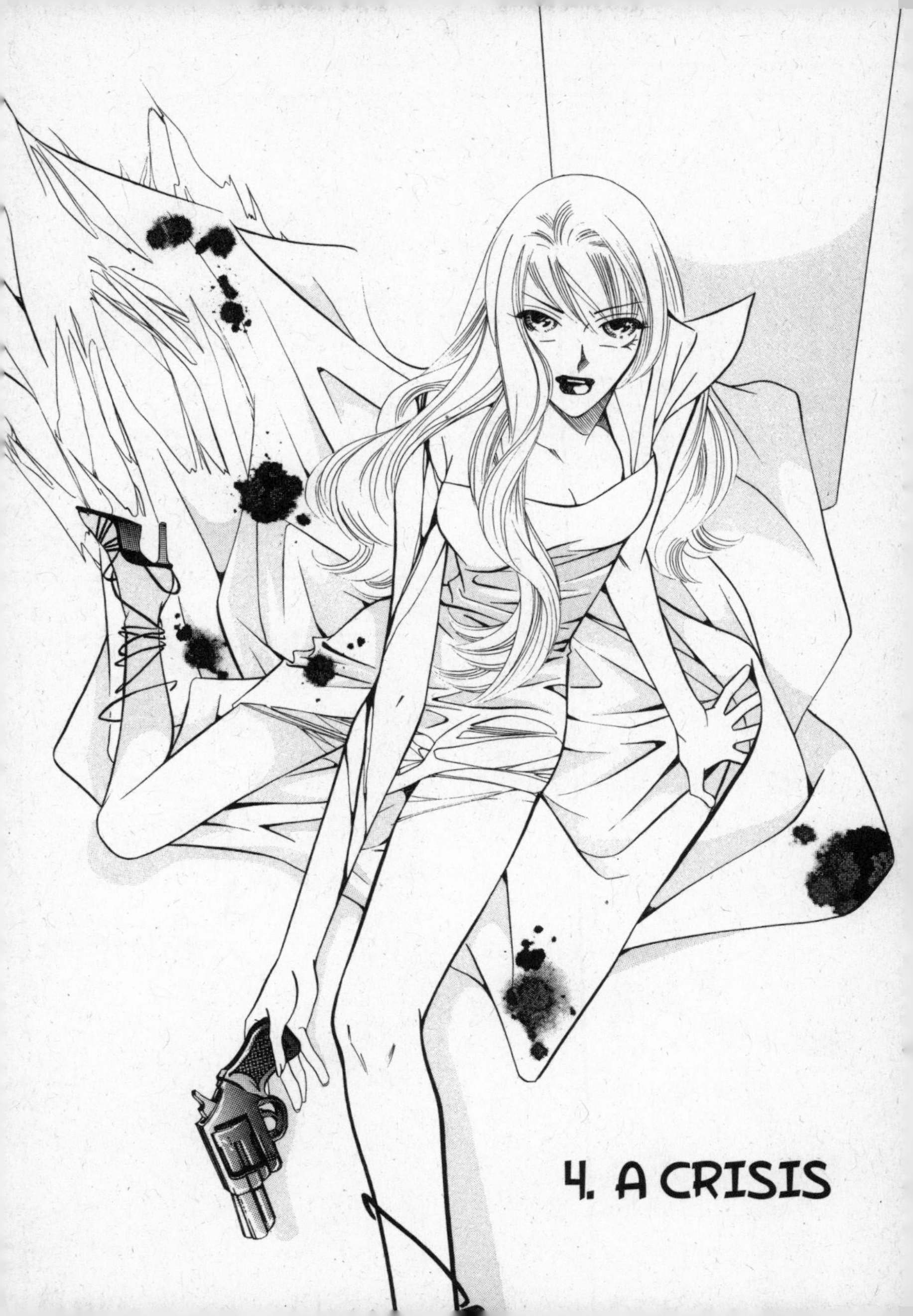

4. A CRISIS

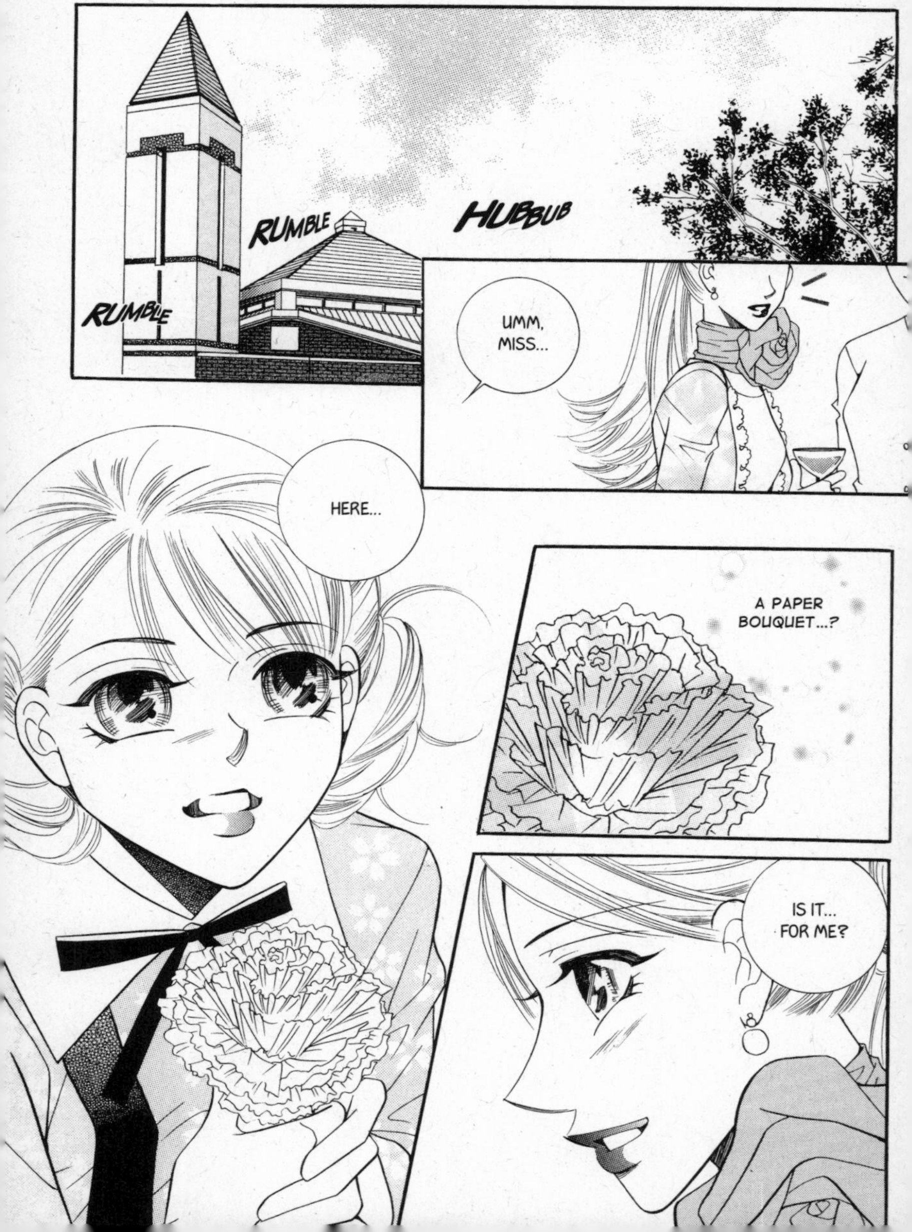
RUMBLE
RUMBLE
HUBBUB
UMM, MISS...
HERE...
A PAPER BOUQUET...?
IS IT... FOR ME?

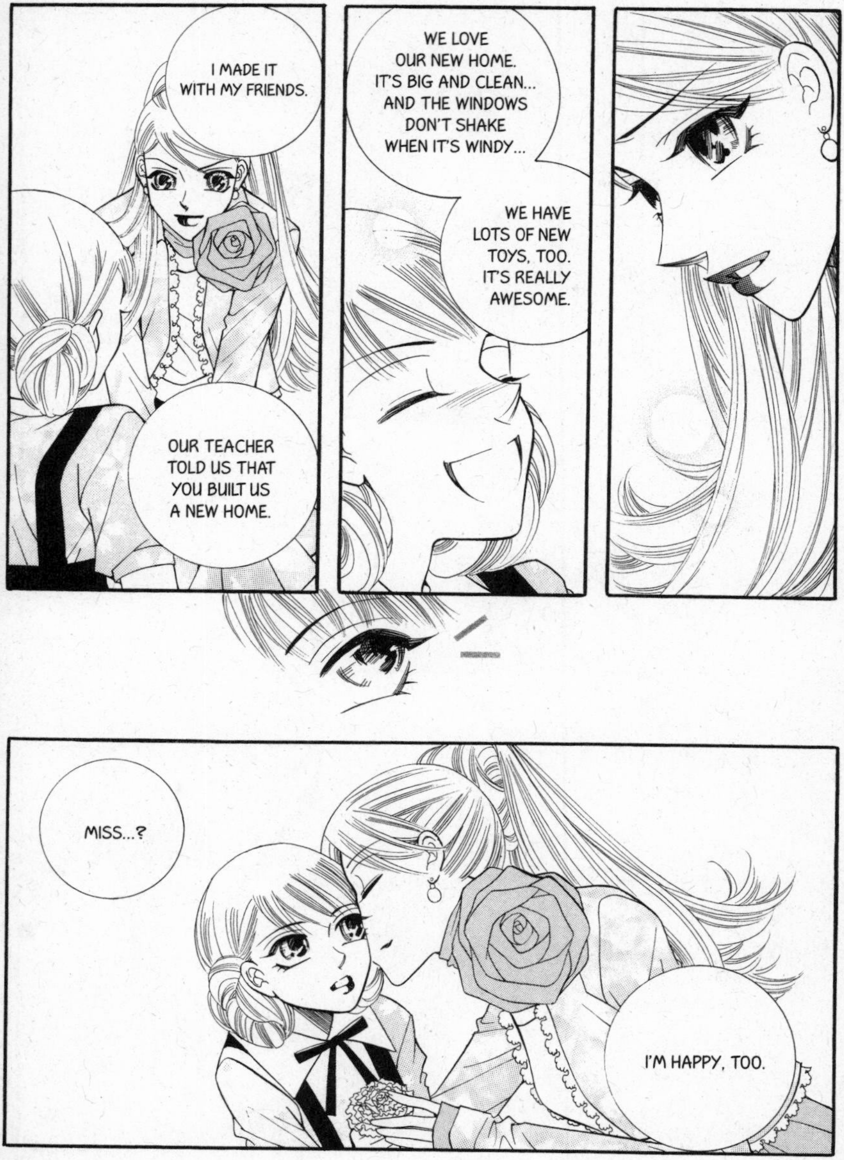
I MADE IT WITH MY FRIENDS.
OUR TEACHER TOLD US THAT YOU BUILT US A NEW HOME.
WE LOVE OUR NEW HOME. IT'S BIG AND CLEAN... AND THE WINDOWS DON'T SHAKE WHEN IT'S WINDY...
WE HAVE LOTS OF NEW TOYS, TOO. IT'S REALLY AWESOME.
MISS...?
I'M HAPPY, TOO.

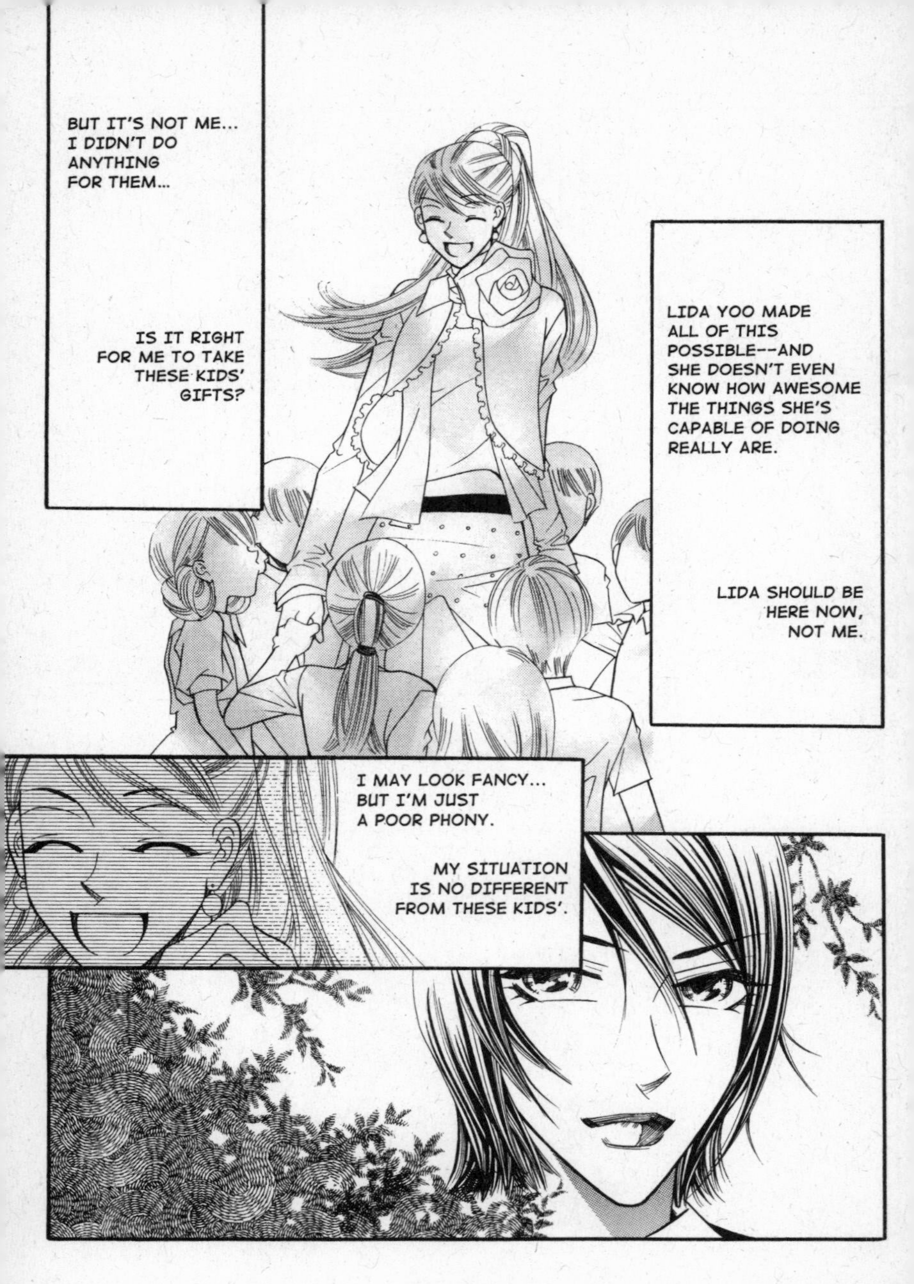

BUT IT'S NOT ME... I DIDN'T DO ANYTHING FOR THEM...
IS IT RIGHT FOR ME TO TAKE THESE KIDS' GIFTS?
LIDA YOO MADE ALL OF THIS POSSIBLE--AND SHE DOESN'T EVEN KNOW HOW AWESOME THE THINGS SHE'S CAPABLE OF DOING REALLY ARE.
LIDA SHOULD BE HERE NOW, NOT ME.
I MAY LOOK FANCY... BUT I'M JUST A POOR PHONY.
MY SITUATION IS NO DIFFERENT FROM THESE KIDS'.

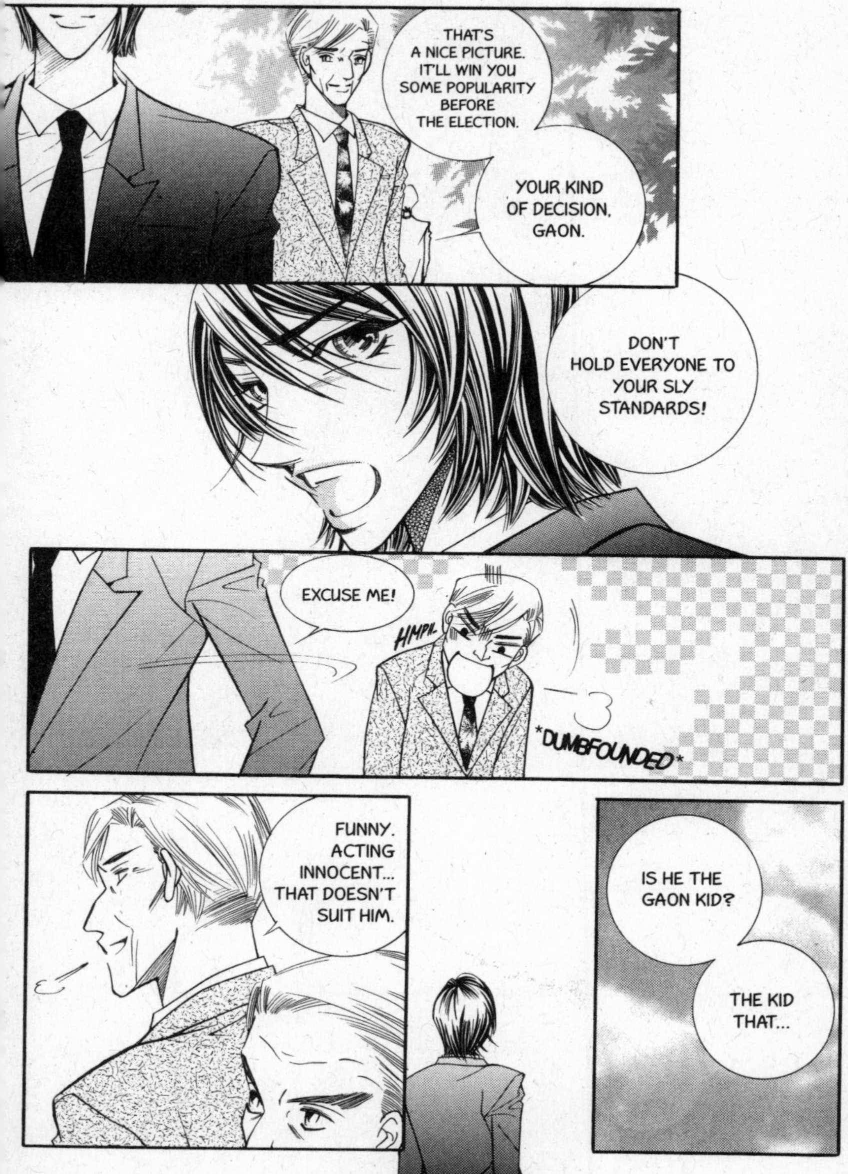
THAT'S A NICE PICTURE. IT'LL WIN YOU SOME POPULARITY BEFORE THE ELECTION.
YOUR KIND OF DECISION, GAON.
DON'T HOLD EVERYONE TO YOUR SLY STANDARDS!
EXCUSE ME!
HMPH.
DUMBFOUNDED
FUNNY. ACTING INNOCENT... THAT DOESN'T SUIT HIM.
IS HE THE GAON KID?
THE KID THAT...

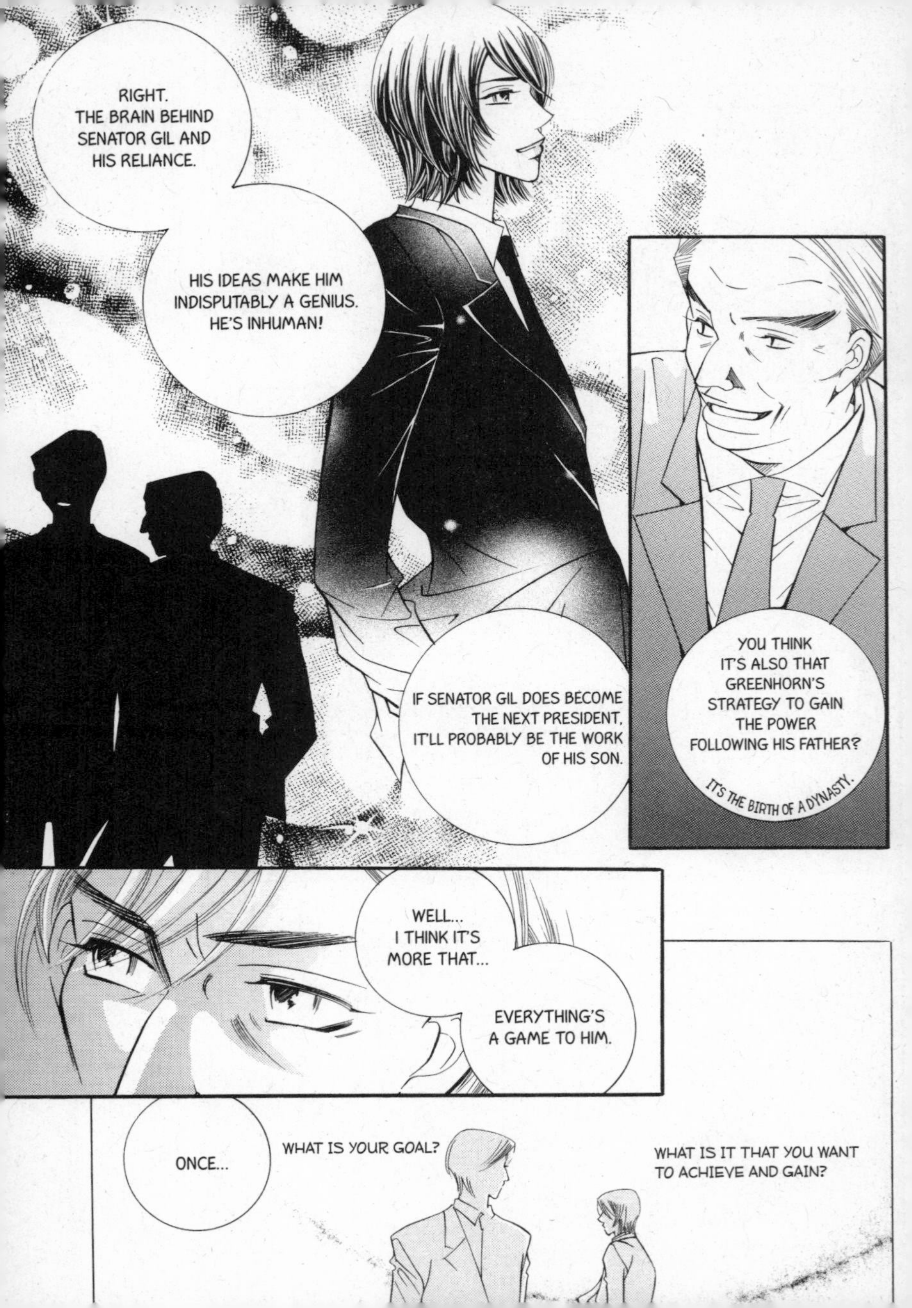
RIGHT. THE BRAIN BEHIND SENATOR GIL AND HIS RELIANCE.
HIS IDEAS MAKE HIM INDISPUTABLY A GENIUS. HE'S INHUMAN!
YOU THINK IT'S ALSO THAT GREENHORN'S STRATEGY TO GAIN THE POWER FOLLOWING HIS FATHER?
IT'S THE BIRTH OF A DYNASTY.
IF SENATOR GIL DOES BECOME THE NEXT PRESIDENT, IT'LL PROBABLY BE THE WORK OF HIS SON.
WELL... I THINK IT'S MORE THAT...
EVERYTHING'S A GAME TO HIM.
ONCE...
WHAT IS YOUR GOAL?
WHAT IS IT THAT YOU WANT TO ACHIEVE AND GAIN?

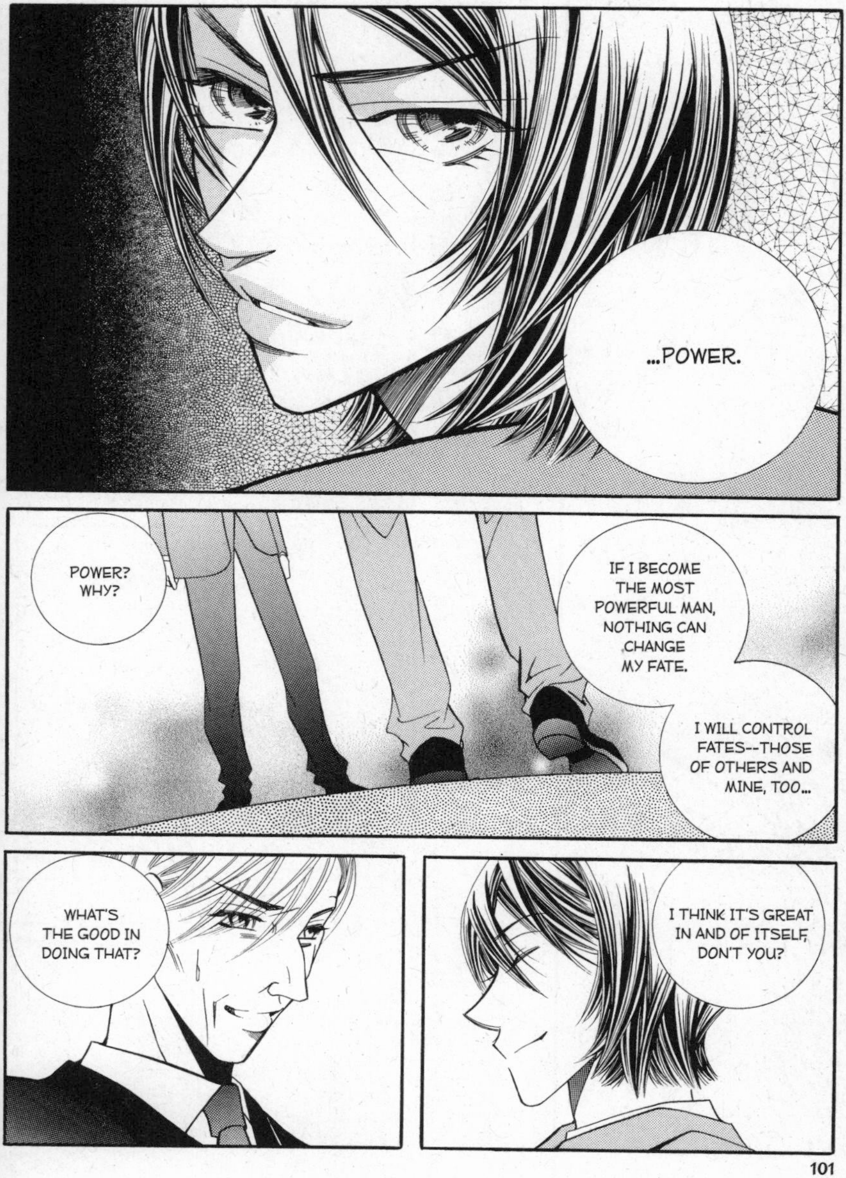
...POWER.
POWER? WHY?
IF I BECOME THE MOST POWERFUL MAN, NOTHING CAN CHANGE MY FATE.
I WILL CONTROL FATES--THOSE OF OTHERS AND MINE, TOO...
WHAT'S THE GOOD IN DOING THAT?
I THINK IT'S GREAT IN AND OF ITSELF, DON'T YOU?

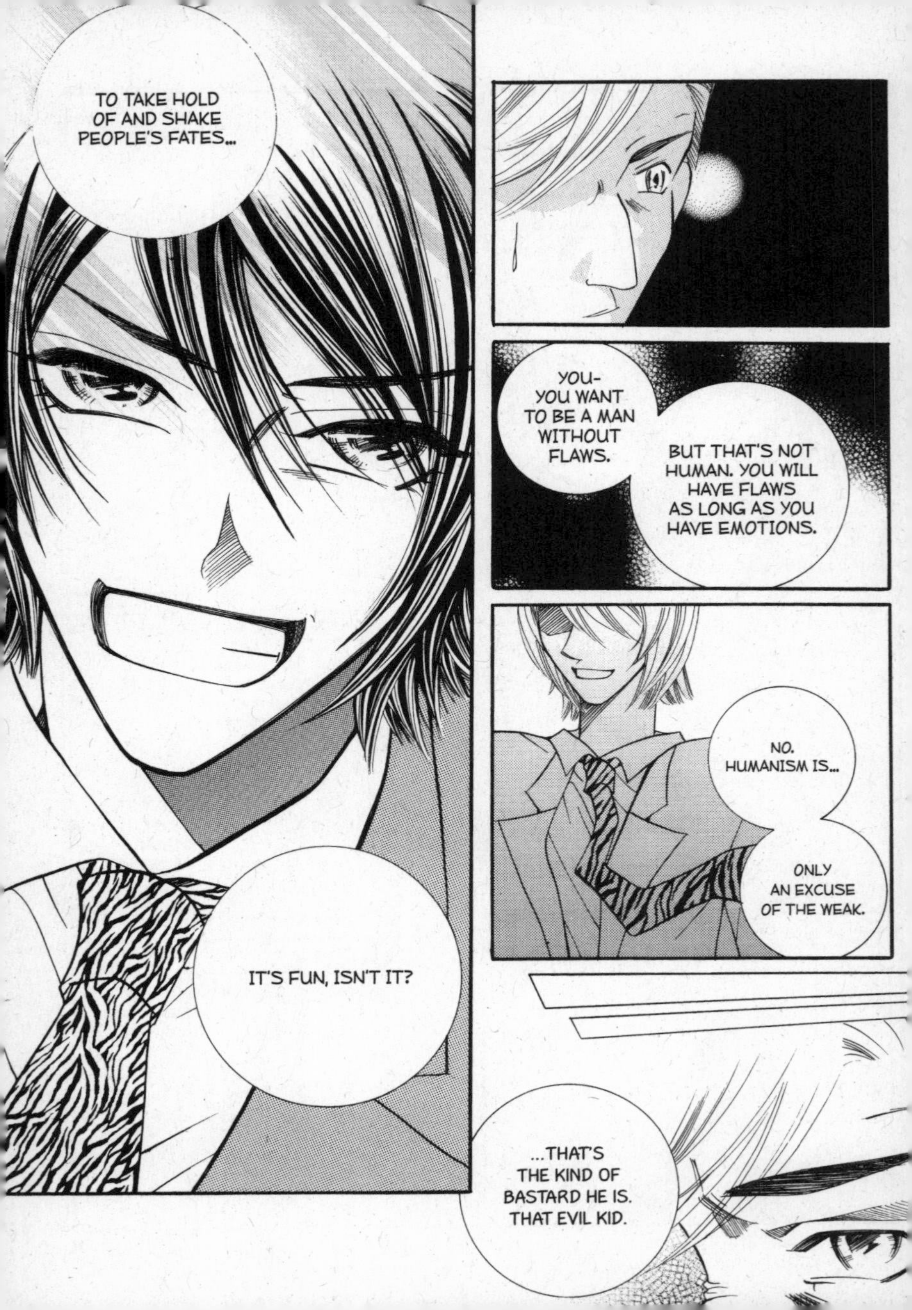
TO TAKE HOLD OF AND SHAKE PEOPLE'S FATES...
IT'S FUN, ISN'T IT?
YOU- YOU WANT TO BE A MAN WITHOUT FLAWS.
BUT THAT'S NOT HUMAN. YOU WILL HAVE FLAWS AS LONG AS YOU HAVE EMOTIONS.
NO. HUMANISM IS...
ONLY AN EXCUSE OF THE WEAK.
...THAT'S THE KIND OF BASTARD HE IS. THAT EVIL KID.

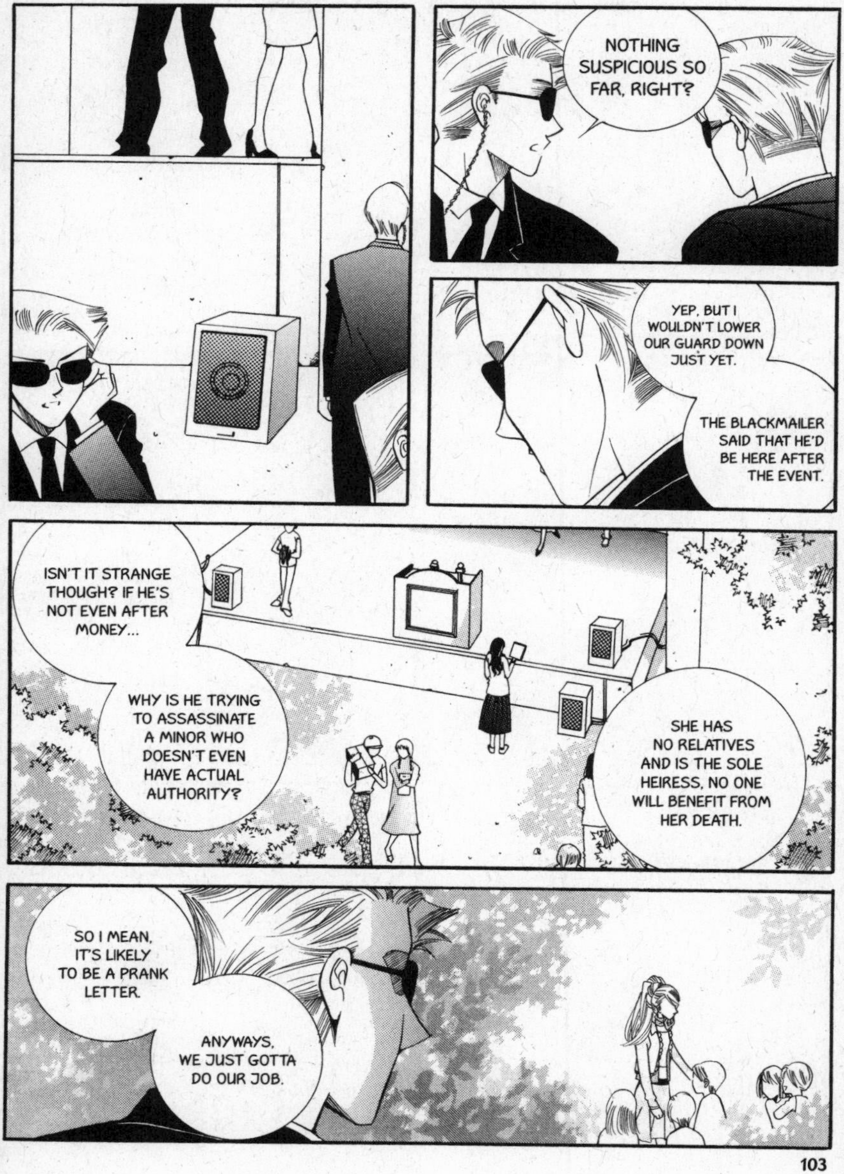
NOTHING SUSPICIOUS SO FAR, RIGHT?
YEP, BUT I WOULDN'T LOWER OUR GUARD DOWN JUST YET.
THE BLACKMAILER SAID THAT HE'D BE HERE AFTER THE EVENT.
ISN'T IT STRANGE THOUGH? IF HE'S NOT EVEN AFTER MONEY...
WHY IS HE TRYING TO ASSASSINATE A MINOR WHO DOESN'T EVEN HAVE ACTUAL AUTHORITY?
SHE HAS NO RELATIVES AND IS THE SOLE HEIRESS, NO ONE WILL BENEFIT FROM HER DEATH.
SO I MEAN, IT'S LIKELY TO BE A PRANK LETTER.
ANYWAYS, WE JUST GOTTA DO OUR JOB.

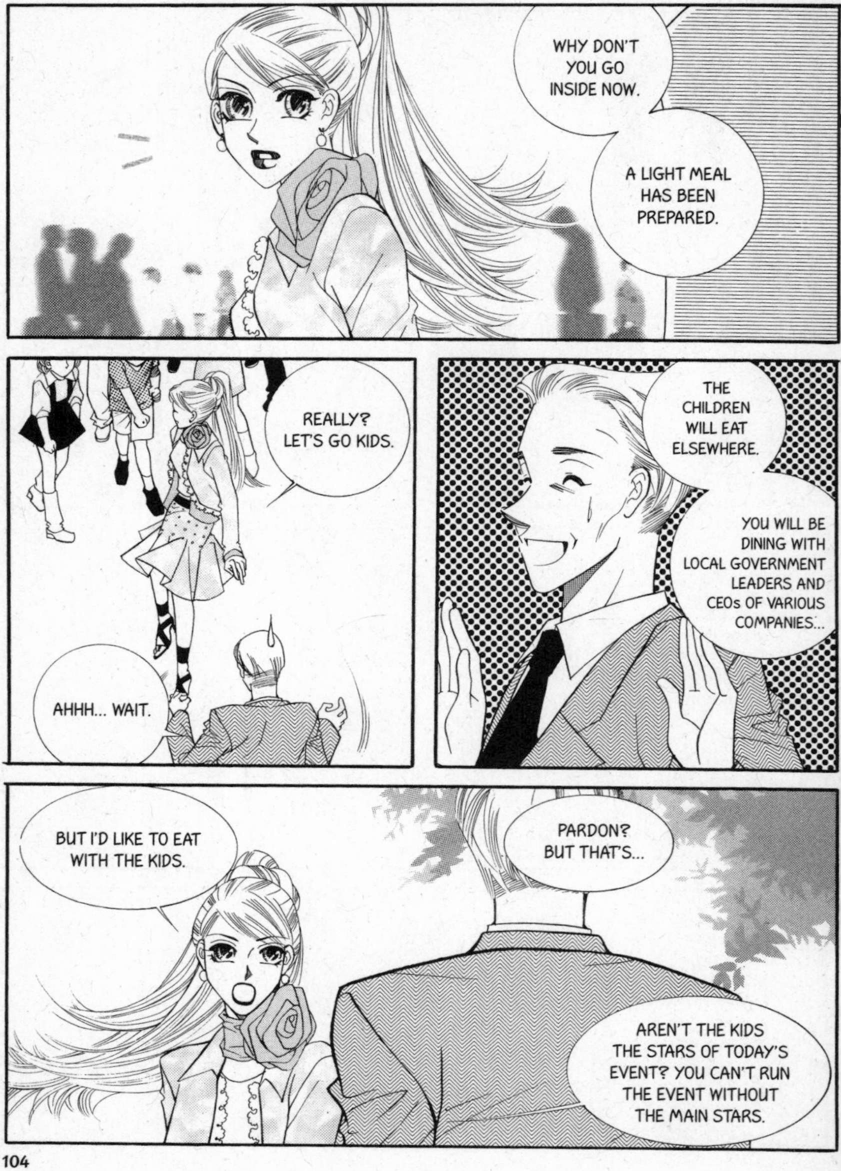
WHY DON'T YOU GO INSIDE NOW.
A LIGHT MEAL HAS BEEN PREPARED.
REALLY? LET'S GO KIDS.
AHHH... WAIT.
THE CHILDREN WILL EAT ELSEWHERE.
YOU WILL BE DINING WITH LOCAL GOVERNMENT LEADERS AND CEOs OF VARIOUS COMPANIES...
BUT I'D LIKE TO EAT WITH THE KIDS.
PARDON? BUT THAT'S...
AREN'T THE KIDS THE STARS OF TODAY'S EVENT? YOU CAN'T RUN THE EVENT WITHOUT THE MAIN STARS.

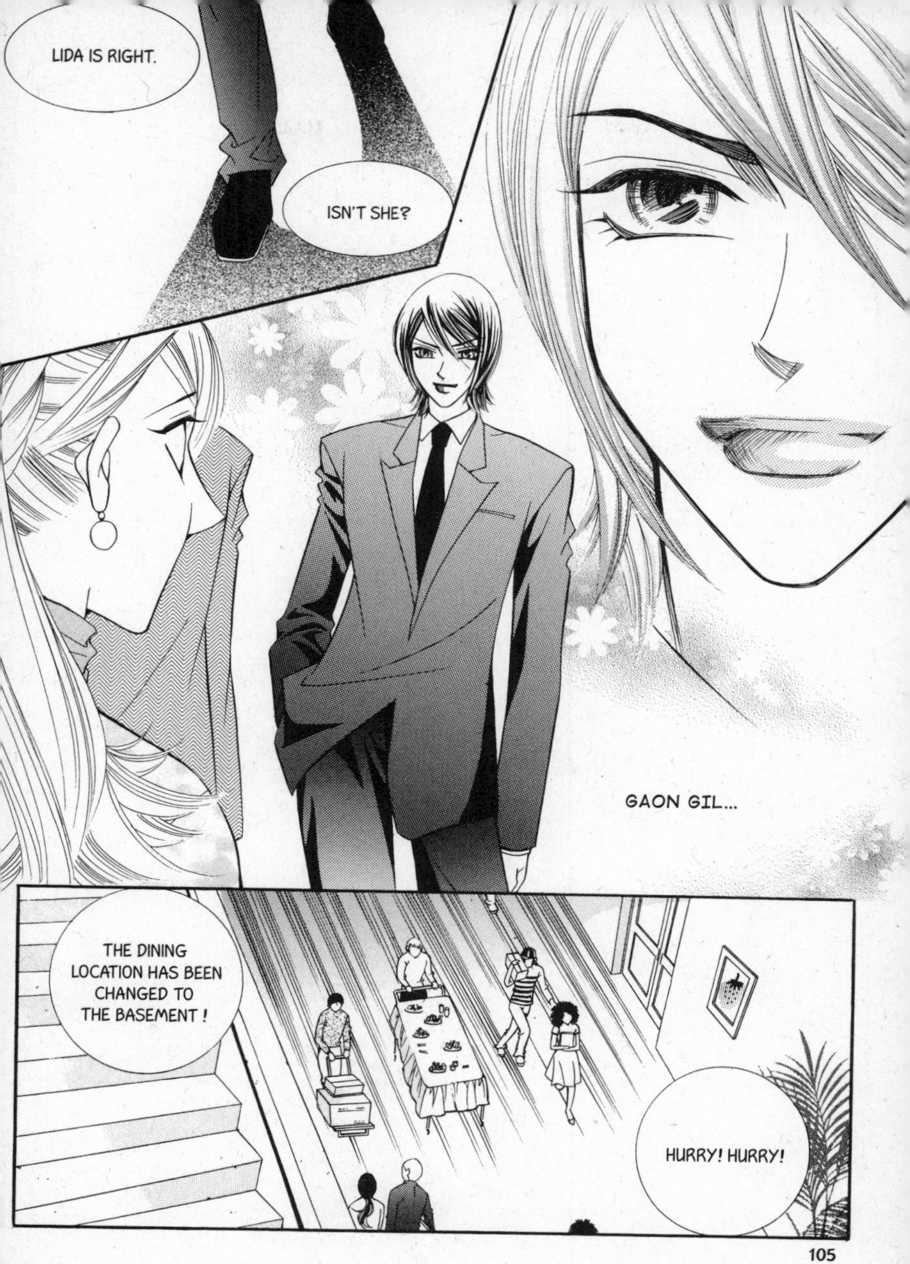

LIDA IS RIGHT.
ISN'T SHE?
GAON GIL...
THE DINING LOCATION HAS BEEN CHANGED TO THE BASEMENT !
HURRY! HURRY!

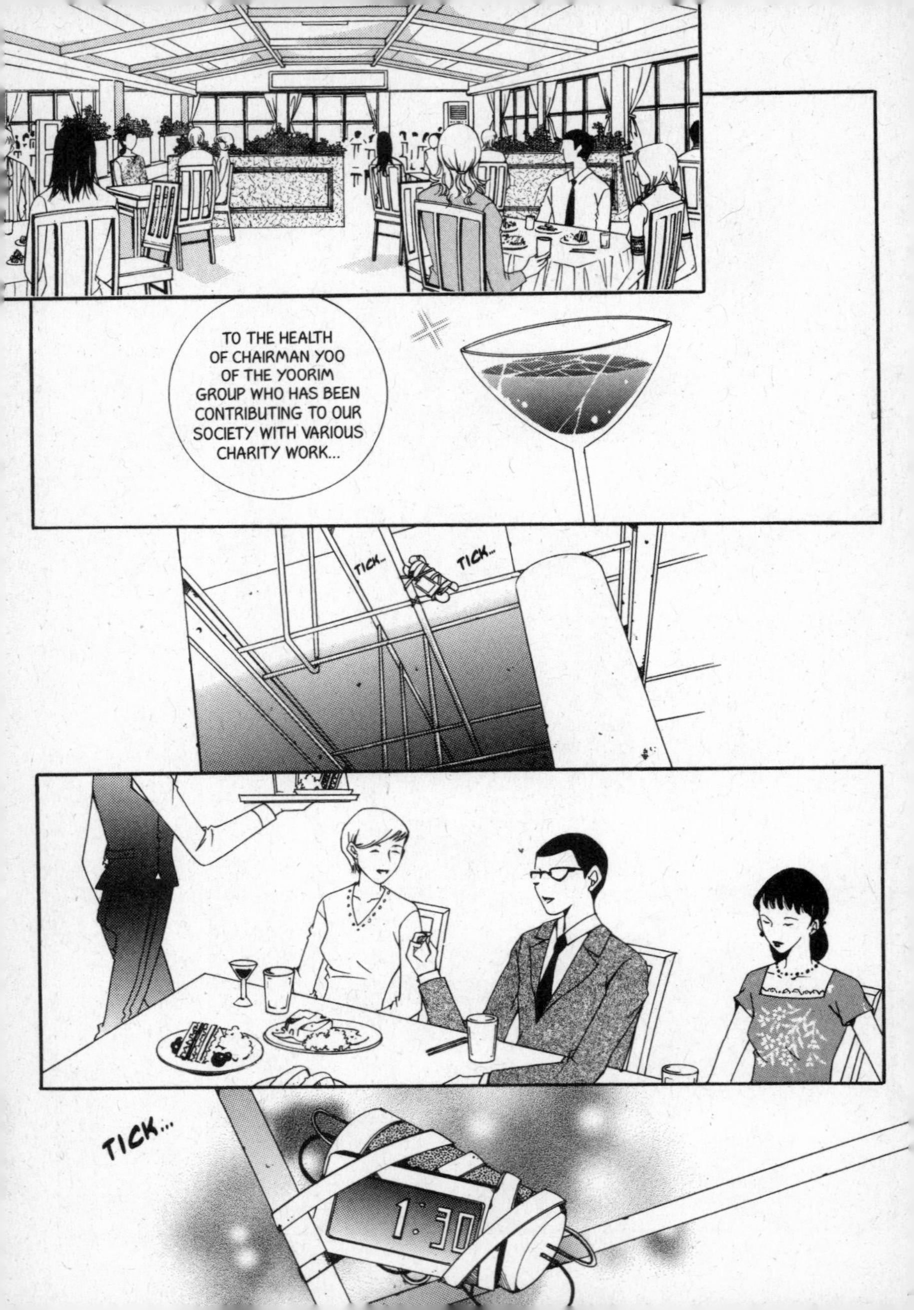
TO THE HEALTH OF CHAIRMAN YOO OF THE YOORIM GROUP WHO HAS BEEN CONTRIBUTING TO OUR SOCIETY WITH VARIOUS CHARITY WORK...
TICK...
TICK...
TICK...
1:30

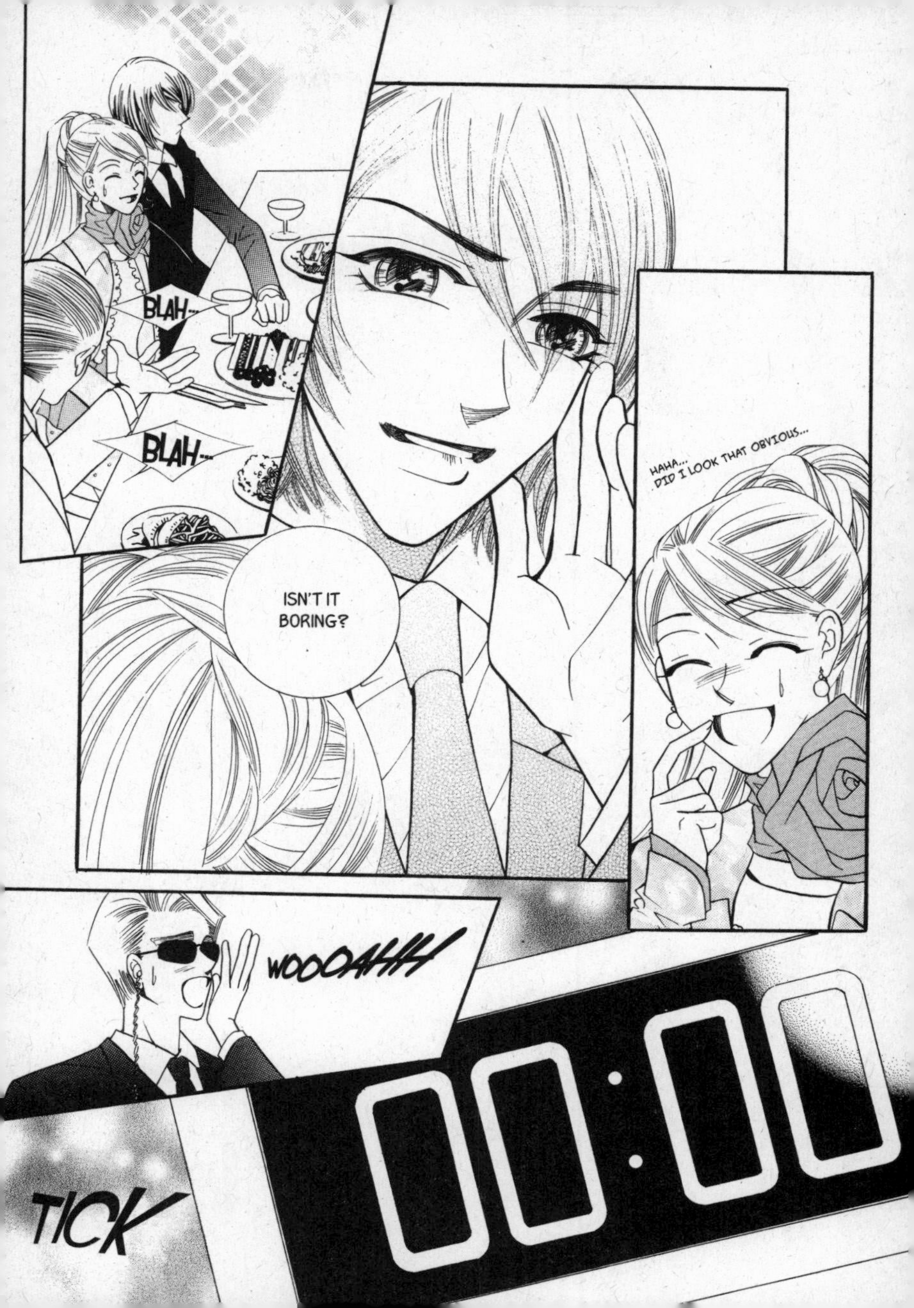
BLAH...
BLAH...
ISN'T IT BORING?
HAHA... DID I LOOK THAT OBVIOUS...
WOOOAHH
TICK
00:00

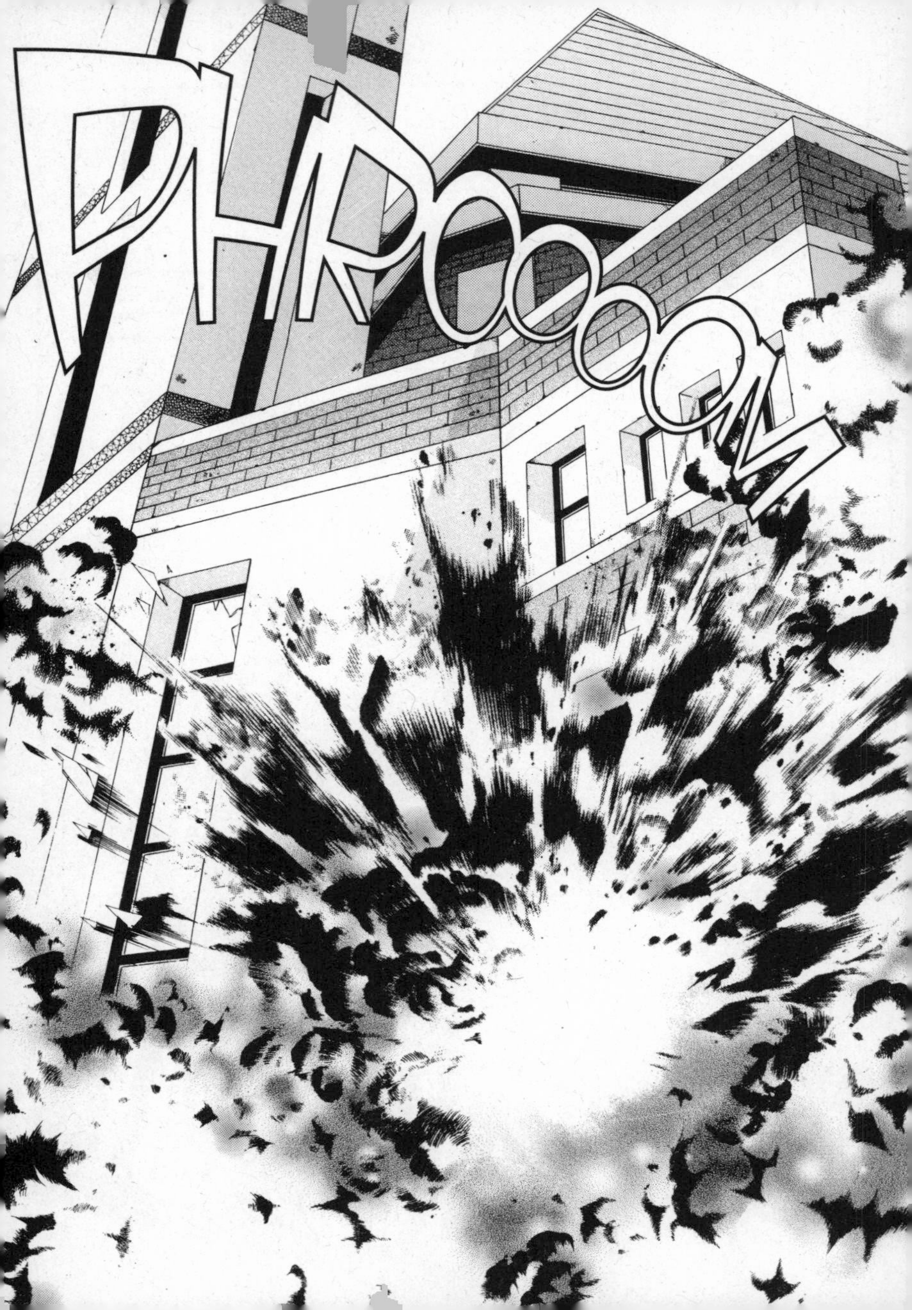
DHROOOOOOM

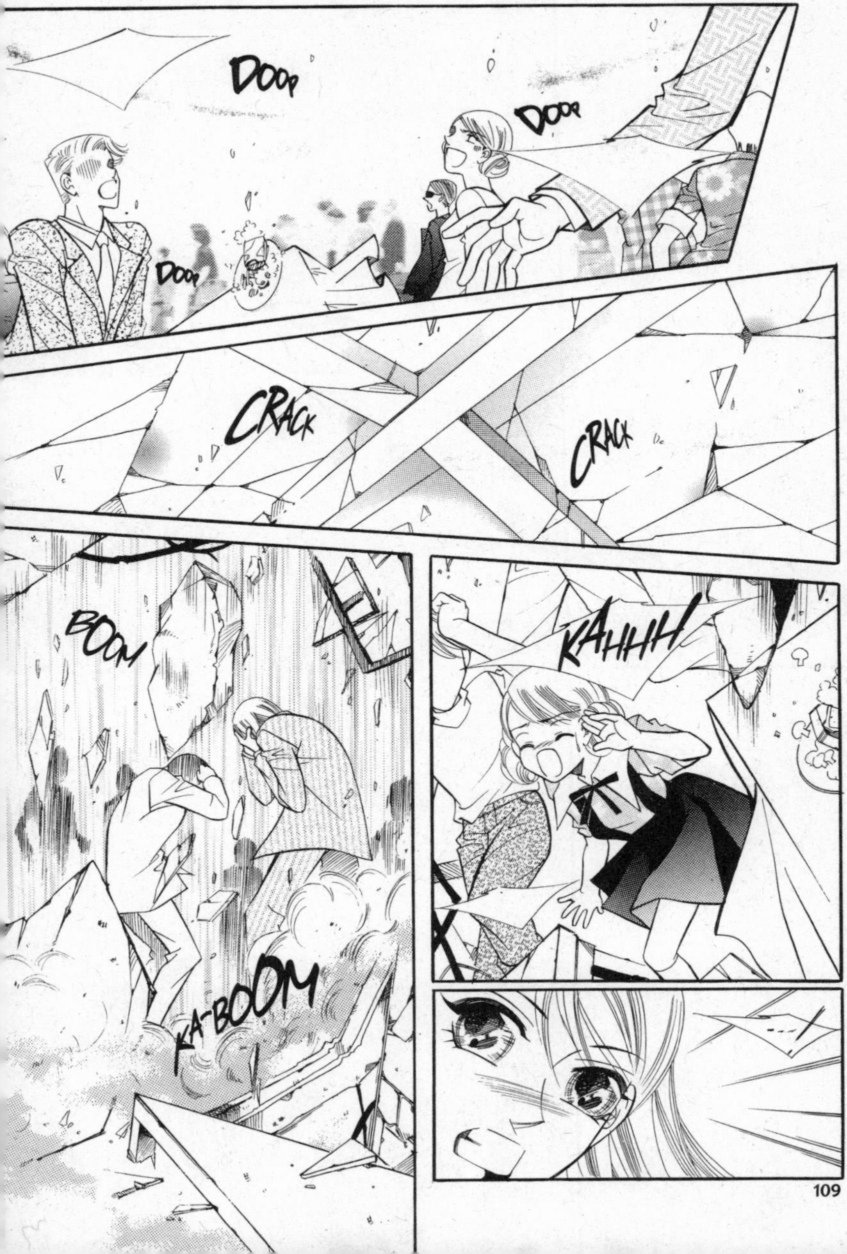
DOOP
DOOP
DOOP
CRACK
CRACK
KAHHH
BOOM
KA-BOOM

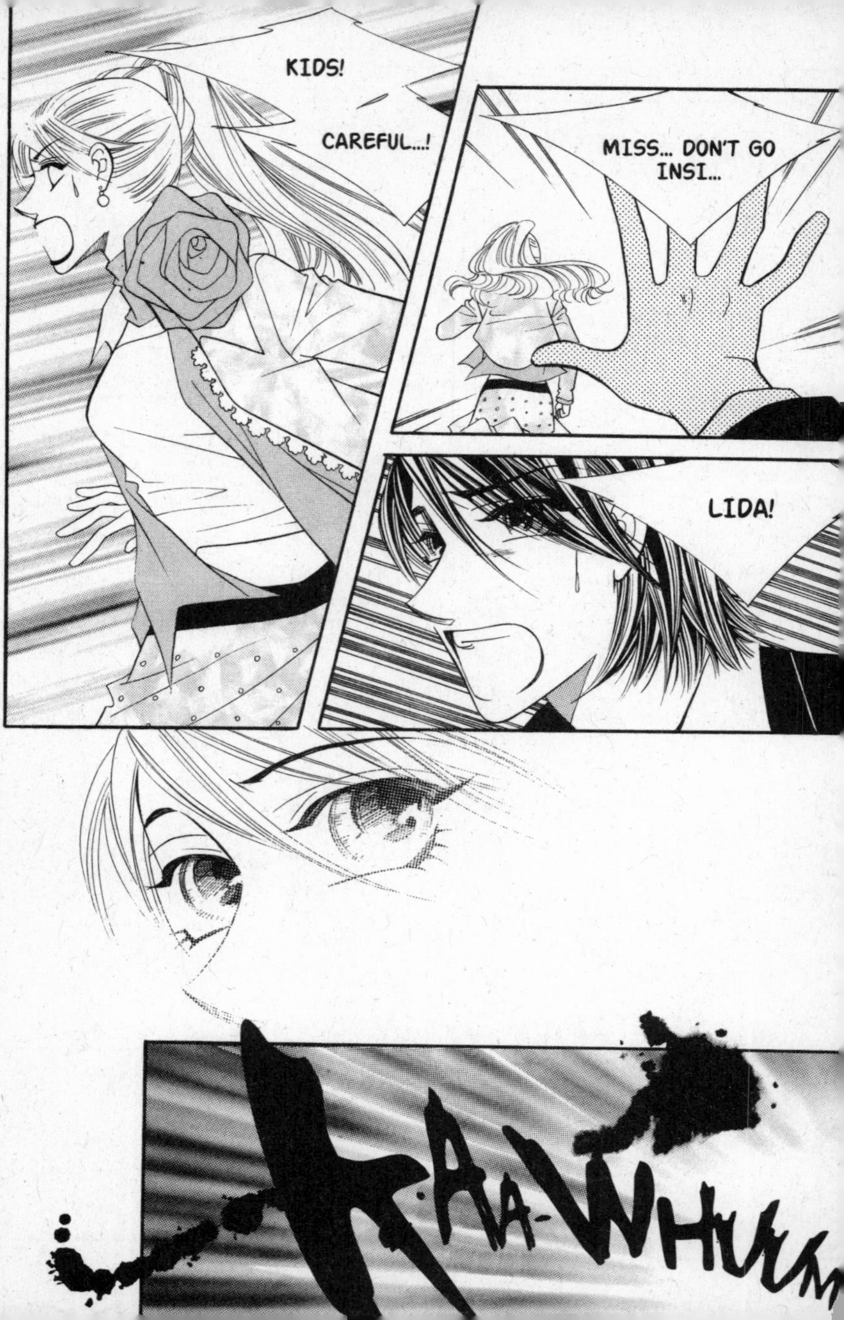
MISS... DON'T GO INSI...
LIDA!
KIDS!
CAREFUL...!

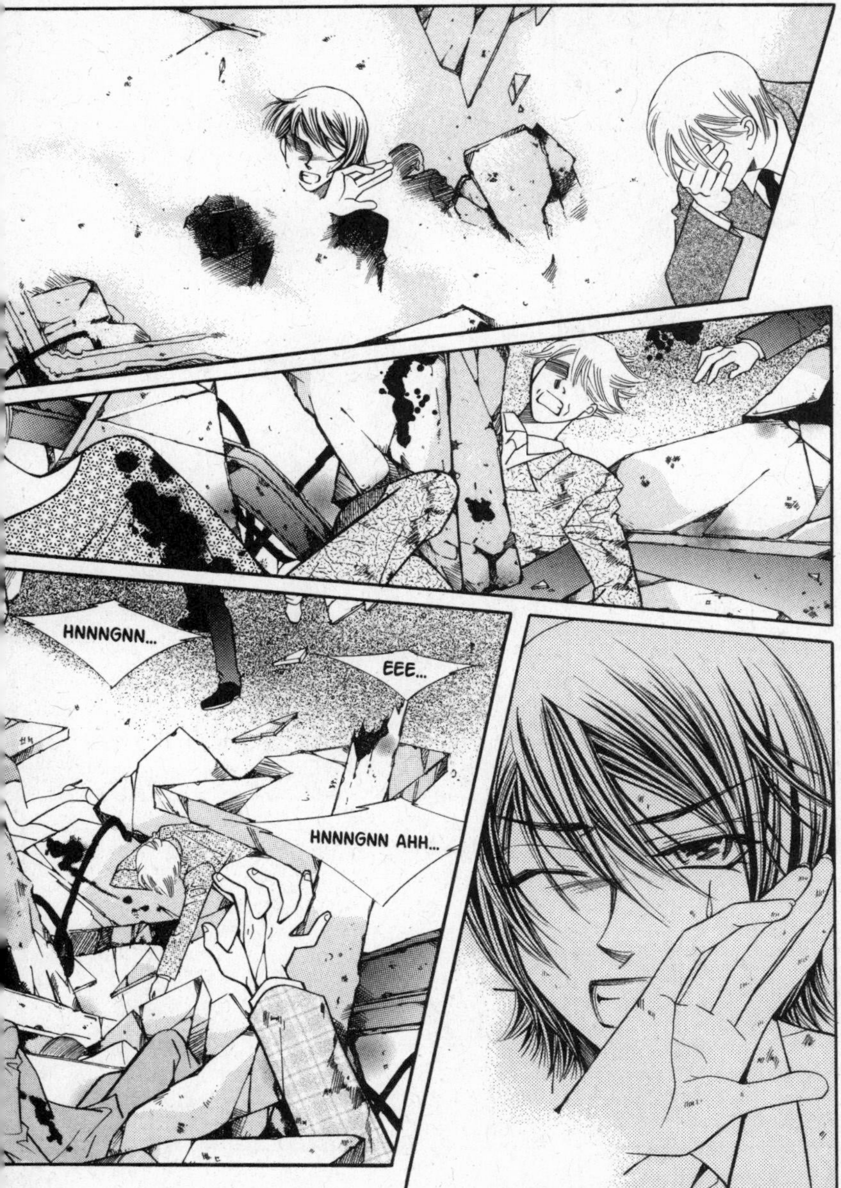
HNNNGNN...
EEE...
HNNNGNN AHH...

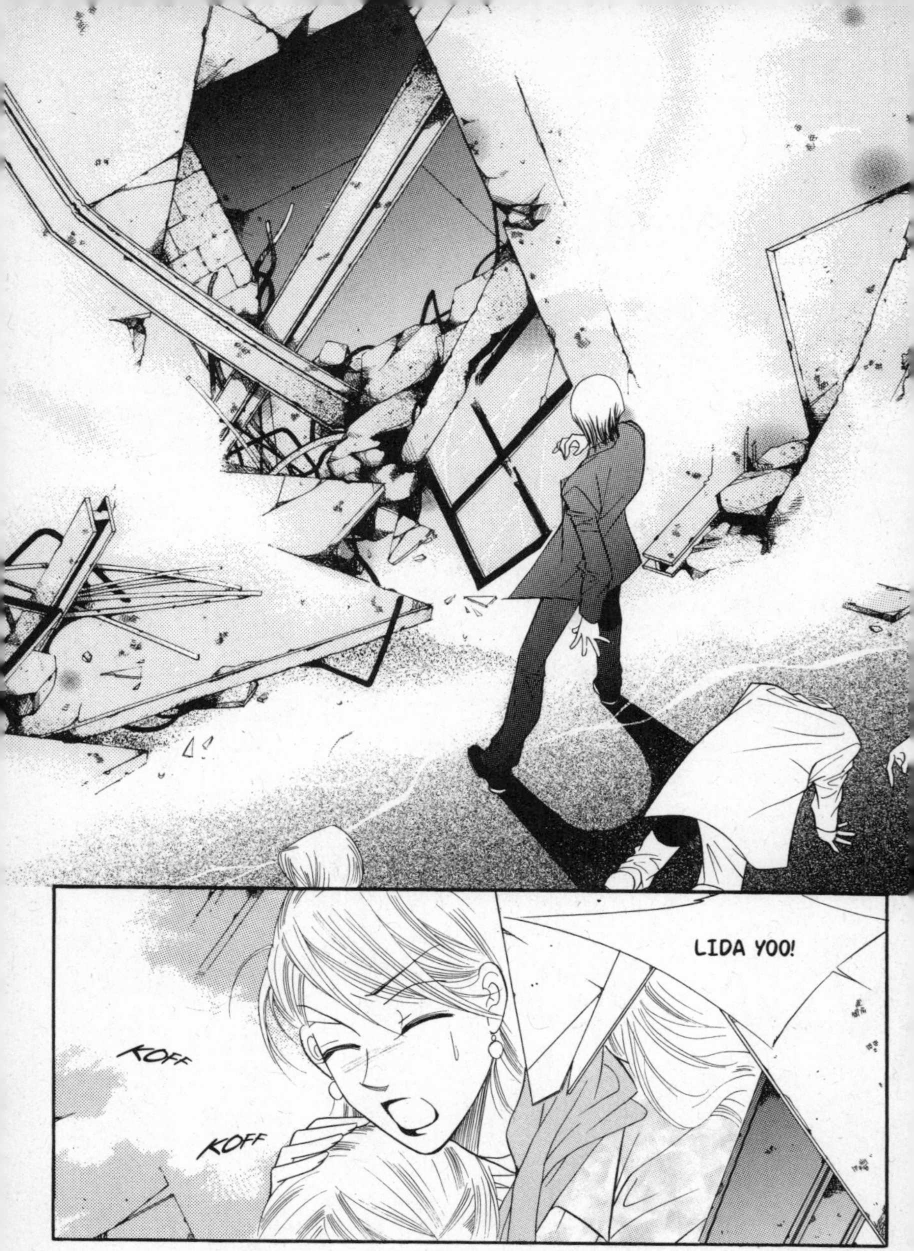
LIDA YOO!
KOFF
KOFF

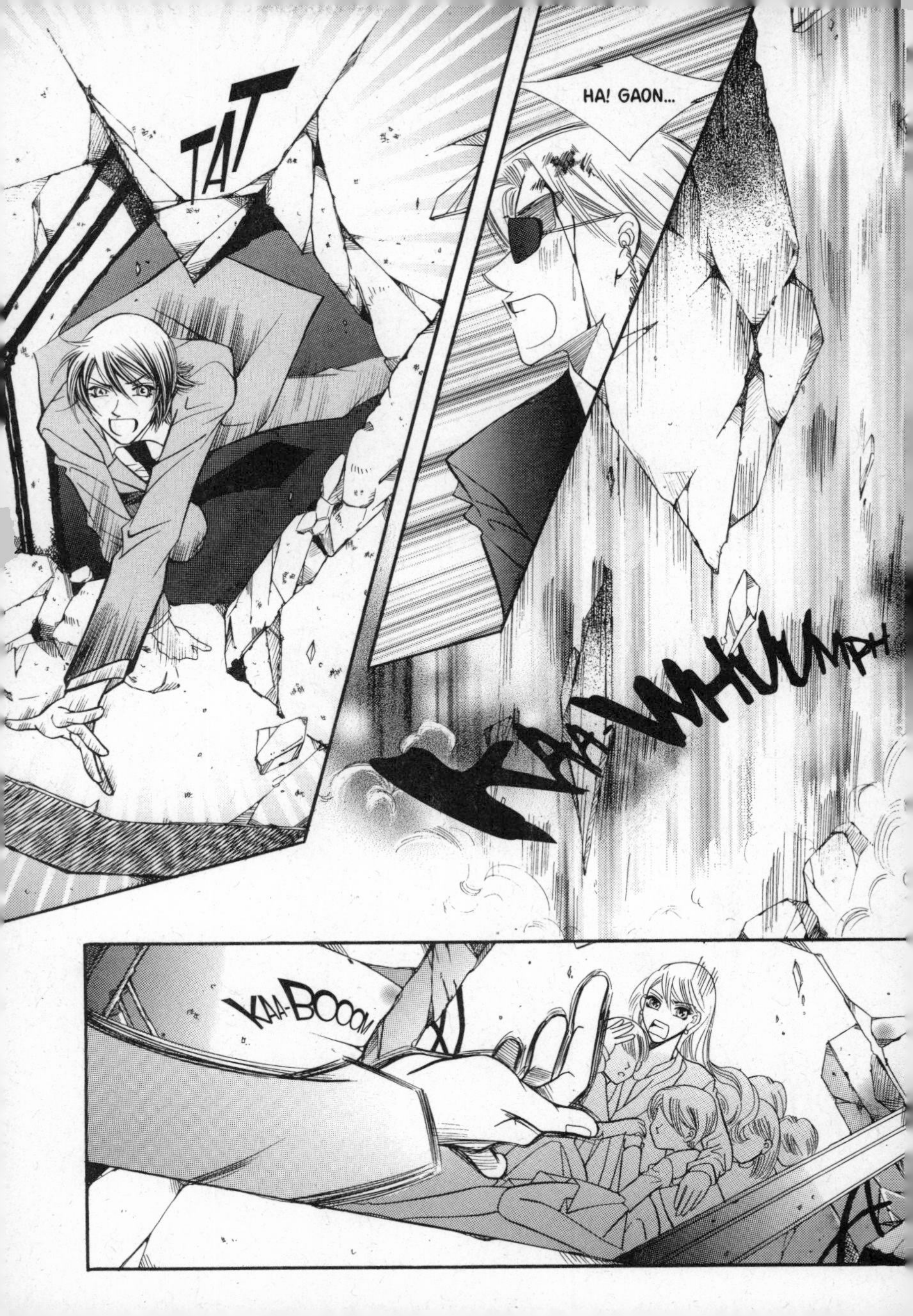

HA! GAON...
TAT
KAA-WHUUMPH
KAA-BOOOM

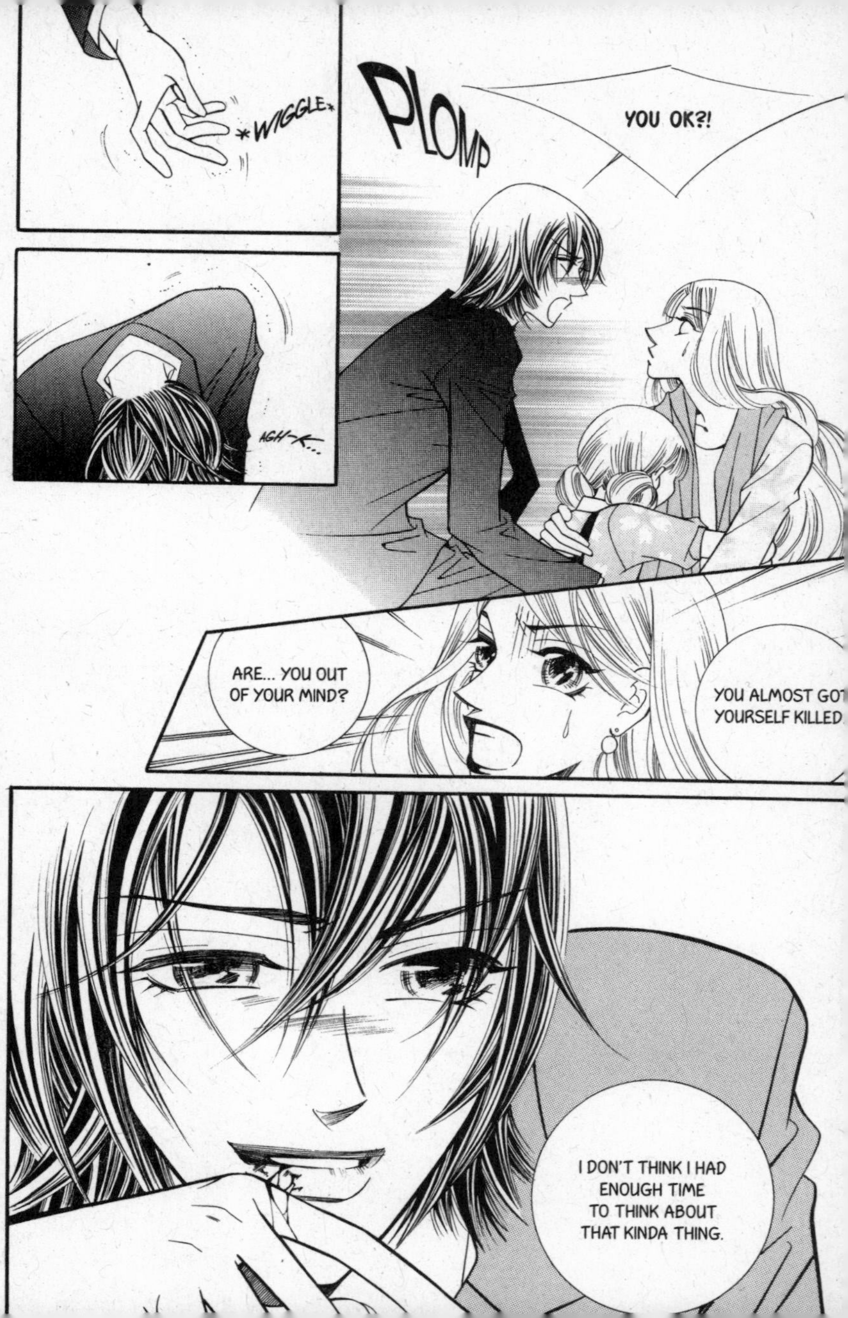
WIGGLE
AGH-K...
PLOMP
YOU OK?!
ARE... YOU OUT OF YOUR MIND?
YOU ALMOST GOT YOURSELF KILLED.
I DON'T THINK I HAD ENOUGH TIME TO THINK ABOUT THAT KINDA THING.

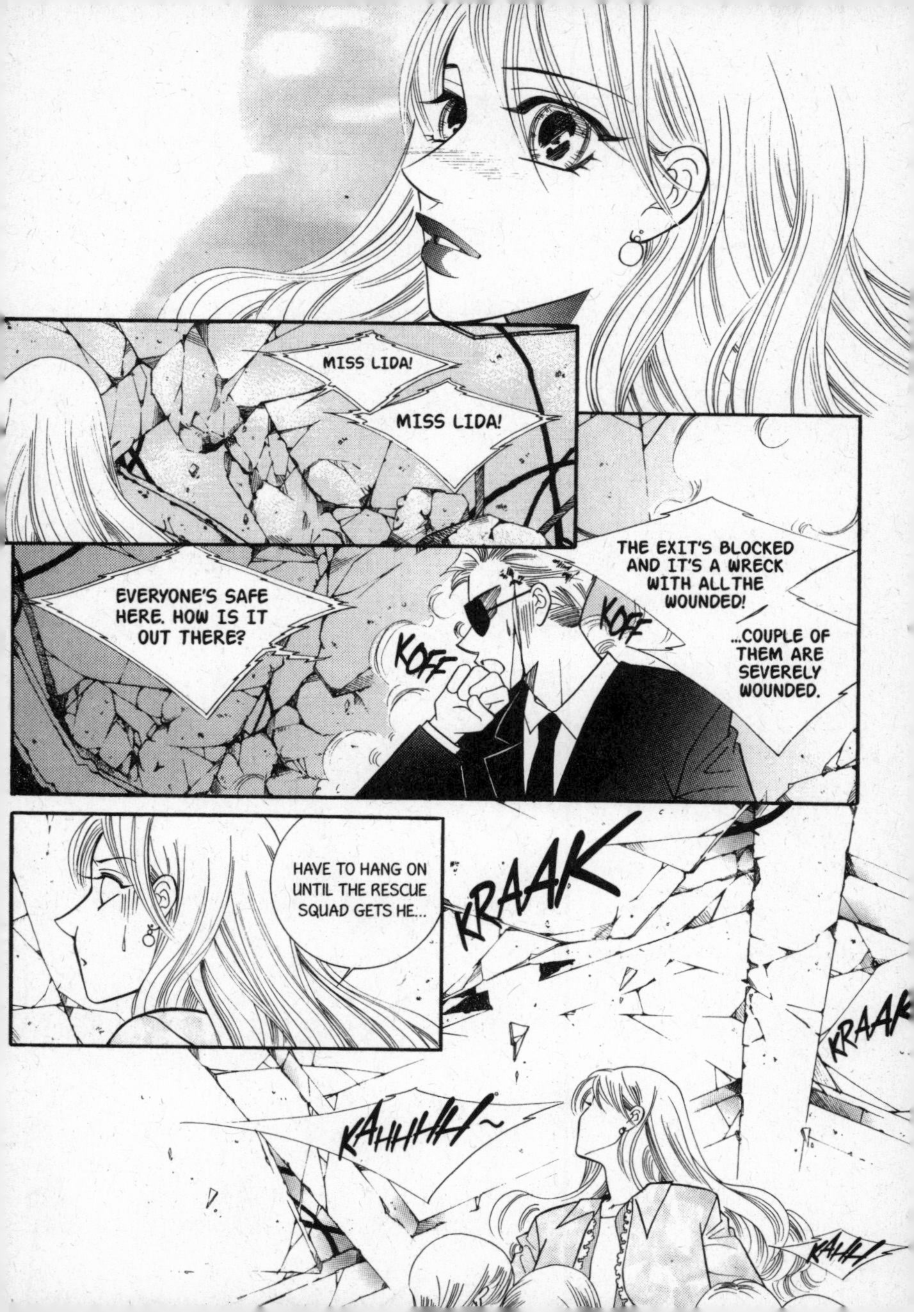
MISS LIDA!
MISS LIDA!
THE EXIT'S BLOCKED AND IT'S A WRECK WITH ALL THE WOUNDED!
EVERYONE'S SAFE HERE. HOW IS IT OUT THERE?
KOFF
KOFF
...COUPLE OF THEM ARE SEVERELY WOUNDED.
HAVE TO HANG ON UNTIL THE RESCUE SQUAD GETS HE...
KRAAK
KRAAK
KAHHHH~
KAHH!

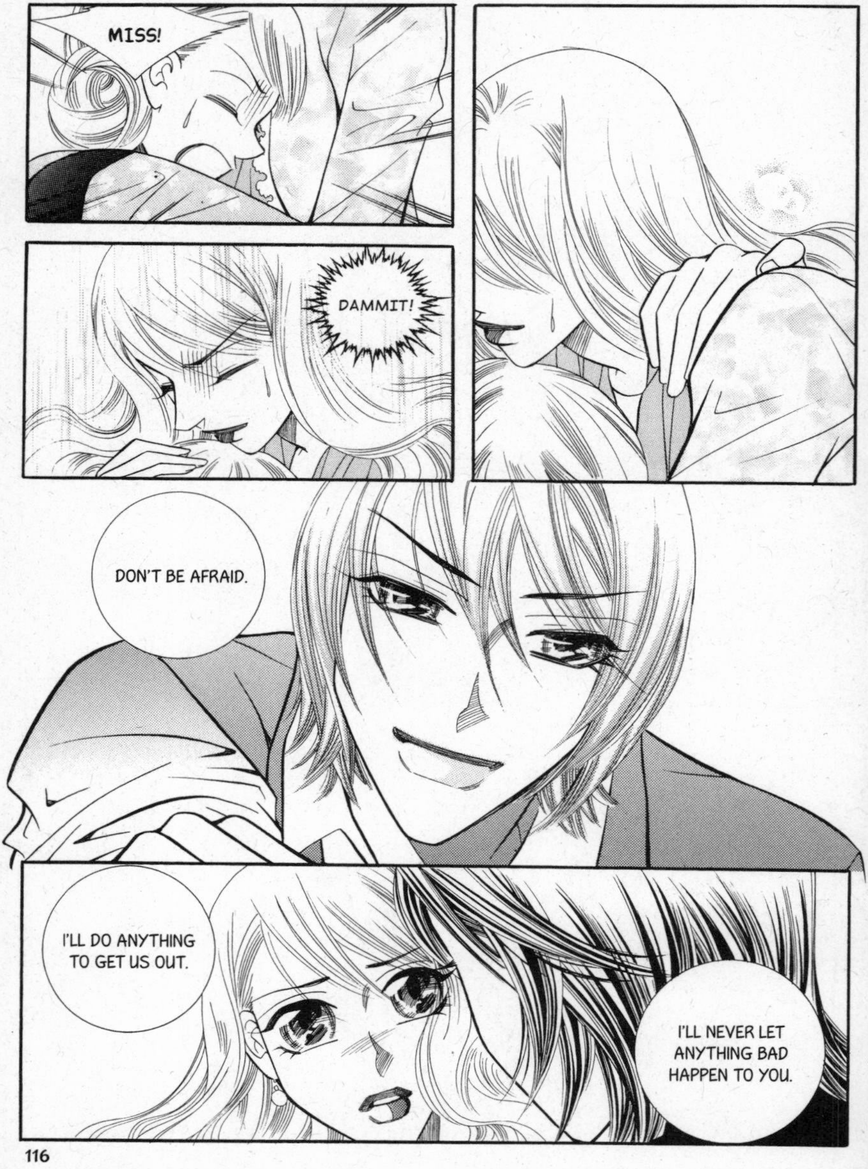

MISS!
DAMMIT!
DON'T BE AFRAID.
I'LL DO ANYTHING TO GET US OUT.
I'LL NEVER LET ANYTHING BAD HAPPEN TO YOU.

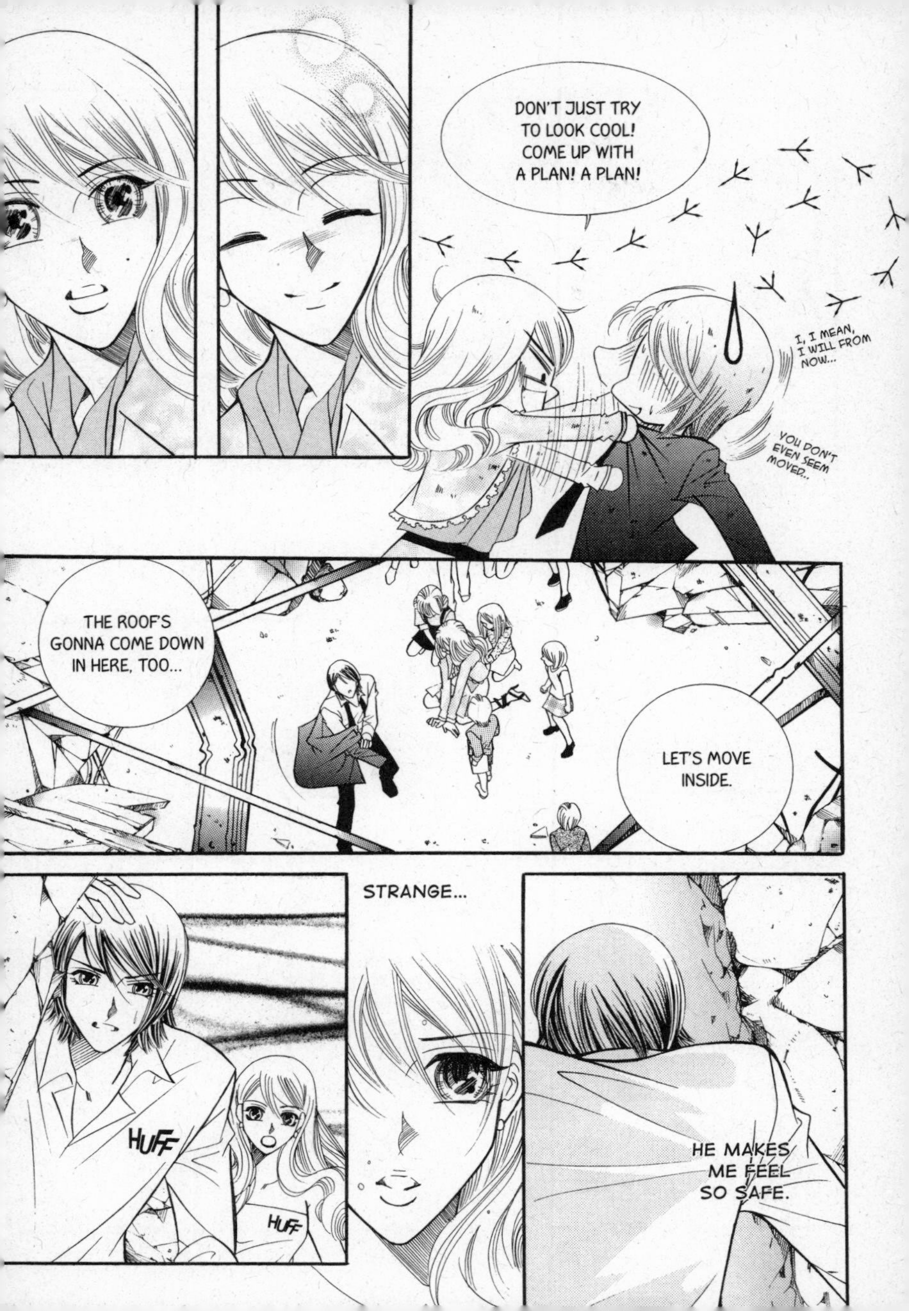

DON'T JUST TRY TO LOOK COOL! COME UP WITH A PLAN! A PLAN!
I, I MEAN, I WILL FROM NOW...
YOU DON'T EVEN SEEM MOVED...
THE ROOF'S GONNA COME DOWN IN HERE, TOO...
LET'S MOVE INSIDE.
HUFF
HUFF
STRANGE...
HE MAKES ME FEEL SO SAFE.

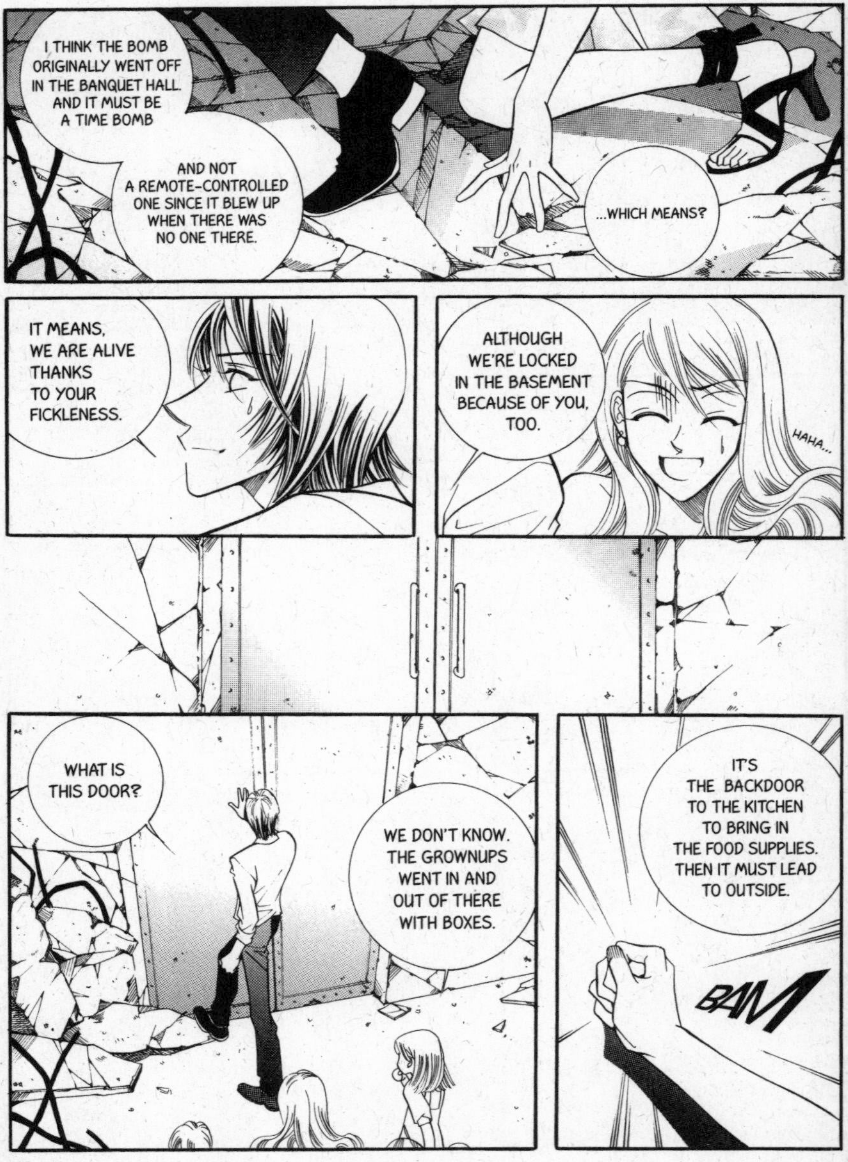

I THINK THE BOMB ORIGINALLY WENT OFF IN THE BANQUET HALL. AND IT MUST BE A TIME BOMB
AND NOT A REMOTE-CONTROLLED ONE SINCE IT BLEW UP WHEN THERE WAS NO ONE THERE.
...WHICH MEANS?
IT MEANS, WE ARE ALIVE THANKS TO YOUR FICKLENESS.
ALTHOUGH WE'RE LOCKED IN THE BASEMENT BECAUSE OF YOU, TOO.
HAHA...
WHAT IS THIS DOOR?
WE DON'T KNOW. THE GROWNUPS WENT IN AND OUT OF THERE WITH BOXES.
IT'S THE BACKDOOR TO THE KITCHEN TO BRING IN THE FOOD SUPPLIES. THEN IT MUST LEAD TO OUTSIDE.
BAM

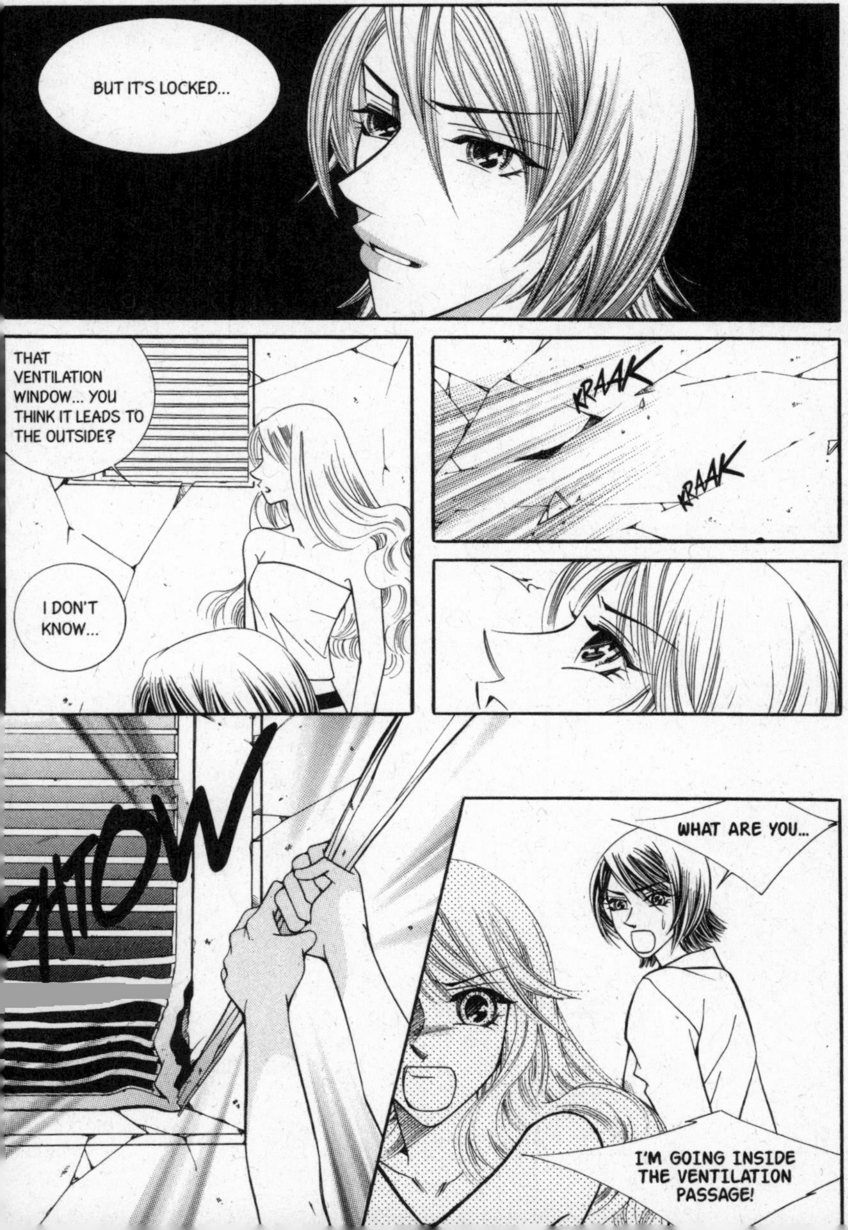
BUT IT'S LOCKED...
THAT VENTILATION WINDOW... YOU THINK IT LEADS TO THE OUTSIDE?
I DON'T KNOW...
KRAAK
KRAAK
PTOW
WHAT ARE YOU...
I'M GOING INSIDE THE VENTILATION PASSAGE!

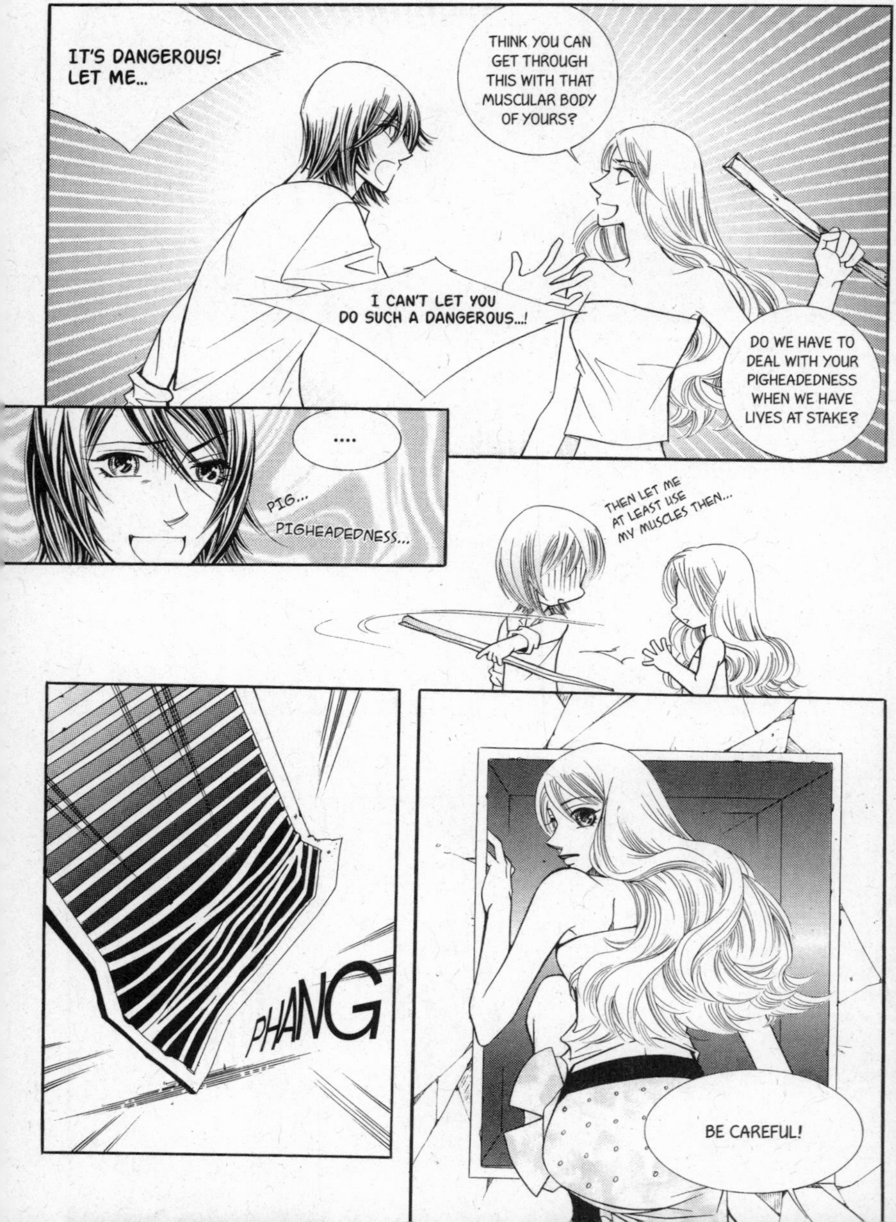
IT'S DANGEROUS! LET ME...
THINK YOU CAN GET THROUGH THIS WITH THAT MUSCULAR BODY OF YOURS?
I CAN'T LET YOU DO SUCH A DANGEROUS...!
DO WE HAVE TO DEAL WITH YOUR PIGHEADEDNESS WHEN WE HAVE LIVES AT STAKE?
....
PIG...
PIGHEADEDNESS...
THEN LET ME AT LEAST USE MY MUSCLES THEN...
PHANG
BE CAREFUL!

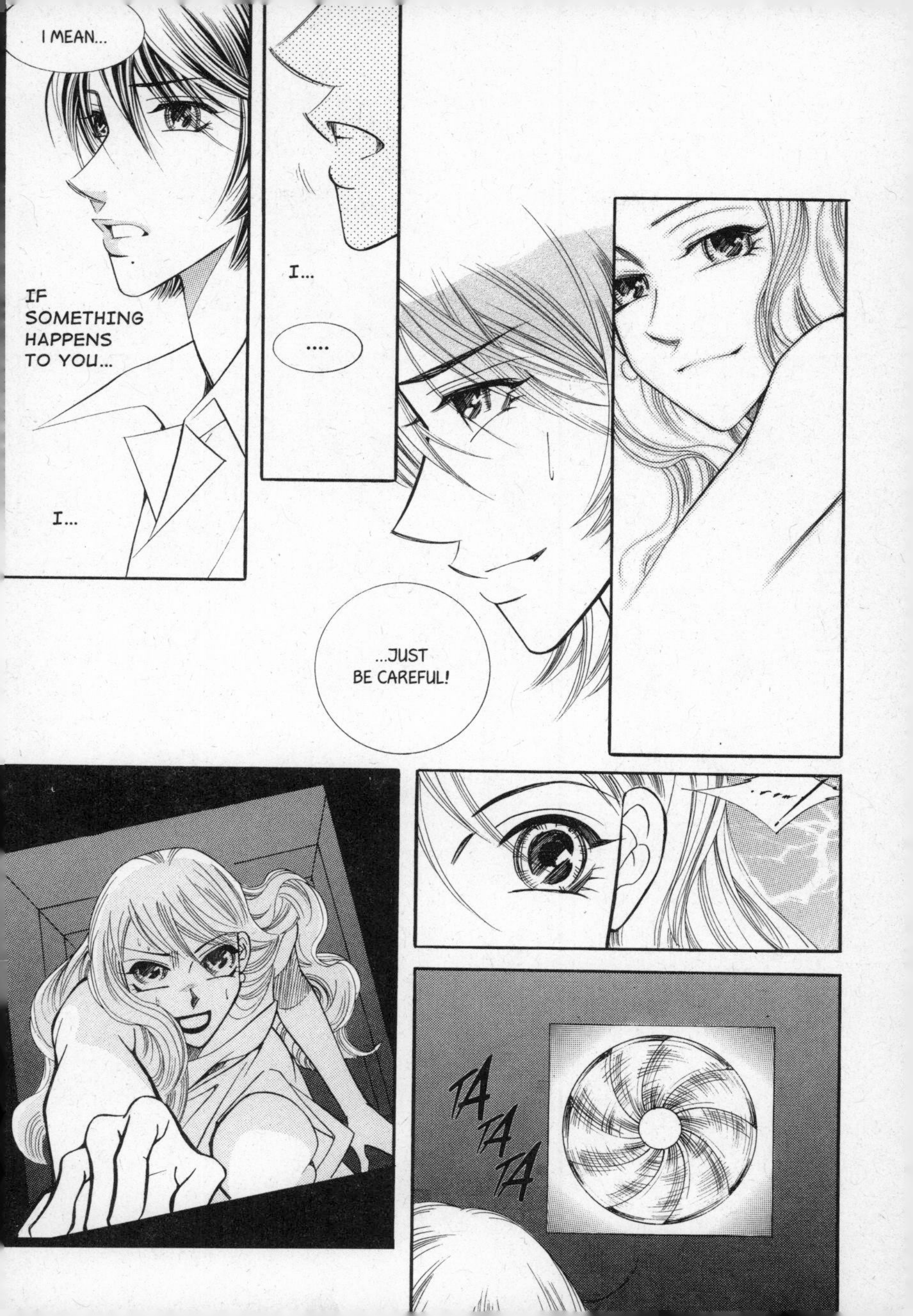
I MEAN...
IF SOMETHING HAPPENS TO YOU...
I...
I...
....
...JUST BE CAREFUL!
TA TA TA TA

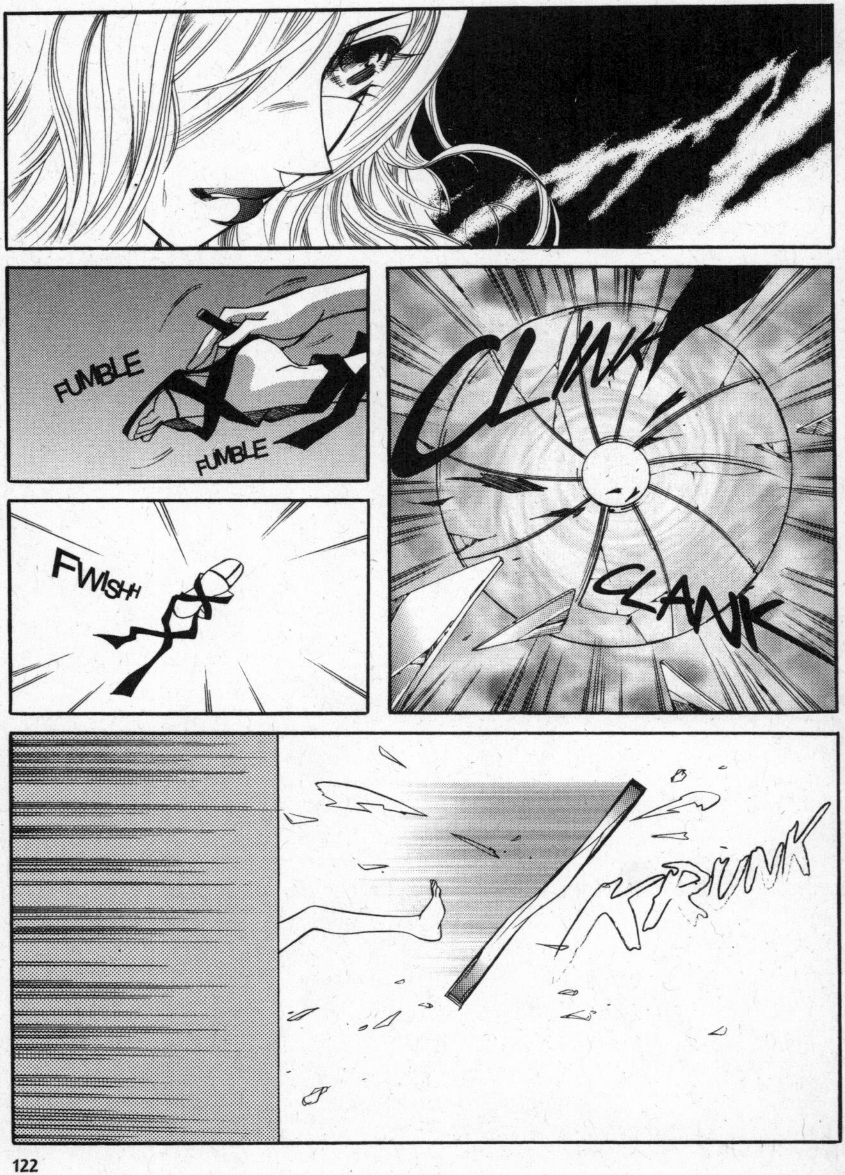
FUMBLE
FUMBLE
CLINK
CLANK
FWISH
KRIINK

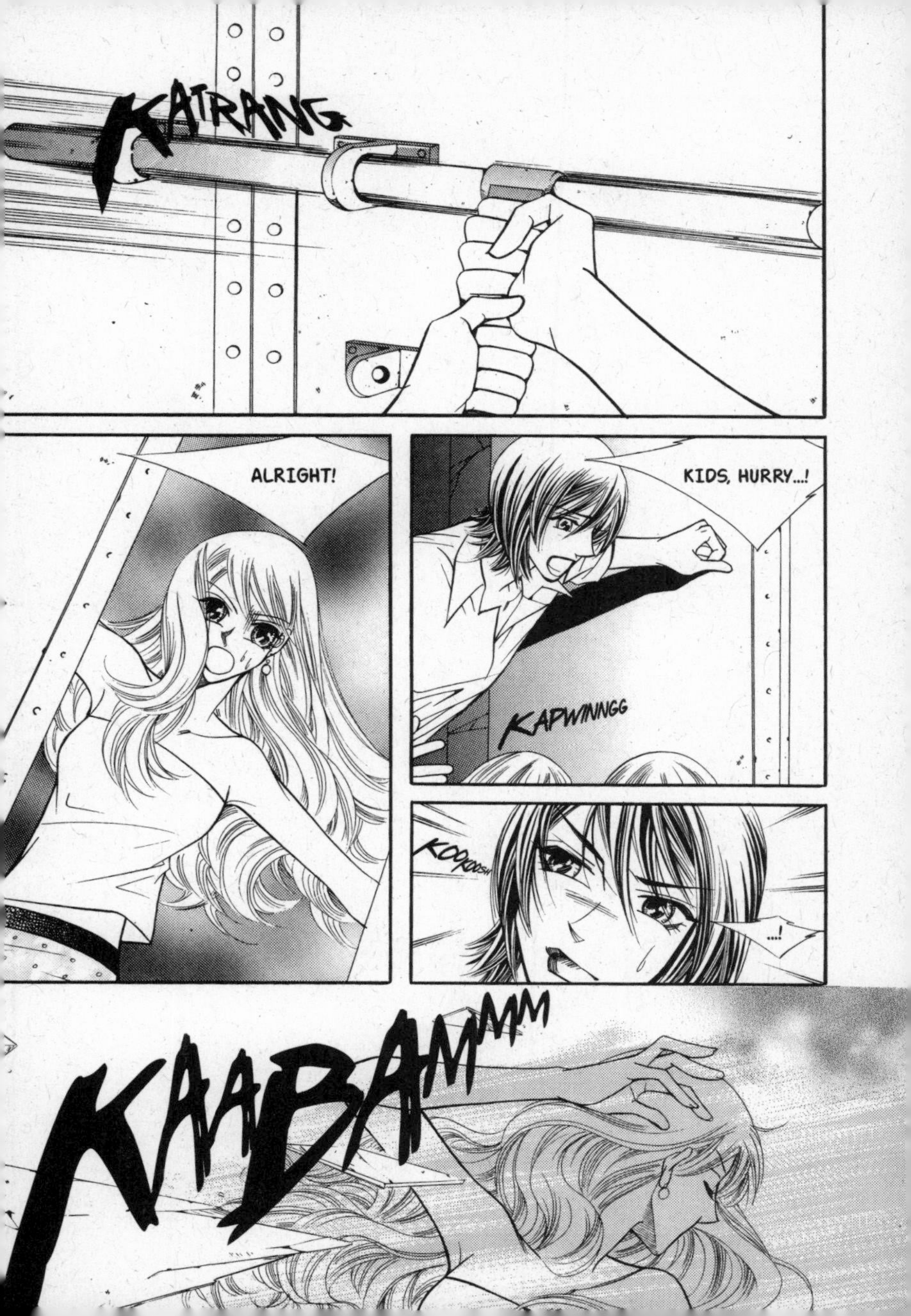
KATRANG
KIDS, HURRY...!
KAPWINNGG
ALRIGHT!
KOOKOOSH
...!
KAABAMMM

YOO, LIDA

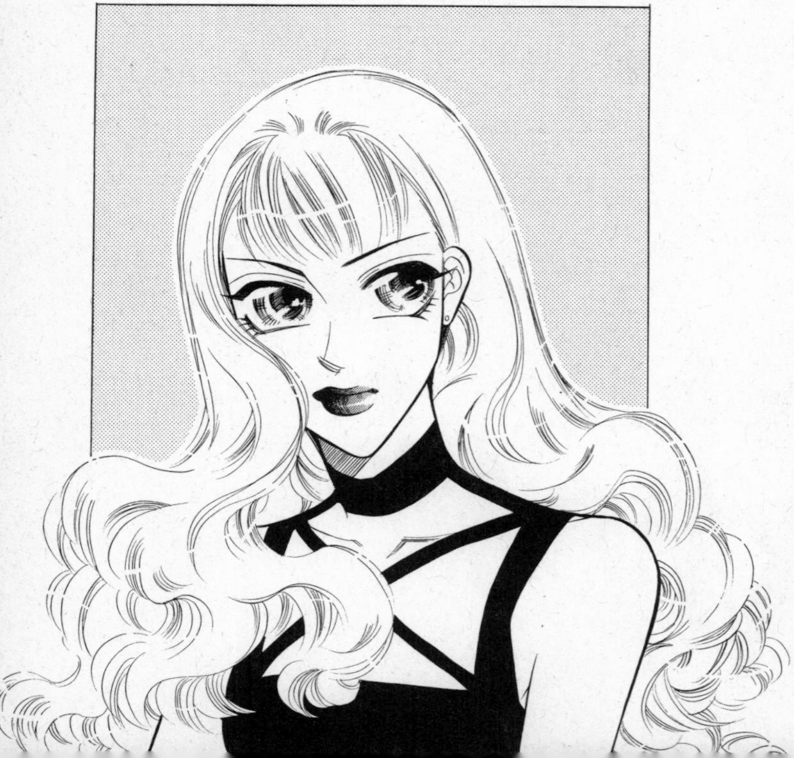

5. IMMERSION

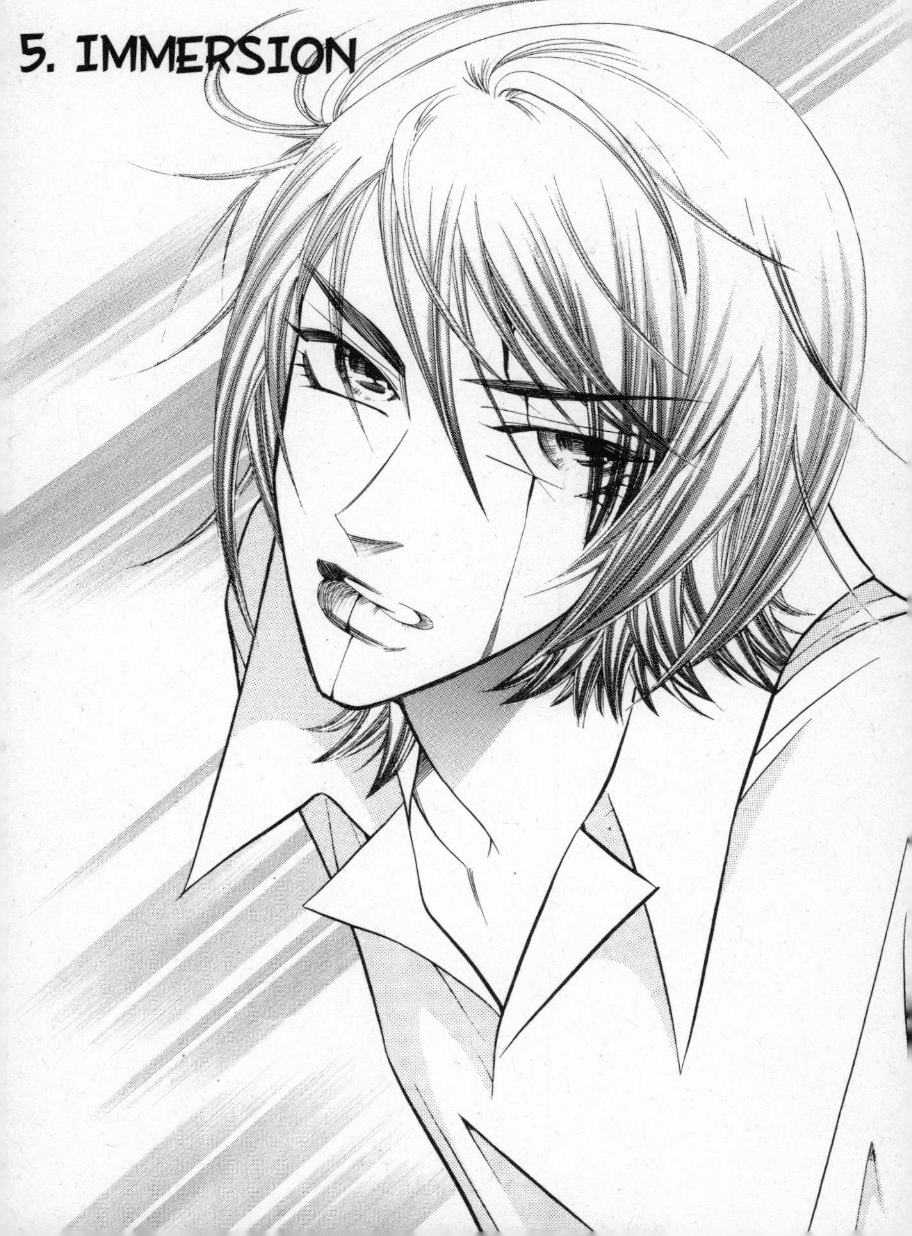

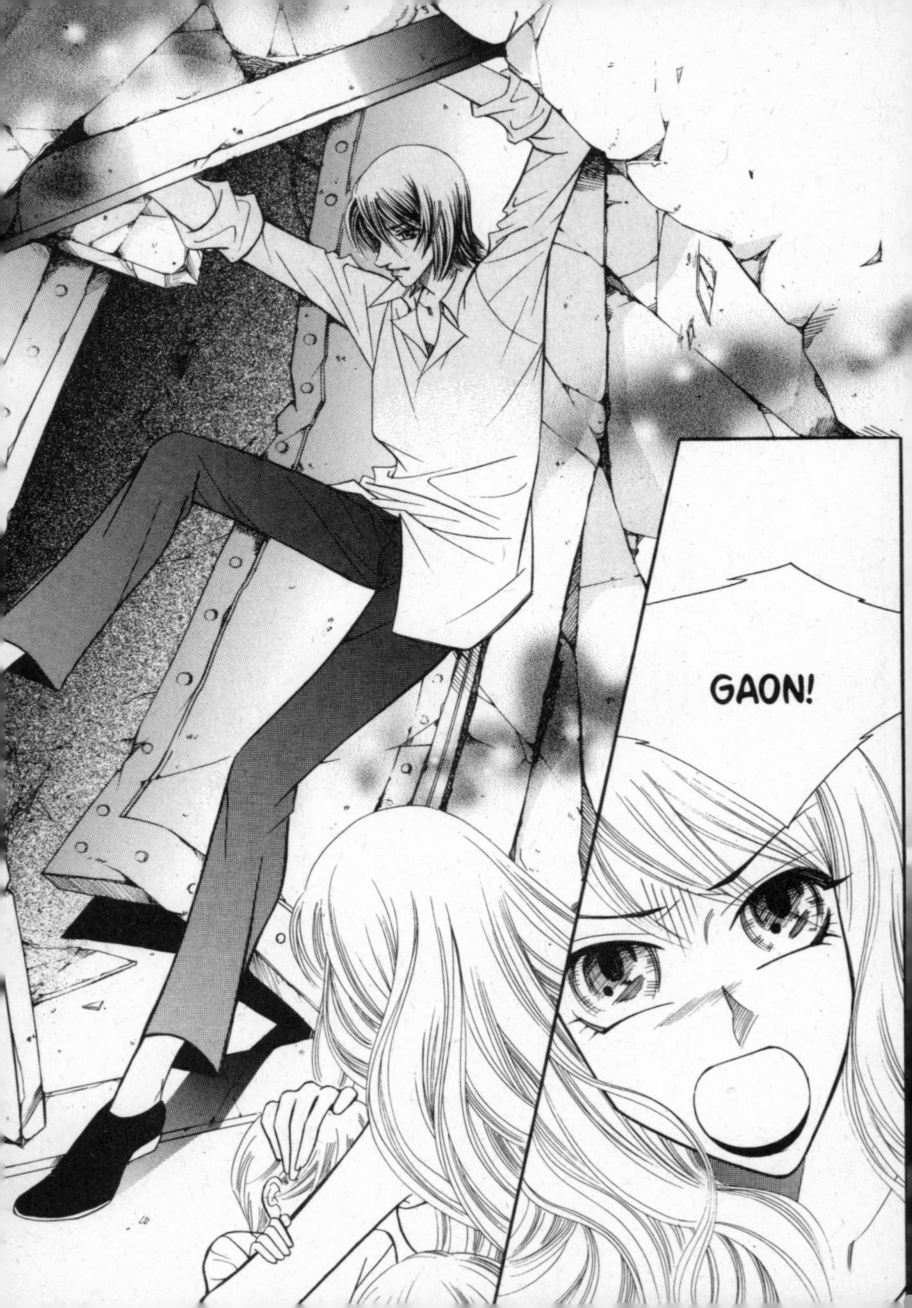
GAON!

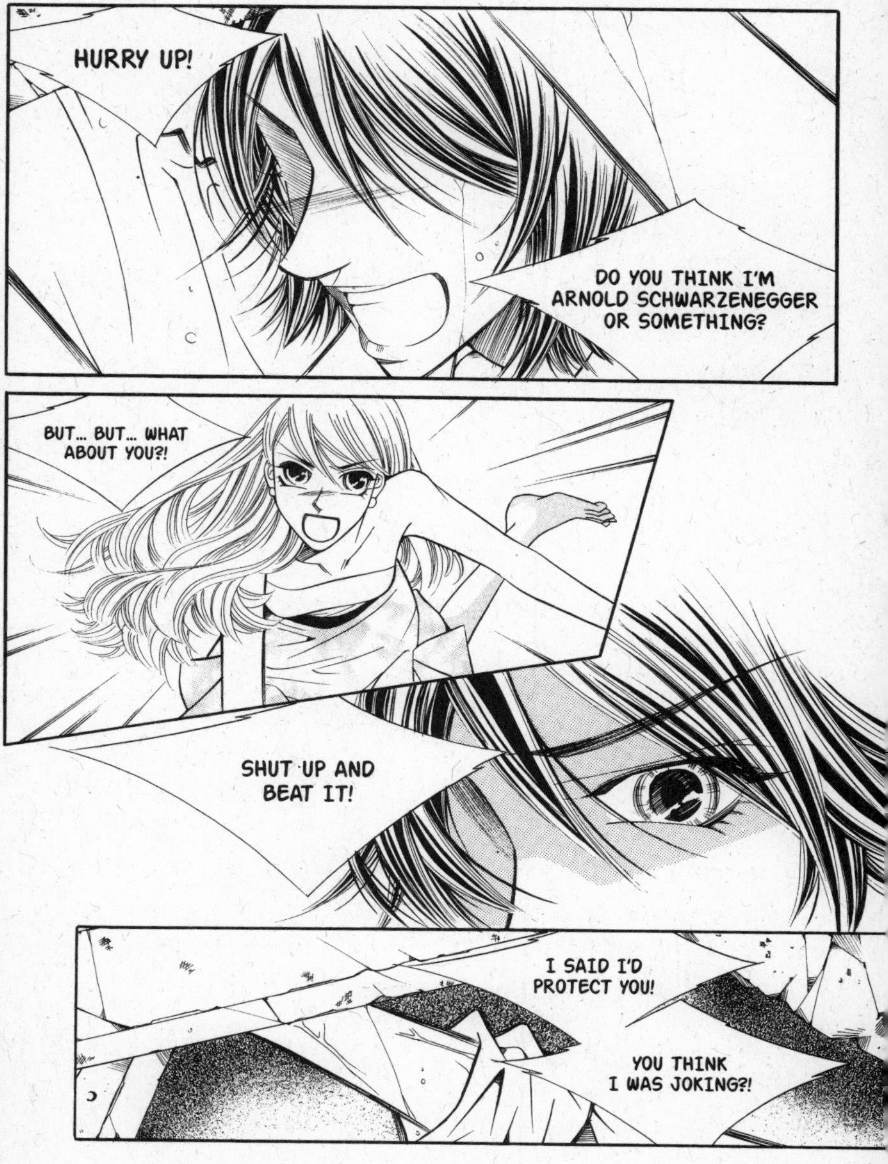
HURRY UP!
DO YOU THINK I'M ARNOLD SCHWARZENEGGER OR SOMETHING?
BUT... BUT... WHAT ABOUT YOU?!
SHUT UP AND BEAT IT!
I SAID I'D PROTECT YOU!
YOU THINK I WAS JOKING?!

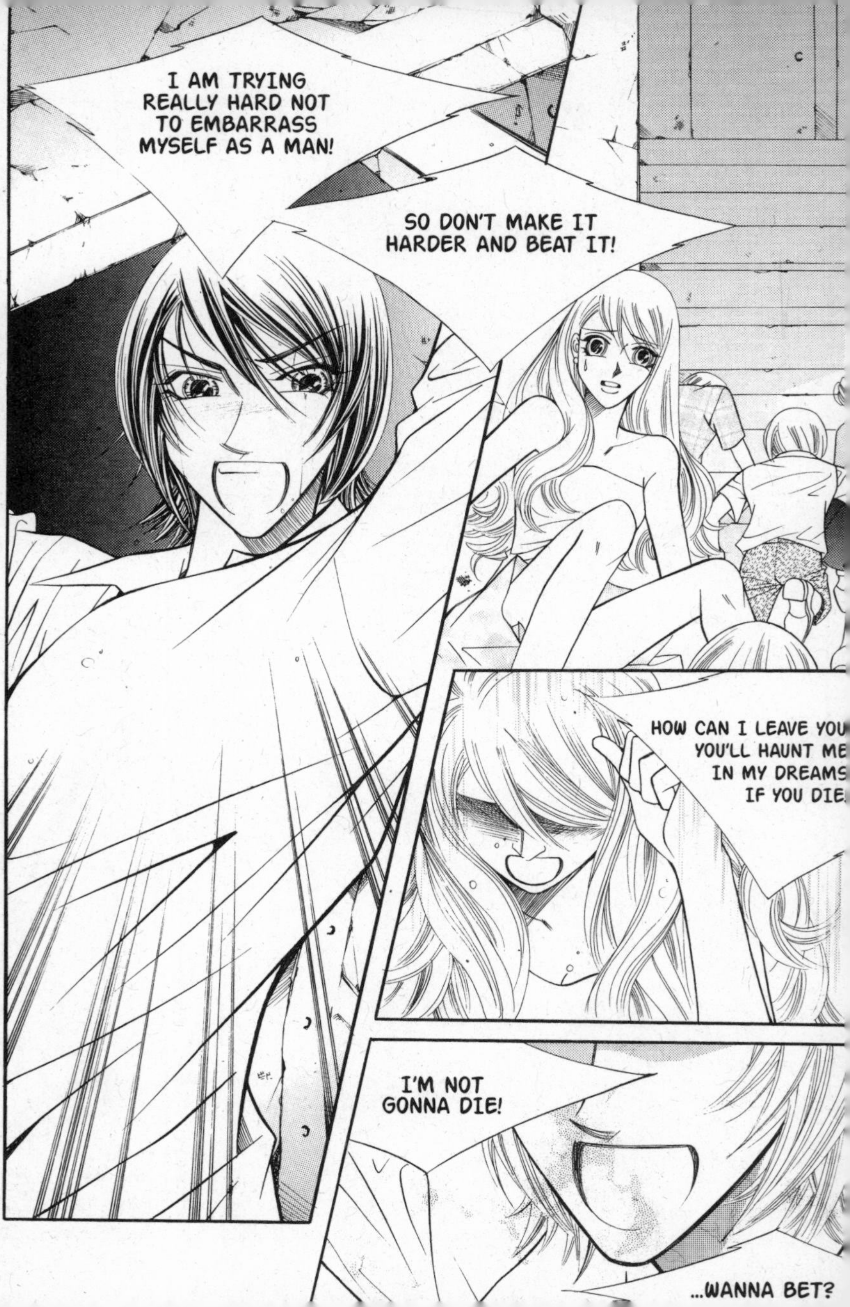
I AM TRYING REALLY HARD NOT TO EMBARRASS MYSELF AS A MAN!
SO DON'T MAKE IT HARDER AND BEAT IT!
HOW CAN I LEAVE YOU YOU'LL HAUNT ME IN MY DREAMS IF YOU DIE.
I'M NOT GONNA DIE!
...WANNA BET?

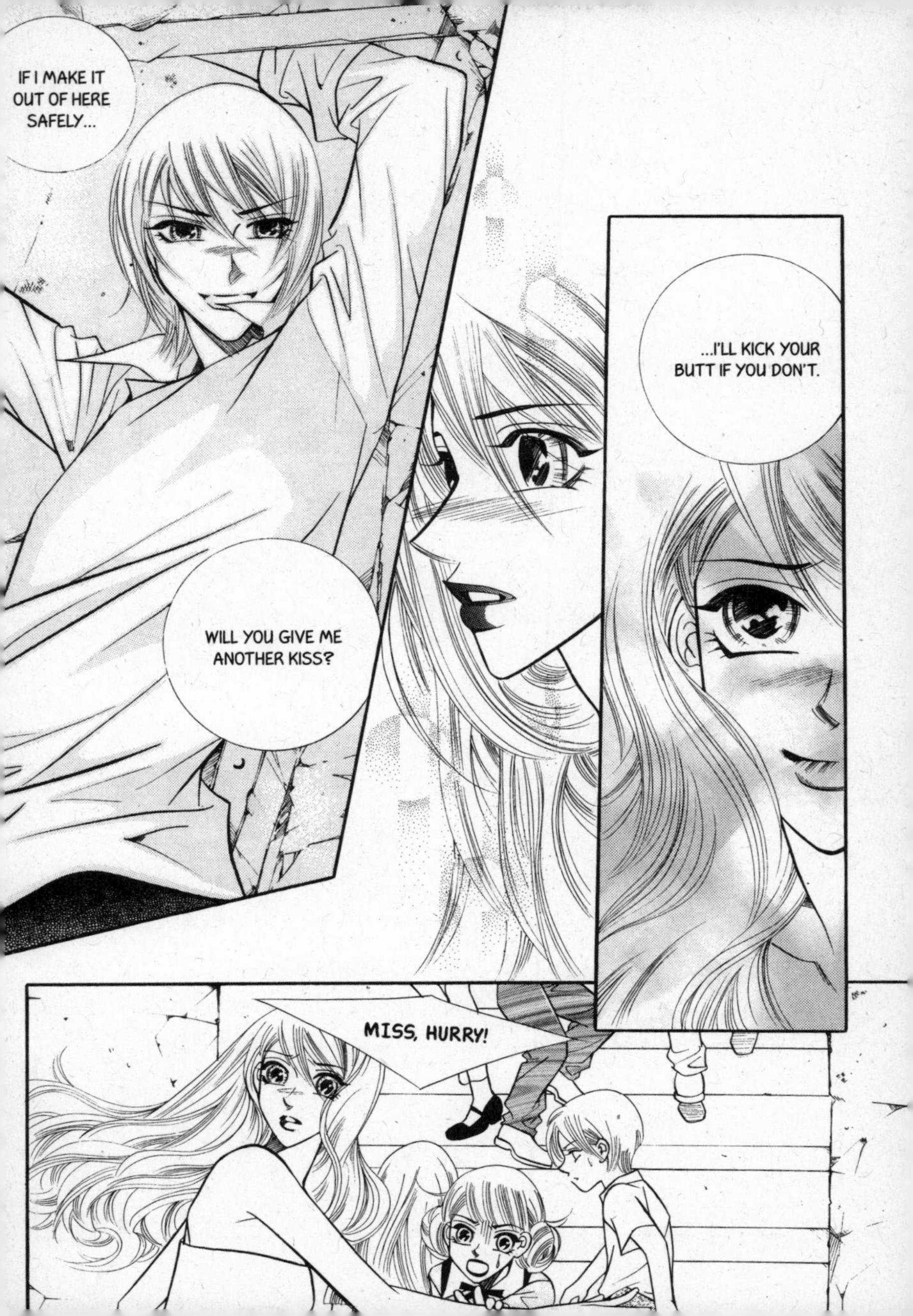
IF I MAKE IT OUT OF HERE SAFELY...
WILL YOU GIVE ME ANOTHER KISS?
...I'LL KICK YOUR BUTT IF YOU DON'T.
MISS, HURRY!

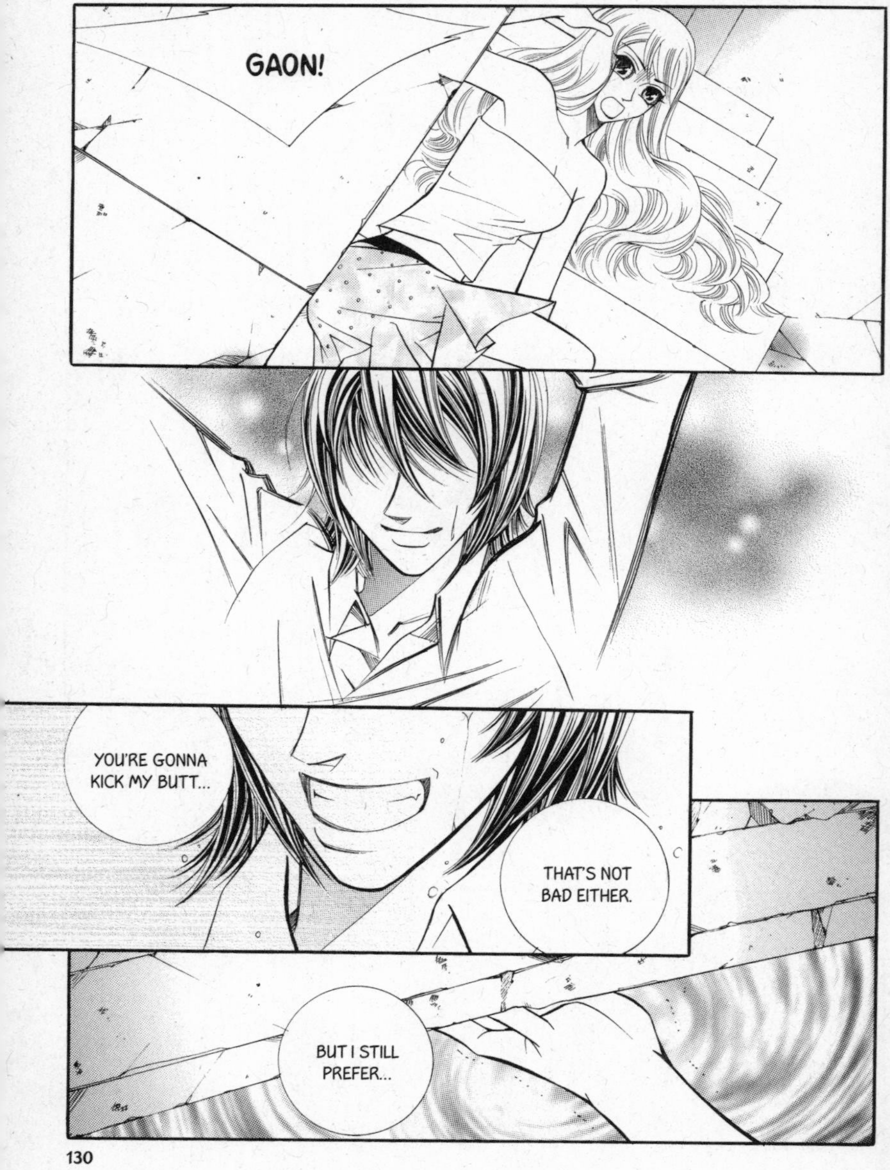
GAON!
YOU'RE GONNA KICK MY BUTT...
THAT'S NOT BAD EITHER.
BUT I STILL PREFER...

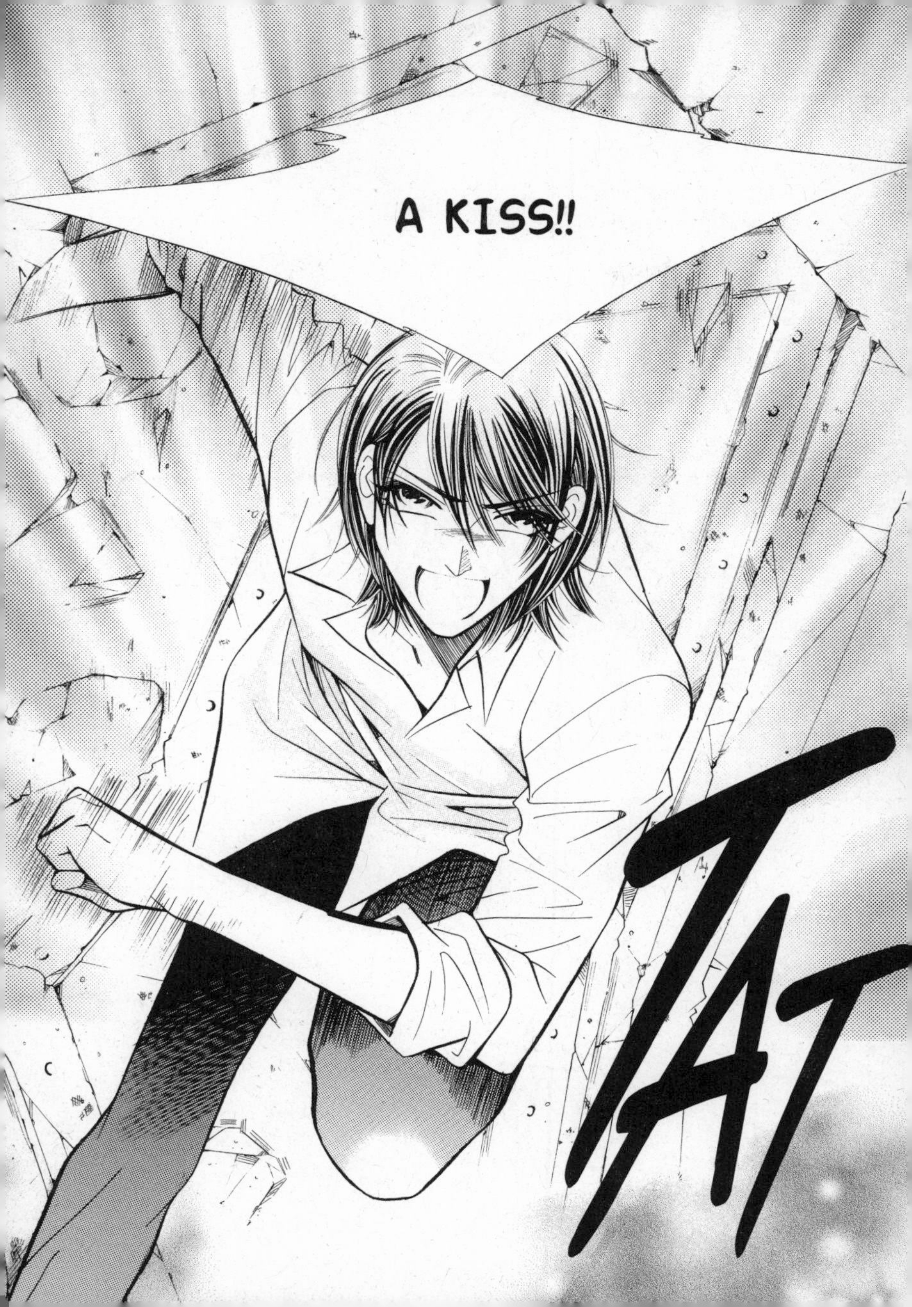
A KISS!!
TAT

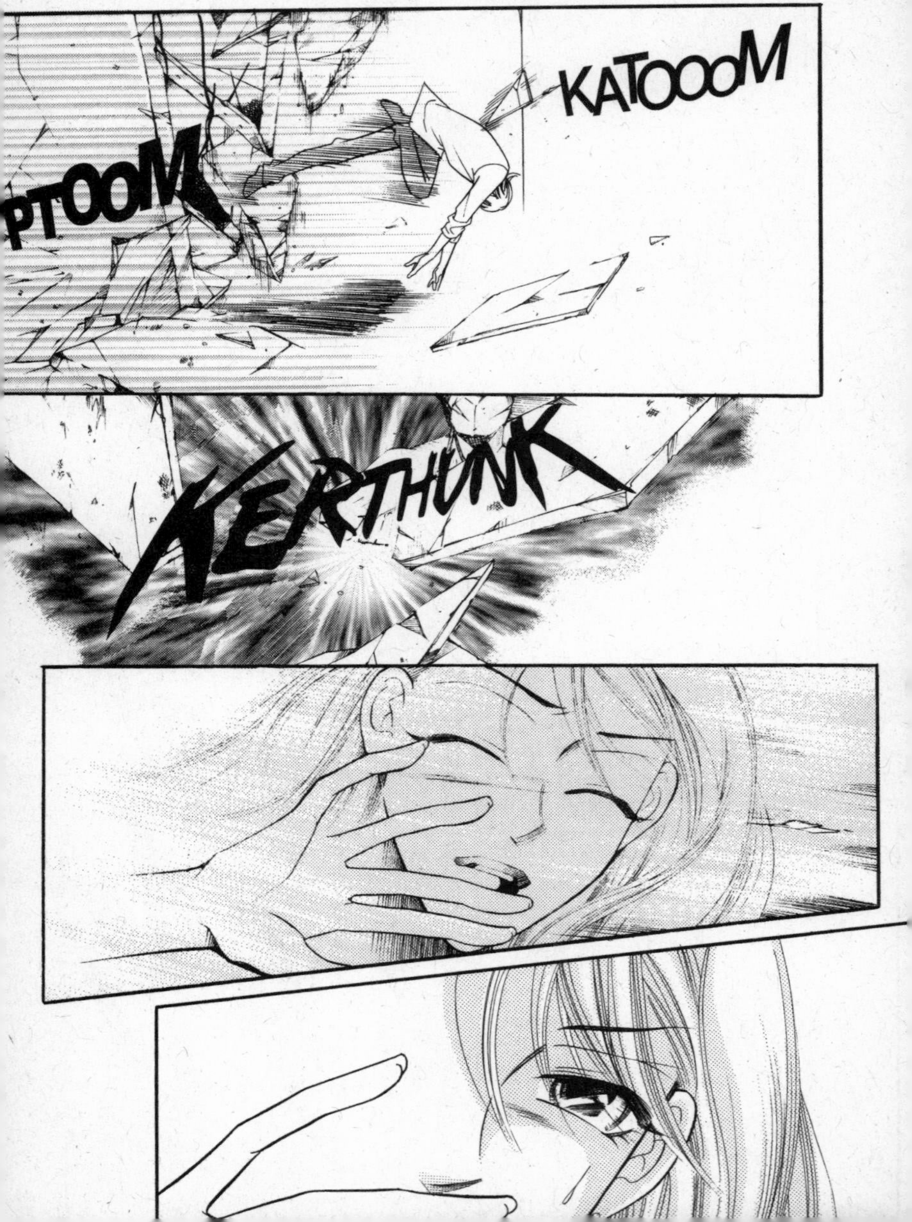
KATOOOM
PTOOM
KERTHUNK

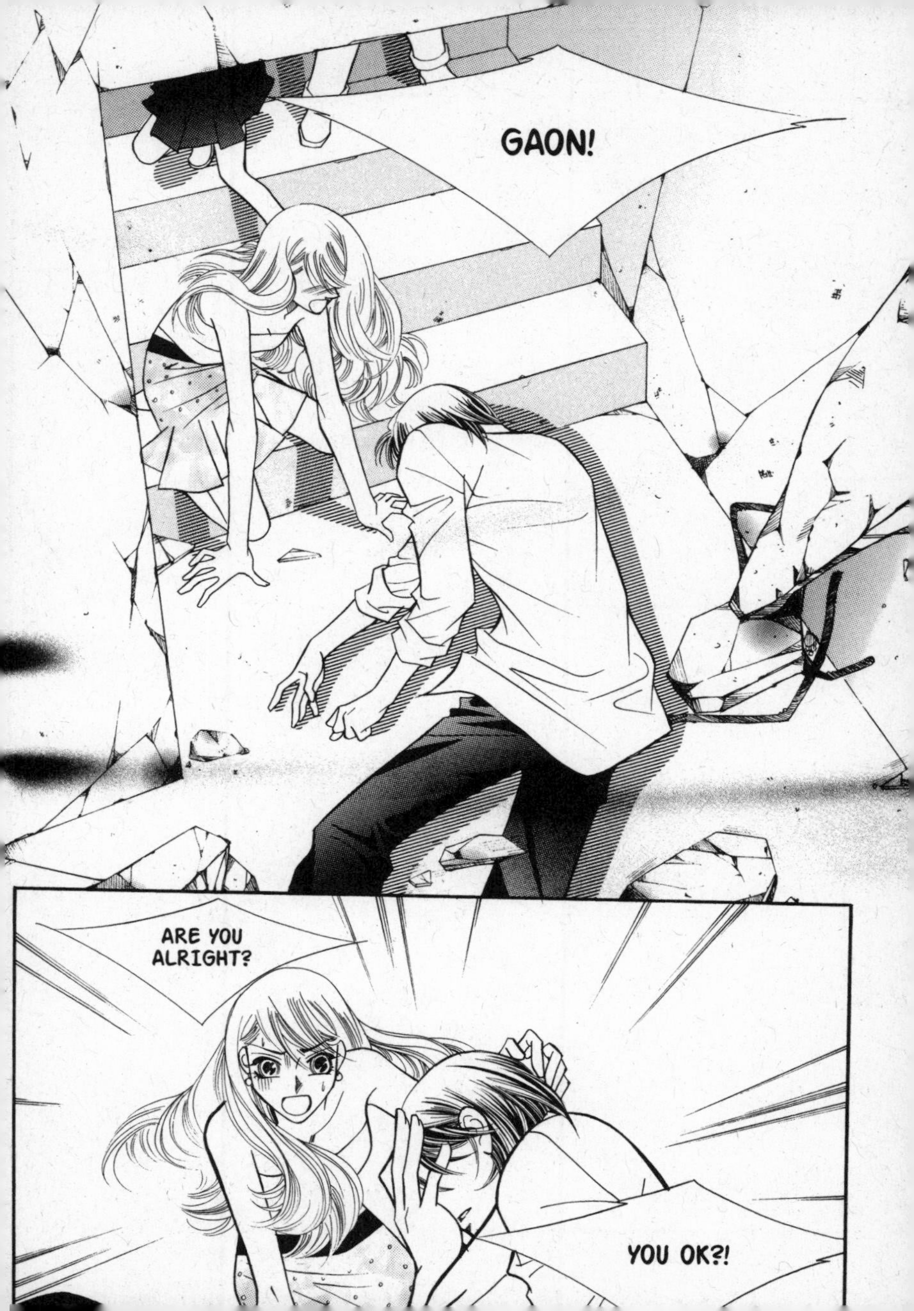
GAON!
ARE YOU ALRIGHT?
YOU OK?!

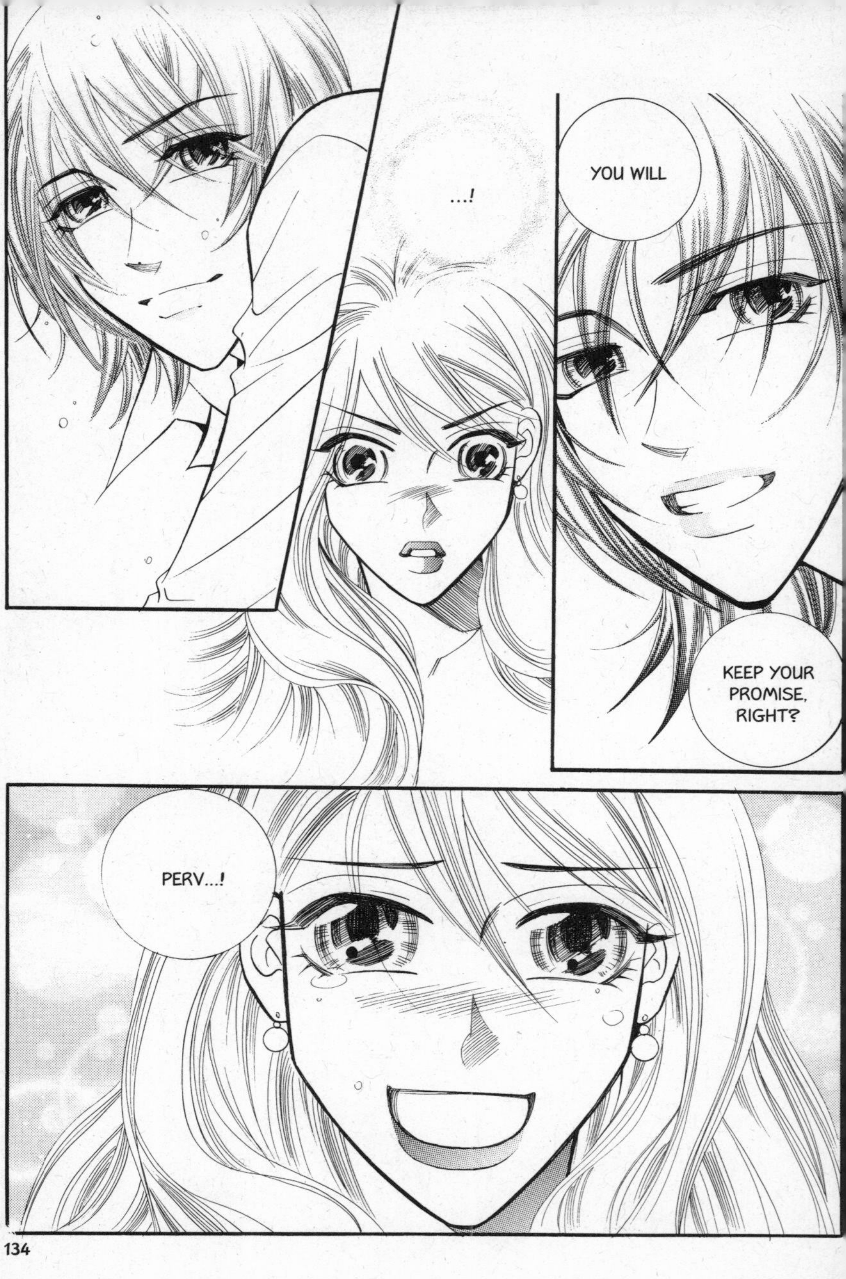
YOU WILL
KEEP YOUR PROMISE, RIGHT?
...!
PERV...!

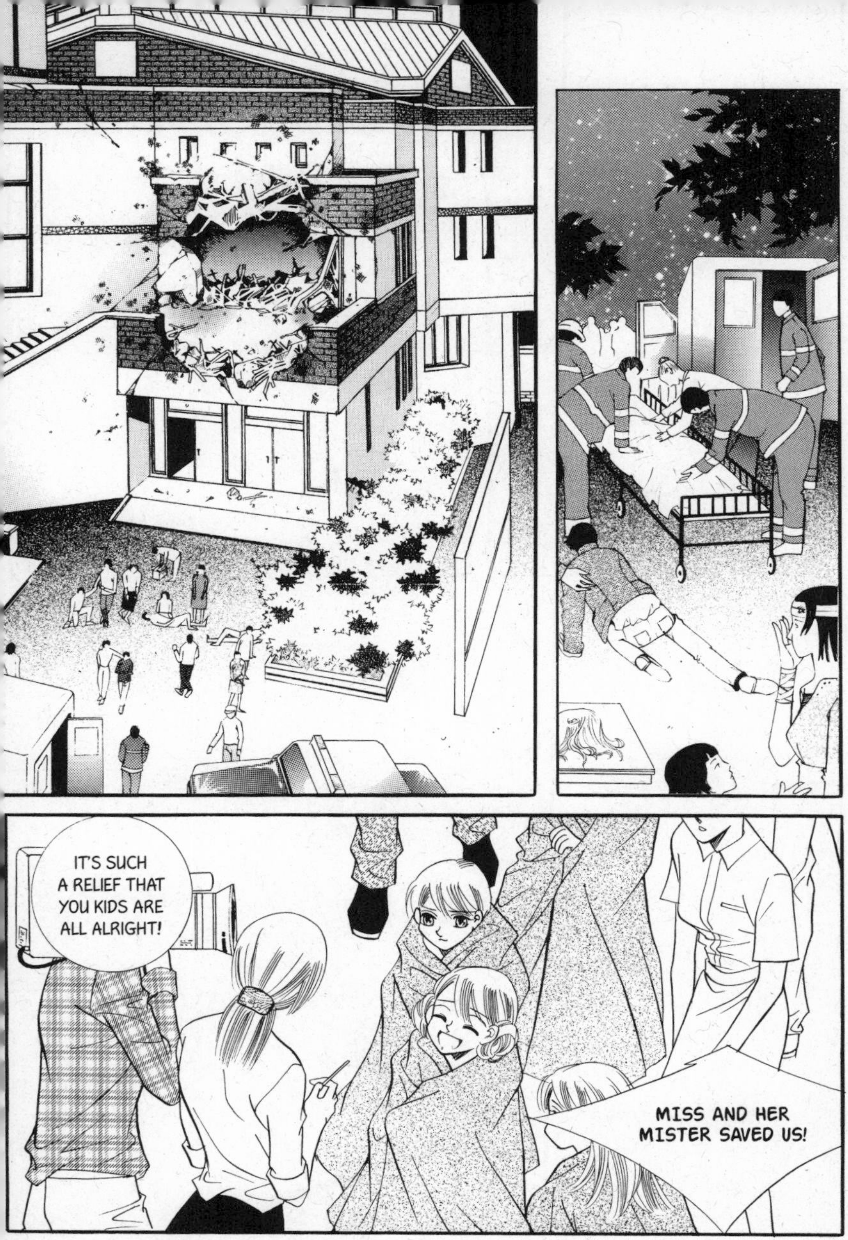
IT'S SUCH A RELIEF THAT YOU KIDS ARE ALL ALRIGHT!
MISS AND HER MISTER SAVED US!

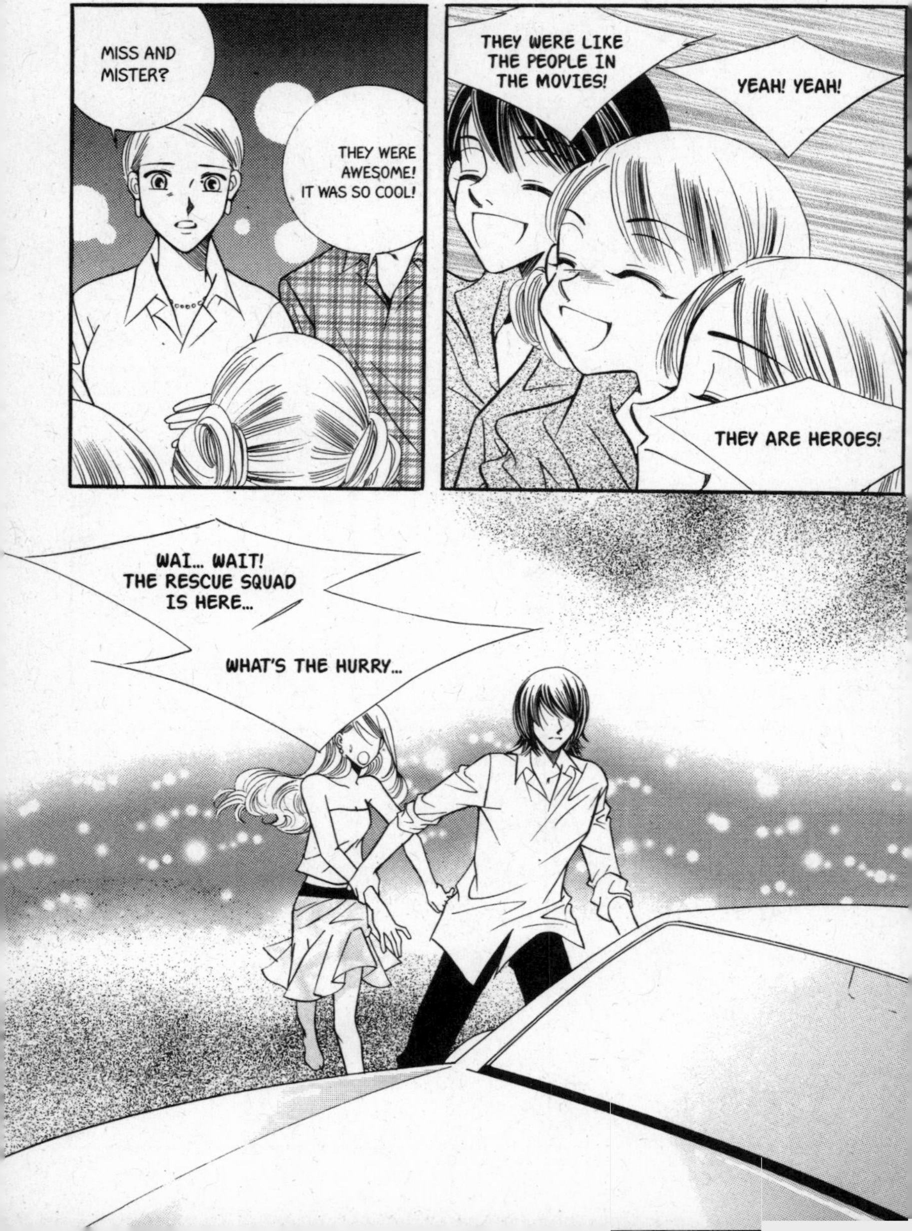
MISS AND MISTER?
THEY WERE AWESOME! IT WAS SO COOL!
THEY WERE LIKE THE PEOPLE IN THE MOVIES!
YEAH! YEAH!
THEY ARE HEROES!
WAI... WAIT! THE RESCUE SQUAD IS HERE...
WHAT'S THE HURRY...

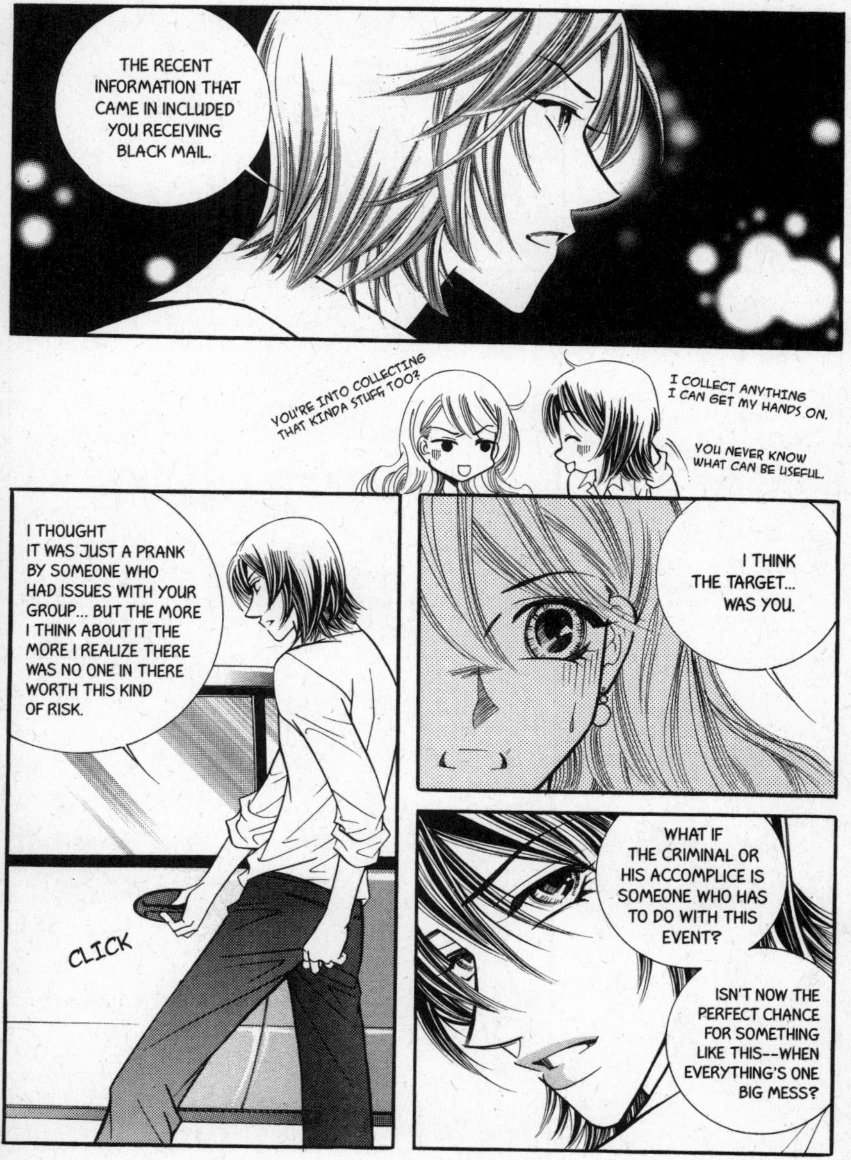
THE RECENT INFORMATION THAT CAME IN INCLUDED YOU RECEIVING BLACK MAIL.
YOU'RE INTO COLLECTING THAT KINDA STUFF TOO?
I COLLECT ANYTHING I CAN GET MY HANDS ON.
YOU NEVER KNOW WHAT CAN BE USEFUL.
I THOUGHT IT WAS JUST A PRANK BY SOMEONE WHO HAD ISSUES WITH YOUR GROUP... BUT THE MORE I THINK ABOUT IT THE MORE I REALIZE THERE WAS NO ONE IN THERE WORTH THIS KIND OF RISK.
CLICK
I THINK THE TARGET... WAS YOU.
WHAT IF THE CRIMINAL OR HIS ACCOMPLICE IS SOMEONE WHO HAS TO DO WITH THIS EVENT?
ISN'T NOW THE PERFECT CHANCE FOR SOMETHING LIKE THIS--WHEN EVERYTHING'S ONE BIG MESS?

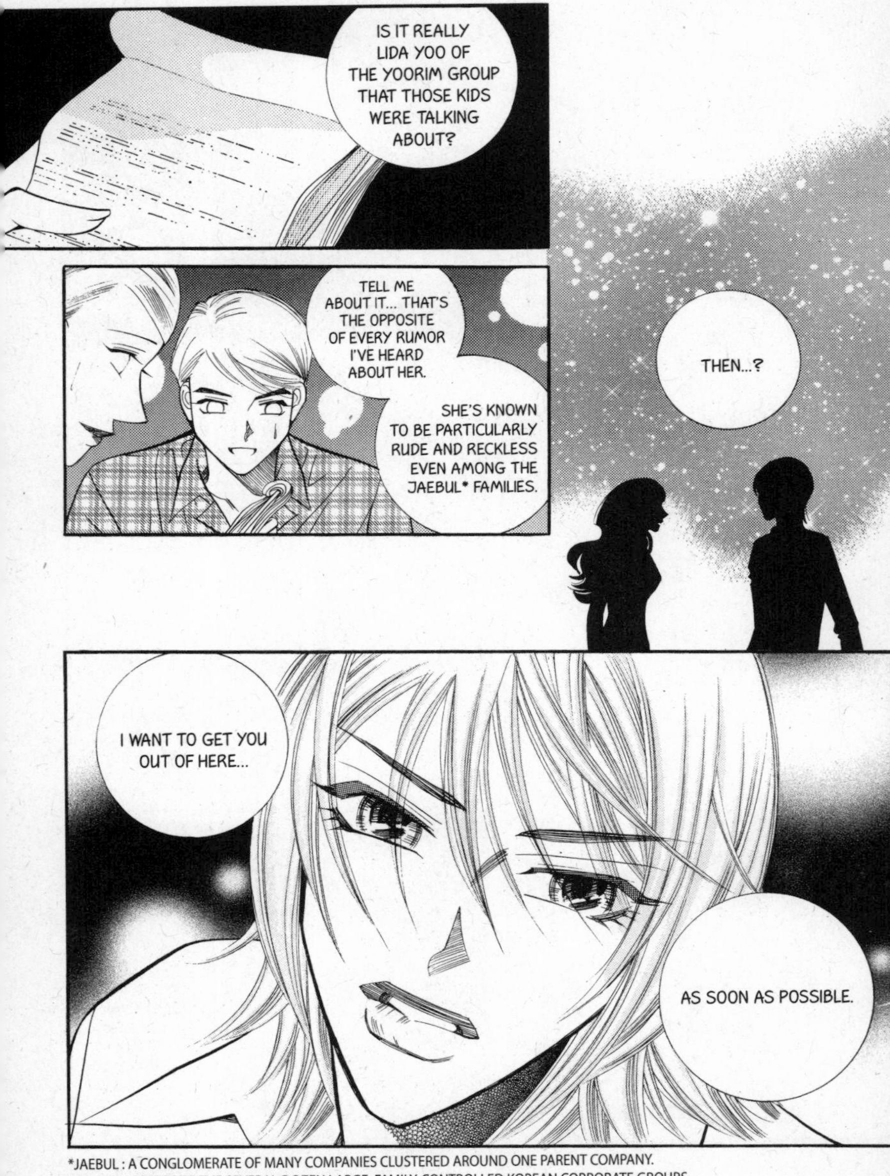
IS IT REALLY LIDA YOO OF THE YOORIM GROUP THAT THOSE KIDS WERE TALKING ABOUT?
TELL ME ABOUT IT... THAT'S THE OPPOSITE OF EVERY RUMOR I'VE HEARD ABOUT HER.
SHE'S KNOWN TO BE PARTICULARLY RUDE AND RECKLESS EVEN AMONG THE JAEBUL* FAMILIES.
THEN...?
I WANT TO GET YOU OUT OF HERE...
AS SOON AS POSSIBLE.

*JAEBUL : A CONGLOMERATE OF MANY COMPANIES CLUSTERED AROUND ONE PARENT COMPANY.
THE TERM REFERS TO THE SEVERAL DOZEN LARGE, FAMILY-CONTROLLED KOREAN CORPORATE GROUPS, AND MEANS BIG BUSINESS GROUP OR PLUTOCRAT.

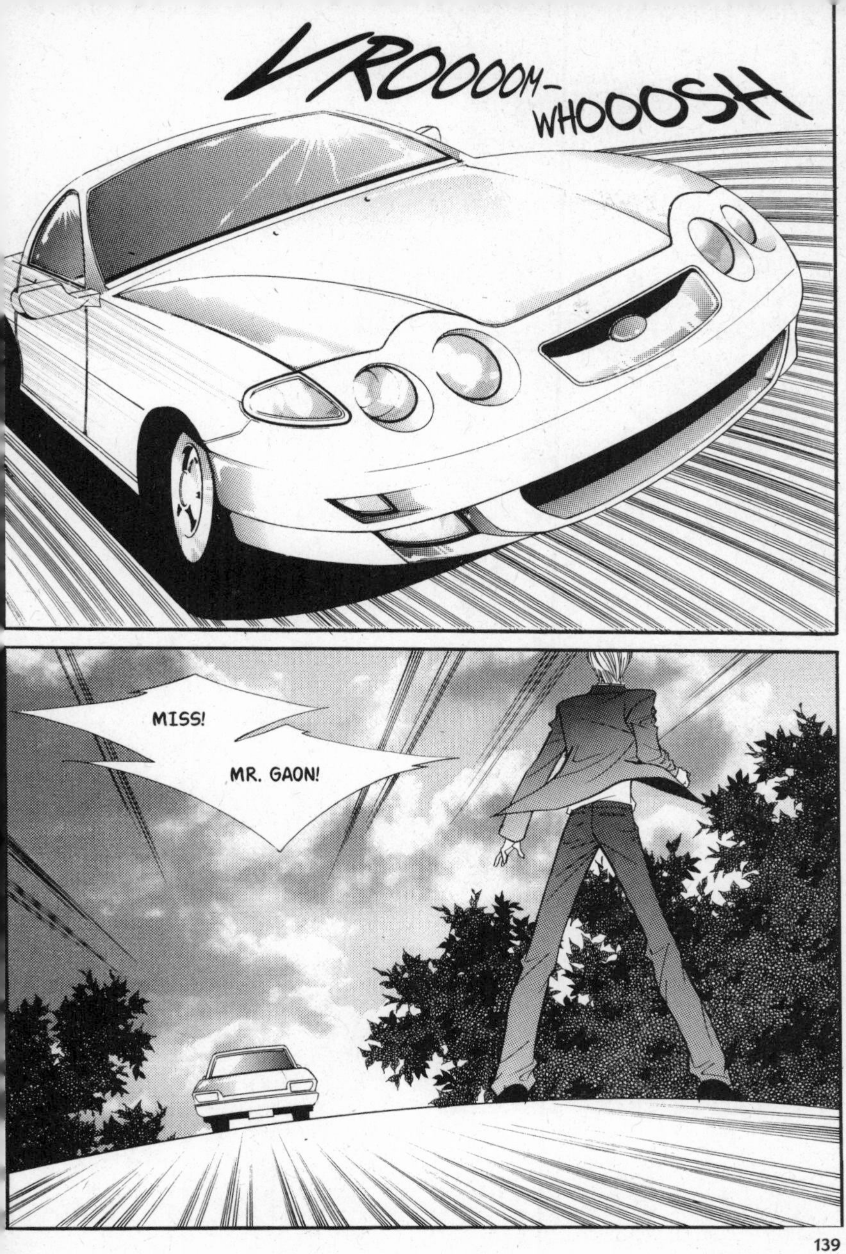
VROOOOM-WHOOOSH
MISS!
MR. GAON!

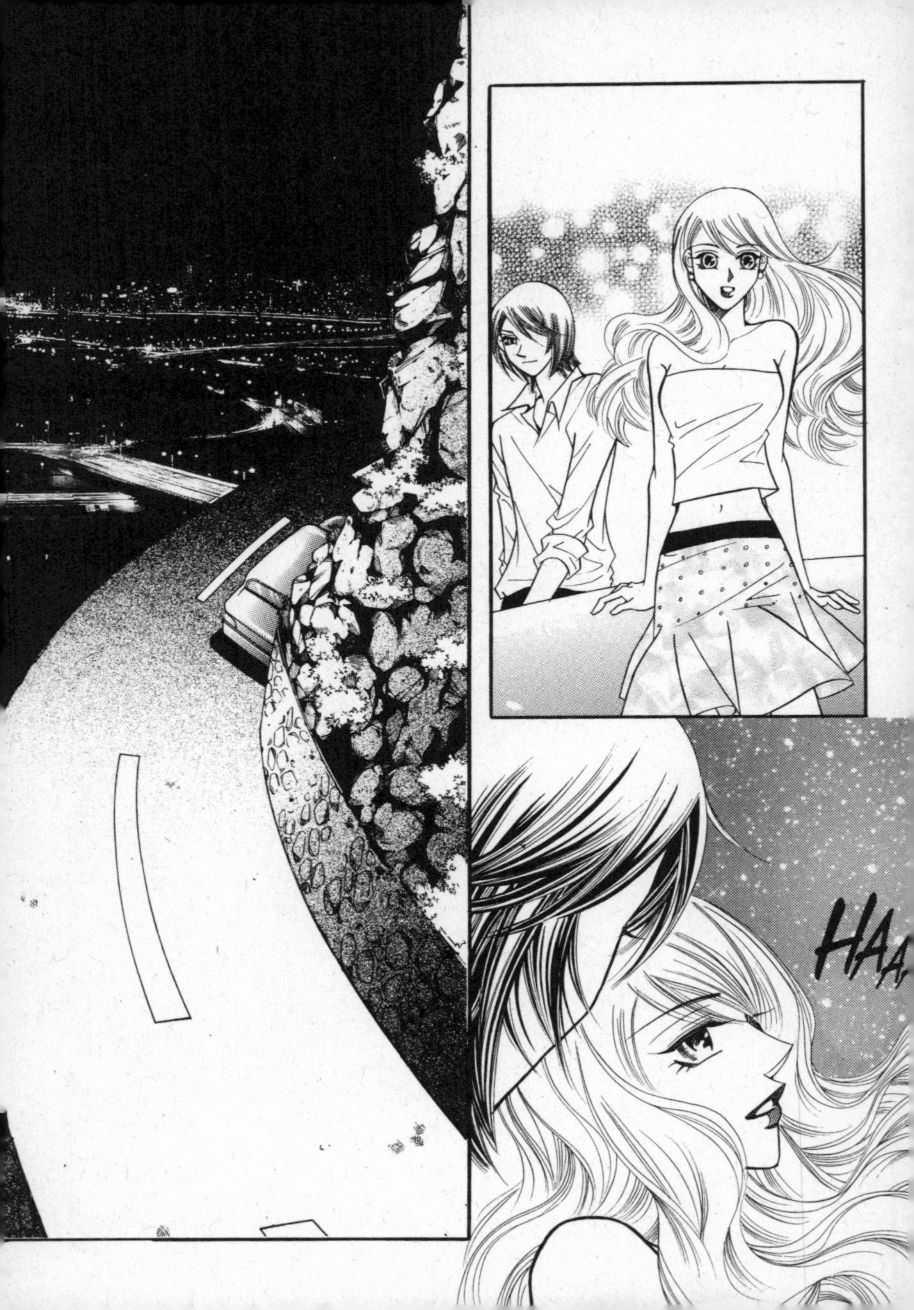
HAA

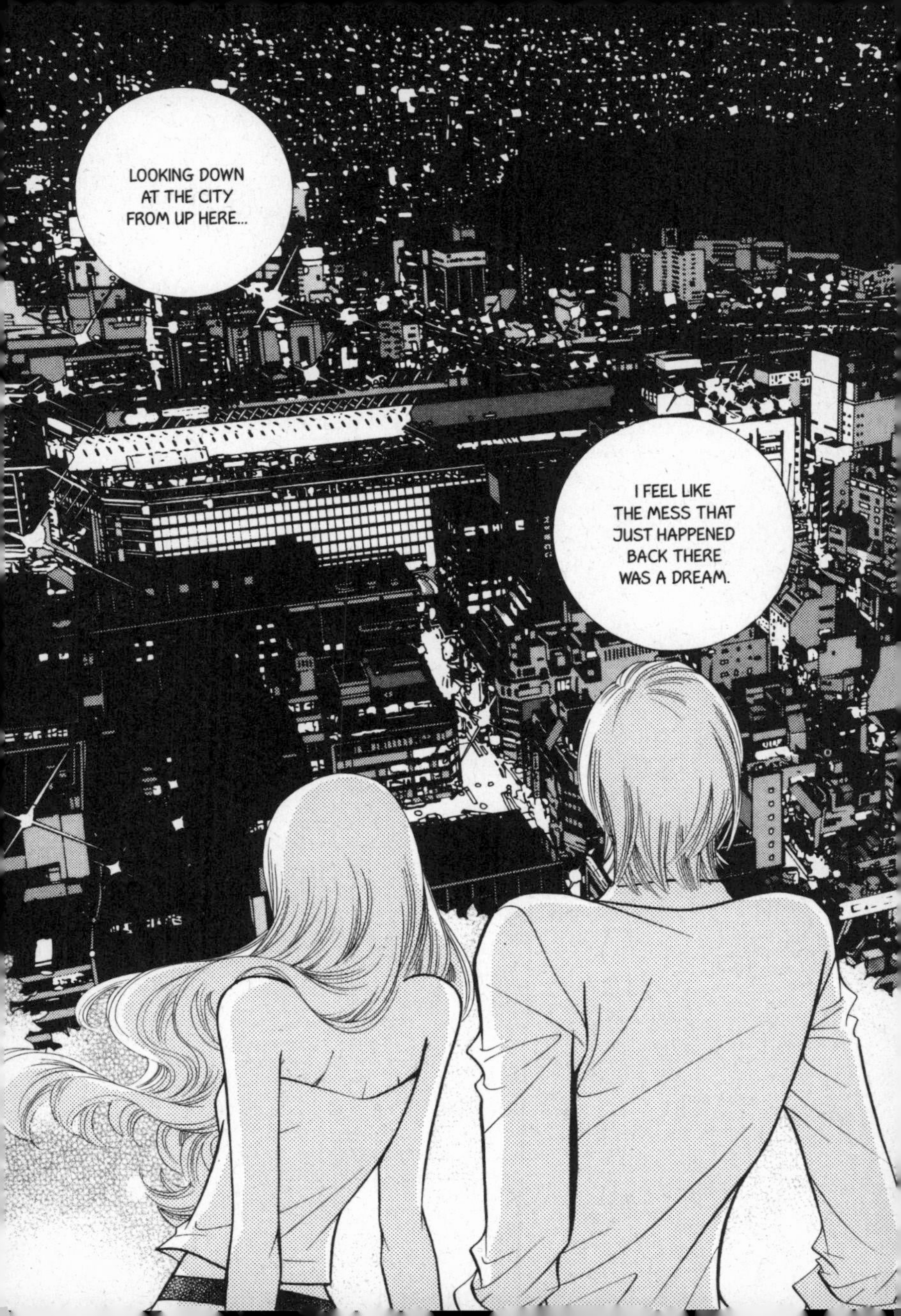
LOOKING DOWN AT THE CITY FROM UP HERE...
I FEEL LIKE THE MESS THAT JUST HAPPENED BACK THERE WAS A DREAM.

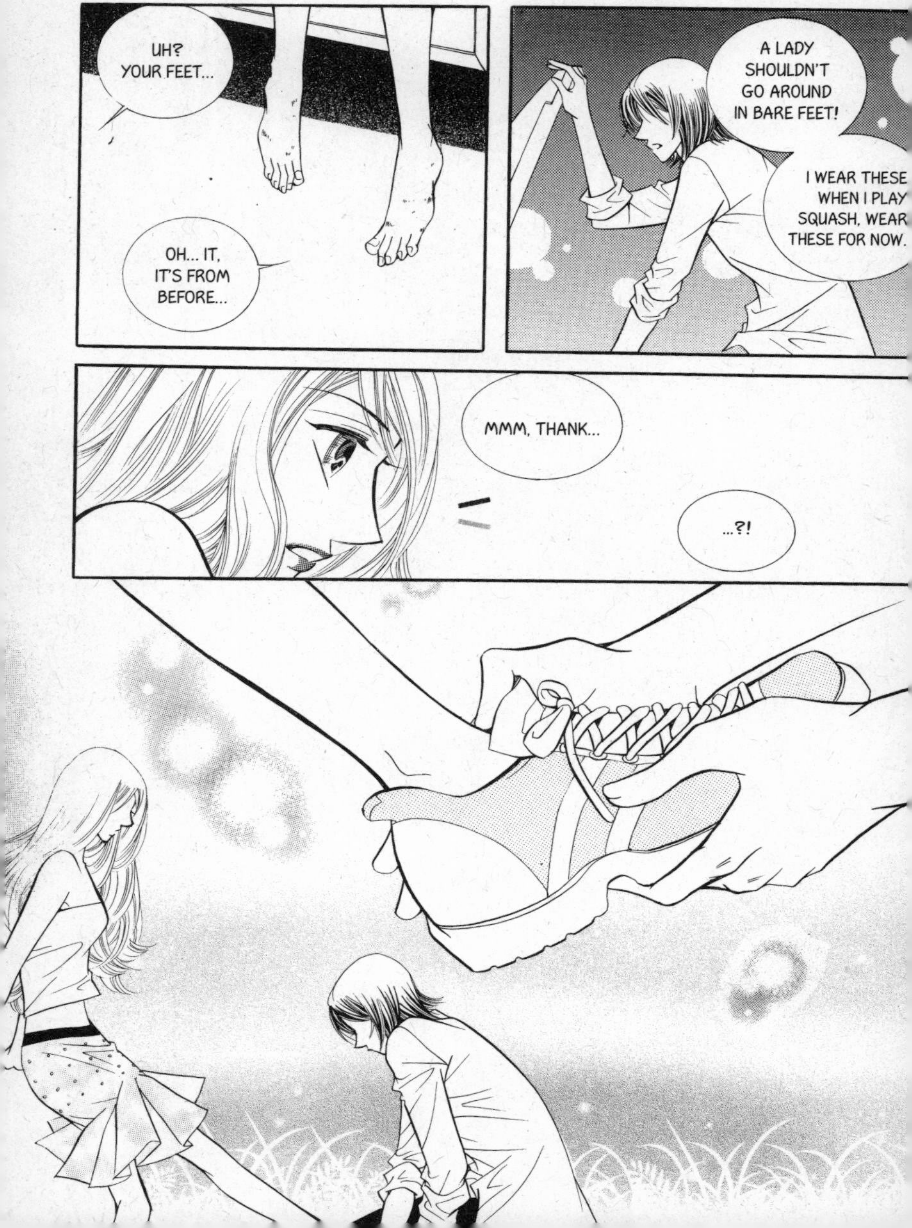
UH? YOUR FEET...
OH... IT, IT'S FROM BEFORE...
A LADY SHOULDN'T GO AROUND IN BARE FEET!
I WEAR THESE WHEN I PLAY SQUASH, WEAR THESE FOR NOW.
MMM, THANK...
...?!

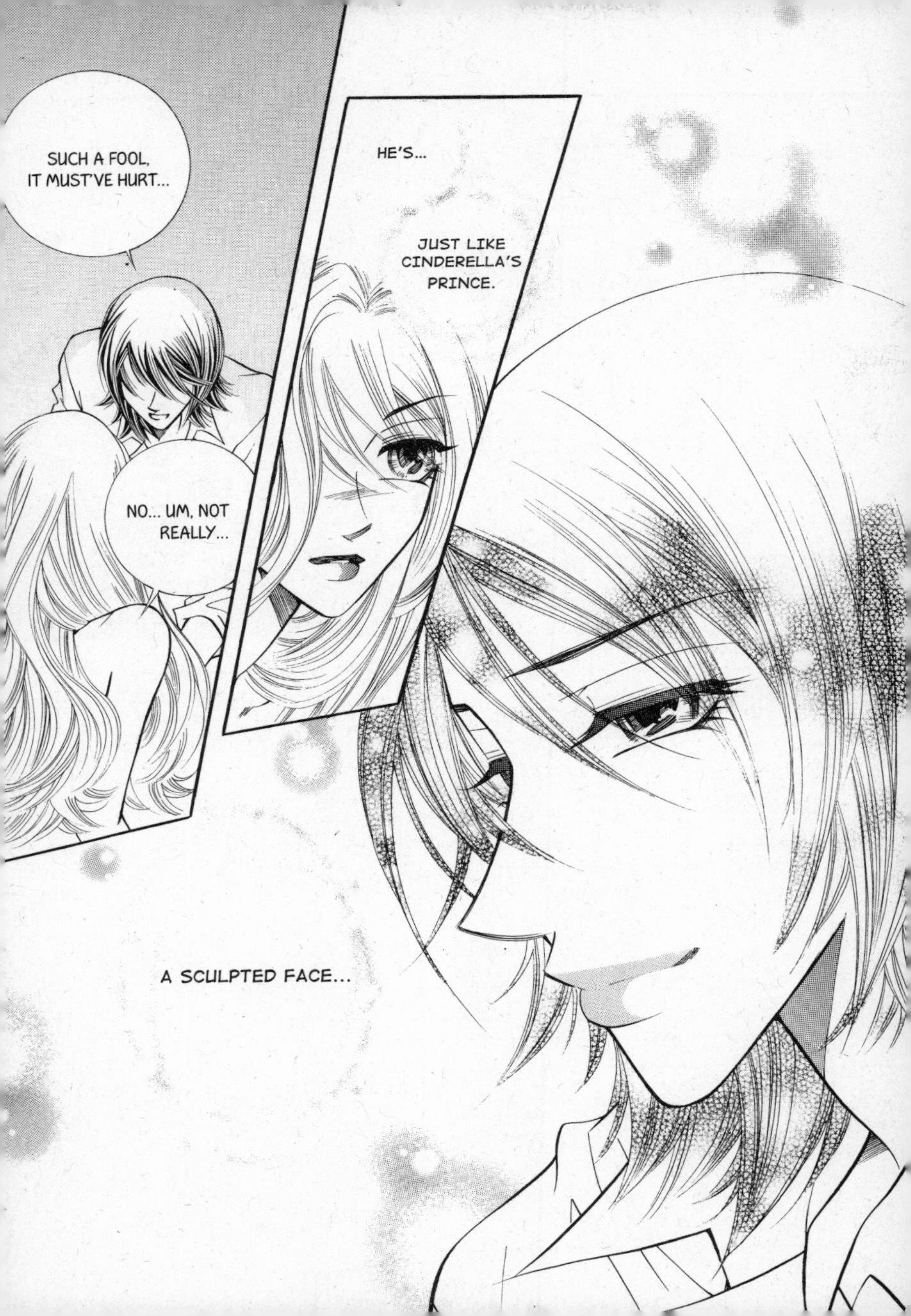
HE'S...
JUST LIKE CINDERELLA'S PRINCE.
SUCH A FOOL, IT MUST'VE HURT...
NO... UM, NOT REALLY...
A SCULPTED FACE...

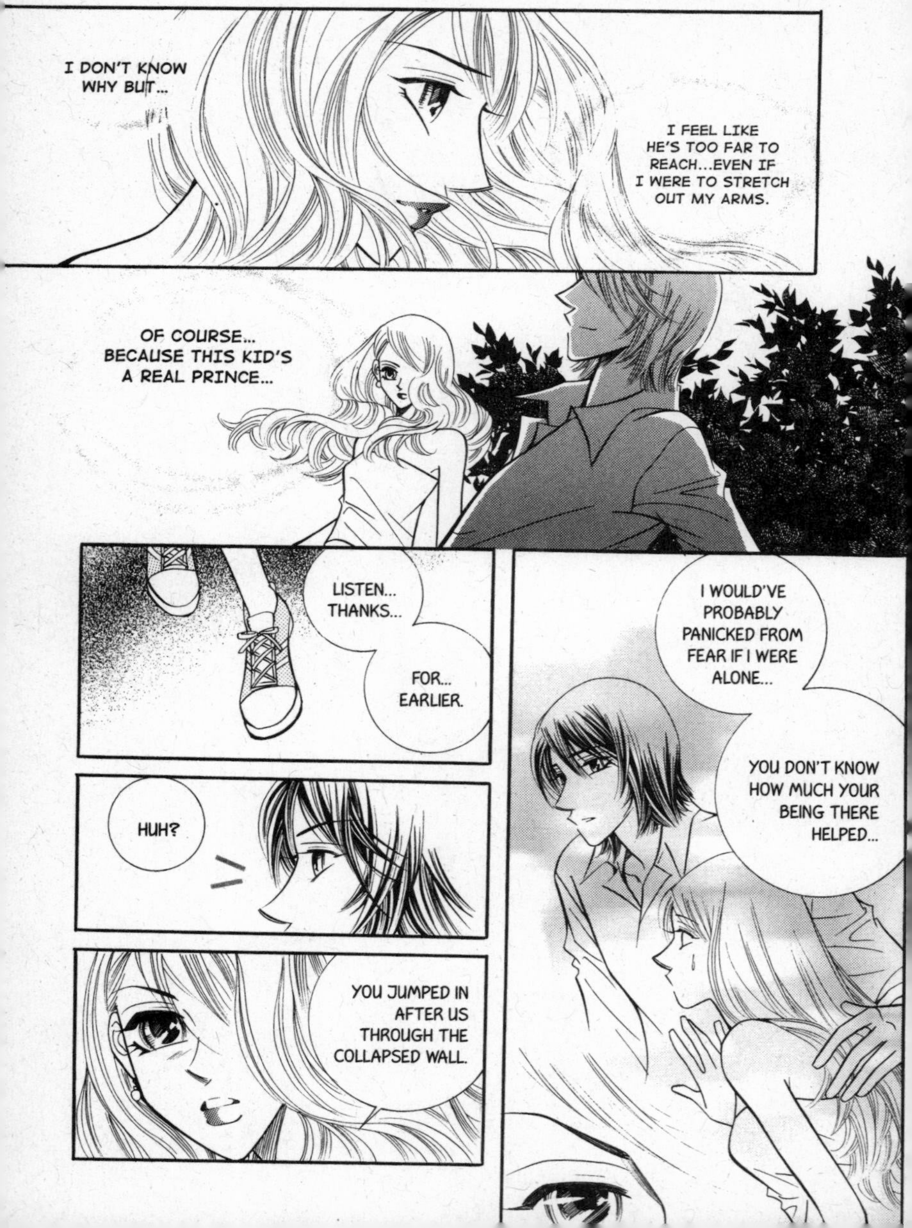
I DON'T KNOW WHY BUT...
I FEEL LIKE HE'S TOO FAR TO REACH...EVEN IF I WERE TO STRETCH OUT MY ARMS.
OF COURSE... BECAUSE THIS KID'S A REAL PRINCE...
I WOULD'VE PROBABLY PANICKED FROM FEAR IF I WERE ALONE...
YOU DON'T KNOW HOW MUCH YOUR BEING THERE HELPED...
LISTEN... THANKS...
FOR... EARLIER.
HUH?
YOU JUMPED IN AFTER US THROUGH THE COLLAPSED WALL.

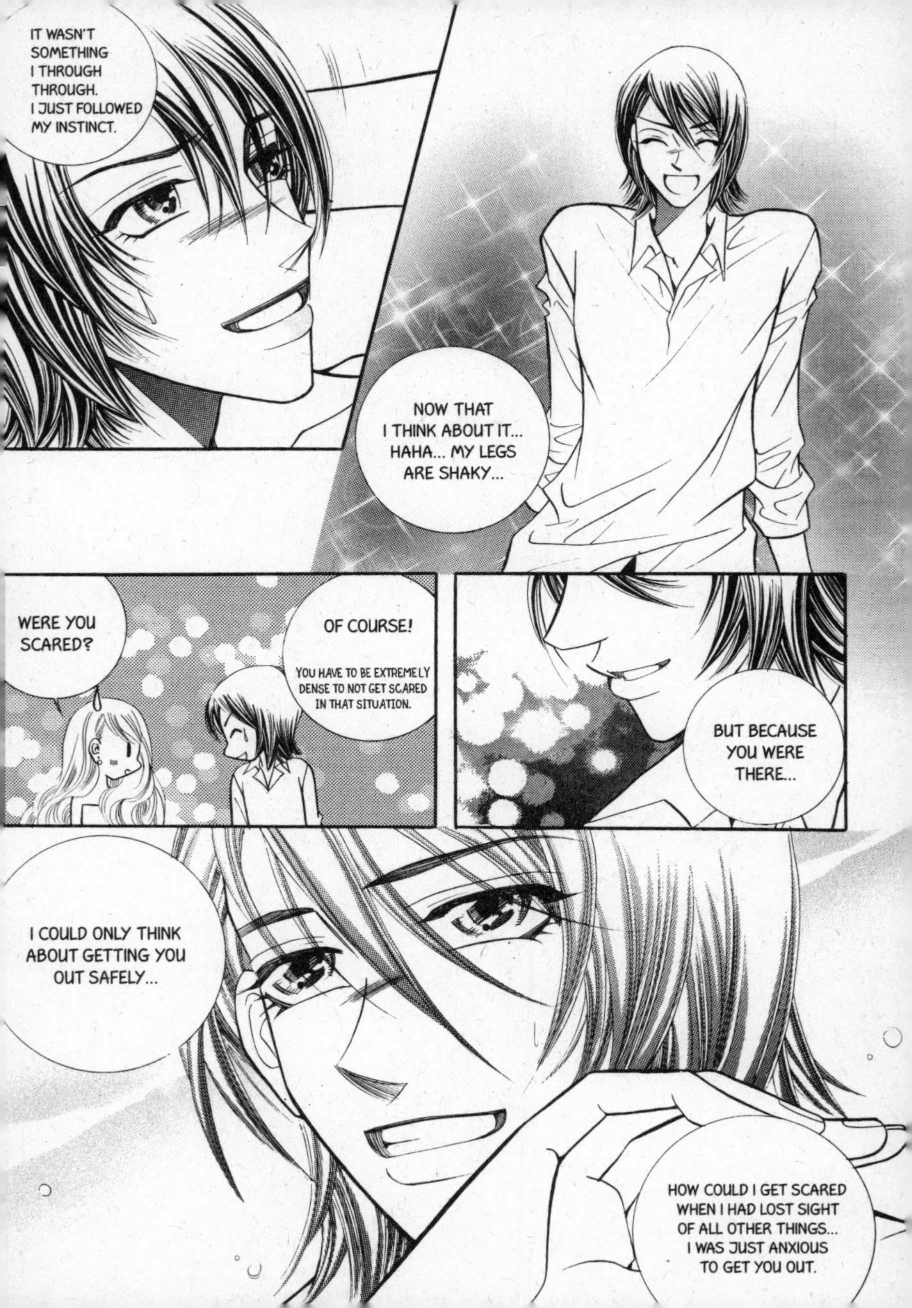
IT WASN'T SOMETHING I THROUGH THROUGH. I JUST FOLLOWED MY INSTINCT.
NOW THAT I THINK ABOUT IT... HAHA... MY LEGS ARE SHAKY...
WERE YOU SCARED?
OF COURSE!
YOU HAVE TO BE EXTREMELY DENSE TO NOT GET SCARED IN THAT SITUATION.
BUT BECAUSE YOU WERE THERE...
I COULD ONLY THINK ABOUT GETTING YOU OUT SAFELY...
HOW COULD I GET SCARED WHEN I HAD LOST SIGHT OF ALL OTHER THINGS... I WAS JUST ANXIOUS TO GET YOU OUT.

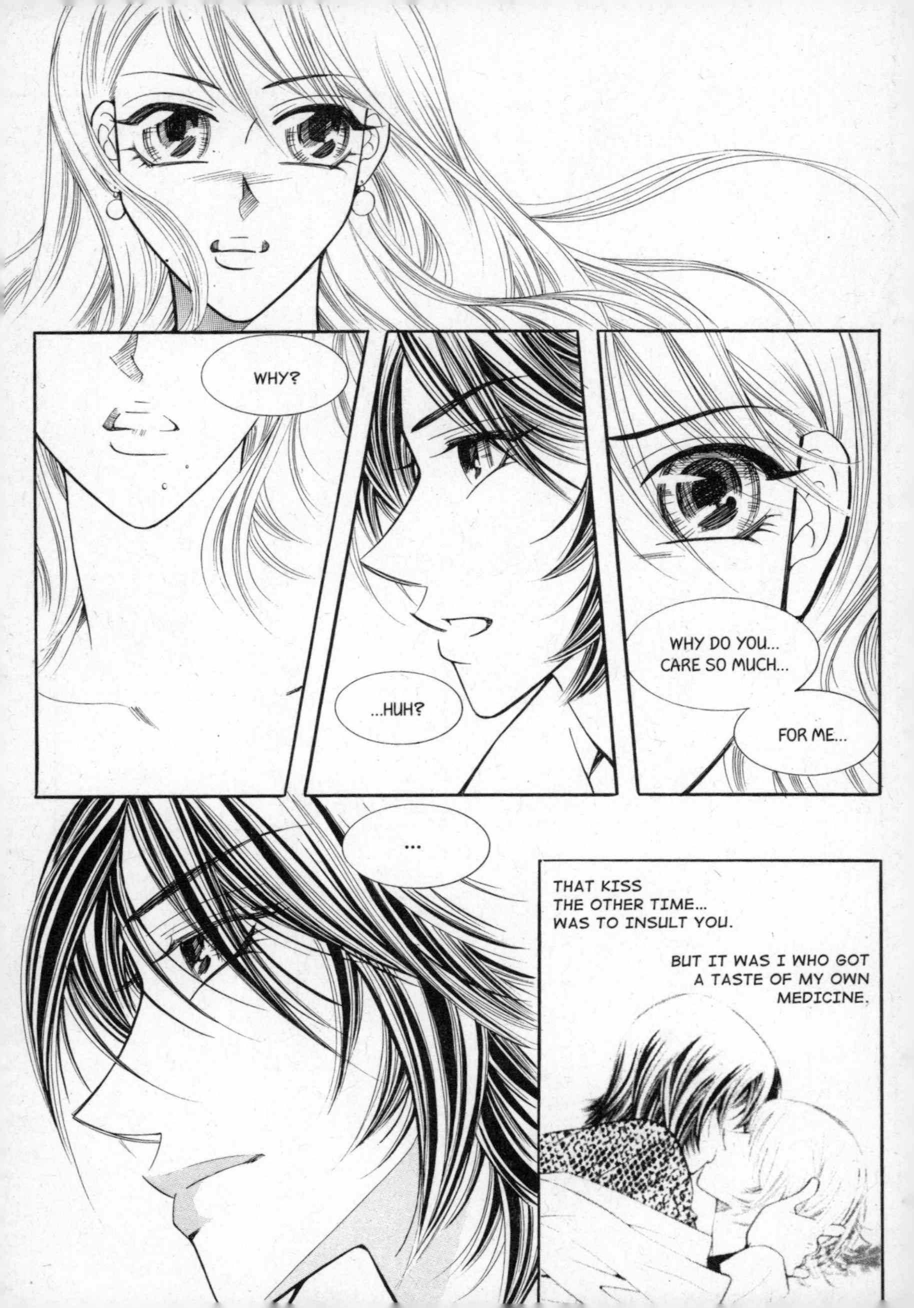
WHY?
...HUH?
WHY DO YOU... CARE SO MUCH...
FOR ME...
...
THAT KISS THE OTHER TIME... WAS TO INSULT YOU.
BUT IT WAS I WHO GOT A TASTE OF MY OWN MEDICINE.

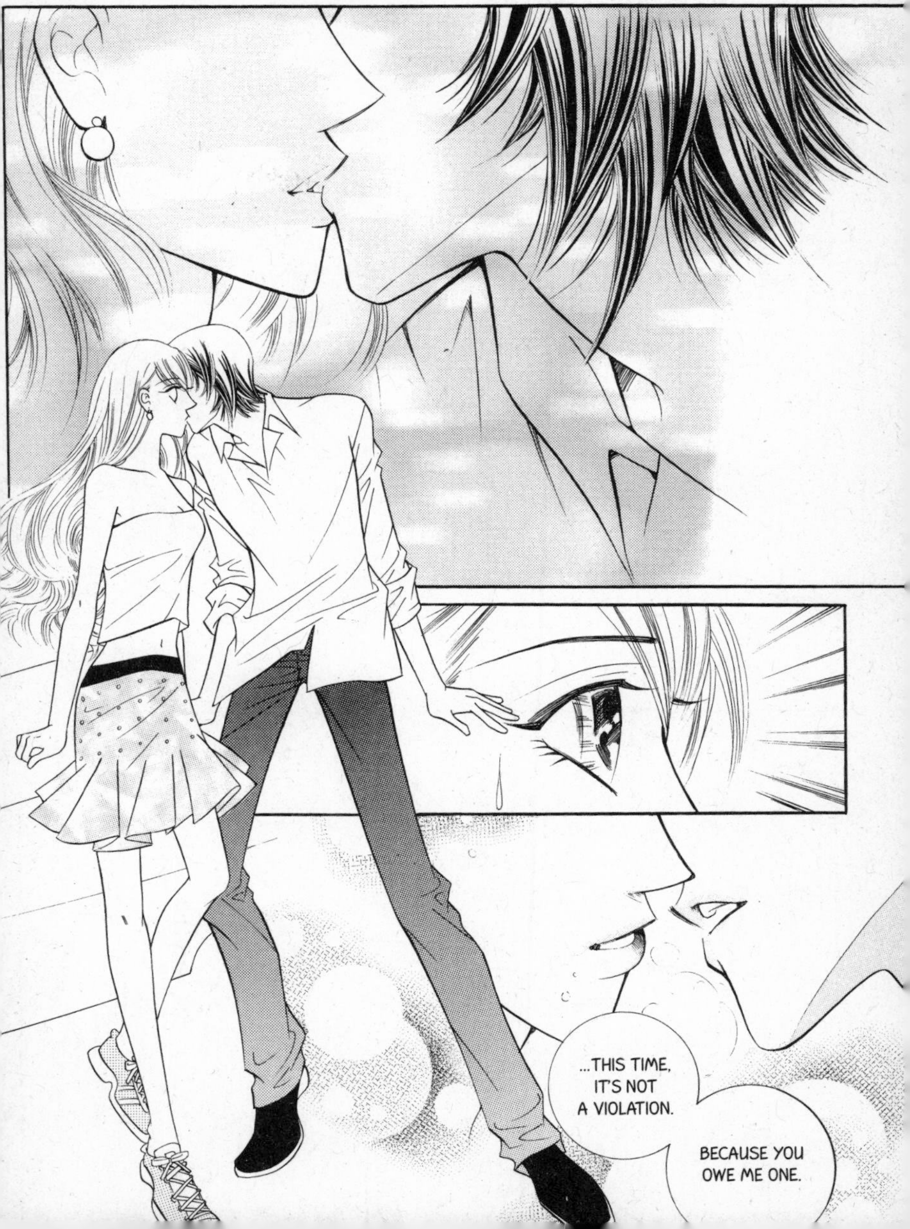
...THIS TIME, IT'S NOT A VIOLATION.
BECAUSE YOU OWE ME ONE.

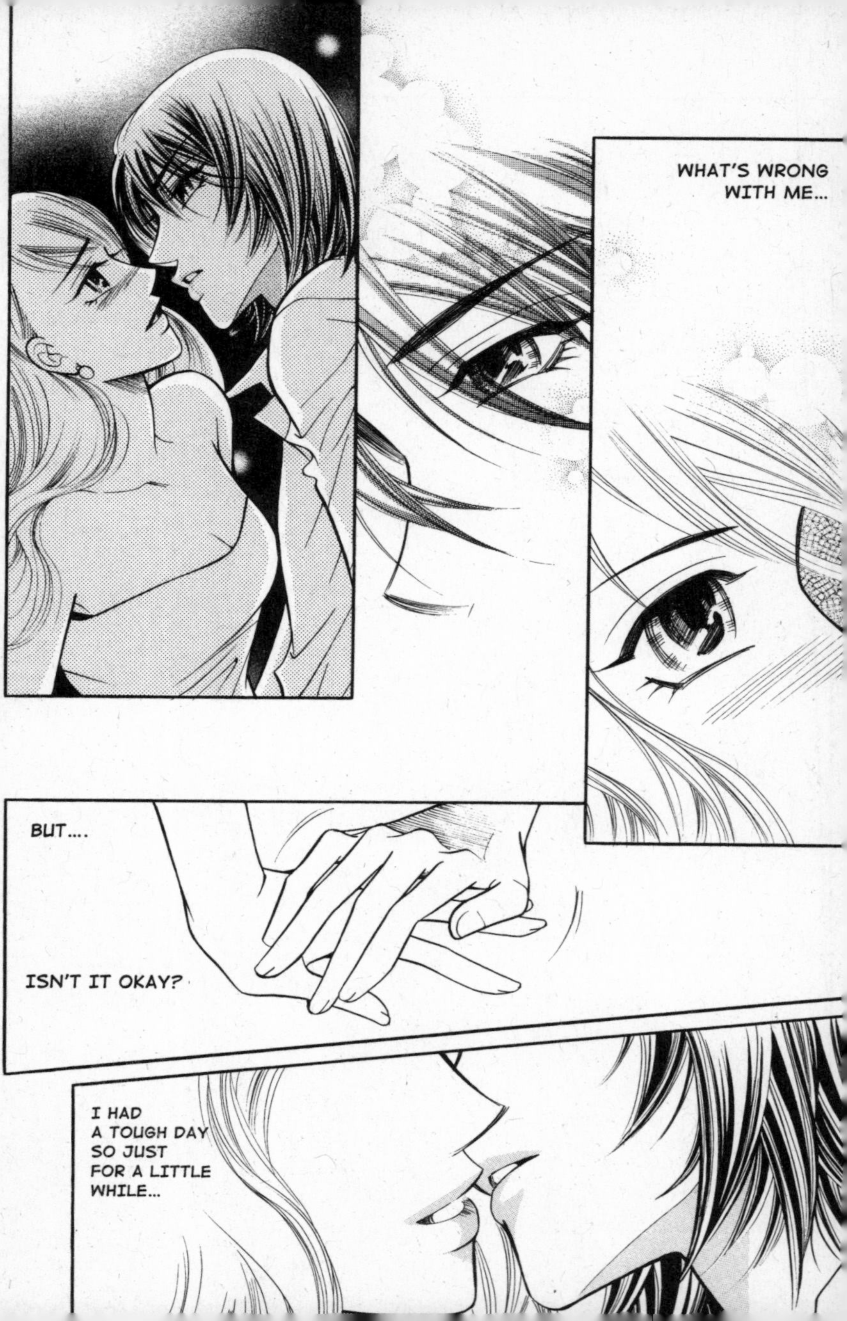
WHAT'S WRONG WITH ME...
BUT....
ISN'T IT OKAY?
I HAD A TOUGH DAY SO JUST FOR A LITTLE WHILE...

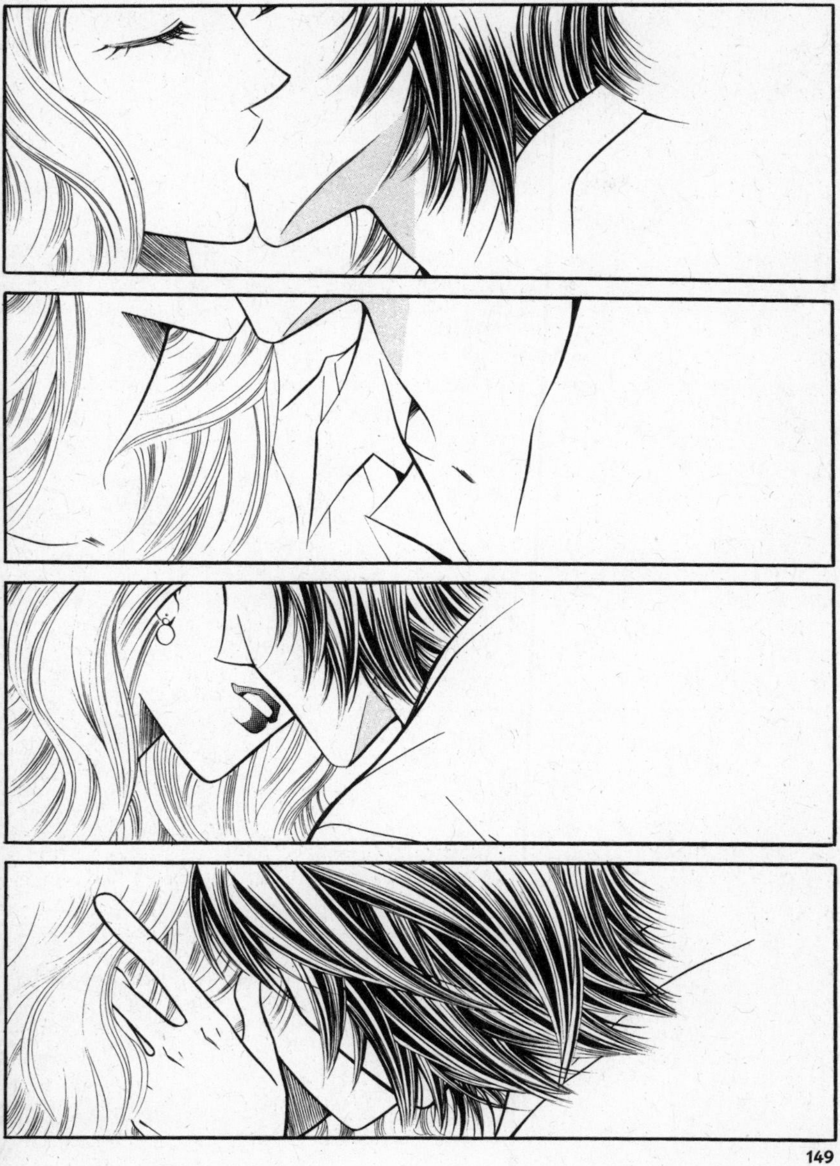

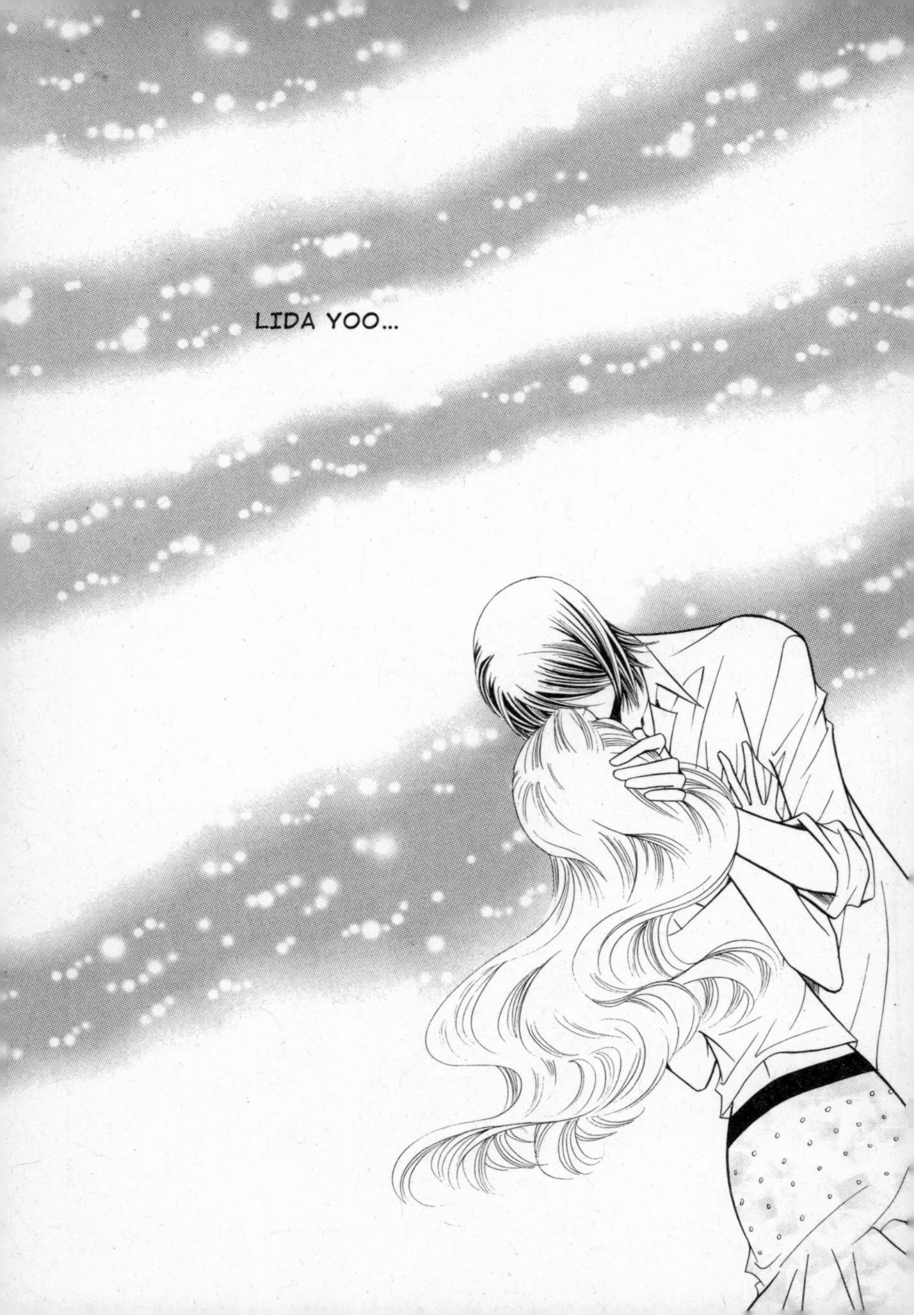
LIDA YOO...

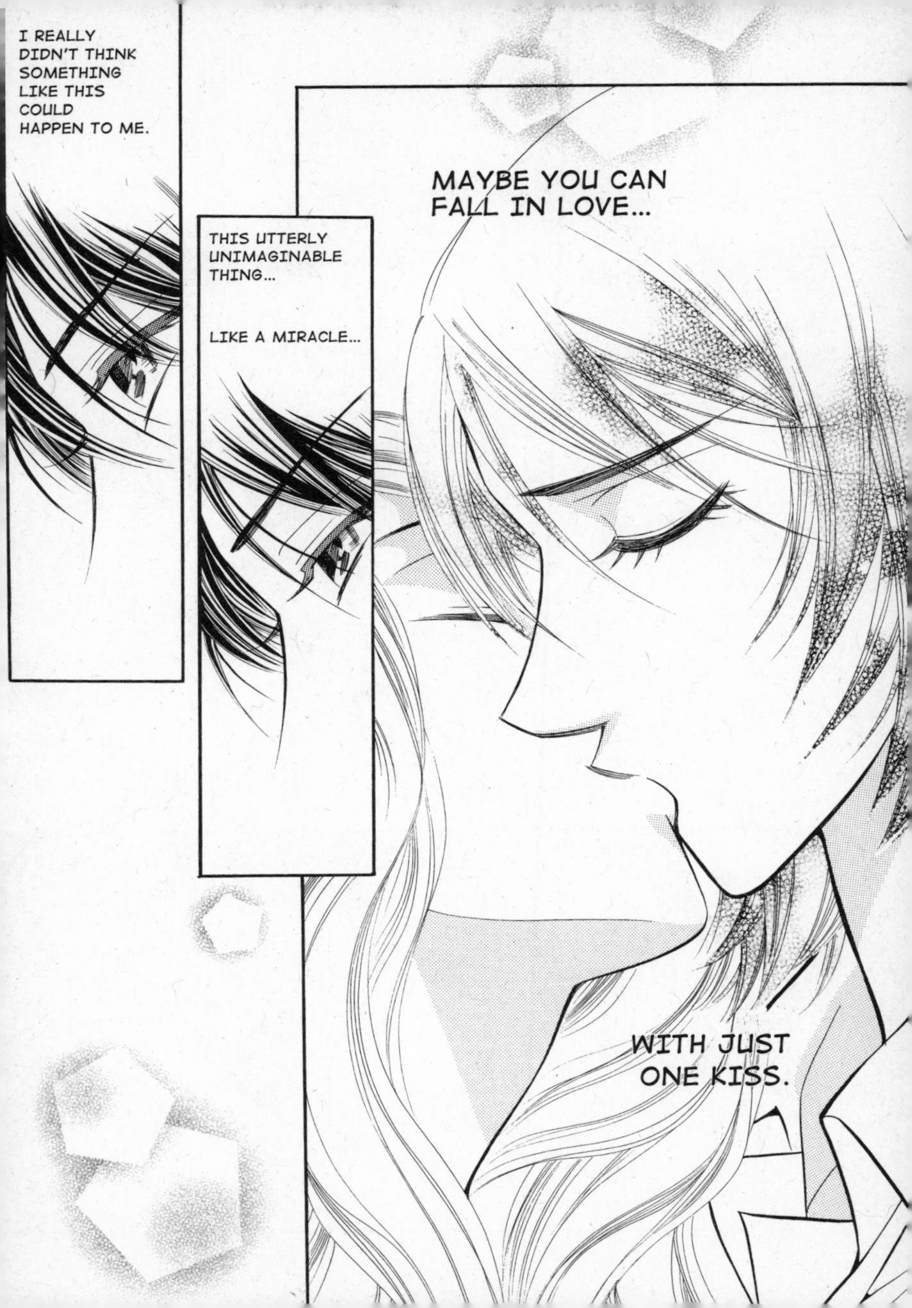
I REALLY DIDN'T THINK SOMETHING LIKE THIS COULD HAPPEN TO ME.
THIS UTTERLY UNIMAGINABLE THING...
LIKE A MIRACLE...
MAYBE YOU CAN FALL IN LOVE...
WITH JUST ONE KISS.

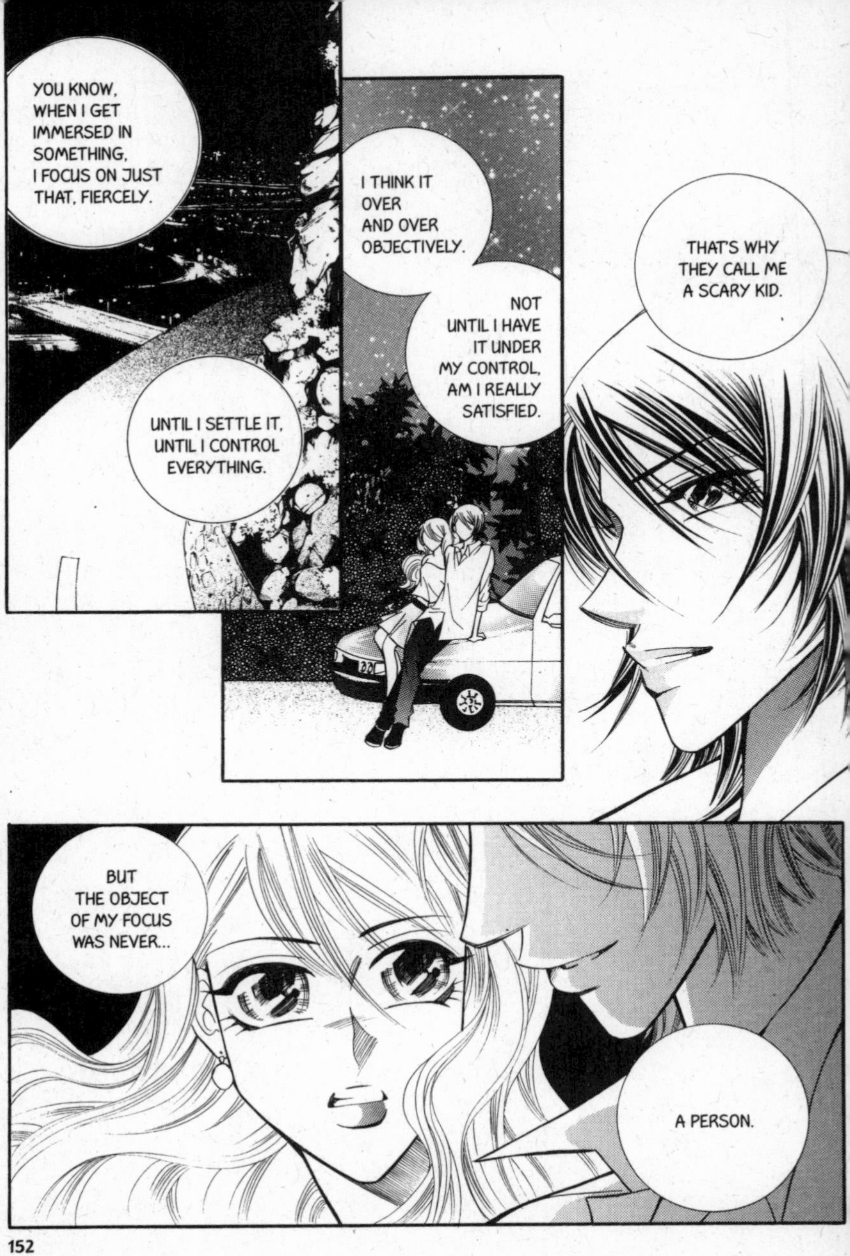
YOU KNOW, WHEN I GET IMMERSED IN SOMETHING, I FOCUS ON JUST THAT, FIERCELY.
UNTIL I SETTLE IT, UNTIL I CONTROL EVERYTHING.
I THINK IT OVER AND OVER OBJECTIVELY.
NOT UNTIL I HAVE IT UNDER MY CONTROL, AM I REALLY SATISFIED.
THAT'S WHY THEY CALL ME A SCARY KID.
BUT THE OBJECT OF MY FOCUS WAS NEVER...
A PERSON.

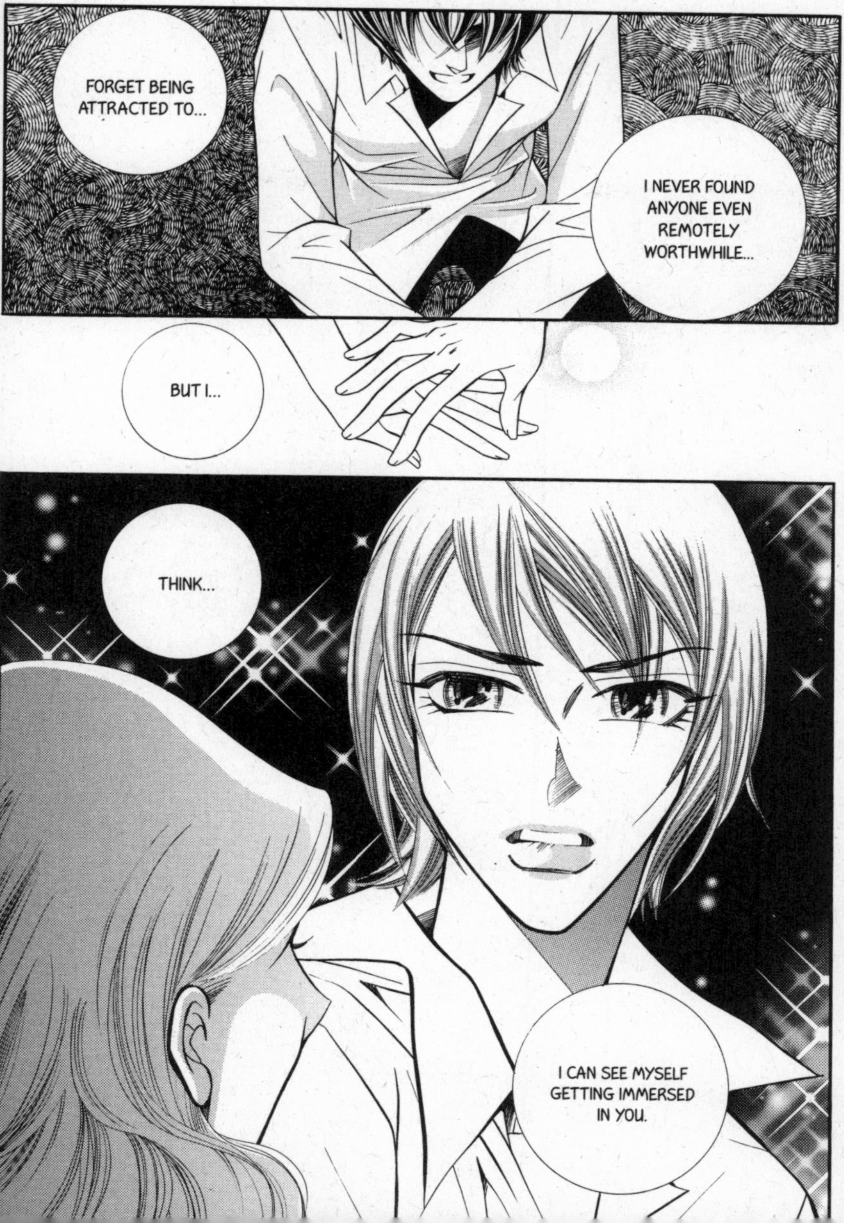
FORGET BEING ATTRACTED TO...
I NEVER FOUND ANYONE EVEN REMOTELY WORTHWHILE...
BUT I...
THINK...
I CAN SEE MYSELF GETTING IMMERSED IN YOU.

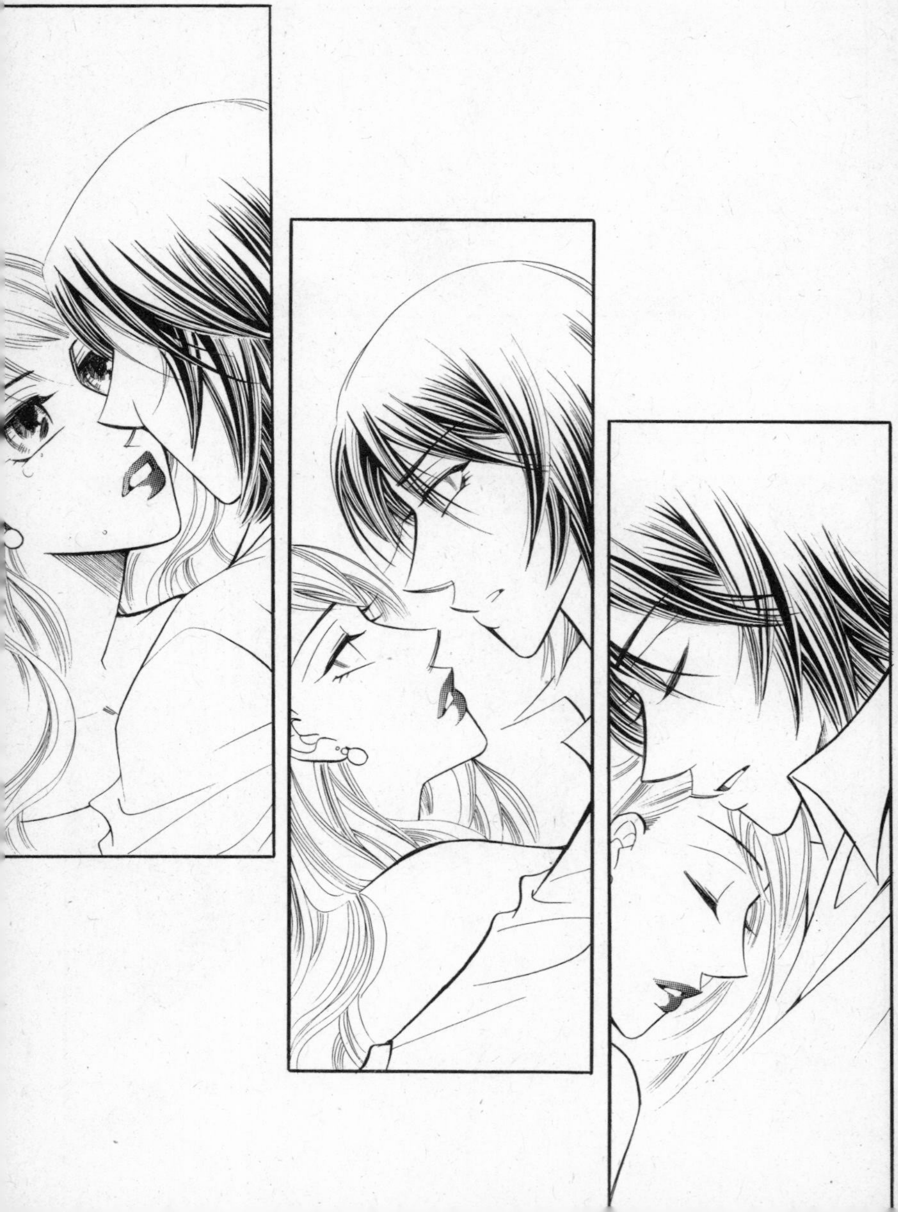

6. A BAIT

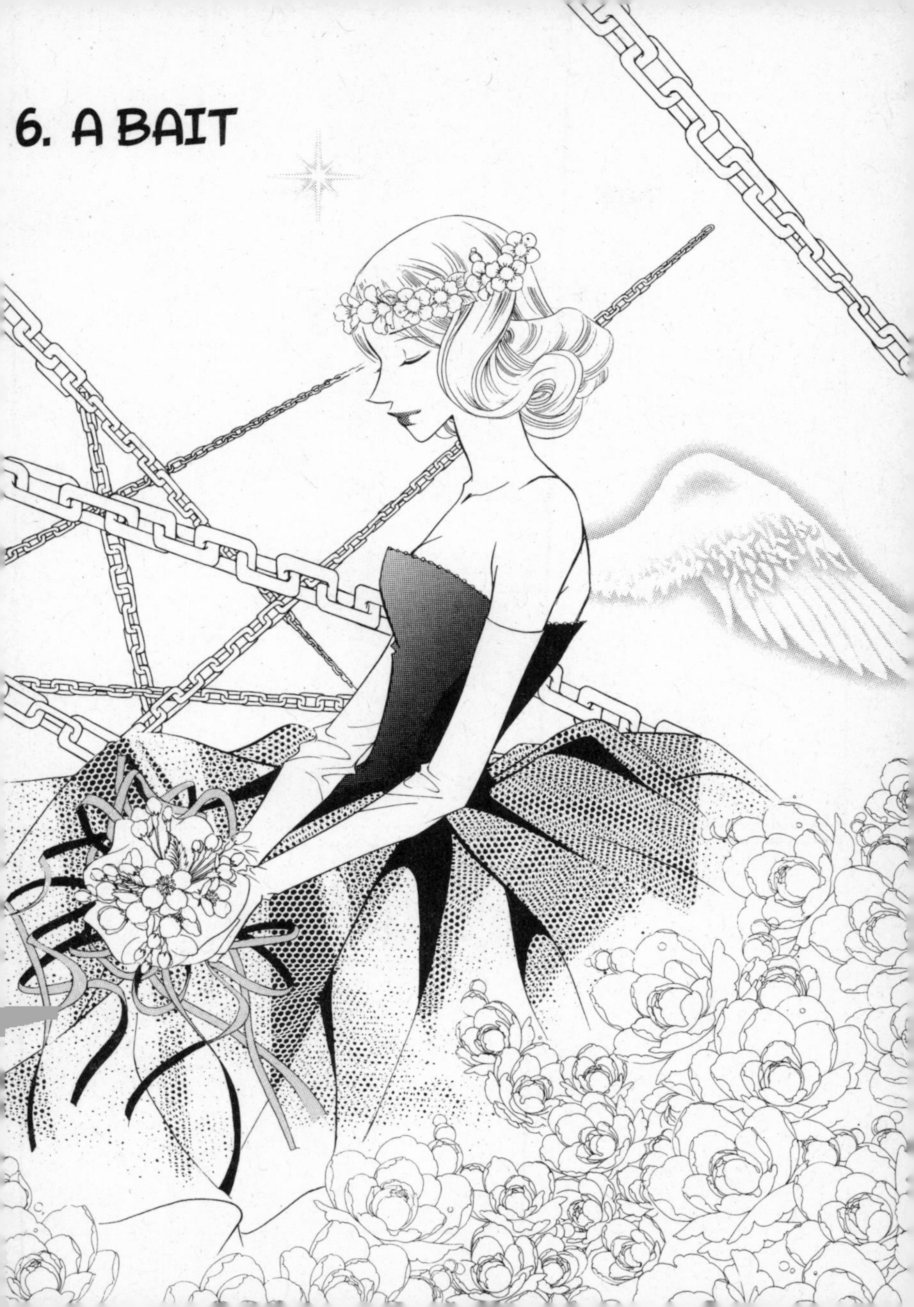

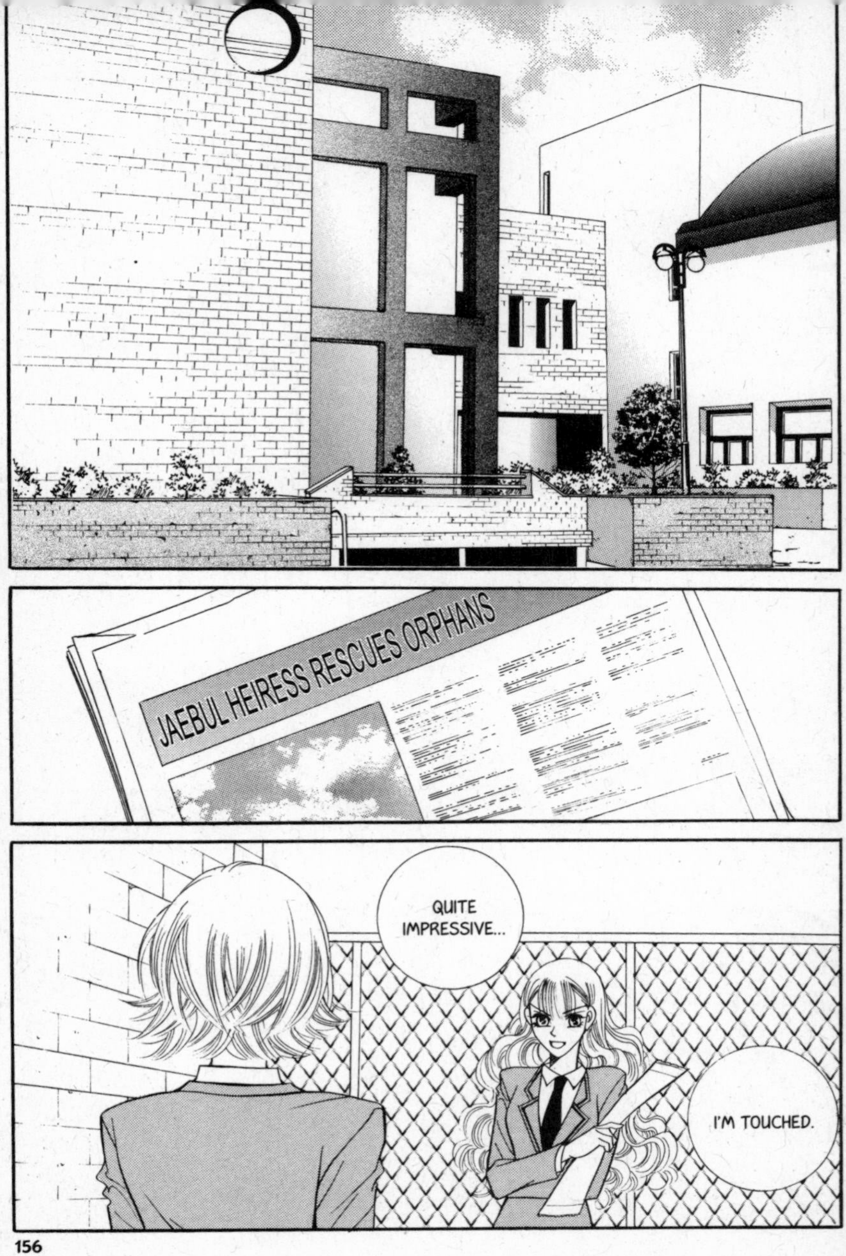
JAEBUL HEIRESS RESCUES ORPHANS
QUITE IMPRESSIVE...
I'M TOUCHED.

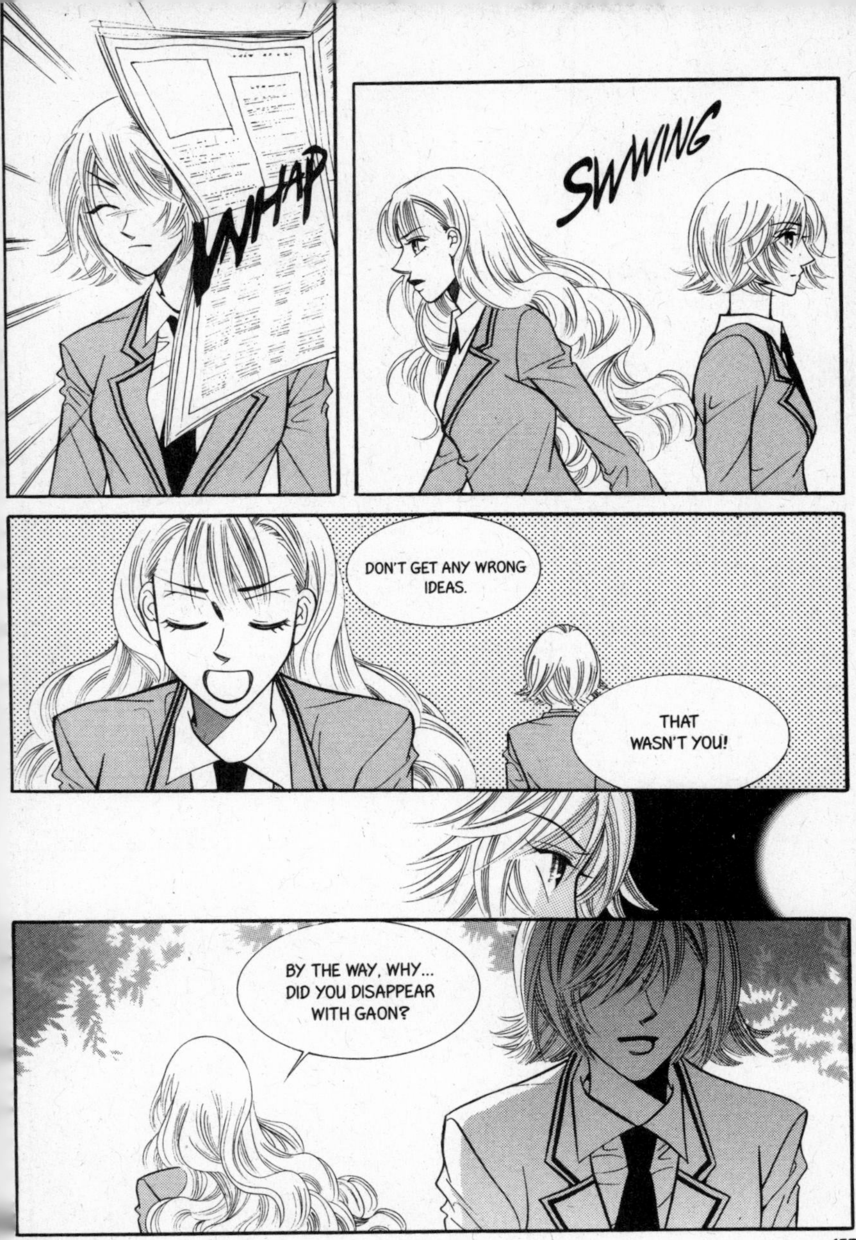
WHAP
SWWING
DON'T GET ANY WRONG IDEAS.
THAT WASN'T YOU!
BY THE WAY, WHY... DID YOU DISAPPEAR WITH GAON?

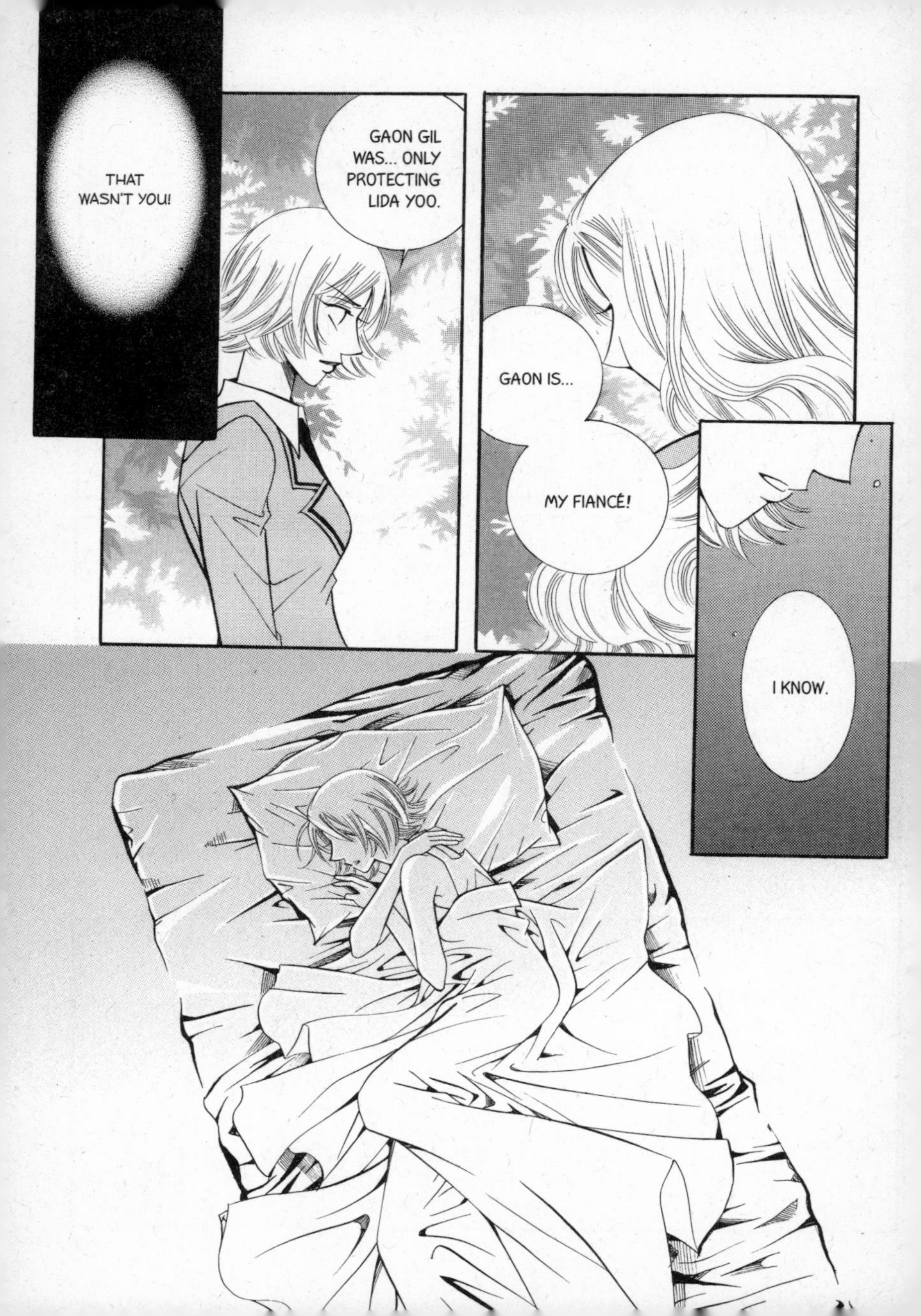
THAT WASN'T YOU!
GAON GIL WAS... ONLY PROTECTING LIDA YOO.
GAON IS...
MY FIANCÉ!
I KNOW.

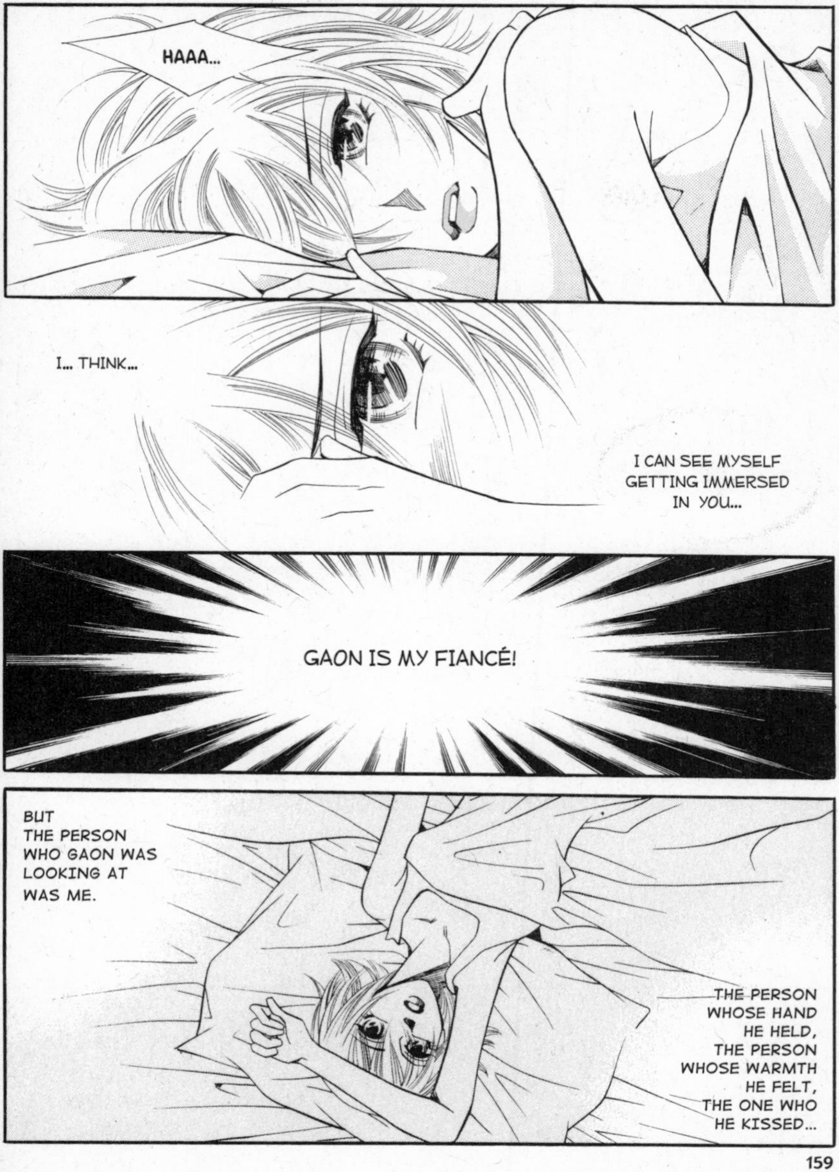
HAAA...
I... THINK...
I CAN SEE MYSELF GETTING IMMERSED IN YOU...
GAON IS MY FIANCÉ!
BUT THE PERSON WHO GAON WAS LOOKING AT WAS ME.
THE PERSON WHOSE HAND HE HELD, THE PERSON WHOSE WARMTH HE FELT, THE ONE WHO HE KISSED...

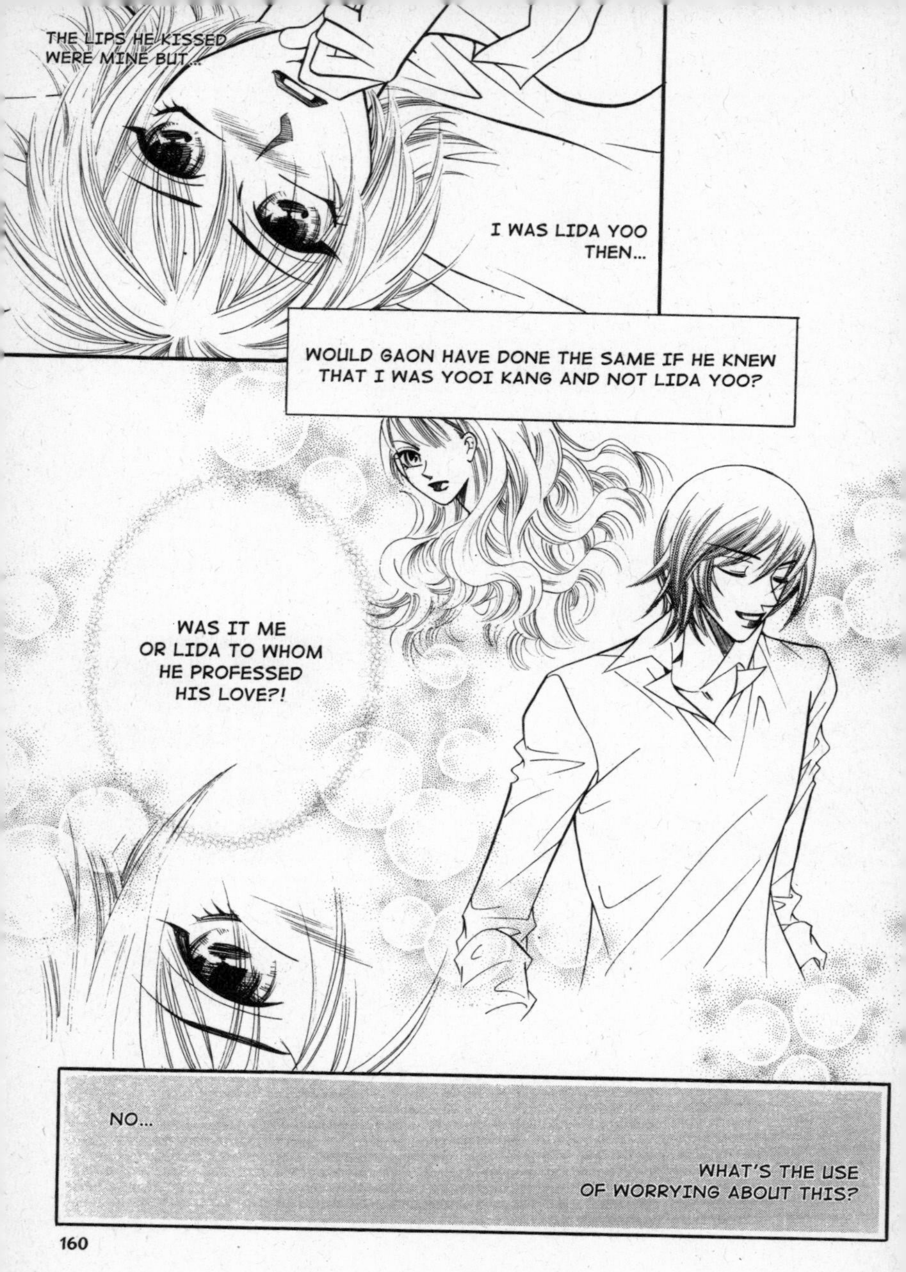
THE LIPS HE KISSED WERE MINE BUT...
I WAS LIDA YOO THEN...
WOULD GAON HAVE DONE THE SAME IF HE KNEW THAT I WAS YOOI KANG AND NOT LIDA YOO?
WAS IT ME OR LIDA TO WHOM HE PROFESSED HIS LOVE?!
NO...
WHAT'S THE USE OF WORRYING ABOUT THIS?

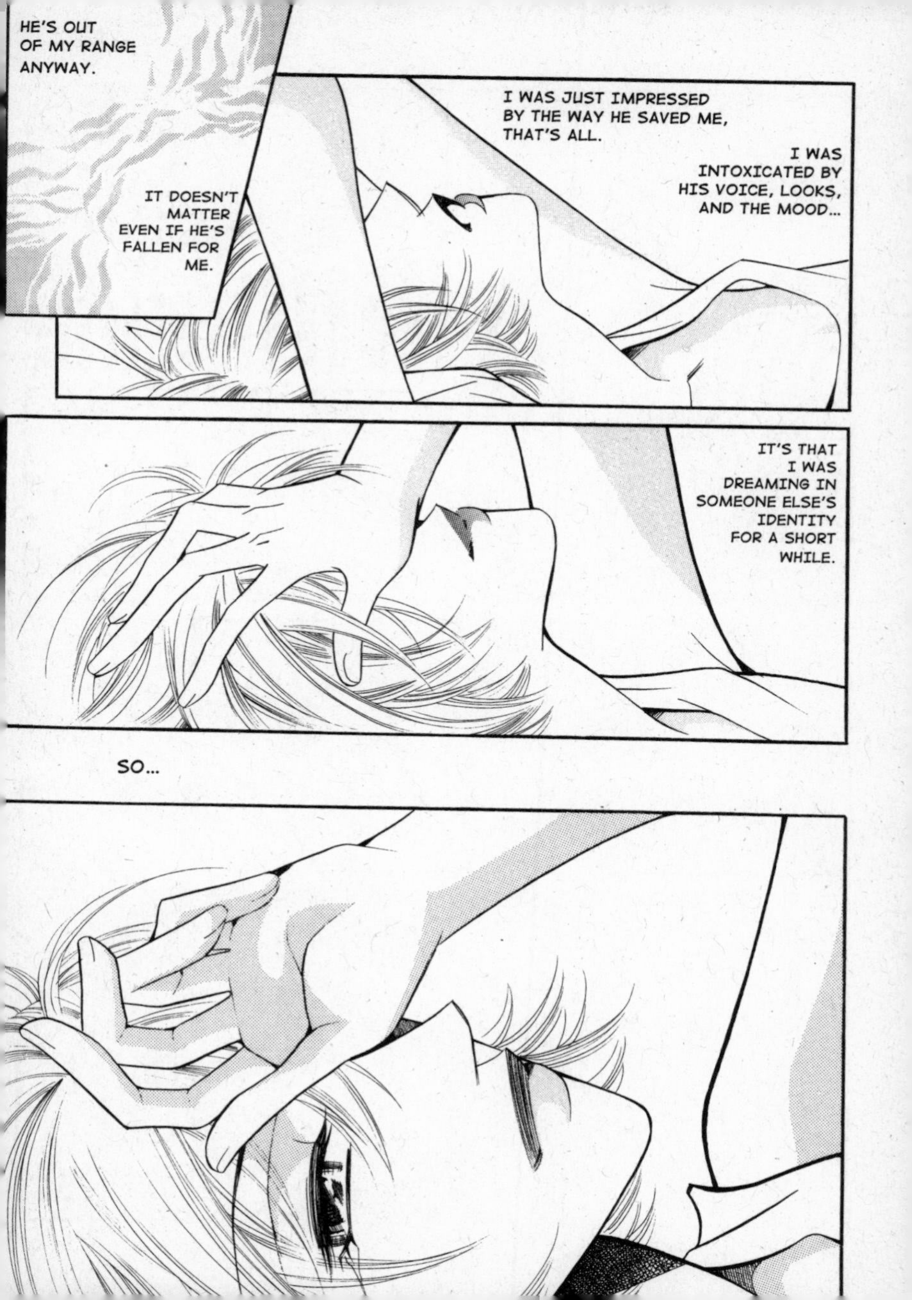
HE'S OUT OF MY RANGE ANYWAY.
I WAS JUST IMPRESSED BY THE WAY HE SAVED ME, THAT'S ALL.
I WAS INTOXICATED BY HIS VOICE, LOOKS, AND THE MOOD...
IT DOESN'T MATTER EVEN IF HE'S FALLEN FOR ME.
IT'S THAT I WAS DREAMING IN SOMEONE ELSE'S IDENTITY FOR A SHORT WHILE.
SO...

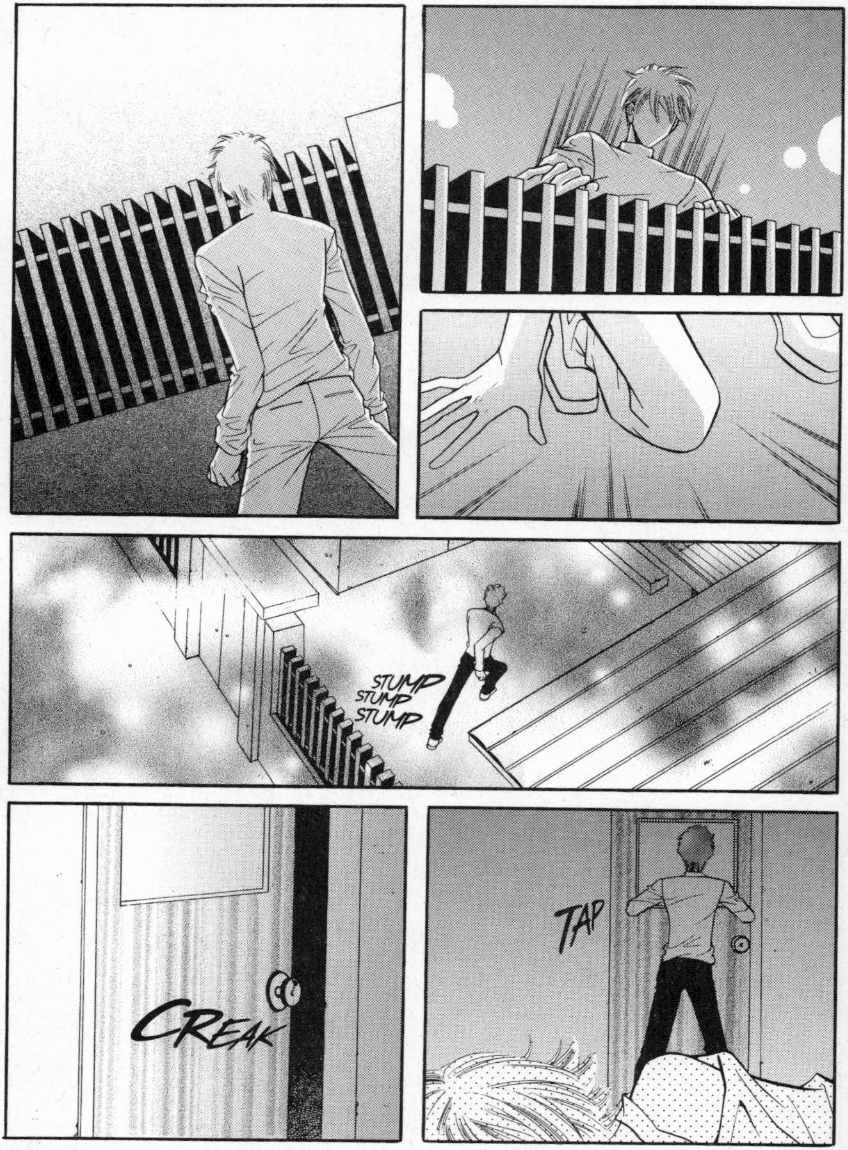
STUMP
STUMP
STUMP
TAP
CREAK

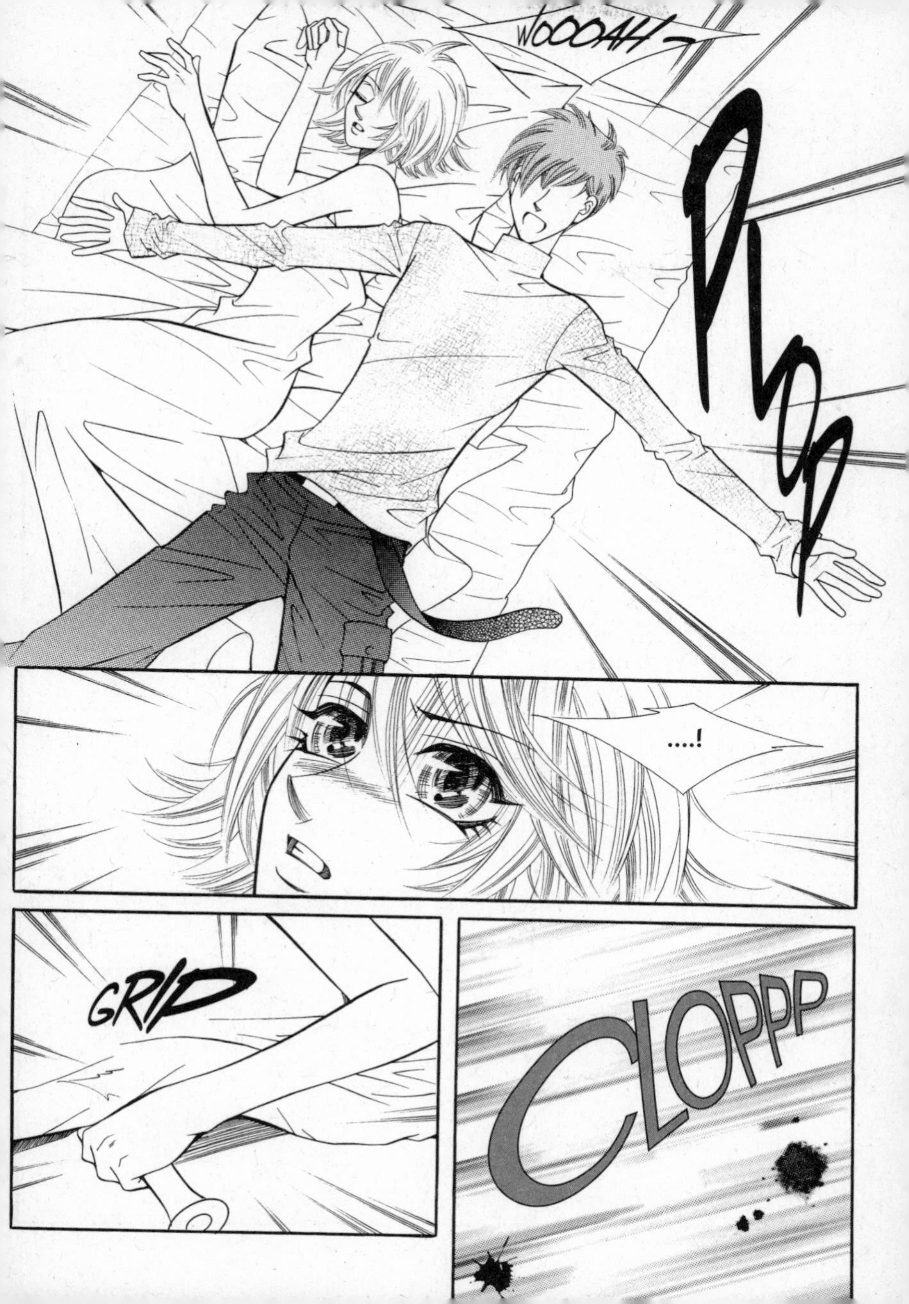
WOOOAH!
....!
CLOPPP
GRIP

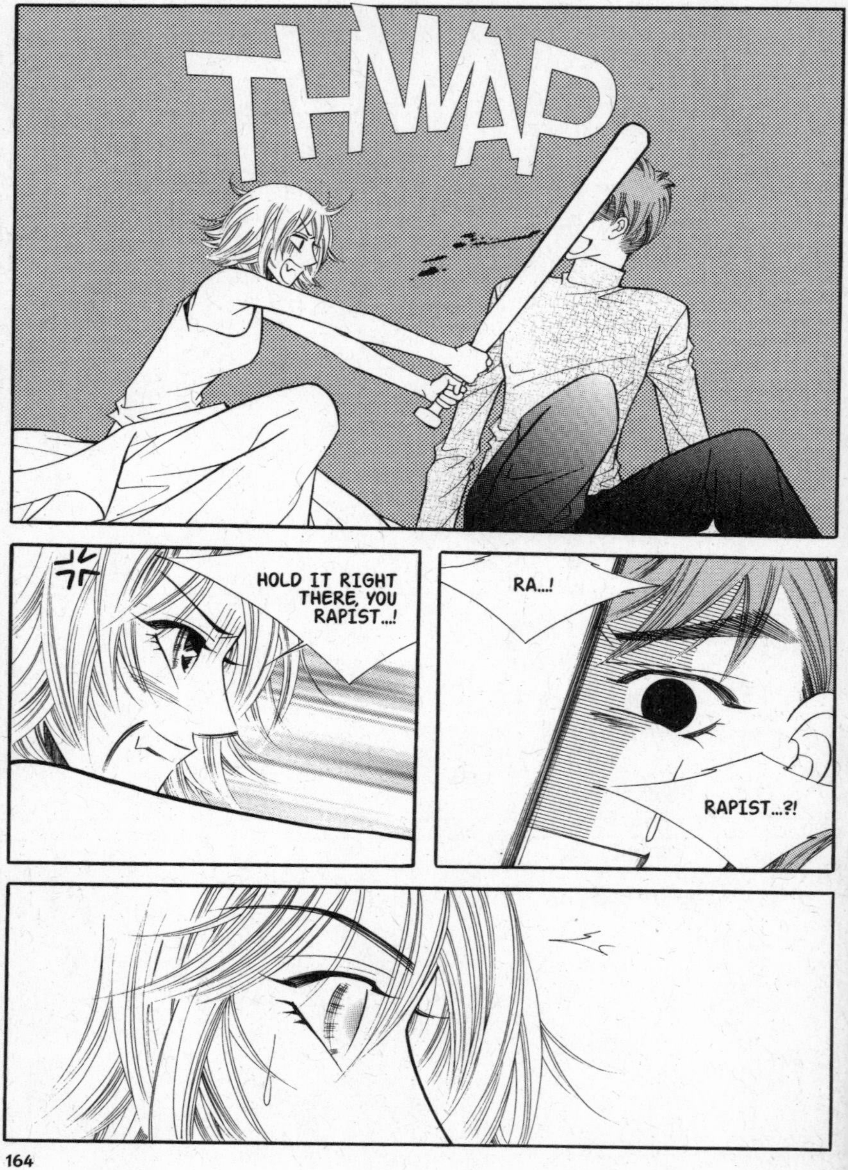
THWAP
HOLD IT RIGHT THERE, YOU RAPIST...!
RA...!
RAPIST...?!

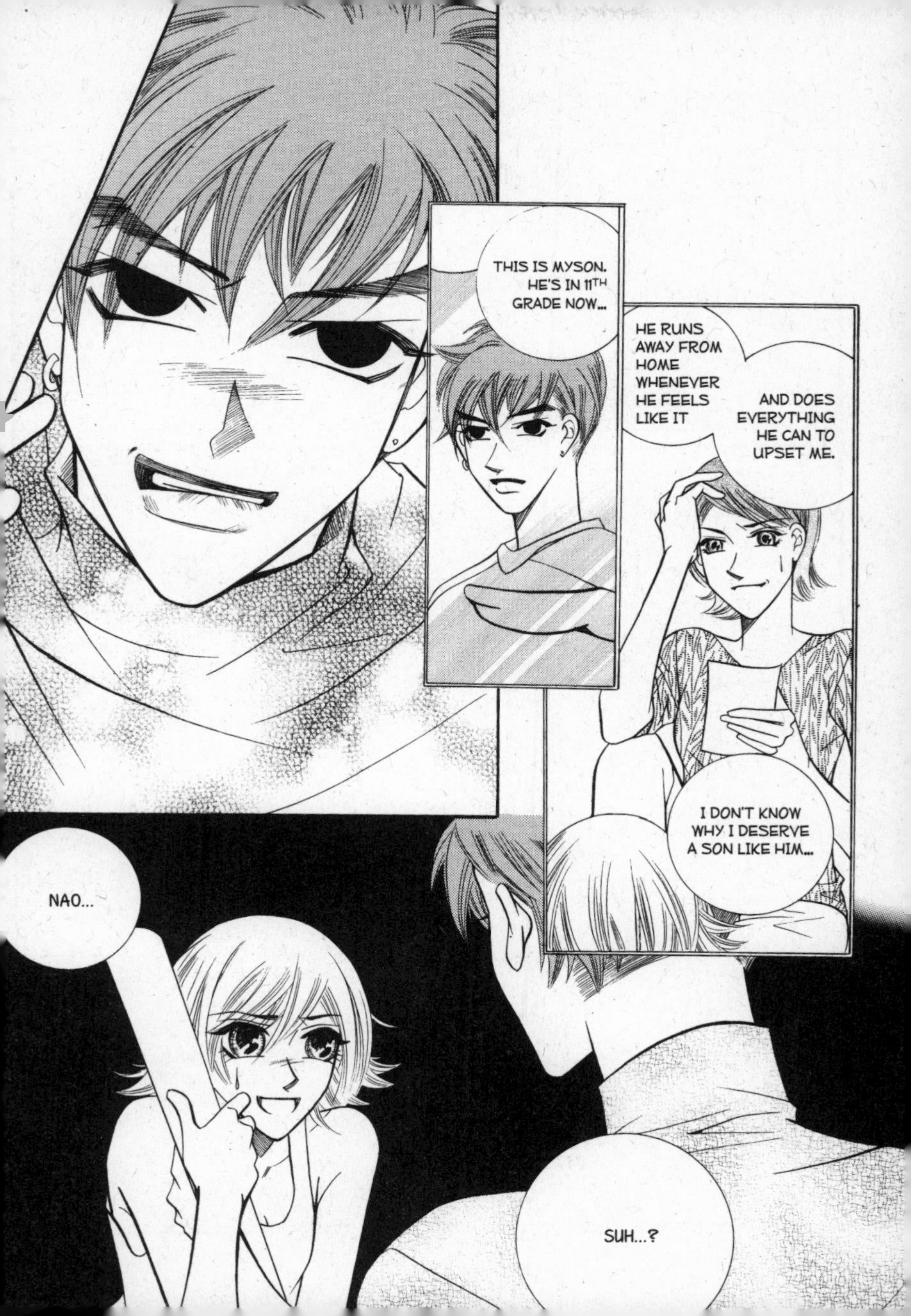
THIS IS MYSON. HE'S IN 11TH GRADE NOW...
HE RUNS AWAY FROM HOME WHENEVER HE FEELS LIKE IT
AND DOES EVERYTHING HE CAN TO UPSET ME.
I DON'T KNOW WHY I DESERVE A SON LIKE HIM...
NAO...
SUH...?

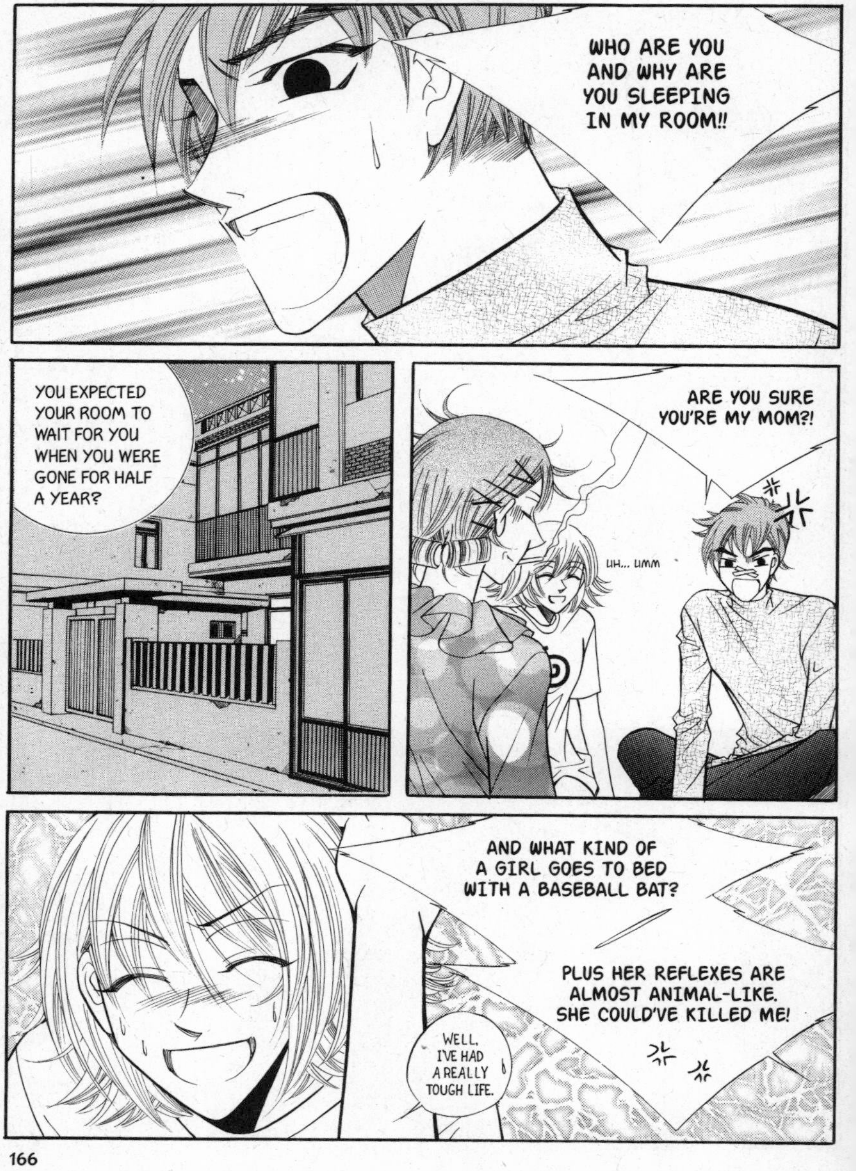
WHO ARE YOU AND WHY ARE YOU SLEEPING IN MY ROOM!!
YOU EXPECTED YOUR ROOM TO WAIT FOR YOU WHEN YOU WERE GONE FOR HALF A YEAR?
ARE YOU SURE YOU'RE MY MOM?!
UH... UMM
AND WHAT KIND OF A GIRL GOES TO BED WITH A BASEBALL BAT?
PLUS HER REFLEXES ARE ALMOST ANIMAL-LIKE. SHE COULD'VE KILLED ME!
WELL, I'VE HAD A REALLY TOUGH LIFE.

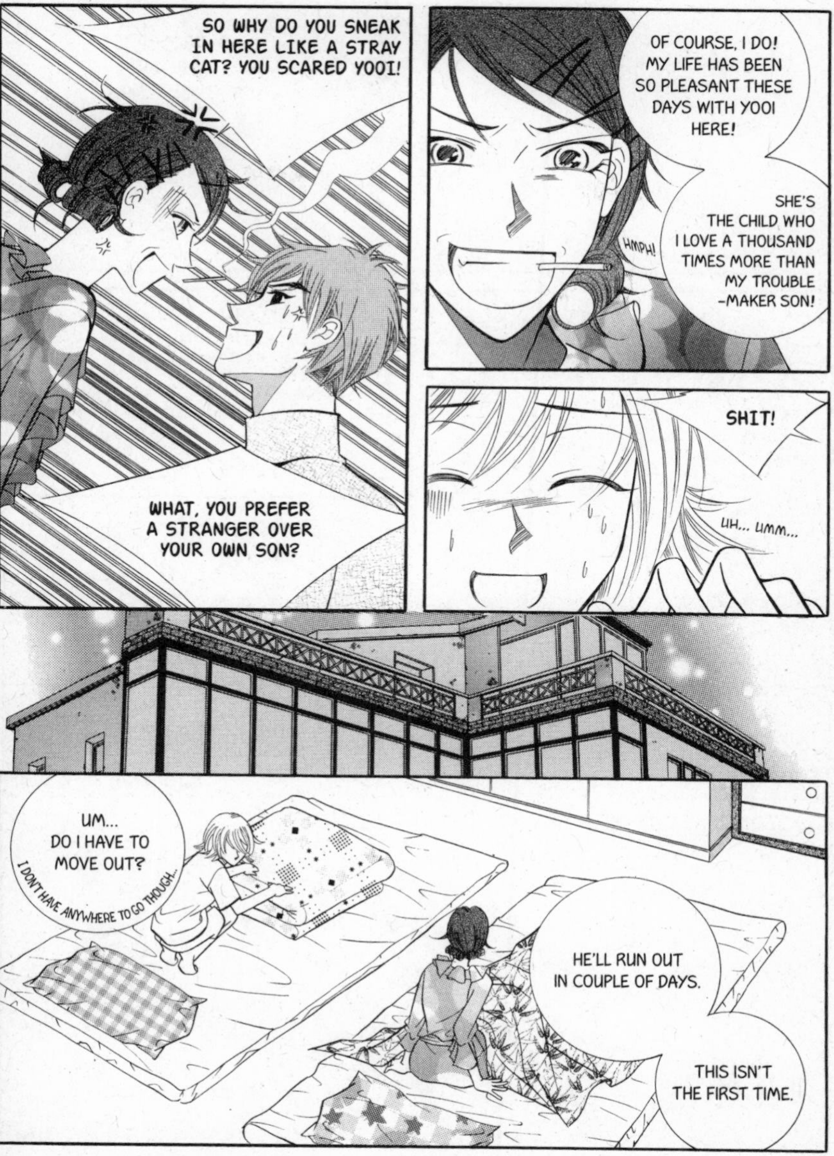

SO WHY DO YOU SNEAK IN HERE LIKE A STRAY CAT? YOU SCARED YOOI!
WHAT, YOU PREFER A STRANGER OVER YOUR OWN SON?
OF COURSE, I DO! MY LIFE HAS BEEN SO PLEASANT THESE DAYS WITH YOOI HERE!
HMPH!
SHE'S THE CHILD WHO I LOVE A THOUSAND TIMES MORE THAN MY TROUBLE-MAKER SON!
SHIT!
UH... UMM...
UM... DO I HAVE TO MOVE OUT?
I DON'T HAVE ANYWHERE TO GO THOUGH...
HE'LL RUN OUT IN COUPLE OF DAYS.
THIS ISN'T THE FIRST TIME.

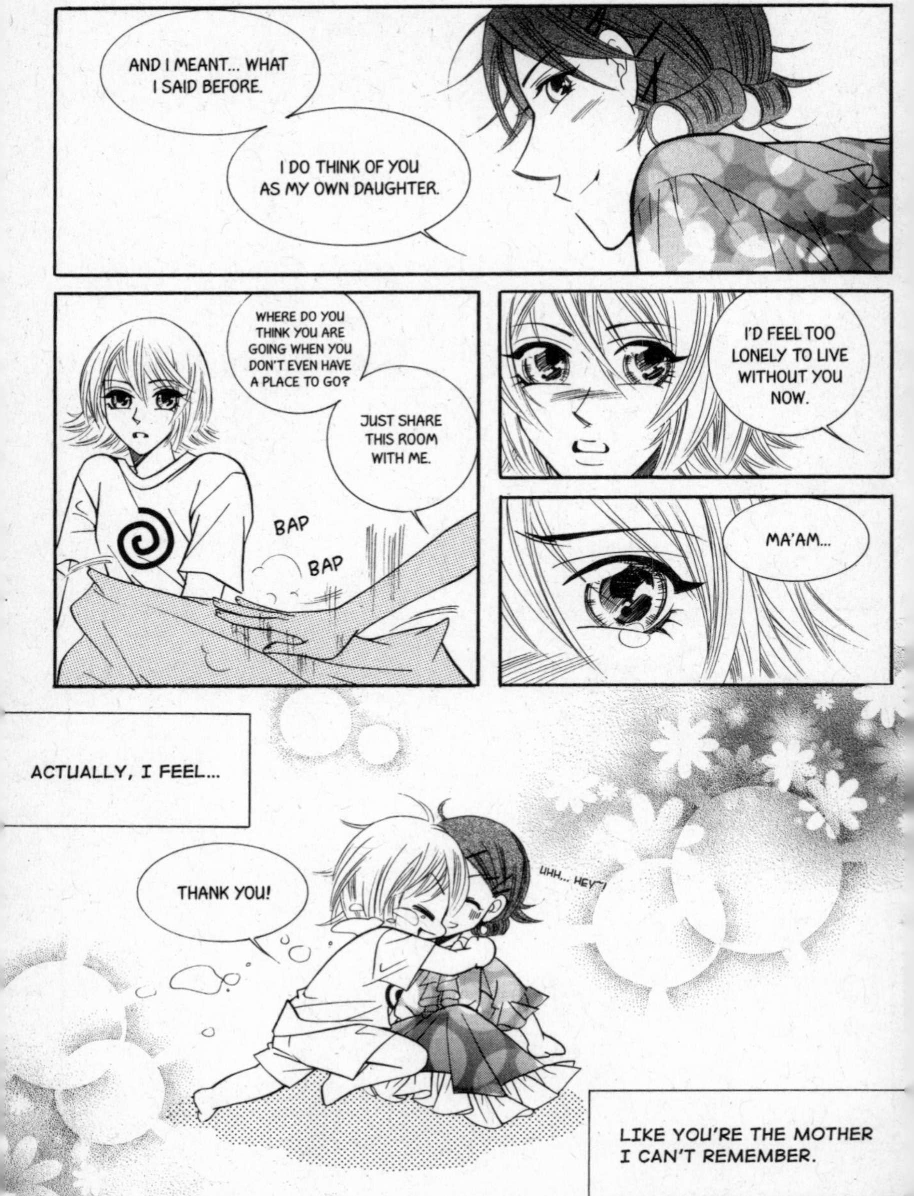
AND I MEANT... WHAT I SAID BEFORE.
I DO THINK OF YOU AS MY OWN DAUGHTER.
WHERE DO YOU THINK YOU ARE GOING WHEN YOU DON'T EVEN HAVE A PLACE TO GO?
JUST SHARE THIS ROOM WITH ME.
BAP
BAP
I'D FEEL TOO LONELY TO LIVE WITHOUT YOU NOW.
MA'AM...
ACTUALLY, I FEEL...
THANK YOU!
UHH... HEY
LIKE YOU'RE THE MOTHER I CAN'T REMEMBER.

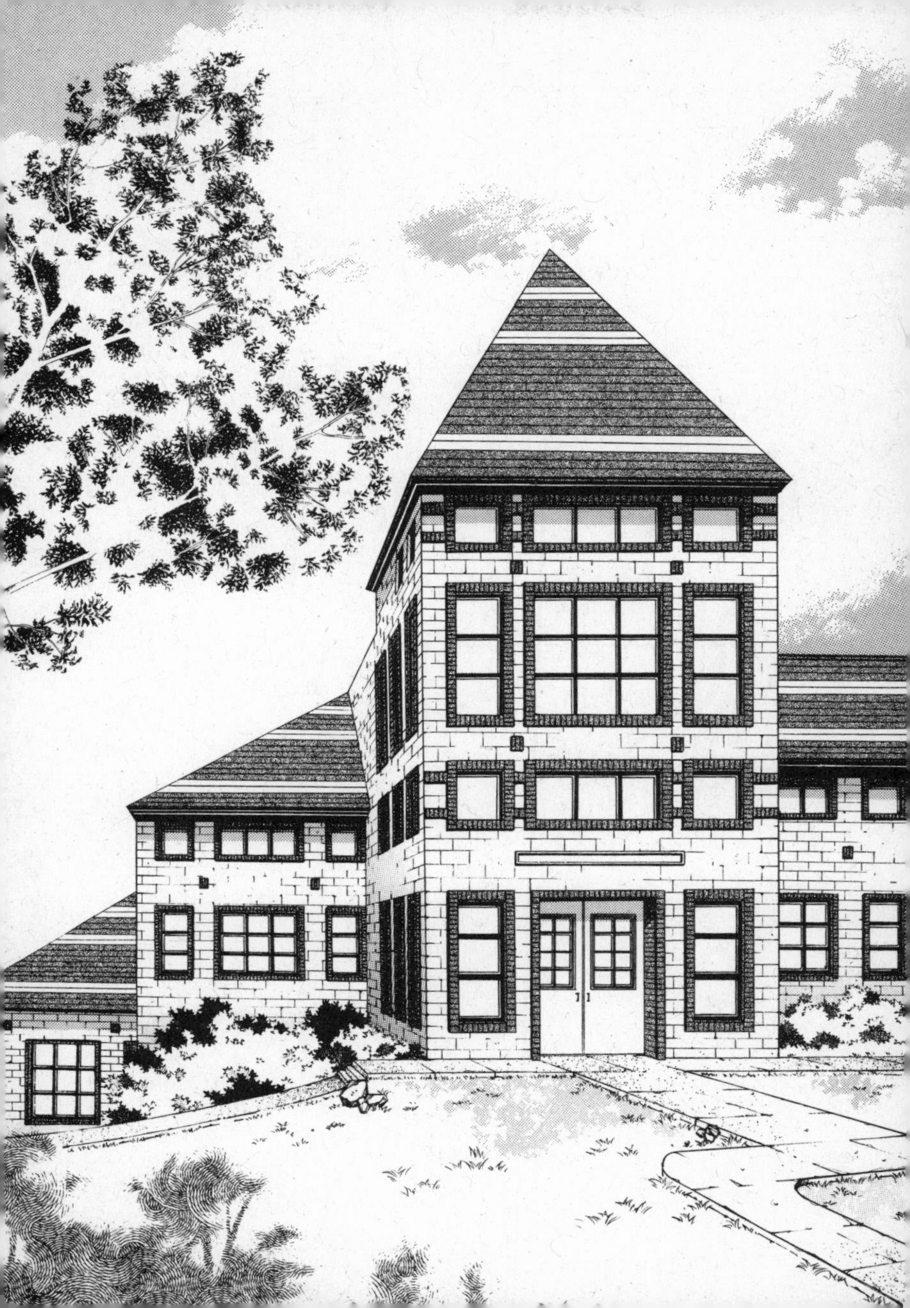

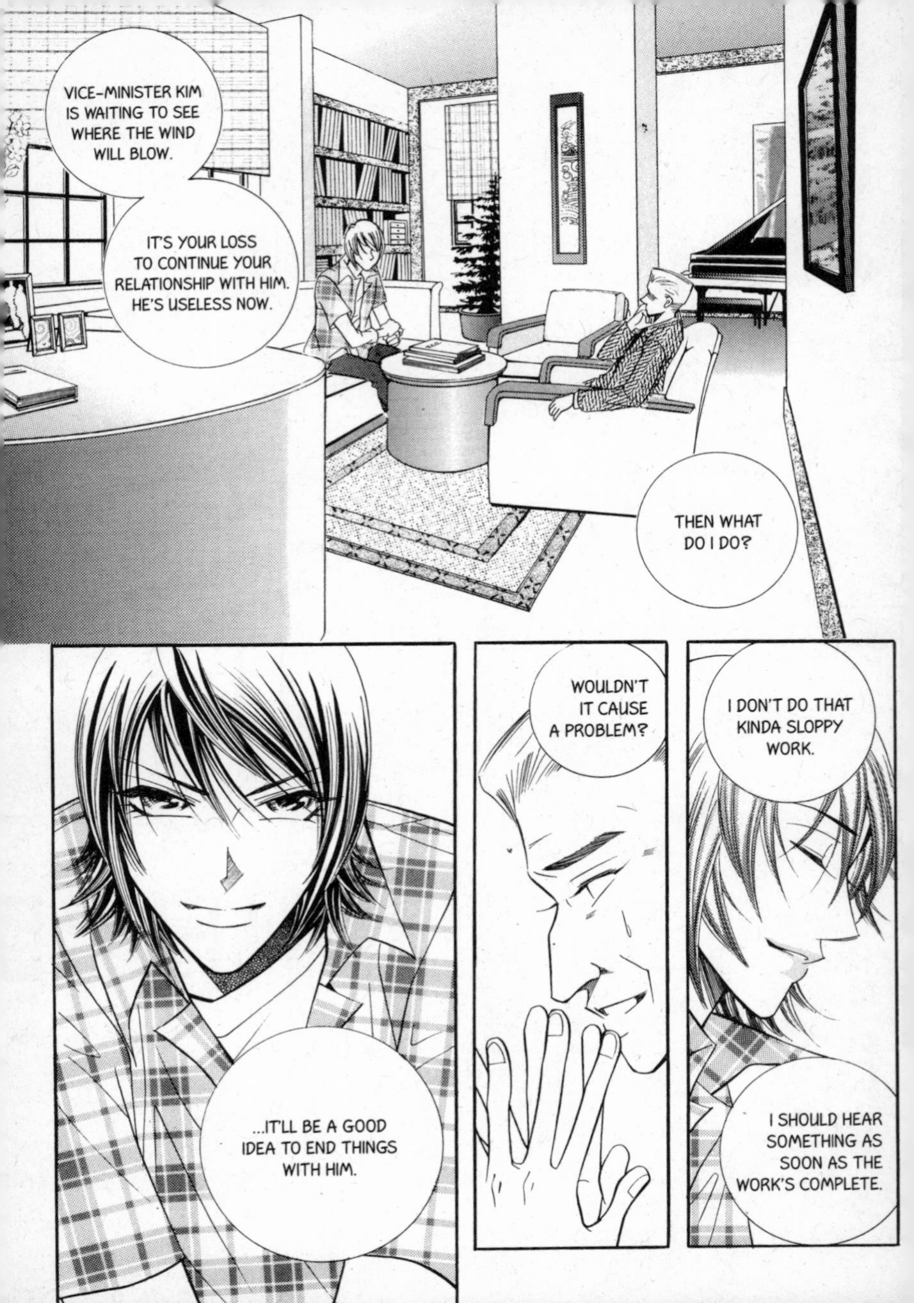
VICE-MINISTER KIM IS WAITING TO SEE WHERE THE WIND WILL BLOW.
IT'S YOUR LOSS TO CONTINUE YOUR RELATIONSHIP WITH HIM. HE'S USELESS NOW.
THEN WHAT DO I DO?
...IT'LL BE A GOOD IDEA TO END THINGS WITH HIM.
WOULDN'T IT CAUSE A PROBLEM?
I DON'T DO THAT KINDA SLOPPY WORK.
I SHOULD HEAR SOMETHING AS SOON AS THE WORK'S COMPLETE.

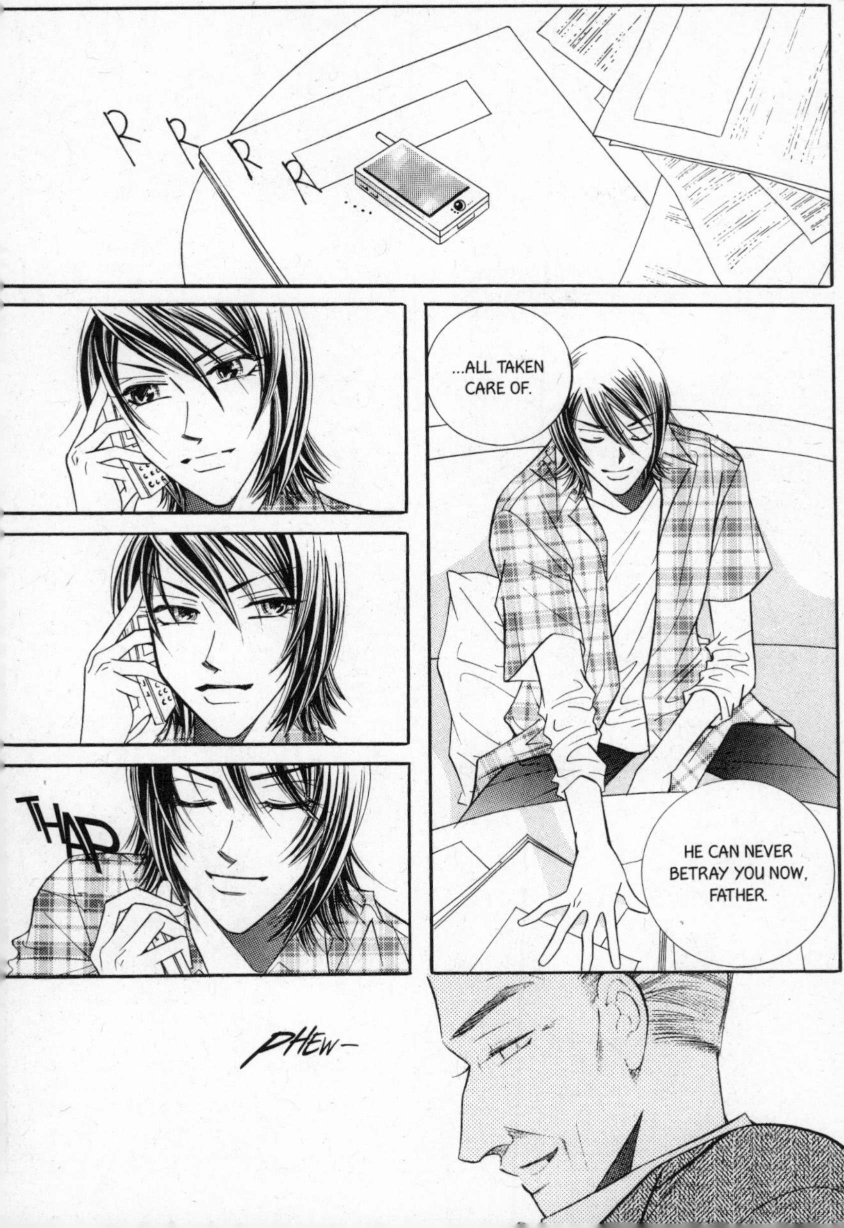
R R R R ....
...ALL TAKEN CARE OF.
THAP
HE CAN NEVER BETRAY YOU NOW, FATHER.
PHEW–

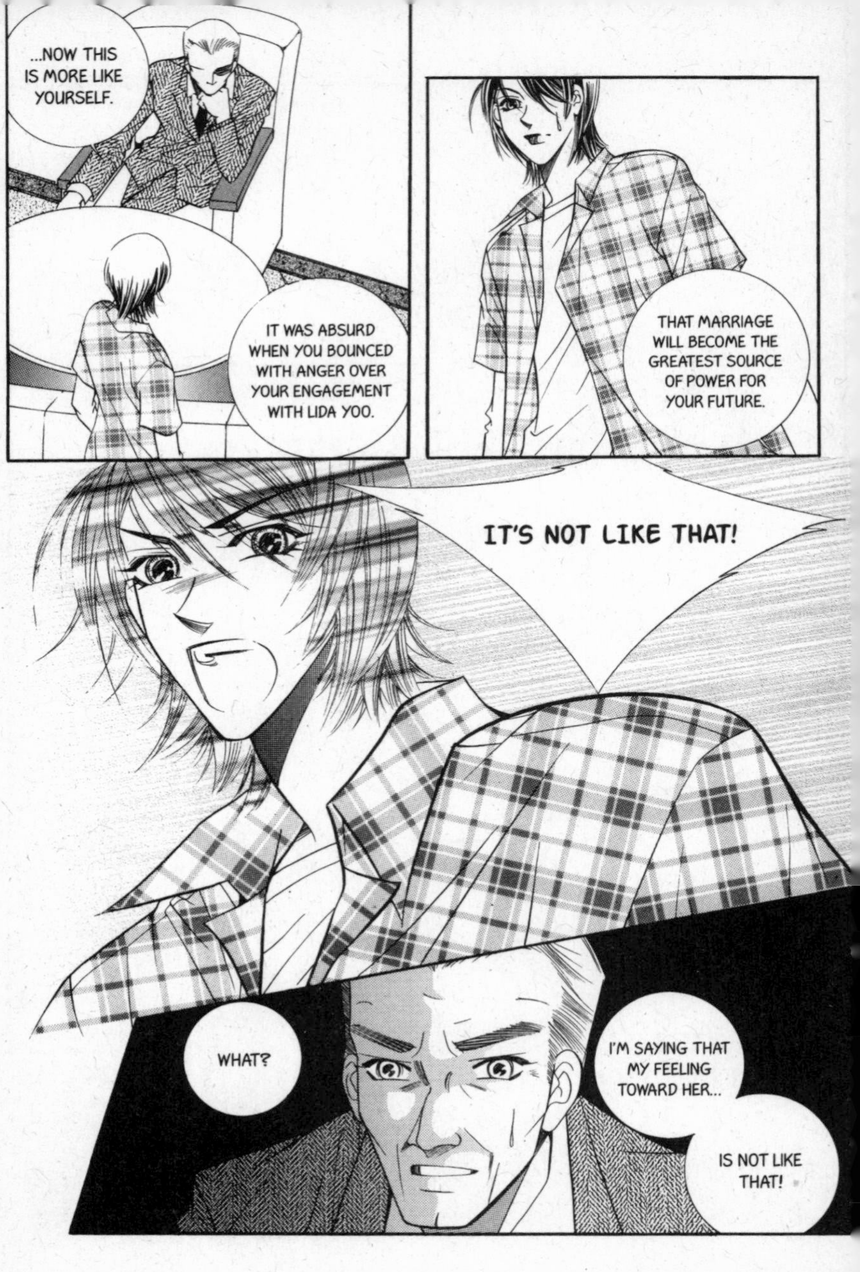
...NOW THIS IS MORE LIKE YOURSELF.
IT WAS ABSURD WHEN YOU BOUNCED WITH ANGER OVER YOUR ENGAGEMENT WITH LIDA YOO.
THAT MARRIAGE WILL BECOME THE GREATEST SOURCE OF POWER FOR YOUR FUTURE.
IT'S NOT LIKE THAT!
WHAT?
I'M SAYING THAT MY FEELING TOWARD HER...
IS NOT LIKE THAT!

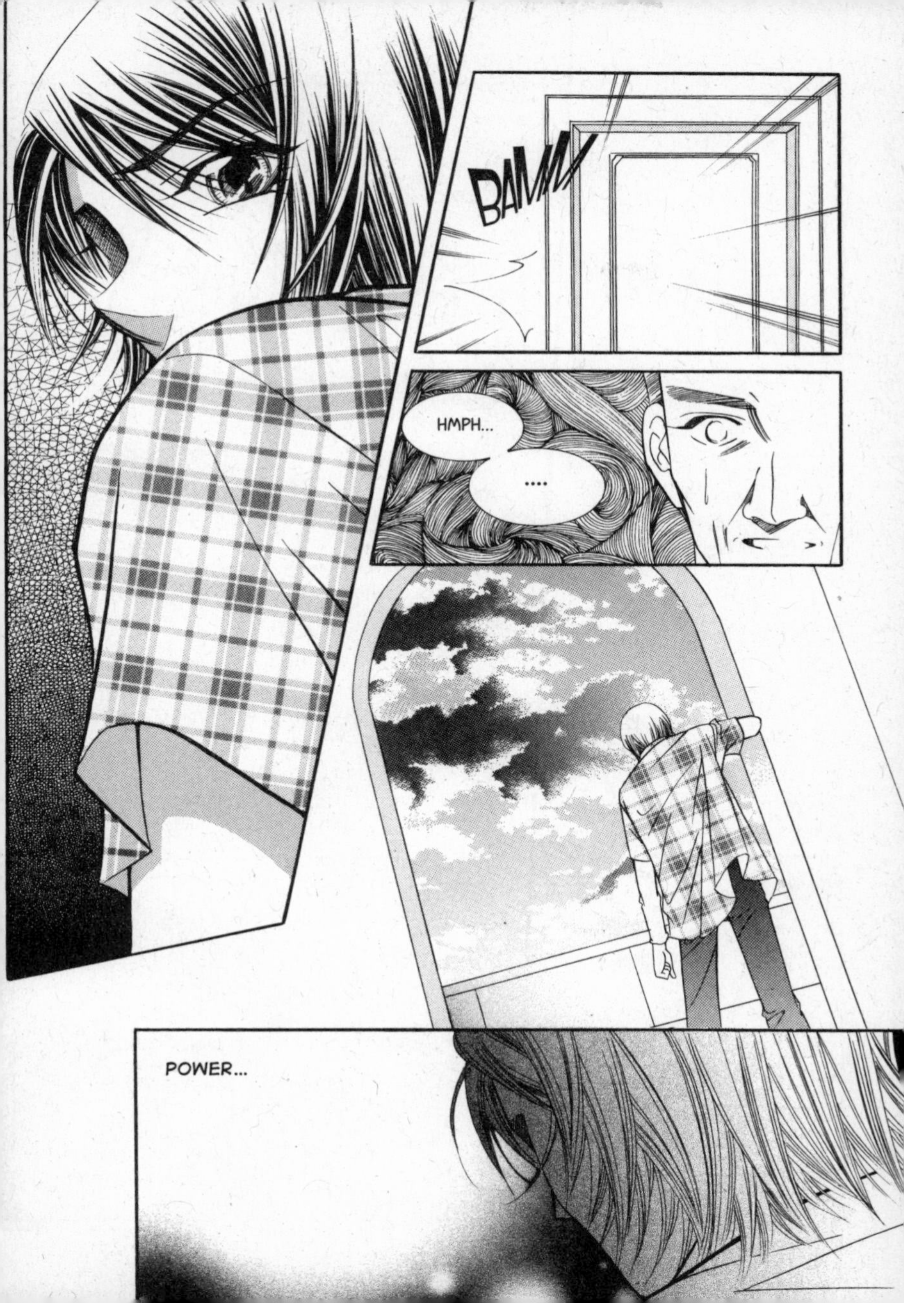
BAMM
HMPH...
....
POWER...

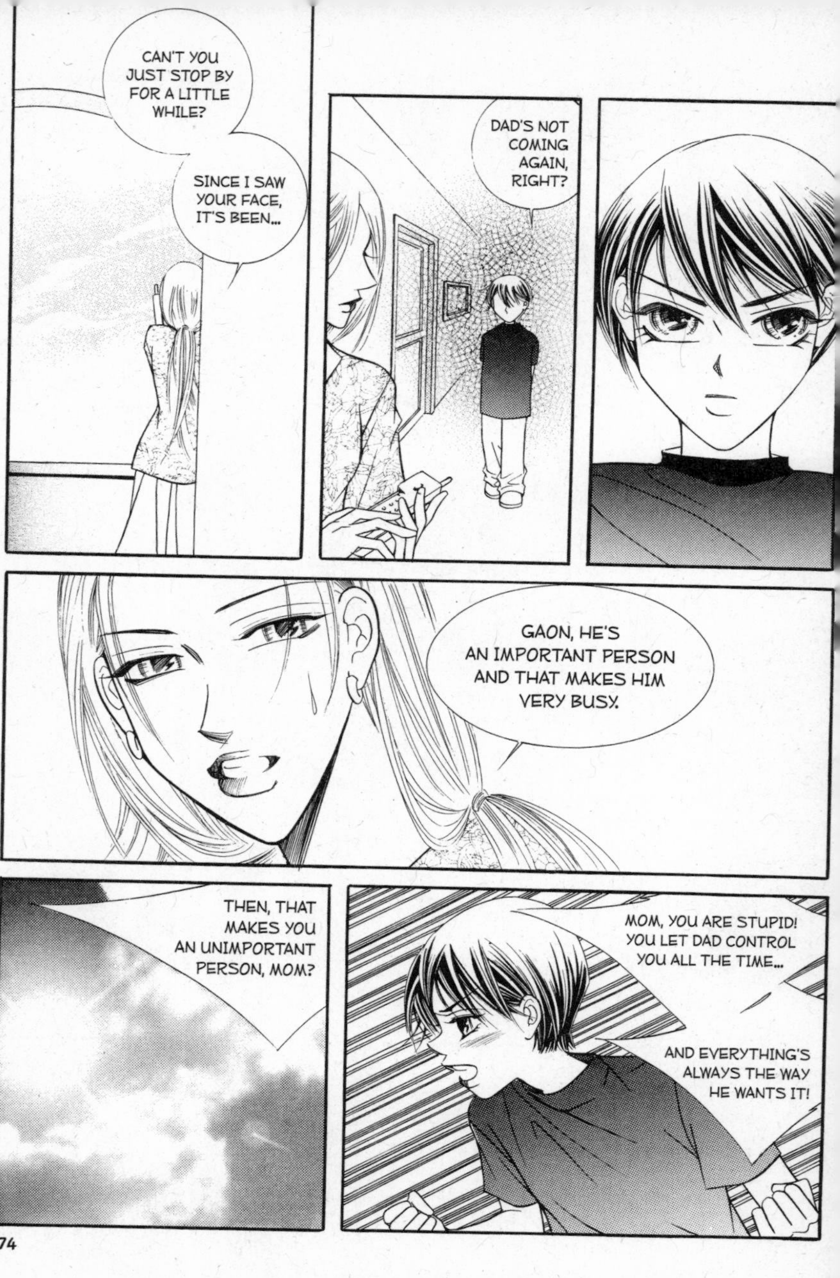
CAN'T YOU JUST STOP BY FOR A LITTLE WHILE?
SINCE I SAW YOUR FACE, IT'S BEEN...
DAD'S NOT COMING AGAIN, RIGHT?
GAON, HE'S AN IMPORTANT PERSON AND THAT MAKES HIM VERY BUSY.
THEN, THAT MAKES YOU AN UNIMPORTANT PERSON, MOM?
MOM, YOU ARE STUPID! YOU LET DAD CONTROL YOU ALL THE TIME...
AND EVERYTHING'S ALWAYS THE WAY HE WANTS IT!

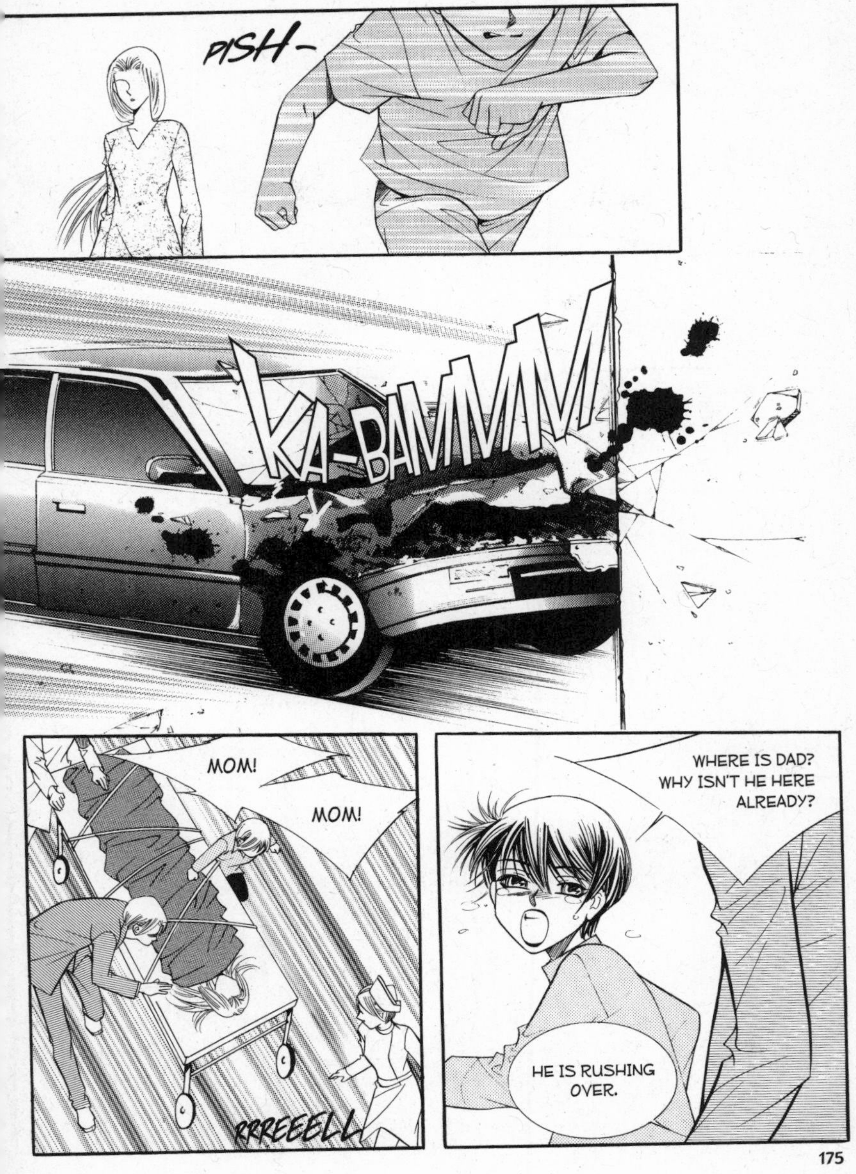
PISH-
KA-BAMMMM
MOM!
MOM!
RRREEELL
WHERE IS DAD? WHY ISN'T HE HERE ALREADY?
HE IS RUSHING OVER.

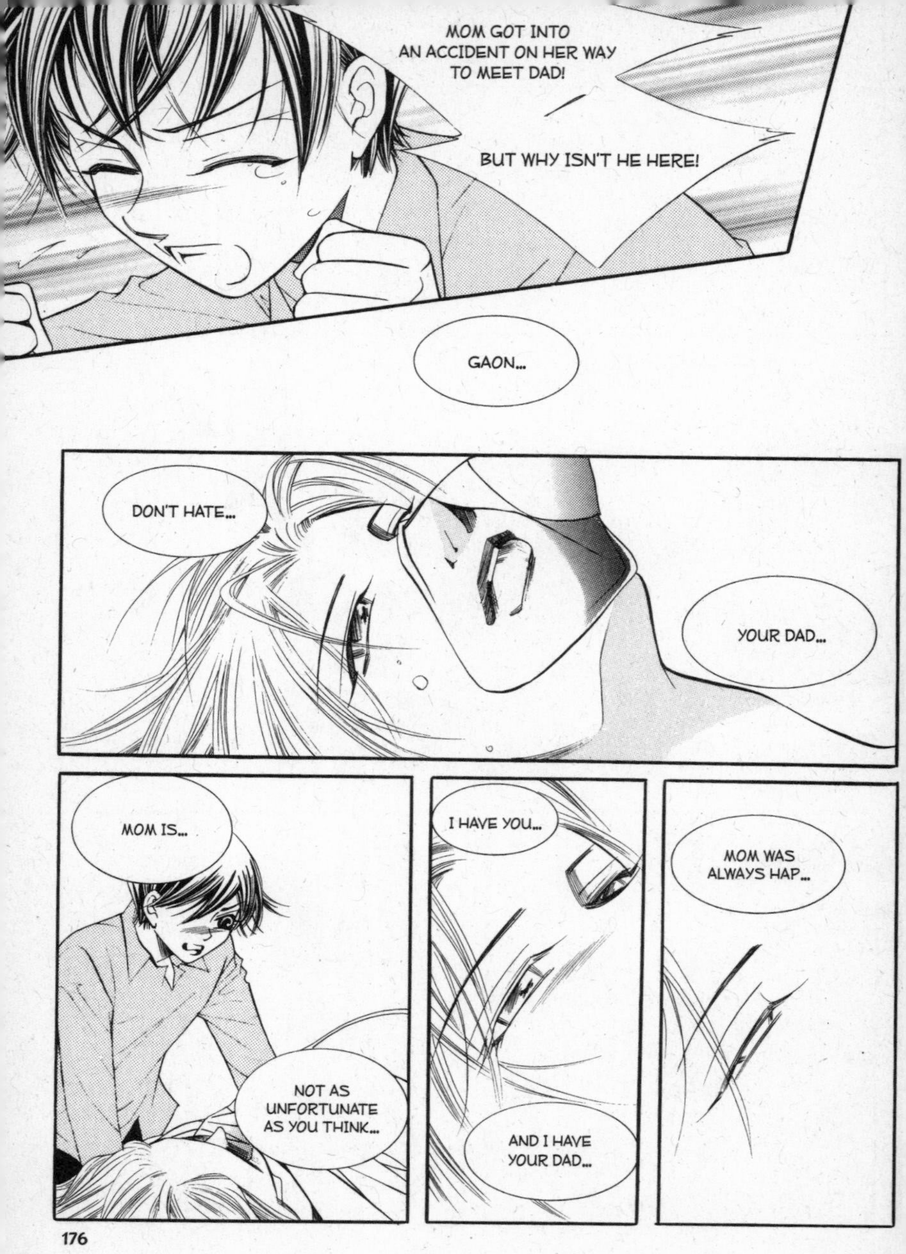
MOM GOT INTO AN ACCIDENT ON HER WAY TO MEET DAD!
BUT WHY ISN'T HE HERE!
GAON...
DON'T HATE...
YOUR DAD...
MOM IS...
NOT AS UNFORTUNATE AS YOU THINK...
I HAVE YOU...
AND I HAVE YOUR DAD...
MOM WAS ALWAYS HAP...

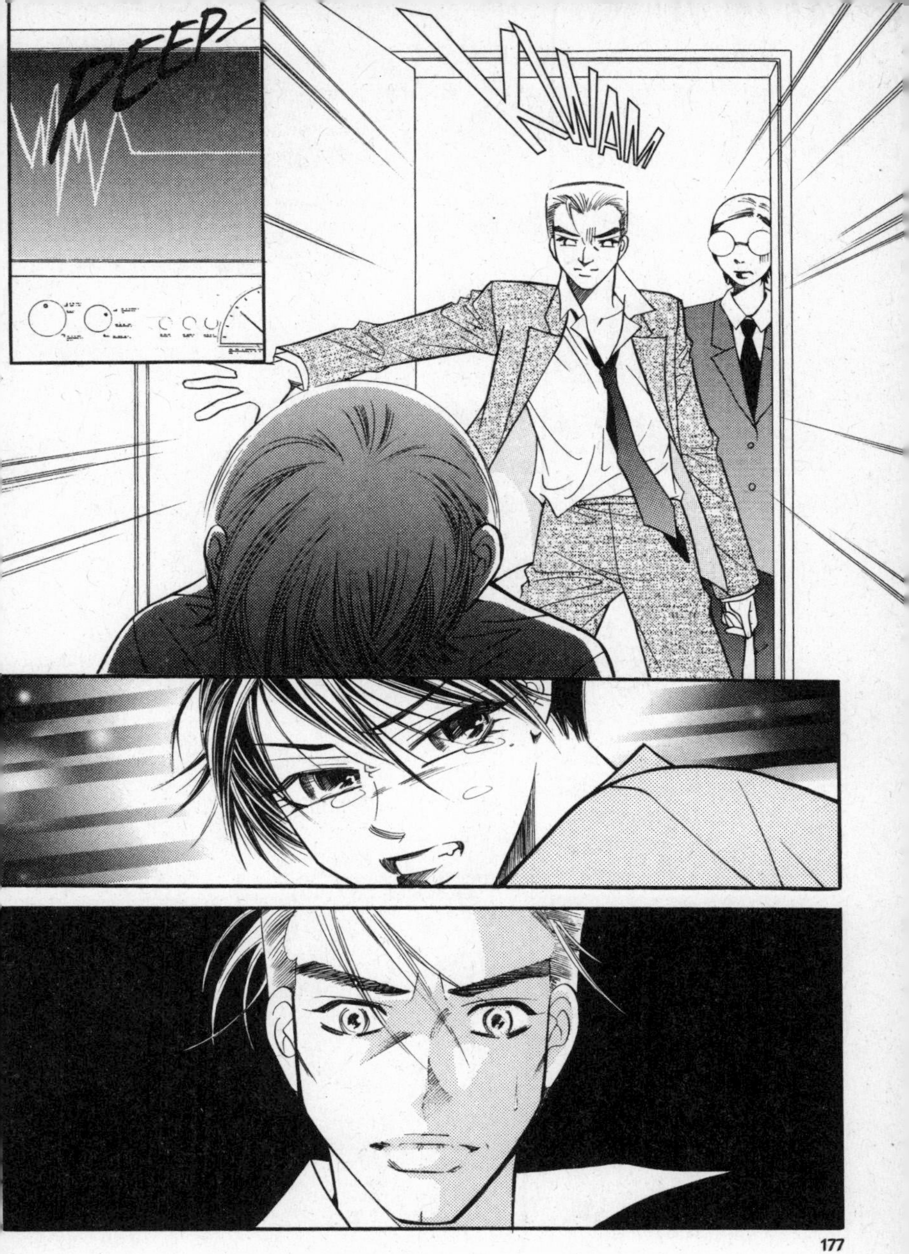
BEEP
WHAM

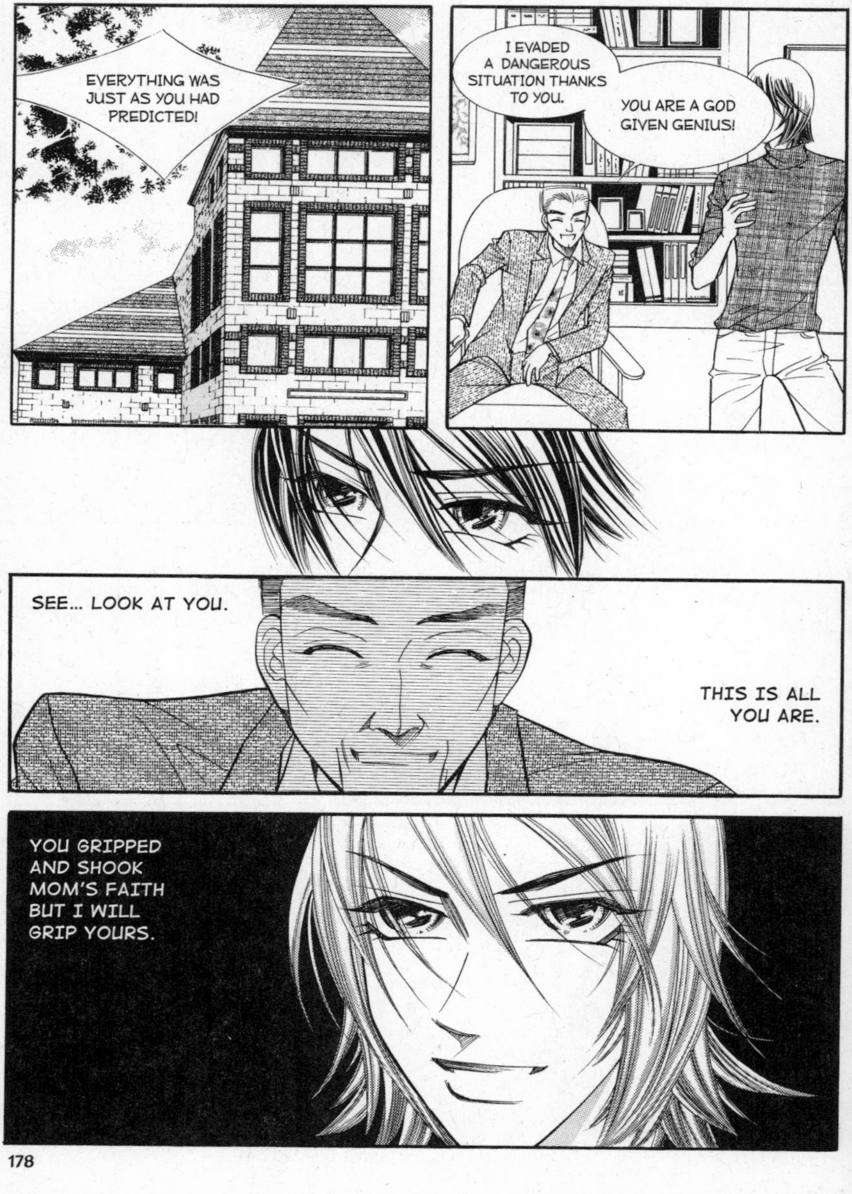
EVERYTHING WAS JUST AS YOU HAD PREDICTED!
I EVADED A DANGEROUS SITUATION THANKS TO YOU.
YOU ARE A GOD GIVEN GENIUS!
SEE... LOOK AT YOU.
THIS IS ALL YOU ARE.
YOU GRIPPED AND SHOOK MOM'S FAITH BUT I WILL GRIP YOURS.

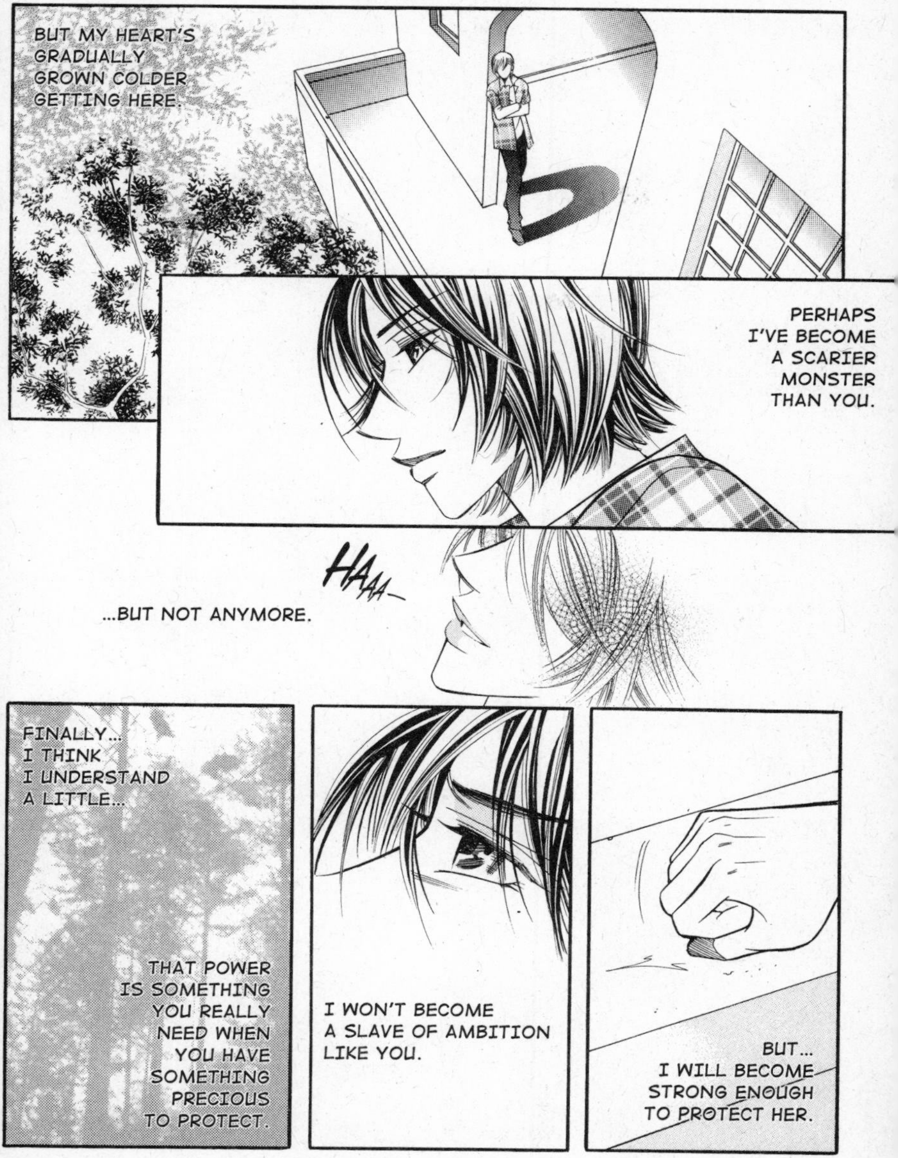
BUT MY HEART'S GRADUALLY GROWN COLDER GETTING HERE.
PERHAPS I'VE BECOME A SCARIER MONSTER THAN YOU.
HAAA-
...BUT NOT ANYMORE.
FINALLY... I THINK I UNDERSTAND A LITTLE...
THAT POWER IS SOMETHING YOU REALLY NEED WHEN YOU HAVE SOMETHING PRECIOUS TO PROTECT.
I WON'T BECOME A SLAVE OF AMBITION LIKE YOU.
BUT... I WILL BECOME STRONG ENOUGH TO PROTECT HER.

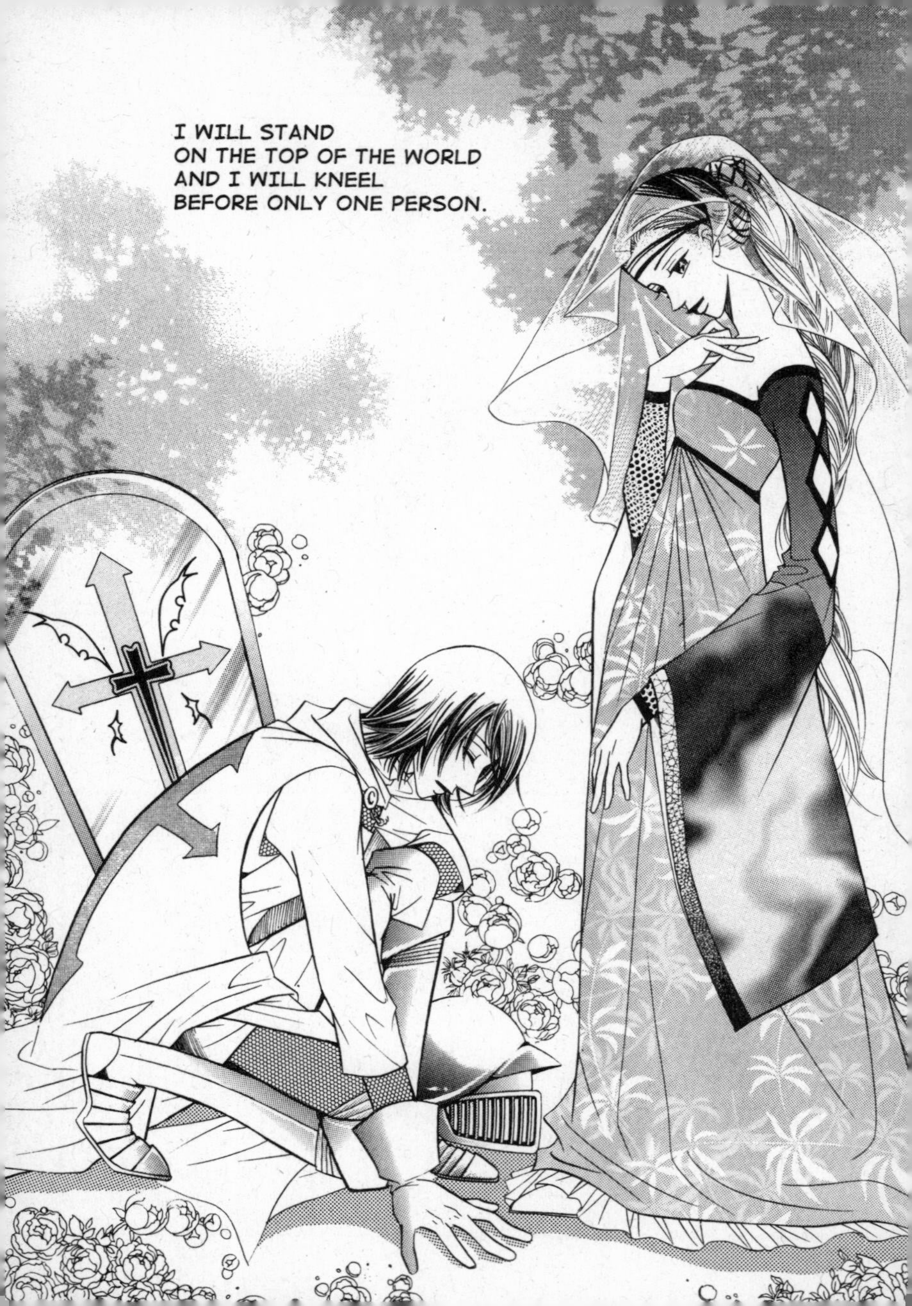
I WILL STAND
ON THE TOP OF THE WORLD
AND I WILL KNEEL
BEFORE ONLY ONE PERSON.

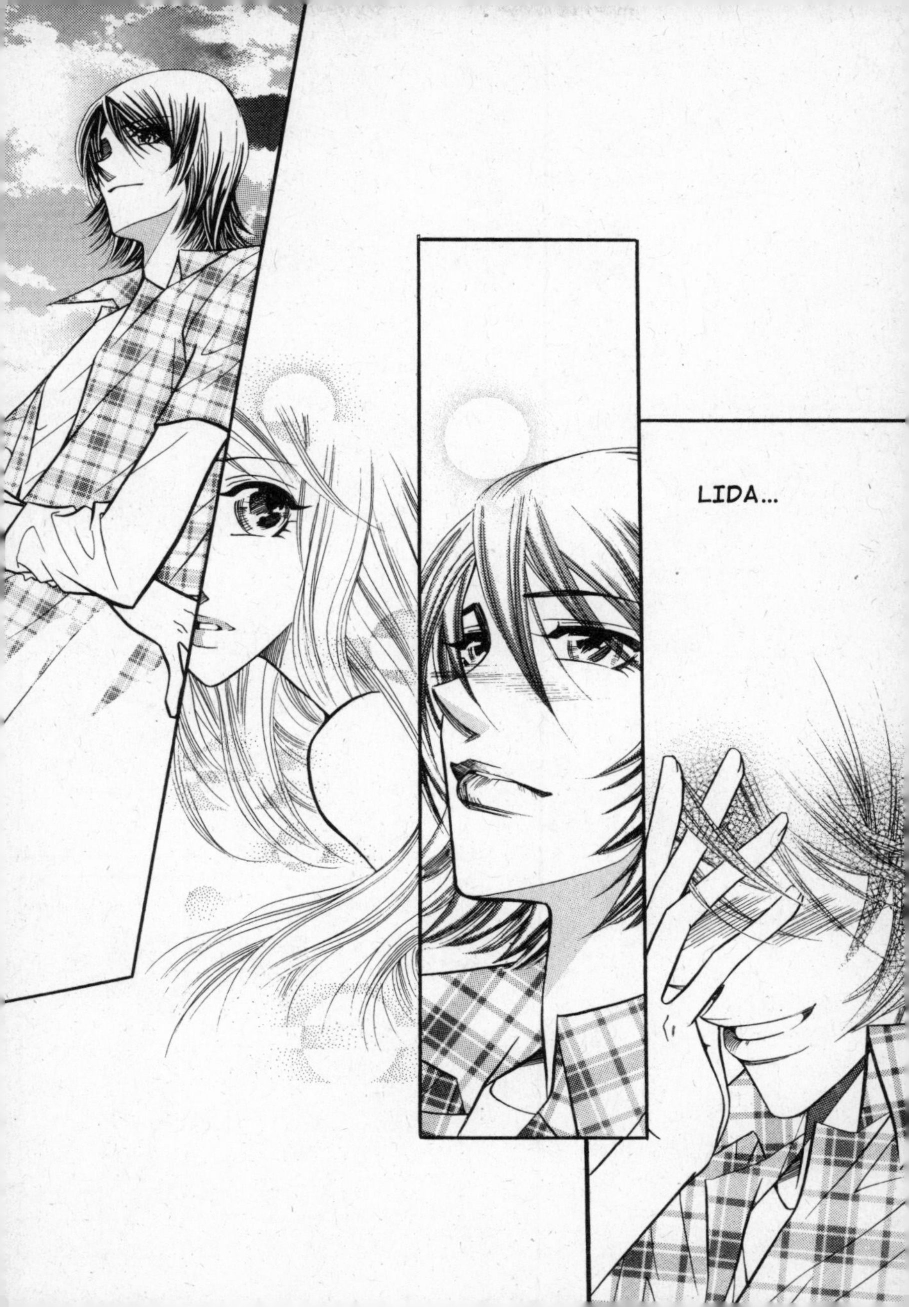
LIDA...

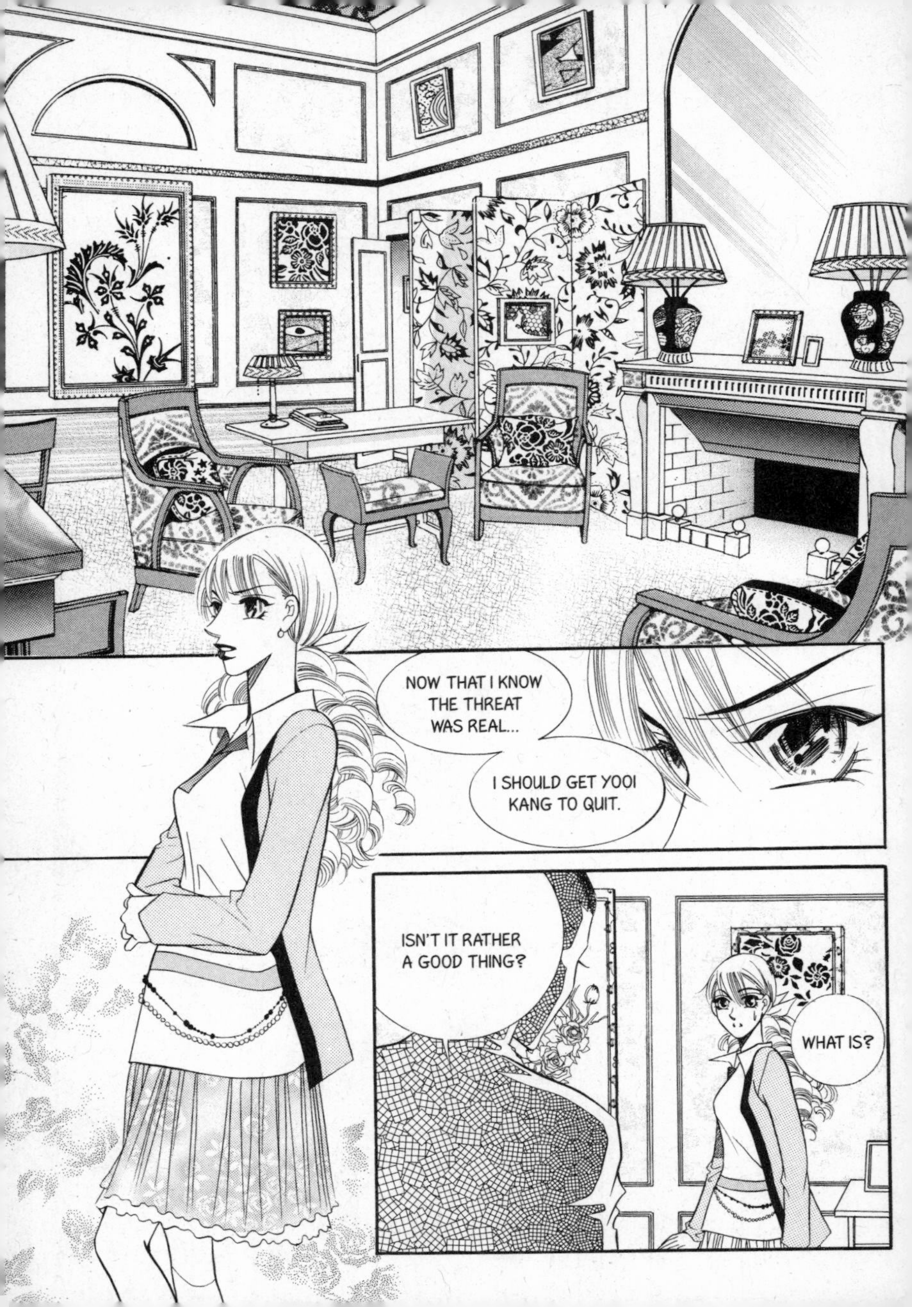
NOW THAT I KNOW THE THREAT WAS REAL...
I SHOULD GET YOOI KANG TO QUIT.
ISN'T IT RATHER A GOOD THING?
WHAT IS?

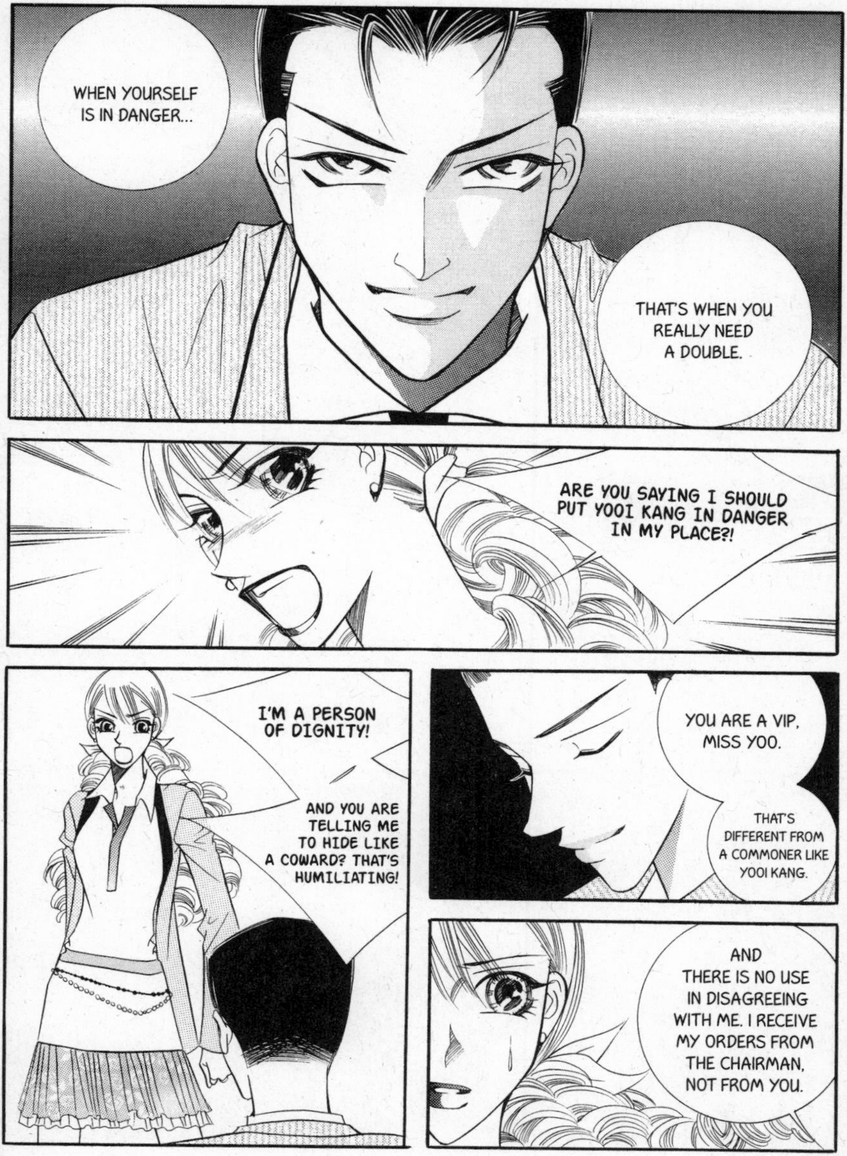
WHEN YOURSELF IS IN DANGER...
THAT'S WHEN YOU REALLY NEED A DOUBLE.
ARE YOU SAYING I SHOULD PUT YOOI KANG IN DANGER IN MY PLACE?!
I'M A PERSON OF DIGNITY!
AND YOU ARE TELLING ME TO HIDE LIKE A COWARD? THAT'S HUMILIATING!
YOU ARE A VIP, MISS YOO.
THAT'S DIFFERENT FROM A COMMONER LIKE YOOI KANG.
AND THERE IS NO USE IN DISAGREEING WITH ME. I RECEIVE MY ORDERS FROM THE CHAIRMAN, NOT FROM YOU.

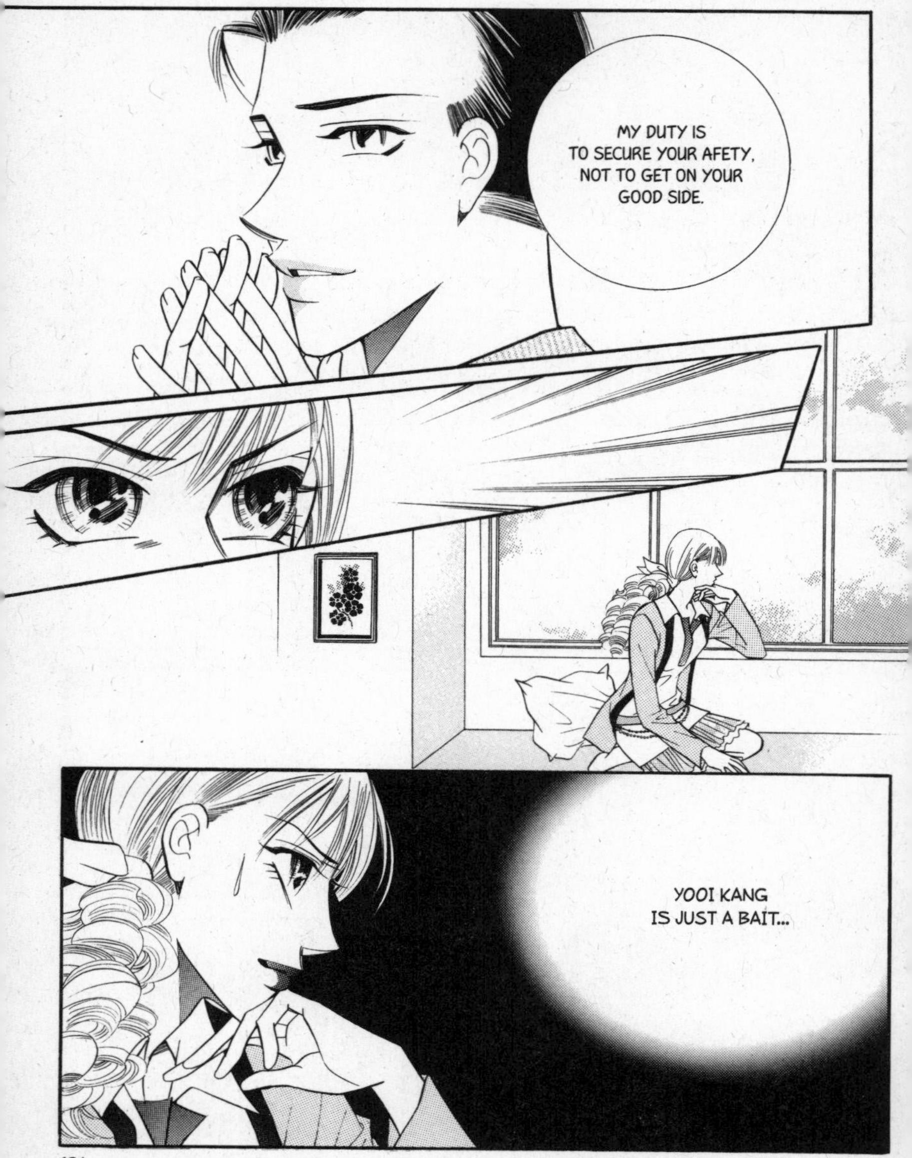
MY DUTY IS TO SECURE YOUR AFETY, NOT TO GET ON YOUR GOOD SIDE.
YOOI KANG IS JUST A BAIT...

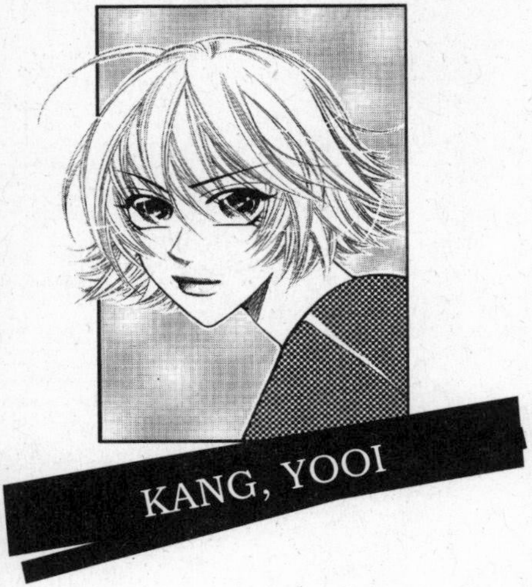
KANG, YOOI

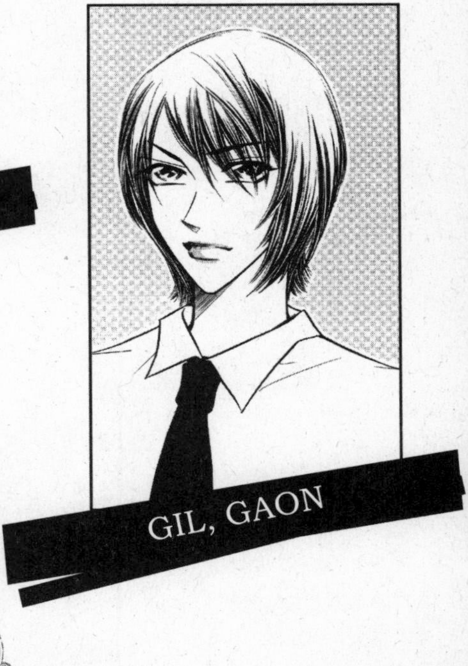
GIL, GAON

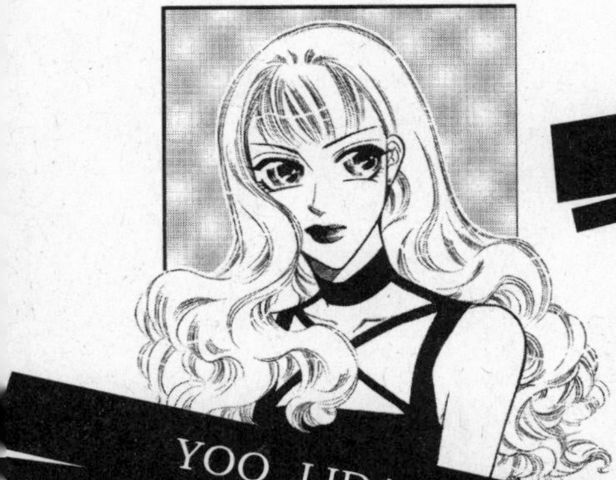
YOO, LIDA

THE END.

To be continued in volume 2 available in June 2006.

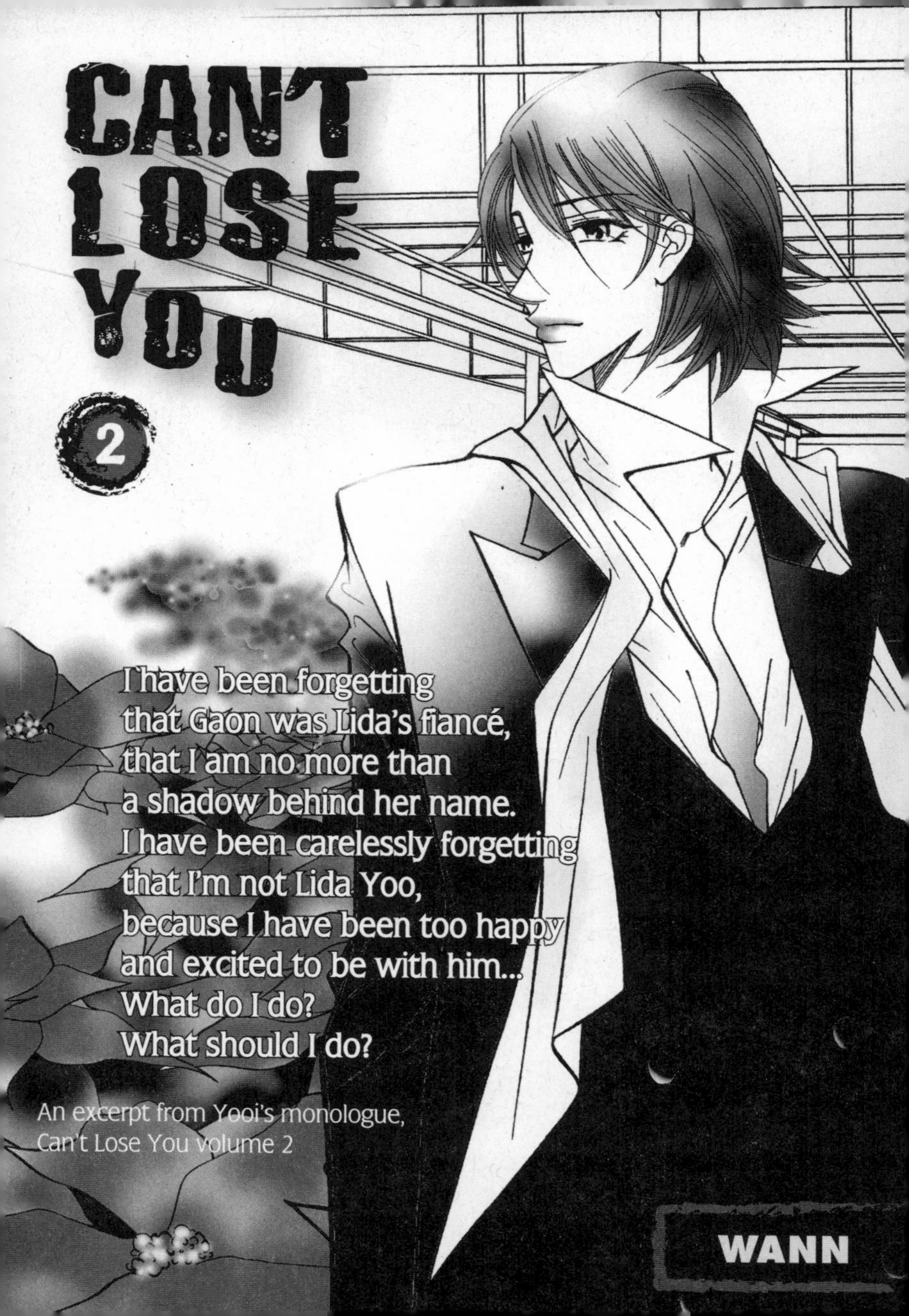
CAN'T LOSE YOU
2
I have been forgetting
that Gaon was Lida's fiancé,
that I am no more than
a shadow behind her name.
I have been carelessly forgetting
that I'm not Lida Yoo,
because I have been too happy
and excited to be with him...
What do I do?
What should I do?
An excerpt from Yooi's monologue,
Can't Lose You volume 2
WANN

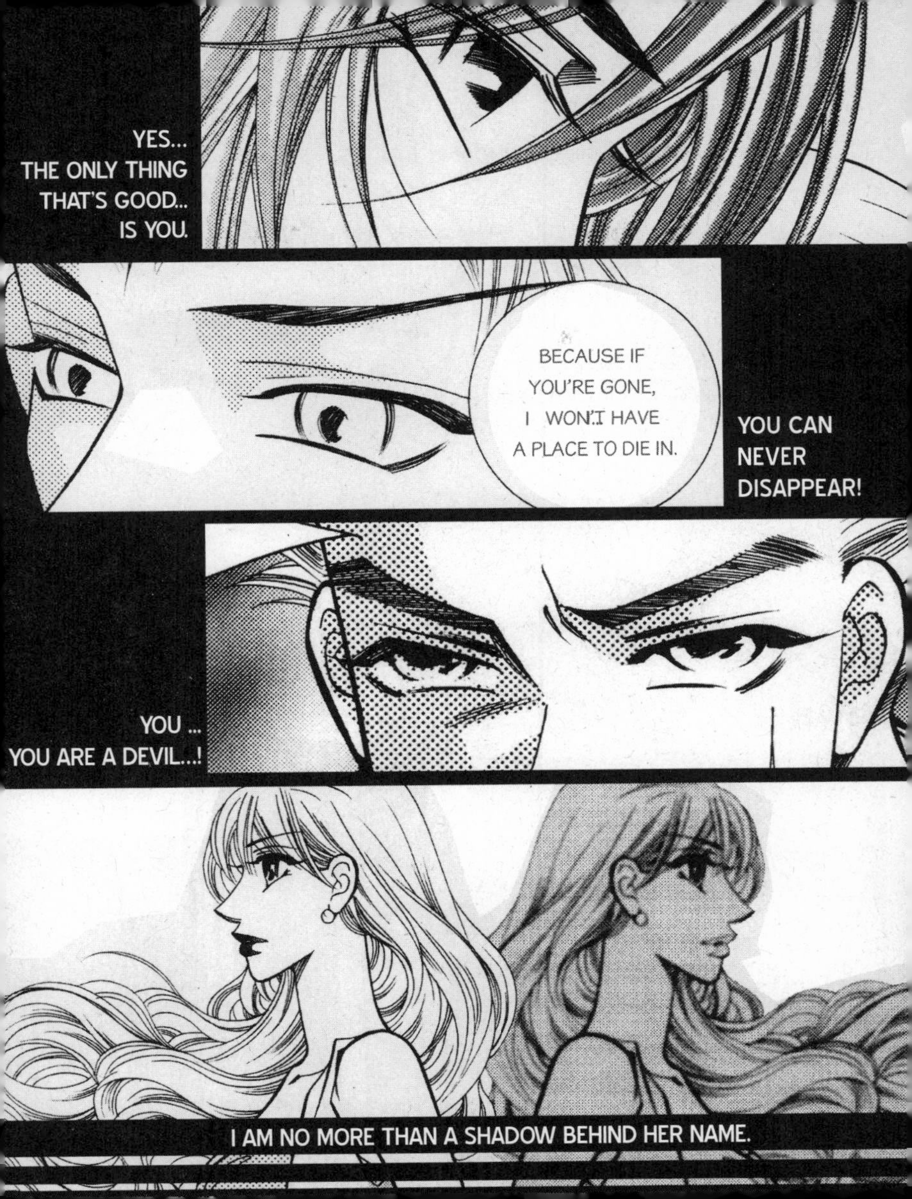

YES... THE ONLY THING THAT'S GOOD... IS YOU.
BECAUSE IF YOU'RE GONE, I WON'T HAVE A PLACE TO DIE IN.
YOU CAN NEVER DISAPPEAR!
YOU ... YOU ARE A DEVIL...!
I AM NO MORE THAN A SHADOW BEHIND HER NAME.

the great
CATSBY

Vol. 1 Created by
Doha

"The Great Catsby is twisted, funny and beautiful. Can't wait to read more."

Scott McCloud, Author, Understanding Comics

Winner of
3 most prestigious awards for manhwa in 2005!

PERSU

HOUNDU

DON'T PULL AWAY!
I WANT TO REMEMBER
THE WRY EYEBROWS
AND THE FACE
AGLOW WITH RED.

DUDE WHO KNOWS
THE ANSWER
EVEN WHEN
HE DOESN'T GET
AN ANSWER.

WILL SHE COME BACK
IF I CALL HER
A THOUSAND TIMES?
...IF IT'S A SPELL
THAT GUARANTEES
HER RETURN,
......I WANT TO.. CALL.

US... WE JUST SLEPT,
RIGHT...?
IMPORTANT, IS IT?

CATSBY

SUN

Korea's most talked-about new series in 2005!
One of the most acclaimed stories in recent years!

Born into a shaman family, Sunbi has inherited the power to see and communicate with spirits just like her grandmother, a notable shaman and savior of their little fishing village in the South Sea. Long shielded from the reality of her power, she finally learns the secret of her mother's death, and why her grandmother was never able to leave their village. Enter Sunbi's eerie world in this mind-boggling psychological chiller .

PROLOGUE. THE UNFAMILIAR FAMILY
CHAPTER 1. THE RITUAL OF THE DRAGON SPIRIT
CHAPTER 2. THE DOKEBI FOOD
CHAPTER 3. THE DEPARTURE

Dokebi Bride

MARLEY

1

PINE KISS VOL.1 / *EUNHYE LEE*

In Pine Kiss, the graceful and endearing series by the celebrated
Eunhye Lee, Orion is the beautiful and mysterious new teacher at
school. He immediately catches the attention of Sebin, the snobby
daughter of a rich gang leader, and Dali, whose first love is Orion.
The passionate triangle between Orion and Sebin and Dali, as well
as the mysterious past of the beautiful teacher is realized in Lee's
elegant drama.

LAND OF SILVER RAIN VOL.1 / *MIRA LEE*

Abandoned in a cabbage patch as a baby, Misty-Rain is saved
from certain death by a witch. She is raised as one of the Dokebi,
a magical race from Korean myth, until one day the enchantment
that had kept the secret of her true identity is broken. She is cast
out to the human world and must find her place among her own
kind. Land of Silver Rain is a captivating tale of love and a
must-read classic for every fan of romance comics.

0/6 (ZERO/SIX) VOL.1 / *YOUJUNG LEE*

At first glance Moolchi is just another unassuming high-school boy.
Then one day, Moolchi's absentee father sends him a 'girl' who calls
herself 'Six' and quickly turns the boy's life upside-down. While
ominous storm clouds gather on the horizon, Moolchi remains
blissfully unaware of his father's dangerous double-life or the
intentions of this mysterious femme fatale.

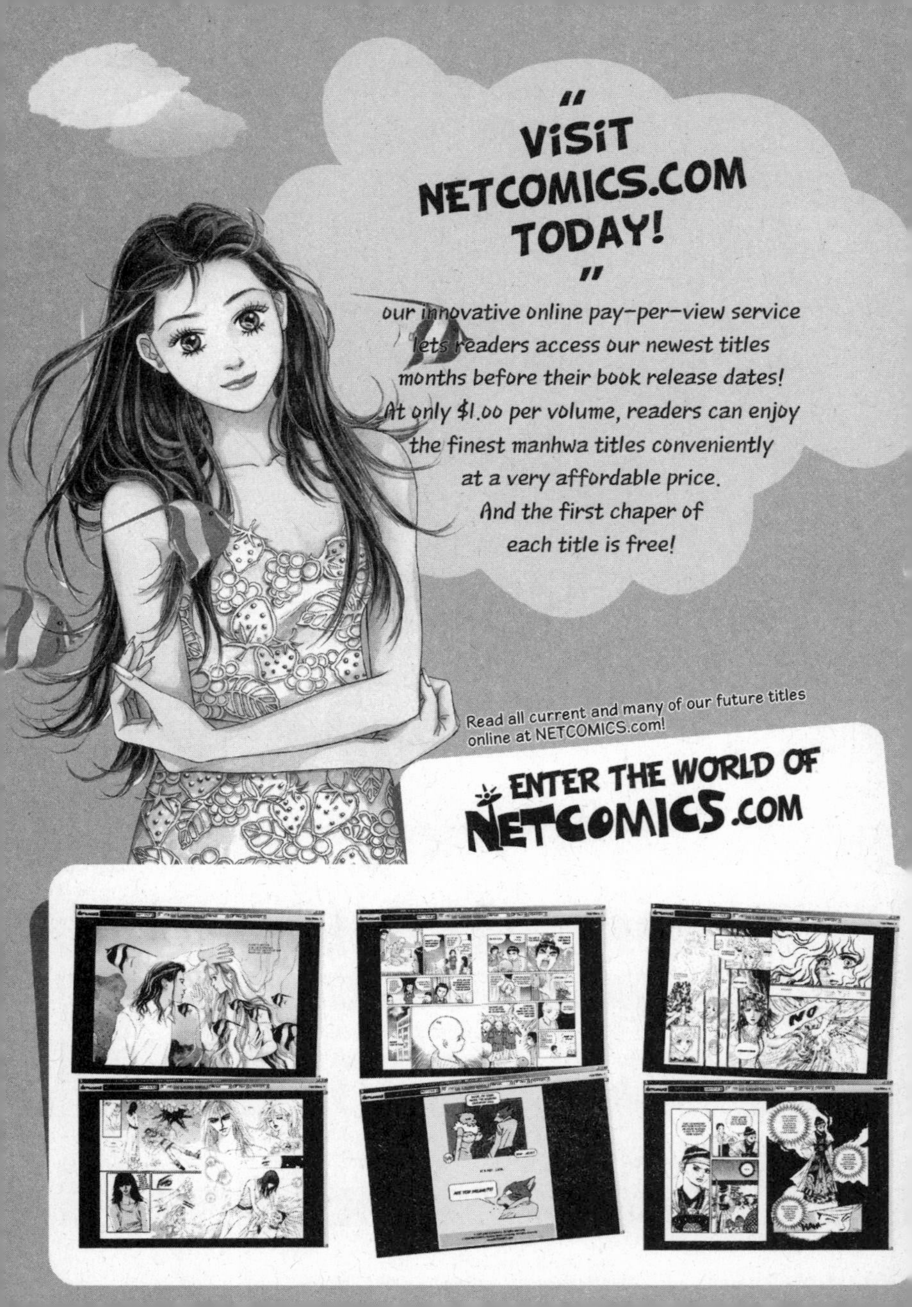
"VISIT NETCOMICS.COM TODAY!"
our innovative online pay-per-view service lets readers access our newest titles months before their book release dates! At only $1.00 per volume, readers can enjoy the finest manhwa titles conveniently at a very affordable price. And the first chaper of each title is free!
Read all current and many of our future titles online at NETCOMICS.com!
ENTER THE WORLD OF NETCOMICS.com
NO